D0884215

The Last Season

A TOM DOHERTY ASSOCIATES BOOK
NEW YORK

The Last Season

RONALD FLORENCE

THE LAST SEASON

This book is printed on acid-free paper.

Edited by David G. Hartwell

Designed by Jane Adele Regina

A Forge Book
Published by Tom Doherty Associates, LLC
175 Fifth Avenue
New York, NY 10010

www.tor.com

Forge® is a registered trademark of Tom Doherty Associates, LLC.

Library of Congress Cataloging-in-Publication Data

Florence, Ronald.
    The last season / Ronald Florence.—1st ed.
        p. cm.
    "A Tom Doherty Associates book."
    ISBN 0-312-84873-0
    1. World War, 1939–1945—Rhode Island—Newport—Fic-
tion. 2. Portuguese American women—Fiction. 3. Children of
the rich—Fiction. 4. Newport (R.I.)—Fiction. I. Title.
PS3556.L5853 L3 2000
813'.54—dc21   00-031793

First Edition: September 2000

Printed in the United States of America

0 9 8 7 6 5 4 3 2 1

For Heather

Part One

I

Everyone seemed to realize that there would never again be a time like that summer of 1941 in Newport.

A few oldtimers pretended that nothing had changed. Tourists still came in droves, asking directions to Bellevue Avenue and Ocean Walk, wide-eyed in anticipation of the mansions of the Astors and Vanderbilts, infamous monuments of an era before income taxes. Newspaper columnists still reported the comings and goings of Society, and townspeople told the tourists the stories they wanted to hear, pointing out the Coogan house on Catherine Street, the site of a notorious 1910 party to which no one had come, now abandoned as a decaying, weed-infested mess in revenge, or the cottage at the head of Bellevue Avenue that functioned as a discreet though pricey pawnshop for those who lived beyond their means. A sharp-eyed observer strolling Ocean Walk might even catch an occasional glimpse of liveried servants, gilded woodwork, or the preparations for a masked ball.

But behind the stone walls and pruned hedges, Newport wasn't the same. For two decades, there had been an open season for new money, and as nearly always happens, new money drove out the old. The first fortunes in Newport, back in the eighteenth century, had been based on the three-cornered trade of slaves, molasses, and rum. But that was long forgotten, and a century and a half later, the remnants of Mrs. Astor's Four Hundred didn't look

kindly on the new arrivals who had made their fortunes as boot-
leggers and speakeasy keepers. The truly rich fled Newport for
more exclusive summer venues like Fishers Island or Bar Harbor,
Maine. Others, facing up to the realities of the income tax and
the Crash, closed their Newport houses without finding substi-
tutes. Early in the summer, Rosecliffe, the fabulous mansion the
Oelrichs had built at a cost of millions, was purchased at auction
by the actress Gertrude Niessen for twenty-one thousand dollars.

The Clambake Club and the Reading Room determinedly
kept the same schedules as in the grand old days, but Blanche's
infamous whorehouse was gone. Members of the Reading Room
watched from their piazza as the trucks carted Blanche's away;
when they recognized the faded wallpaper of the Peacock Room,
where generations of well-dressed gentlemen had awaited their
choice of ladies, they raised their glasses in tribute. The exclusive Gooseberry Island Club, whose fourteen gentlemen members had once retreated to Easton's Point for swims in the nude
and catered luncheons with selected women guests, was also
gone, a victim of the hurricane of 1938. Newport had changed
too much to see it rebuilt. Even Bailey's Beach had been reor-
ganized. The old stratifications of rank were now under such
siege that in the newly rebuilt clubhouse they were enforced by
formal classes of membership: eighty Class A members had
outside cabanas, two-hundred Class B members got the less desirable inside cabanas, and the hoi polloi of *hobereaux* were restricted to use of the locker room.

For those who stuck it out in Newport, the newspaper head-
lines conspired against a decent season. France had fallen to the
Panzer divisions, England was hanging on by a thread, ferocious
battles waged across a thousand miles of North Africa and a
two-thousand mile front in the Soviet Union. The outcome of
the fighting was so obscure that the newspapers had adopted an
all-purpose cynical expression, "as clear as the Russian front." If
the U.S. hadn't actually mobilized, the President had already
declared a State of Emergency, Hildegarde was singing "The Last
Time I Saw Paris" at the Savoy Room in New York with unmistakable emotion, and the talk everywhere had shifted from

if to when the U.S. would enter the war in Europe. Even the weather was terrible. The summer was a relentless series of storms, punctuated by steamy, humid days that stretched tempers to the limit.

People were desperate for diversions. While the rest of the country wondered how long handsome young New York Yankee outfielder Joe DiMaggio's amazing streak of games with hits could go on, or how long the equally handsome Boston Red Sox outfielder Ted Williams could bat over .400, and a few who knew baseball marveled that the great southpaw pitcher Lefty Grove was closing in on his three hundredth victory, the men of Newport pondered the sorry state of the world from the cockpits of yachts in Brenton Cove, where paid hands polished the brasswork to a patina that new money could not buy. They talked of the glorious days of the America's Cup, when the fleet had gathered off Brenton Reef to witness the valiant challenges of Sir Thomas Lipton and T. O. M. Sopwith. The last races for the Cup had been in 1937, and with Britain still cleaning up the rubble left by the Messerschmidts and Heinkels, it looked like the Brits wouldn't be ready to mount another challenge for a long time. How long, the worthies of Newport asked one another, would the damned foolishness in Europe go on?

A stalwart few tried to ignore the signs. Floppy-brimmed hats, pleated skirts, spaghetti straps, and two-piece taffeta bathing suits were the rage in fashion that summer, and boxes were hard to come by for tennis matches at the Casino. Still, no one disputed the harrumphed verdict of Gladys Worthington, veteran of thirty-seven seasons, when she announced that she would no longer accept invitations to parties because they weren't fun anymore.

The third Sunday in July was a day to make Newport forget its woes. There hadn't been a better day for racing all summer. The air was clear and dry, more like autumn than midsummer. Cottony cumulus clouds scattered a chiaroscuro of shadows on the water and crisp northwesterly puffs scudded across the harbor, lifting hat brims and pleated skirts on the varnished spectator boats. Across the harbor the breeze snapped ensigns on

the gray lines of warships that stretched from Fort Adams up to
the U.S. Navy Training Station and the Naval War College on
Coaster's Island, and shook scales from the patched nets of the
tired draggers and trawlers of the fishing fleet tied up two and
three deep next to Long Wharf. In the middle of the harbor, a
fleet of Monohulls, quick one-man sailboats, danced around the
committee boat like moths around a light as the sailors waited
for the start of the final race. It was a time for strong young
men to show off their prowess to the young beauties on the
spectator boats.

Along the edge of the spectator fleet, close by the starting
line, Navy Lieutenant Russell Westcott III hiked back as he
eased the mainsheet on his Monohull, using the long muscles of
his legs and stomach to hold his body parallel to the water. He
had anticipated the puff, spotting the dark patch on the water
from the corner of his eye; his reactions on a boat were instinctive, as automatic as lifting a foot to take a step. Like most things
he chose to do, sailing came easily to Russell Westcott III.

Russell was one of those souls blessed—some would say
cursed—by an extraordinary beauty and grace. Even as a child,
his hair was thick and blond, his pale blue eyes were set off by
long lashes, and his precociously steady smile and gaze capti-
vated visitors and relatives alike. But Russell was only one of
many pretty children in Newport. He was adept at sports, when
his aggressive competitiveness did not drive playmates away, but
his childhood body and face were burdened with a layer of fat
that left his face too round and full, and his jaw and neck too
fleshy to be handsome. Not even his mother thought him extraordinary as a child.

It was with puberty, when the rapid changes in their bodies
left other boys ungainly, that Russell was transformed. In a single
summer at Newport, the baby fat seemed to melt away. He grew
five inches that summer, and his features abruptly fell into place,
as if they had been awaiting the wave of a magic wand. The
blue of his eyes deepened, strong cheekbones and a finely lined
jaw fought their way out from under the once puffy baby
cheeks, and the steady smile, which some had found almost
frightening in a child, became a beguiling grin.

His body too changed: the muscles of his back and shoulders and limbs emerged from under the disappearing layer of baby fat to leave him proportioned not as a temporarily mismatched adolescent, but like an athlete at the peak of his training. Those who hadn't seen Russell for even two months were shocked: the pudgy little boy was suddenly a young man of shocking grace and beauty, tall and golden, with skin so smooth and hair of such luxurious curls that he seemed a statue come alive.

Russell was himself unaware of the changes until one August morning when his mother, Sybil, came up to his room early to rattle off her plans for the week. He was standing in his undershorts when she barged through the doorway. A tiny gasp rose from her throat as her eyes traced the lines of his body. He stood as still as a statue, soaking up her gaze as if it were applause from a theater audience.

"We'll talk downstairs," she said. "When you're dressed."

It took Russell a long time to come downstairs. For close to an hour, he studied himself in the full-length mirror he had never used before.

"Try not to strut so," his mother said when he came into the breakfast room. "You're not the only stallion in the stable."

Three days later, a divorced friend of his mother named Caroline Fiske, who fancied herself an artist and for years had tried to organize a salon with Sybil Westcott, asked Russell to pose for some sketches at Bailey's Beach. Caroline had rakishly short black hair, long fingers that were always grazing arms and shoulders, and lips that got bigger and wetter as she spoke. After half an hour of sketching, she said the afternoon light wasn't right and took Russell to her studio in a house near the head of Bellevue Avenue. It took little persuasion to get Russell to pose in the nude under a skylight. He had been admiring his own body for days and welcomed another admirer. Caroline needed no persuasion to take her own clothes off. By the end of the afternoon, Russell's childhood was over.

The spectator fleet that Saturday was bigger than usual, not just the regulars from the Yacht Club, but the blazer set from Bellevue Avenue, the respected souls who knew, as if from hor-

monal signals passed down in the blue blood, when one ought
to be at the races, just as they knew when to go to the Casino
or Bailey's Beach or the Clambake Club. Monohulls, athletic
one-man boats that were raced in the Olympics, weren't usually
included in the races the Ida Lewis Yacht Club ran on Sundays
and Wednesday afternoons. The anticipation of handsome
young athletes had drawn a crowd that would have passed up
the usual races of sedate Herreschoft 15s.

As he waited for the start sequence, Russell tacked and jibed
back and forth around the anchored boats, nodding when he
saw familiar faces. Even the mysterious Mr. Raymond was there,
on an anonymous but perfectly respectable launch, dressed im-
peccably, as usual, in stiffly creased white trousers, a jaunty blue
cap, and a fine wool blazer with an innocuous crest on the
pocket. It was hard to peg Mr. Raymond. He was an outsider,
but always correct: somewhere he had learned how to dress and
how to behave, even the subtle rules of where to position himself in the spectator fleet, close enough to the starting line to
see the races and to be seen, but not so close that it would
offend the Yacht Club regulars with their rigid notions of protocol.

As Russell sailed under the transom of a straight stemmed
cruiser with a covered cockpit, he heard his name called out.

"Russell!" It was a woman's voice, young and crystalline. "Russell!"

Over his shoulder he could see hanging plants in the cockpit
of the cruiser, above a wicker table holding a sterling champagne
bucket. At the stern rail, a portly figure in Navy dress whites
was engaged in an impromptu lecture to a semicircle of Newport worthies.

"The situation is potentially serious," the voice pontificated.
"The Japanese are a bellicose race, in cultural isolation from
Western Civilization as we know it. . . ."

Behind the dress whites, Russell saw a streak of gossamer scarf
float in the breeze. He jibed around, coming alongside the boat
as another puff scudded across the harbor. The woman at the
rail reached up with a gloved hand for her floppy-brimmed hat.
Her other hand halfheartedly batted down her skirt. The effort

was casual enough to reveal long, shapely legs, the ankles thin, the thighs milky white. *Inviting* was the word that came to Russell's mind as he waited to see the face shaded beneath the hat.

The lecture in the stern went on, oblivious to the flutter of Russell's sail. "Make no mistake. The Japanese are virile and determined, circumscribed by their insular existence, poor in resources. The limitations of their markets and vital supplies may force them into a war, which ultimately. . . ." The phrases were naggingly familiar. It took only one more sentence for Russell to recognize the voice of Captain Horatio Breedlove, Professor of Strategy at the Naval War College.

The woman, Russell concluded, had to be Breedlove's daughter Nicole. In his office in Mahan Hall, Breedlove had said Nicole was only seventeen. The emphasis had been on "only," as if she were obviously too young to have anything to do with the randy officers in the junior course at the college. Fathers in Newport had a healthy respect for the effect that handsome Navy officers in dress whites had on nubile young ladies. Russell, with his lean body and easy smile, the effortless charm that came from growing up with money and privilege, rarely needed the extra advantage of the uniform.

One of the worthies on the yacht, with the straw hat and cheeky jowls of an ex-commodore of the Yacht Club, glanced over at Russell. "Well, Westcott! You going to win this regatta or not? That Portagee looks good." The words came out in a blustery gargle. About two hours of steady drinking, Russell guessed.

Without waiting for an answer, the ex-commodore turned back to Breedlove. "Good God, Breedlove! You don't really think *That Fellow Down in Washington* is fool enough to get us into another war? Bad enough a socialist in the White House; hate to think he's a madman too. We haven't had a challenge for the Cup since '37. At this rate, it'll be ten years before the Brits get another effort mounted!"

"The President may have no choice. The geo-economic constraints on the Japanese . . ."

Russell had already turned back to the milky thighs of Nicole Breedlove.

Seventeen? She was a ripe seventeen-year-old. Her thin sweater was a size or two too small—the rage that summer, along with uplift bras made out of thin fabric that revealed the outlines of nipples—and she held her shoulders back, thrusting her impertinent breasts out in a taunt. When she knew she had Russell's eye, she flashed a wide, toothy smile, rolling the tip of her tongue around the corner of her mouth. The gesture, from some movie with Humphrey Bogart, had swept Newport. Nicole Breedlove had it down perfectly.

A cannon fired on the committee boat, signaling the beginning of the start sequence for the third and final race. Russell broke off the flirtation with a quick grin, an open-ended invitation for after the race. Glancing back as he bore away for the start line, he could trace the shape of Nicole Breedlove's thighs through the clinging fabric of her skirt. Women like that, he thought, made up for the inanities of a billet at the Naval War College.

There were fourteen boats in the racing fleet, and only one that Russell worried about: the sailor that the old commodore had called the Portagee. Russell had beaten most of the Sunday Monohull fleet regularly throughout the season. And he had done it his way. The conventional wisdom said the way to win a series was to sail consistently, to place well week after week without taking chances. But conservative tactics weren't Russell Westcott's style. He sailed aggressively in every race, risking gambles that could have left him in a windless hole or on the wrong side of the course when the wind shifted. To the astonishment of experienced observers, he had gotten enough firsts to outweigh the times when he took a flyer and tanked.

The Portagee was on a new boat, not from the club, but launched off the beach just before the race. There had been guffaws from the spectator fleet when an old Ford pickup truck backed down to the beach below the Ida Lewis Yacht Club, and laughter mixed with cheers when the boat slid off the rack on the back of the truck into the water with an enormous splash. The Portagee climbed aboard in the water, wearing a pair of cutoff dungarees and an undershirt instead of the white shorts and polo shirts that were a uniform for the other sailors. He rigged the boat himself, and sailed over to the starting area.

The laughter stopped when the newcomer came in a close second to Russell in the first race. The spectators and the other sailors took a good look then at the new boat, a beautifully finished hull, with coat after coat of hand-rubbed varnish that stood out from the plain vanilla paint of the other Monohulls. Those who had laughed loudest when the boat was launched began covering their bets.

Russell had watched the other boat during the race. Sometimes luck could put a boat into a surprise finish. Being on the right side of a windshift, even if it was an accident, could leap-frog a boat from the bottom of the pack to first place. But the success of the varnished boat was no fluke: the Portagee had good speed and solid tactics, and sailed in a tricky breeze with the decisive self-confidence that separates the winners from the losers in any sport.

Russell asked around in the interval after the race and found out that the Portagee was named Jake Werth. Supposedly, he had built the boat himself. Some said they had seen him in Newport before, crewing on big racing boats. Werth was shorter than Russell, and stocky, with thick, dark hair that stood up like a brush, and the tough, creased hands of a workman. His thighs and biceps looked powerful, not the lean muscles of a college athlete, but the knotted muscles of a laborer. The few spectators sober enough to follow the races had nicknamed him the Por-tagee because of his tanned arms and face, and his one shrieking fan on an old Portuguese fishing boat on the east side of the harbor. But up close he didn't really look Portuguese. And when he answered a playful taunt of Russell's as they jockeyed before the start, Werth's accent sounded more like an Ivy League un-dergraduate than a workman.

When the gun went off for the second race, Russell was just able to slap a close cover on the varnished boat, doggedly staying between the Portagee and the next mark. During the first two legs of the race, the boats were never more than a boatlength apart, so close that by peeking under his sail, Russell could check whether the other sailor was rattled by the aggressive sailing.

They rounded the third mark that same boatlength apart. The last leg was to windward, and Russell was sure that the Portagee would initiate a tacking duel, flipping from one tack to the other in the hope that he could break out of the close cover. There was no other way the Portagee could win.

Russell was also sure he could outtack anyone in a Monohull. He had been on his way to the Olympics in 1940, until the war in Europe canceled the games; during the brief training period, he so outdistanced the competition that the coaches agreed that he was headed for a medal.

"May the best man win," Russell shouted as he sheeted in for the windward leg.

Werth smiled back, and Russell thought, or hoped, he detected a trace of resentment, maybe anger, in the quick grin.

As soon as they were around the mark, Werth tacked. Russell tacked to cover, keeping himself between Werth and the finish, and Werth tacked back. When Russell covered that one, Werth held for a minute, tacked, and as soon as Russell followed him, flipped back onto his original tack. In five minutes, they had tacked five times. There was enough breeze to make the tacks hard work. Russell could feel his chest heaving. In the next five minutes, Werth threw four more tacks. This wasn't an ordinary tacking duel.

Tacking slows a boat. The two of them should have seen the rest of the fleet catch up. But they were so quick in their moves, so efficient in the way they used the weight of their bodies to roll the boats into each tack instead of flinging the rudder over, that they were able to maintain their lead over the rest of the fleet. Russell stopped counting at ten tacks. He was concentrating so intensely that he hardly noticed the ache in his legs and stomach, or the pounding in his chest. He was sailing on pure adrenaline.

The duel went on for more than twenty tacks, until the finish line, with the cluster of waiting spectator boats, loomed ahead of them. Werth and Russell were still separated by the same boatlength that divided them at the last mark. When it was obvious that he wouldn't break through, Werth broke off the duel and began to concentrate on speed. In quick glimpses under his sail, Russell saw the other sailor tweak lines and ooch his weight forward and aft on the gunwale to fine-tune the boat. It hardly mattered. With the boats that close to the finish, Russell knew he was safe. Werth could never squeeze by. At best he might close the margin between the boats. He was beaten.

"Tired?" Russell shouted. The finish line was less than one hundred yards away.

Werth's answer was another tack, done quickly, without a hint of preparation. Russell instinctively tacked to cover, wondering why Werth would risk looking foolish with a desperate and futile gesture at the finish. When he peeked under his sail, expecting to see the other boat safely below him, he realized that Werth hadn't tacked. He had only gone head-to-wind, faking the tack. Russell swung his head around to see Werth still on the original tack, borne off slightly for speed, and heading for the finish. Russell watched, helpless, as Werth broke out of his windshadow into clear air, squirted ahead, and crossed the finish line.

The silence was punctuated only by scattered groans from those who had lost bets. Then a cheer came across the harbor, a throaty, indecipherable shout from a rusty fishing boat tied up on the seawall. By the time Russell tacked back and crossed the line, two full seconds behind Werth, men and women on the spectator boats were laughing, their fingers pointing to the tired fishing boat in the distance, a most unlikely gallery for a yacht race in Newport harbor.

Russell's father was waiting at one end of the finish line in a mahogany runabout. Wes's white flannels and sweater were immaculate. As usual, there was an attractive young woman with him in the cockpit, and an open bottle of champagne in a gimbaled silver bucket on the bulkhead. "Beaten by the Portagee, Russell?" he said. He didn't shout. Russell Westcott, Jr., never shouted. He expected people to listen to him, and to hear what he said.

"He's fast," Russell answered. He was still breathless from the exhausting tacking duel. For a moment he let himself forget that his father rarely expected an answer to anything he said.

"He's not that fast, Russell. He's hungry, and willing to work for what he wants. That's why he won." Having finished with his son, Russell Westcott, Jr., turned to his attractive companion, speaking loudly enough for his son to hear. "I suppose it's not a bad idea to let outsiders sail in our regattas. Keeps our boys on their toes. Young Russell needs something to focus his energies."

Young Russell. The girl in the cockpit might have been his age. *Might.* Russell's fingernails dug into his palms as he chalked up one more reason he had to win the final race.

When the boats began their jockeying for the third start, Russell watched Werth up at the weather end of the line. The varnished boat was head to wind, testing the breeze for a last-minute windshift. Werth had done it twice before, at one-minute intervals. It was the right thing to be doing.

The Olympic coaches had told Russell that he was going to have to sail smart if he wanted to win, that in competition at the international level it wasn't enough to be strong and fast. Every day in practice they had given him a checklist of prepa-rations for the starts: check the wind, calculate oscillations, trace shift patterns, test the current, analyze the competition. Maybe they were right, he told himself, but he couldn't bring himself to sail that carefully, to make an intellectual exercise out of sail-boat racing. He liked to win by sheer force, by sailing faster, taking more chances, overpowering the other boats. It was like winning a fleet exercise with a frontal attack instead of skir-mishing.

Russell had been watching Werth so intently that the final gun of the starting sequence caught him by surprise, a full boatlength shy of the starting line. Werth, closer to the wind, approached the line fast, driving over two other boats so that he was right on the starting line and moving fast at the gun. In seconds, Werth was in a controlling position, ahead and to windward of Russell, close enough to keep Russell from tacking. It was like a rerun of the last race, this time with Werth in the lead.

They sailed parallel to one another for two minutes, until the breeze shifted to the west, one of those dramatic shifts that come in a northwesterly, and that can throw a race to the wary. Werth tacked on the headed breeze, as if he had expected it.

Russell followed, and the two boats split from the rest of the fleet to sail toward the east side of the harbor. Russell was half a boatlength behind and a boatlength to leeward of Werth.

Russell debated whether to try breaking through. A tacking duel this early in the race might let someone else in the fleet steal the lead. The smart move was to stay with Werth and wait until the last leg. But being behind nagged.

He tried a quick tack, then peeked under his sail to see if Werth followed. The varnished boat sailed on, with no more than a glance back.

Why didn't he cover me? Russell thought. Is he letting me get away? Russell sailed for two long minutes, concentrating on his speed, before he looked under the sail again.

Werth was still heading toward the east shore of the harbor.

Russell remembered how careful Werth had been at the start. There must be a reason he's holding that tack, Russell thought, as he tacked back to follow the varnished boat. In the shifted breeze, he was farther behind than he had been before he tacked away. *I let him rile me*, he thought.

As they approached the row of draggers tied up on the east shore of the harbor, just off Long Wharf, Russell heard a shout from one of the rusty tubs, the same throaty voice he had heard when Jake finished ahead in the last race. "You've got him, Jake. He'll never break through."

Russell looked over and saw a figure in dungarees and a blue workshirt, standing under the patched nets at the stern of a boat. Whoever it was knew more about yacht racing than two-thirds of the spectators on the Yacht Club fleet.

"He's in your pocket, Jake. Stuff him!"

The second taunt was enough. Russell tried a pair of quick tacks, hoping to break the close cover. Werth matched each tack, flipping his boat as quickly as Russell. Werth was safely ahead on port tack and safely to windward on starboard. Each tack earned him a cheer from the fishing boat.

"Who's your fan club?" Russell shouted.

Werth glanced over his shoulder at Russell. His smile was easy. The trace of hostility Russell had detected earlier was gone. Werth's concentration was unbroken.

As they sailed on toward the row of draggers, each sailor tried
little tricks to eke more speed from the matched boats, trimming
lines, bearing off for speed, or hardening up by fractions of a
degree in patches of flat water to point closer to the wind. At
times one boat would squeeze a few inches, perhaps feet, ahead;
within minutes, the other boat would catch up. Russell could
see the rest of the fleet far in the distance, on the other side of
the course. One big windshift and he and Werth would be tied
for last place. But all that mattered now was beating Jake Werth.

And that wasn't looking easy. Russell had squeezed up to
leeward of Werth until he was so close he couldn't tack without
hitting Werth's boat. If he fell off to give himself room to clear
the stern of Werth's boat, he would just be farther behind. Russell had no choice but to sail on, tucked under the other boat,
controlled, hoping that if he held off until the last moment,
when they were right under the sterns of the draggers, Werth
might sail in far enough to lose his wind in the shadow of the
hulls of the fishing boats.

From the distance, he could hear frail shouts from the spectator fleet in Brenton Cove. The voices were too faint to make
out with the wind ahead of him. His own fans probably, like
Nicole Breedlove and the other splendid women in their peek-
aboo hats and pointed bras. Russell loved the attention, the
shouts, the waves, the grand gestures of the old yachting salts
who bowed and tipped their hats to a winner. Most of the
women rarely understood what was happening on the course,
and a good number of the men were so into their cups that they
paid little attention to the race until the boats converged on the
finish line. Still, they cheered.

Up ahead of him, the shouts from Werth's fan on the rusty
dragger, one voice strong but upwind, were clear and loud, the
voice hoarse from shouting:

"Go for it, Jake! Sit on him! Give him a dose of dirty air!"

It felt like a conspiracy. Russell was losing his concentration
as he fumed over being beaten by the newcomer, the humiliation compounded by the taunts from a rust-streaked tub. Fishing
boats were the bottom of the nautical pecking order in Newport. He could remember watching the fishermen steam into

the harbor, their boats reeking with the stench of rotting fish scraps, the men on deck in dirty oilskins cursing because they had to dodge their way around a racing fleet. When the Navy frigates went out on maneuvers, it was a ritual to scatter the fishing fleet with a pull on the steam horn.

Glancing over his shoulder, he saw Werth looking up at the dragger. Acknowledging the cheers? Russell thought. It angered him out of all proportion that at this corner of the course he wasn't the favorite.

He craned around to follow Werth's eyes. He had to scan over the rust patches and the tangle of cables, winches, and nets before he could make out the figure in dungarees on the stern deck. The pant legs were rolled up to the knees, over bare feet. Russell slowly raised his eyes, until he was staring at the most beautiful girl he had ever seen.

2

Girl? She was young, no older than the flirts like Nicole Breedlove who waited on the dock at the Yacht Club after the races in their undersized sweaters, rolling their tongues over their lips, peeking mischievously from under the brims of their floppy hats, and throwing kisses with mannered and practiced gestures. But this dusky-skinned woman stood out from the Nicole Breedloves the way a twelve-meter sloop would stand out from a fleet of workboats.

Her skin was tawny, not just tanned from the sun, but mysteriously radiant, like a gypsy. Her eyes were dark and luminous, the whites bright and clear. Thick black hair hung loose below her shoulders, wild from the wind, strands blowing across her cheek and forehead. A flash of teeth peeked from behind her lips. The inviting smile was hard not to answer.

She stood with her long neck cocked to one side, her shoulders square, thrust back. He couldn't remember seeing that much confidence in a woman before, except in those wretched matrons of Bellevue Avenue who saw the world down the slope of their noses.

A man's workshirt was tied around her waist. Underneath she wore what looked like a man's undershirt, thin white cotton that followed the rounded curves of her body, hugging breasts that were soft and beckoning, not the hard pointy bullets that had become such a fashion among the stylish young ladies of Newport. The heavy material of the dungarees didn't hide the long grace of her legs. One bare

foot was lifted, arched over the other, as if she were a dark
heron, standing in the shallows, alert, watching, uncommitted.
Yet for all the sparkle in those dark eyes and bright teeth, there
was something taunting and distant in her gaze, a haughtiness
that puzzled Russell until he realized that this girl in dungarees
and a man's shirt, perched under the ragged nets and deck
winches of a rusty dragger, was mocking him.

Still, he couldn't take his eyes away. She was magnificent.
Russell had known countless women since that August day in a
Thames Street studio when his mother's artist friend Caroline
had introduced him to a world of pleasure he had only suspected. He had never seen a woman like this, never seen a bearing so aloof and enticing, a smile at once so beckoning and
remote. Where was she from? he wondered.

Could she be Portuguese? He knew the fishing boats were
Portuguese. He had driven by the multistoried, colorful houses
where they lived, neat and cared-for, not at all like the rust-
streaked boats. The women were always dressed in shapeless
black housedresses. He could remember old women and children, and men who looked like common laborers. Someone had
explained that most of the Portuguese weren't really from Portugal, but from the Azores and the Cape Verde Islands, closer
to Africa than Europe. Many of them were black, and kept at
that wary arm's length of separation reserved for black people
in Newport, where remnants of guilt from the centuries of slave
trading had put a gloss of civility onto the cautious relations of
blacks and whites. Russell couldn't remember ever seeing young
Portuguese women, but then he had never thought about them.
At parties, someone was always saying that the Portuguese made
the best gardeners if you could get them to forget the sea. What
could those houses and rusty boats and wrinkle-faced crones in
black have to do with a woman like this?

Finally, her eyes caught his. Her expression didn't change: the
smile, alluring and unreachable, still seemed to mock him. He
waited for a gesture, but she didn't wink, didn't run her tongue
across her lips, not one move from the repertoire that he had
seen so often, the forced antics that the rich girls of Newport
borrowed from the movies and thought irresistibly sexy.

Then, as suddenly as her eyes had found his, she turned away. Russell watched her search for the varnished boat. She shouted, her voice throaty and hoarse: "Beautiful, Jake. Beautiful. You've got him. Go for it!"

Russell fumbled for words to answer the taunt. Then he felt his boat swing upright, wallowing in the chop off the seawall.

"Shit!" He said it out loud, a curse that only he and the girl could hear, as he realized what had happened: he had sailed too far into the windshadow of the fishing fleet. For long enough to cost him dearly, he had forgotten the race, forgotten where he was, forgotten everything.

His instincts took over. He pulled himself up onto the gunwale, delaying his tack just long enough to catch her eyes when she turned back after her last shout of encouragement to Jake Werth. The glance lasted only an instant. The beguiling smile was just as he remembered, but something ineffable had changed—he was sure of it. Perhaps a sparkle in those dark eyes, a flush in that dusky skin, a tilt of her head that let the mane of black hair tumble onto her shoulders. He wasn't sure exactly what he had seen, but he knew what it meant. She had seen him, not a competitor on another boat, a challenger to the boat she was cheering, but Russell Westcott III. Russell grinned, flashing his teeth back at her, then pushed the tiller down hard.

His boat spun and the sail filled on the opposite tack, leaving the girl on the dragger behind him. When he trimmed in on the new tack, Werth was three boatlengths ahead of him, in the clear.

The rest of the leg was a parade. Werth and Russell were well ahead of the rest of the fleet, which had sailed up the middle of the course. By sailing out to the corner, right to the layline of the next mark, there were no more tacks for them on this leg. No more tacks meant no chance for Russell to catch up to Werth.

From behind him, Russell could hear the cheers of the black-haired girl, urging Werth on. He forced himself not to look back. He didn't need to: those long legs, the beckoning smile, the thin shirt stretched over those gently rounded breasts, the hair blowing across her face, the cocky tilt of her head were etched in his mind.

He and Werth rounded the mark the same three boatlengths apart, their positions unchanged since Russell tacked under the fishing fleet. Russell knew he couldn't break through by sailing over Werth on the reach, so he bore off to a low, conservative course. It wasn't his style—he liked to sail aggressively on the offwind legs, attacking any boat that was near him—but he was too far behind to win by attacking. And winning mattered now. It was all that mattered.

The wind was up to a steady fifteen knots, with gusts over twenty, and a sea had built up in the outer harbor. That gave him a chance, Russell thought. Every sailor looks good in eight or ten knots of breeze and flat water, but when the wind builds up, skippers start to clinch. They see the choppy waves and the black puffs, especially on the offwind legs, and they make mistakes, sailing too high to avoid an accidental jibe, or waiting for a lull instead of jibing on a puff.

Maybe Werth would botch his jibe, Russell thought. In that breeze, a mistake would mean a capsize. Werth was probably a good enough sailor to recover, but it would cost him the lead.

In the distance, Russell could see the committee boat and the spectator fleet beyond. He imagined the conversations on the spectator boats and at the Ida Lewis Yacht Club after the race, the inebriated postmortems that would explain his every mistake, how he had botched the start and let Werth sucker him into the shadow of the fishing boats. Some pundit would say that he should have stayed lower on the reach, or that he shouldn't have attacked Werth from behind. Wes would announce that his son had lost his upwind speed or his ability to tack the boat quickly. "Young Russell lacks focus," he would say, in the same tones he used to pronounce on a horse or a new skeet gun.

Russell tried to concentrate on tactics, on what he could do to break the cover and the lead of the other boat, but all he could think of was the long-legged girl. He remembered the smile, the fleeting sense—now a certainty—that she had reacted to him. He had to win the race now. Winning and the girl had become the same thought.

He watched Werth reach out to the corner of the course. *I'd go now*, Russell thought, putting himself on the varnished boat. An instant later, a stiff puff scudded across the harbor, and Werth jibed. The boom slammed across the cockpit of his boat, and the varnished hull heeled sharply. If the end of the boom went into the water, it would mean certain capsize.

But Werth never lost control. And he had a good angle coming back toward the mark. He would clear Russell easily, rounding the mark at least two, maybe three boatlengths ahead. Then it was a straight shot to the finish. Werth had it sewn up. If he was ahead at the last mark, there was no way Russell could catch him on the final reach.

Unless . . . It was a long shot, but there was a way Russell could win the race.

Yacht racing is governed by rules. The rules are arcane and complex, with one essential goal: to avoid collisions and injuries on the racecourse. Protests are permitted, and juries in blazers hold formal hearings in yacht club committee rooms to settle the issue, but the burden in most situations is on the competitors, who as "gentlemen"—it is assumed that anyone who can afford to race a sailboat is a gentleman—are supposed to police themselves, to yield when they do not have the right of way, and to disqualify themselves if they violate the letter or the spirit of the rules.

Experienced yacht racers know the rules well enough to use them to their advantage. If they can approach a potential collision on starboard tack, which has the right of way, they will, using a loud hail of "Starboard!" to remind the other skipper of the obligation to yield. Timing the shout, or bluffing a boat that might cross safely, is part of the game, a perfectly legitimate tactic. At a mark rounding, a boat that is clearly ahead within two boatlengths of the mark has the right to the favored inside course around the mark; experienced sailors who have not established the necessary overlap still try to bluff their way inside.

Russell rarely needed the fine print to win races. Between his talent at the helm, his instinctive tactical sense, and his aggressiveness, he could usually cow his competition before a protest situation arose. Skippers who had been beaten often enough by Russell Westcott yielded from instinct, from a sense that of course he was in the right. Russell had become accustomed to the authority and power.

But Werth didn't seem a patsy, and Russell wasn't close enough to establish an overlap before the imaginary two-boatlength circle around the mark. Werth had already hardened up to a course that would bring him close to the back side of the mark, a heavy, rusted bell buoy. It was a smart tactic. By rounding close, he would get a good angle for the next leg.

As they approached the mark, Russell bore off slightly, to make the angle between the boats look more threatening. The breeze was close to twenty knots, and the boats were covering water rapidly. The timing was critical. He waited until Werth was close to the mark, then jibed on a puff, putting his own boat on a parallel course to Werth's.

"I'll take room at the mark," he said, with a jaunty tone in his voice, as if it were a fait accompli.

Werth glanced over his shoulder and said, very calmly, "Un-uh. You didn't have an overlap in time." Werth had calculated his own course to just clear the back of the mark. There was no room for another boat between him and the mark, which meant that Russell was now headed straight for the bell buoy.

"Give me room!" Russell shouted. This time his voice was edgy.

It was pure bluff. Russell had no rights in the situation: he didn't have an overlap in time and wasn't entitled to room to round the mark inside of Werth. Werth had a fraction of a second to decide: if he held his course, Russell would hit the mark or hit him. Someone might be hurt. One or two boats would be smashed up. There would surely be a protest. With only their own boats in a position to see what happened, and no witnesses close enough to corroborate the testimony, being right didn't always suffice. Smart sailors try to avoid that sort of protest. That was Russell's gamble.

Russell was inches from the mark when Werth bore away,

letting Russell in. Russell grinned as he took the inside on the rounding. Being inside put him in the favored position for the last leg.

The last leg was short. Russell was only a half-boatlength behind and overlapped to windward of Werth as they rounded the bell buoy. It was the ideal position: within two boatlengths of the mark he had blanketed Werth's wind and shot ahead. Werth tried to attack from behind, but Russell was just fast enough to avoid the windshadow of the other boat.

Russell won by half a boatlength. As he crossed the line, even his father allowed a barely audible, "Nicely done, Russell," with a lift of his champagne glass.

All Russell thought about was the girl on the dragger.

Russell knew the party at the Ida Lewis Yacht Club would go on for hours. Spectator boats were rafted up three and four deep on the moorings and docks. Members and friends, many of whom could hardly climb from one boat to another after an afternoon of champagne in the sun, drifted through the fleet, sampling canapés and talking of the coming season.

Lovely young ladies in floppy hats and pleated skirts and too-tight sweaters waited outside the clubhouse. As he sailed by the dock, Russell saw Nicole Breedlove hovering by the door of the clubhouse. Her hat was tipped so that her face was in the shade, and the wind pressed her skirt against her legs. He remembered the invitation her smile had offered before the race.

A winner is supposed to collect his laurels and accolades. Russell flashed smiles and nodded, acknowledging the waves and blown kisses. He knew that once he stepped on the dock, fingertips and breasts would graze his arms, that he would get caught up in conversations that never went past two phrases each, take sips from half-a-dozen champagne glasses, and hors d'oeuvres from white-gloved hands and fingers with carefully painted red nails.

It was tempting, but he sailed past, toward the beach at the far end of Brenton Cove where Werth's truck was parked. The course he picked was instinctive. Russell wondered what drew him. Did he expect to see the girl? Or was it the noblesse oblige of a victor?

He saw Werth up to his knees in the water, stripping the rigging from his boat. A man in a blazer and crisp white flannels was standing on the beach, talking to Werth.

Russell beached the bow of his own boat twenty yards down the beach, leaving the sail luffing in the breeze. Werth glanced at the noisy sail, then turned back to the man in the blazer.

It surprised Russell that Werth didn't seem angry. He was used to men starting fights for far less. Russell always said that he never wanted a fight, but ever since Cavite he had gotten a reputation. Other men, even those who didn't know about Cavite, seemed to read it in his face or his moves.

But Werth paid him no attention. He worked steadily on the varnished boat, with deliberate, economical moves. Werth seemed the kind of man who would have provoked one of Horatio Breedlove's favorite clichés: "Still waters run deep." Sybil, Russell's mother, would have twisted her admiration into a wisecrack, but she would have shared Breedlove's opinion. Sybil liked thinkers.

The man in the blazer said to Werth, "I saw you sailing on *Ranger*, didn't I? In the America's Cup. Middeck was it, or foredeck?"

"Mostly middeck. I steered in practice." Werth tied up the rigging of his boat and coiled lines while they talked.

The man in the blazer laughed. "Is that why the boat was so fast?"

Werth smiled at the compliment.

"I'm James Putnam." The man in the blazer said, as if anyone would know the name. "I've got a motorsailer over at the club that could use a good looking over. I'm told you're the man for the job."

"I can take a look," Werth said. "Is she at the dock or on a mooring?"

"On a mooring, but I can have her laid alongside if that would suit you better. I'm hoping you'll be available soon."

"Sometime later this week all right?" said Werth.

"Anytime. Shall I give you a ring?"

"I don't have a telephone," said Werth.

"Well, just come up when you have a chance and take a look at her. Start with a proper survey so I know what needs tending. I'm sure she'll want some rigging work. Let me know if anything else needs attention. Here's my card."

Werth stopped working on his own boat only long enough to take the card and shake hands.

Russell waited for the man in the blazer to get into a waiting sedan. Then he walked a few steps closer and said, "Nice boat." His own Monohull, like the others at the club, was painted white, one of a fleet that had been ordered together. Except in its dimensions, it was nothing like Werth's carefully fitted and varnished hull. "Did you really sail on *Ranger*?"

Werth nodded, with a hint of a smile. He's proud of that, thought Russell.

"What was it like?"

"The boat was terrific."

"I take it something else wasn't terrific."

"I pulled strings and heaved canvas. The white shoes in the back steered and called the shots. We went faster in practice than in the races."

"With you at the helm?"

Werth answered with an easy smile.

"Well, well. Did you ever try out for the Olympics?"

"I brought this boat up for the tryouts."

"In Monohulls? I don't remember you."

"When I turned in my entry, some guy with a white mustache pointed out that I hadn't filled in the name of a yacht club. I told him I was unaffiliated and he asked, 'Where is that?' "

Russell laughed. "Probably so far into his cups he thought it was a new club. The ones who drink too much to sail become sticklers for rules. What club do you sail for now?"

"Stonington Yacht Club."

Russell raised his eyebrows. "Sorry, I've never heard of it."

"The facilities are pretty limited. We've only got about fifty sheets left."

"Fifty sheets? I don't get it."

"I needed a club to race, so I had a box of stationery printed up with a phony name."

Russell laughed. "Your secret is safe. I'm glad for the competition."

Werth turned to face Russell, and stopped working on the rigging of the boat. "Are you?"

Russell was embarrassed by Werth's direct gaze. "You had me out there," Russell said. "Why did you give me room at the bell buoy? You knew I was bluffing."

"I don't like to smash up boats."

"With a boat like that, I can see why." Russell hesitated, then said, "Sorry about what happened. Call it bad judgment."

"Does winning matter that much?"

"Does it matter?" Russell expelled air through his lips in an exasperated, silent whistle. "My father comes out to watch me win, rides me if I don't. My mother expects laurel garlands for her golden boy. It's the same at the college. They call it an exercise, but I'm supposed to win at war games."

"The Naval War college?"

Russell wasn't surprised by Werth's raised eyebrows. The Naval War College was one of those places everyone had read about and seen at the head of the harbor; no one knew what they studied there. "It isn't a real college," he said. "Nothing like the coeds in *Life* magazine. And I'm not sure anyone there knows much about war." There was nothing more he could or wanted to say about the college. "You do all right in a boat. If you don't sail to win, why race?"

Werth carefully tied the last hold-down on the hull and looked back toward the Yacht Club. His long silence made Russell uncomfortable.

Russell glanced over his shoulder toward the Yacht Club. As his eyes swept down the curved beach, he saw the black-haired girl walking ankle deep in the wavelets. She must have walked all the way along the waterfront, he thought. He watched her until she looked up. Her eyes caught his and she smiled, the same teasing grin he remembered from the race. It lasted only a moment.

"All set?" she asked Jake Werth. She waited for his nod, then got into the front seat of the truck.

Werth turned back to Russell and winked. "I like to win too," he said.

It took ten minutes of kisses, waves, sips of champagne, and nibbles of hors d'oeuvres before Russell could sneak away from Nicole Breedlove and the other beauties on the club dock. From the clubhouse, he walked alone down the causeway that connects the clubhouse to the mainland, then along the edge of the harbor toward the fishing boats.

He had driven by, sailed by in everything from a Monohull to a cruising schooner, sculled by in a shell, motored by in launches and speedboats, once even been rowed by in an admiral's gig with the oarsmen pausing after every pull on the oars. He had seen the fishing boats from the bridges of minesweepers and frigates, from the ferry, from the porticos of houses on Ocean Drive. He had never before looked closely.

From the seawall, the boats all looked the same, rust streaks down the sides of the hulls, heavy machinery on deck, the planking of the topsides sprung, misaligned, sorely in need of caulking and fairing. The finish of each boat was crude, the paint bright, in colors that would never appear on a yacht. One had green topsides, another was royal blue with a yellow stripe. The names were handpainted on the bows in bold letters: *Joseph & Maria, Josinha, Divino Mar, Ancora Praia.* Russell could hear a loud pump aboard one boat, and wondered if they needed constant pumping to stay afloat. A man had to be stupid, or brave, to go to sea in a boat like that.

Two men were working on the deck of the third boat, sitting on wooden crates, one man pulling lengths of net from the dock onto the deck while the other man sewed. One of the hands reaching for the net was missing fingers. The men worked stead-

ily and silently. The rhythm as they pulled the net was mes-
merizing.

"*Eh, marinerho blanco!*" the man with missing fingers called
out.

Unsure what it meant, Russell didn't answer.

"You, white sailor! Didn't you ever see a man who lost some
fingers?"

"I didn't mean to stare," Russell said. Some manners are instinctive. "You're pretty adept with that hand."

"A man does what he has to do." The man gestured to his
companion. "Josué has only half a leg. He can still work like
four white sailors."

The other man's leg was propped up on a box, with the net
draped over it. Looking closely, Russell saw that the leg ended
at the knee, with an old-fashioned wooden peg below. The man
returned Russell's glance and said, "A shark ate it." Then both
men laughed, rolling their heads back and slapping their knees.

"You ever go to sea, white sailor?" The man without fingers
could hardly stop his laughter to talk.

Russell knew his faltering self-confidence was like a neon sign.

"It's okay, sailor. You don't have to be afraid of the sharks.
The fingers went in a donkey engine. The leg was eaten by an
otter board. Like that." He pointed to an enormous wood and
iron panel that dangled from a derrick over the deck.

Russell imagined the heavy panel coming down on his leg,
and shuddered. "I'm looking for a girl," he said. "With black hair.
She was on one of these boats earlier this afternoon."

"A girl?"

"She was watching the sailboat races. In the harbor."

The two men chatted in rapid nasal language. Then both
laughed. More lengths of net moved across the deck.

"Don't dirty your pretty white uniform," said the man with
the missing fingers. "She's not from here. She's from Stonington."

"Stonington?"

"In Connecticut. It's a fishing town."

"Do you know her name?"

The fisherman stared at Russell, as if in amazement at Russell's persistence, or perhaps pity at the futility of it all. "Her name is Sera," he said. "She's the daughter of a fisherman. She won't look twice at a Navy boy who's afraid of sharks."

3

A gray sedan pulled up too quickly, bouncing over the gravel drive and screeching to a stop in a cloud of dust. Jake Werth watched the driver crease his fedora, take a thick leather briefcase off the seat of the sedan, and step gingerly onto the gravel of the boatyard.

Jake and Bernardinho had been working on Joseph Costa's boat since six that morning. From the amount of work they had done, it could have been weeks, or even months, that the boat had been in the yard, but it had all started the afternoon before, when Costa had come over late in the afternoon with a face longer than a cod.

"I got a problem," he told Jake.

"How much is she leaking?" Jake asked.

Costa shook his head. "Too much. I got men with families fishing with me. They'd go out if the deck was under water. But that's not right, Jake. I don't want to lose them or her."

Jake understood what he meant. Costa fished with four other men. If the boat didn't go out, five families would have no food on the table. Like almost every other boat in the fleet, it was mortgaged to the gunwales. The boat got roughly forty percent of the profits of each trip for fuel, upkeep, and to pay loans. Without that share, it wouldn't take long before Costa lost her.

Jake hauled Costa's boat that night, on the high tide. She was barely up the rails when he could see seams wide enough to drain the bilge like an open seacock. Jake was gentle with the old hull, but it took only a few minutes of probing with an awl to discover that one section of the portside garboard plank had the consistency of wet cardboard.

"How long it takes?" Costa asked. "Two days, Jake. No more."

"Joe, she's an old girl."

"I owe the boys already. I had to take from their shares for a new pump. If it's more than two days, I got to fish like she is."

"A boat has to be right, Joe."

"The time it takes you to do a repair *right*, a man could build a new house."

"When you build a house, you can cut corners. Houses don't sink."

Costa rolled his eyes in exasperation. "Just like your father. It's a workboat, Jake, not a yacht."

"She's still a lady," Jake said. "You have to treat her right."

Jake worked until long after midnight, stripping off the waterlogged plank, cleaning out the old bedding compound underneath, rigging electric fans to dry the wood. Three frames in the way of the plank were starting to go too. A builder long ago had cut corners by not putting drainage holes in the stringers, so that pockets of fresh water from the melting ice in the hold would get trapped against the planking. The price for those shortcuts was being paid now. It took Jake most of the morning to shape new oak and sister it to the old frame ends.

Most boatyards would have taken weeks for the job, even with a full staff of carpenters. But these weren't normal times. Prices were down. Fishermen up and down the coast were hauling everything with fins on it to market. With all the war talk and the sightings of German submarines, there were rumors that the Coast Guard would restrict the fishing grounds. If war came, the rumors said, the Coast Guard and the Navy would seize fishing boats for patrol duty. It was now or never for fish.

"One more try," Jake said, as he and Bernardinho leaned into the heavy plank. The old Portuguese had been working in the yard as long as anyone could remember. His perpetual three-day beard was gray now, and his arms no longer had the strength to muscle heavy timbers, but Bernardinho had an instinctive feel for wood that couldn't be taught.

Jake had measured, planed, remeasured, and replaned the plank four times. The bevels were right. The plank fit perfectly at every station. But perfect fit didn't mean the plank would take the shape the boat demanded, at least not willingly. Jake's shirt had come off hours before. His back and chest and arms were covered with sweat and sawdust. "I'll lever," he said to Bernardinho. "You tighten the clamps, one frame at a time, nice and easy."

"She's coming," Jake said, mostly to himself. He was using a long pipe and blocks to bend the plank against the frames. "Funny, Bernardinho. An old girl like Costa's boat, you bring her out of the water she's so loose you can see through her. Then you try to squeeze in a new garboard plank and she's like a scared virgin."

Bernardinho flashed a quick grin, showing his yellowed, ground-down teeth. Bernardinho's arthritic fingers wouldn't straighten anymore, but they did what they had to do. He knew by feel how tight each clamp could go without crushing the wood.

"Mr. Werth? Jake Werth?" The voice had the sharp, clipped intonation of the city, of a man used to being answered immediately. Jake had forgotten the gray sedan.

Jake looked over his shoulder. The stranger was wearing a pinstriped, double-breasted gray suit and a starched shirt. His carefully creased hat perched over a trimmed-sidewall haircut. His polished leather shoes were covered with yard dust. "Give me fifteen minutes," Jake said.

"Fifteen minutes." The man said it precisely, glancing at his watch. Jake watched him walk off through the boatyard.

It wasn't an impressive yard anymore, not compared to what it had once been. The big shed was gone—the hurricane in '38 had finished what years of neglect had started—and the only buildings still standing were the rigging shed, a lumber rack, and the cottage. Still, there was nothing to be ashamed of. The wood in the rack was straight and dry, wood a man could trust in a boat. The tools in the shed were sharp, oiled, each in its place, ready. Jake's father had a saying: "Lips lie, tools don't." If the man knew anything about boats and boatyards, he would have known a lot about Jake Werth from a few minutes in the yard.

A careful observer could have spotted the remnants of the corner posts of the big shed, but the stranger didn't know how to look. He wasn't interested in the rigging shack or the lumber rack; he walked right by the stacks of selected mahogany and cedar without a second glance, pacing the ground as if he were measuring it off. From the railway, he walked to the far edge of the yard, then took a ninety-degree turn and paced down to the tideline. Jake wondered if he was a tax assessor.

A wooden boat is more than the naval architect's lines and the builder's craftsmanship. The boat takes on a life of its own, a delicate balance between the tensions and grains in the wood and the unpredictable loads of rigging, engines, wind, and seas. Planks and frames breathe and sweat, reacting to weather and stress like an arthritic knee. When the ravages of time and the sea have gone too far, the boat needs nurture and care.

The boatwright must be both diagnostician and surgeon, searching for causes beneath the symptoms before he patches the traumas of a collision or tries to reverse the decay of old age. An awl and hammer are his stethoscope; the saw, plane, and fastenings are his scalpel and sutures. With the right care, a wooden boat can stage a recovery every bit as wondrous as the miracles of modern medicine: leaks suddenly disappear, frightening noises and motions subside, and an old girl with years and miles under her keel behaves and looks as though she just came down the ways. To play a role in that miracle is to realize that the lumber, caulking cotton, screws and paint that become a boat are alive. But in a boatyard, as in the hospital, the miracles of surgery take time.

"Mr. Werth!" The voice was louder this time, with a honed edge of exasperation. "I've been waiting for thirty-five minutes."

Jake twisted around, holding the long lever with his arms.

The plank was seated against the first four frames. Patience and a steady hand would set it now, and he and Bernardinho were close. The stranger still had his hat on. His tie was cinched in a fat Windsor knot.

Jake said, "Sorry about that. Every day that this boat isn't in the water, Joe Costa and his crew can't put food on the table. Something tells me you get paid while you wait." The gray-suited man's mouth twitched, until the man stifled his anger into a tense smile and walked back toward the railway.

It took another twenty minutes of coaxing before enough clamps were on the plank to keep it seated.

"Can you drive the fastenings yourself?" Jake asked Bernardinho. "Don't force them. That plank is stressed; she won't want screws driven in hard."

"Go see the man. I'll take care of her."

Jake put on a shirt and wiped his hands on a rag before he offered one hand to the stranger. "I'm Jake Werth. What's on fire?"

The answering smile was mechanical and measured. "Biddle. Steven Biddle, Manning-Biddle Ship Brokers." He pumped Jake's hand twice. "Is there somewhere we could talk?"

"My office?"

Biddle looked pleased, until he discovered that the office was Jake's cottage, two rooms on the edge of the boatyard. The front room was a living room, library, and office, with a narrow galley kitchen along one wall. The back room was furnished with a cot, bureau, built-in lockers, and a chair. Both rooms were paneled with butternut out of a wrecked cruiser. One wall of the back room had portlights instead of windows.

Years before, the two rooms had been the office for the yard, and the walls were still covered with drawings, plans, sketches, and carved half-models of boats. Whatever space was left between the old drawings and models Jake had filled with renderings and plans for designs he hoped to build.

Like most visitors', Biddle's gaze went to the drawing over Jake's worktable, a framed watercolor of a mahogany rum-runner driving through an angry sea. The sketch was the work

of a draftsman rather than an artist, but the power and beauty
of the boat were obvious, even to someone who knew nothing
about boats.

"Beautiful boat," said Biddle. "She looks fast."

"She was."

"Was? What happened to her?"

It seemed rudely personal for a stranger to call the boat "her."
Men who knew boats, and the sea, didn't take such easy famil-
iarities.

"She sunk," Jake said. There was nothing to explain to a
stranger.

Biddle handed him a business card. Plain block letters, with
raised ink.

> **Steven Biddle**
> **President**
> **Manning-Biddle Ship Brokers**
> **Bristol, Rhode Island**

"Manning-Biddle?" said Jake. He had never heard of the yard.
"What do you build?"

"We're looking for a yard location to build fast attack boats
for the Navy."

"You mean you don't have a yard?"

"Building the boats is only one step in the process. Working
with the Navy on contracts of this scale is big business. We
contract the actual construction."

Jake half smiled, nodding. He knew how to listen. Rapt attention and an occasional question leads people to say more than
they intend.

"We aren't talking about a fishing boat here and a yacht there.
There's a war on in Europe, Mr. Werth, in case you haven't
noticed. We expect to be building hundreds of these attack
boats. Did I say hundreds? Could be thousands. A yard building
these boats under subcontract could make a lot of money."

"I'm not sure we're what you're looking for," said Jake. "We're
a yacht yard."

"Doesn't look like much of a yacht you were working on out there."

Jake bristled. "It's an honest boat."

Biddle said, "We understand that there's a large Portuguese workforce available in this community. From our experience, the Portuguese are good boat builders."

"The best," said Jake.

Biddle nodded, welcoming the agreement. "You've got a good location here. Sheltered water, access to major shipping facilities, close to the research and training facilities at Newport and New London. This could be the opportunity of a lifetime for you."

"Who told you the yard was for sale?" Jake asked.

"We're not talking about purchase, Mr. Werth. The yard would be under a contractual production arrangement. I can't make any guarantees, but given the way the Navy works, once we've filled the contracts, the Navy doesn't care what happens to those facilities. You would end up with a lot of expensive equipment at little or no cost to yourself." He unsnapped the latch on his briefcase and brought out some papers. "Here's the design we're working on, plywood over sawn frames."

Jake said nothing as he turned the blueprints around. It didn't take long to see what kind of boats Biddle was talking about. Jake shook his head.

Biddle forced a smile. "Mr. Werth, I hope you aren't shaking your head at getting this boatyard rebuilt at no cost."

"Every boat a man builds has his name on it. I wouldn't want my name on hulls like those. I'd rather build boats that a man can trust."

"How many men do you have on your payroll?"

"Bernardinho is on salary. He works part-time at the fish dock. I wouldn't count myself, because I don't pay myself a regular salary."

"One and a half people?" Biddle laughed. "Within three months, we would have fifty, seventy-five people working here. This could be a real boatyard."

Jake got up. "You're not talking about a boatyard. You're talking about a factory. If you'll excuse me, Mr. Biddle, right now I

have a boat out there that has to get in the water the day after
tomorrow."

"Don't you feel any obligation to your town, Mr. Werth? This
contract could provide a lot of jobs."

Jake opened his eyes wide, questioning.

"Nobody can cheat history," said Biddle. "Before the year's
over, the U.S. will be building fifty thousand airplanes a year,
more boats and ships than you can count. What's wrong with
keeping some of the jobs here?"

"Are you sure those are the jobs they want around here? Why
don't you ask around town and find out how many men want
to work in a factory?"

Biddle folded the drawings and started to put them back in
his briefcase. "You're passing the chance of a lifetime, Mr.
Werth. What do you think all these deals with the British are
about?"

Jake raised his eyebrows, encouraging Biddle to continue.

"FDR may have two legs that don't work, but he's going to
show everybody he's got something between them. The man
loves the Navy. They say his study is filled with ship models and
prints of ships. What does he wear in pictures? A Navy cloak.
He calls the Navy 'us' and the Army 'them.' And he's not the
only one who wants a war. It doesn't matter whether anyone
wants a war against us. FDR wants it enough to start one. And
when he does, a Navy contract is going to be like owning your
own mint."

"Sounds like your contracts are a sure thing."

"Damn close. And you know why? Because this country loves
a war. Uncle Sam, marching bands, uniforms, war bonds—sure
beats breadlines. And this time, it's going to be like nothing
you've ever seen. Those who get on the bandwagon are going
to make a bundle."

"Is that what war is about, making a bundle?"

"No, it's about winners and losers. And not just on the bat-
tlefields. Who do you think will be driving these attack boats,
Mr. Werth? The Navy is going to recruit every rich Ivy League
kid they can find. After all, rich kids with speedboats are the
only ones with experience on small, fast boats. After the war,

when those kids go back to working for daddy's bank and start ordering pleasure boats for themselves, what boat builder are they likely to trust? The guy who built the boat they drove in the war."

"Sounds good. Do you think we can win a war with boats like that?" Jake pointed at the drawings that Biddle was folding into his briefcase.

"What's the matter with them? They'll carry four torpedoes, a heavy machine gun, and do thirty-five miles per hour."

"Your engineers do nautical speed in miles per hour?" Jake pointed to the blueprints. "Plywood laminations won't hold up at speed in a seaway. Those panels have no longitudinal stiffness. They're disposable boats."

"So? Build them, use them, and build some more. I'd call that good business for a boatyard."

Jake held the door open for Biddle. "Only if you're planning to put disposable men in them."

Outside, Bernardinho was cleaning tools.

"Bernardinho," Jake said, "this man wants to build a boat a day here."

Bernardinho shook his head. He looked down at the tools he was oiling.

"He'll pay you three, maybe four times what I pay you. And he'll pay on time every week."

"I rather stay like it is," said the old Portuguese.

Jake looked over at Biddle and shrugged.

Jake watched Biddle walk to his car. The car wheels churned up another cloud of dust as he left. The man doesn't even know how to drive in a boatyard, thought Jake.

How is she?" Jake asked Bernardinho.

Bernardinho said, "That plank was good, like your father cut wood. I always said that if the Lord had known how it would come out, he wouldn't have made the world in a week. He would have taken a year or two instead and let your father build it right." He waited for Jake's laugh.

How many times had Bernardinho said it? A hundred? A thousand? Jake always laughed.

"Do you know how your father hired me? I didn't know any English then. Your father couldn't speak any Portuguese. It didn't matter. Men who know boats can talk without words. He took a scrap of paper—always for him it was an old envelope or a wrapper from a lunchbox, and a broken pencil that he had to sharpen with a knife before he could use it—and he drew a box, with dovetail joints and a rabbet along the top edge. Then he showed me the scrap woodpile and the toolshed. It took me all afternoon to build that box.

"When I finished, your father looked at it like a Portuguese woman looks at a fish in the market—top, bottom, front, back, inside, outside. He ran his fingers along the joints, then he put it on the floor and jumped on it. It didn't break, but one joint opened up a little. I thought, Oh no, I'll never get this job. How could a man want a box strong enough to jump on?

"But he didn't throw me out. He took me to the workbench and took the box apart, showed me how to build a joint that wouldn't give even when you jump on it. He cut a groove behind the rabbet so the two pieces lock together. It takes a whole day to build a box with joints like that, but that was the kind of work he wanted. From that day, I never wanted to work anyplace else.

"You're like him, you know. Except he only knew how to build with his hands. You know with your head too."

Jake hugged the old man when he said goodnight.

Alone, Jake wandered toward the water. He stopped to run his fingers down the seams of Costa's boat. The plank they had set that morning was fair. When the red lead primer set it would take a good caulk. Was it all worth it? he wondered. Were there still customers who appreciated the beauty of a fast hull, the craftsmanship of a boat built as a work of art? Or would the only customers be men like Biddle who wanted factory boats built out of cardboard?

He ended up at his Monohull, sitting on the rack next to the truck. He hadn't seen Sera since Saturday, but the boat made him think of her, of how she looked on the deck of her uncle's dragger, of the sound of her voice over the water.

"Take care of her." It was the last thing Paul had said before he left for the Pacific. Jake and Paul had seen one another rarely in the years when Jake was at MIT and sailing, and Paul had quit school to go fishing, but the roots of a childhood friendship never withered. When Jake came back to Stonington to take over the old yard, he and Paul picked up the friendship as if Jake had never been away. They were the same age, rivals in sports, pals in everything else, and they loved the water, loved anything to do with boats and the sea. With Paul's kid sister Sera tagging along, they had been the three musketeers of the Sound, fishing, sailing, swimming, anything to be near the sea.

It had taken guts for Paul to leave Stonington. Jake knew he wasn't getting along with his stepfather, but to give up the chance to inherit a dragger, to trade the only world he knew for the deck of a tramp freighter in the Pacific, had been a bigger break than anyone in the village could imagine. To the other fishermen, who rarely ventured beyond the confines of the village and the range of their draggers, it was as if Paul had fallen off the edge of the earth. Paul had written Jake twice in the year that he had been gone, and the letters were lonely, asking about the village, about the boatyard, the fishing. Each ended with the same line: "Take care of her."

That summer, Sera had started stopping at the yard on her way home from her job at the velvet mill. When the late afternoon breeze was right they would take a boat out in Fishers Island Sound, ghosting in fading evening breezes and setting off in blows that would have frightened most sailors. Sometimes on a Saturday afternoon, when she got off at the mill, he had taken Sera with him when he repaired boats in Newport or Fishers Island. He could remember how her eyes turned to saucers when she saw the flawlessly varnished boats, the huge houses filled with art and music and servants and carpets. Newport was only three hours by car, including the ferry, but the yachts of the Ida Lewis Yacht Club and the mansions on Bellevue Avenue were a world away from the village of Stonington. Fishers Island was only an hour by workboat, but he remembered watching Sera's eyes when she saw fifty-room houses built of solid mahogany, with picture windows of glass that had been custom-bent in Belgium, and an eighty-foot cruiser that had gold-plated fixtures in the heads and a parquet-floored ballroom on the upper deck.

Of course, Sera didn't know the other side of the rich. She had never met men like that lieutenant Jake had raced against on Sunday. She had never heard the pat speeches about "the good of the sport" and "a gentleman's honor" from people who would cheat on the race course to win a plated cup.

The lieutenant was right: winning mattered. Losing that race had hurt because Sera was watching and cheering. Jake had seen her eyes on the other boat. He had seen the lieutenant eyeing Sera. What man wouldn't?

Jake could half-read Sera's feelings. Her stepfather had forbidden her to come to the boatyard, and still she came, sometimes to watch and talk while he worked, or to go for a sail. Together they laughed about their old antics, the days when Sera had trailed after him and Paul. But theirs was a relationship that had started down one track—she was the kid sister of his best friend—and couldn't easily be shunted to a different track. He could remember when they had sailed one evening during the Perseid showers, ghosting along in a breeze so soft that it left scarcely a ripple on the water, lying on their backs in the cockpit and watching the meteors streak across an inky sky. Her thigh pressed against his, her breasts caressed his arm. Was she still too young? he wondered. In the eyes of the village, she was already a woman. Did she think of him only as a friend, as Paul's buddy?

He loved Sera so much it hurt.

4

The light bounce of Manuel's feet told Sera what to expect. The front steps of the house were wooden, long resilient planks that resonated under the weight of footsteps. For as long as Sera could remember, those steps had tolled early warnings.

When her father was alive, she could tell from his footfalls on the treads what kind of catch he had made that day. On good days, he bounded up the steps, eager for the door, ready always with a hug, and with time for stories before supper. He would tell of the hurricanes, the storms on the banks, the heroics of the codmen who had fished alone from dories. Most of the stories she had heard a thousand times. She and her brother Paul would sometimes race to see who could fill in the next line first. Yet as many times as she heard them, there was a reassurance in those stories. Just hearing of men who were out three or four nights alone in a dory on the banks seemed to make the village a bigger place.

On bad days, her father would linger on the front steps, and she would count each heavy footfall. He could always force a smile when he saw her, but there were no stories those days, and her own spirits would fall with her father's. Sera had learned the moodiness of men from the sounds of those steps.

Manuel had first started coming to the house a year after Sera's father died. His footsteps were timid at first, the polite shuffle of a gentleman caller. He was the captain of his own boat, and not a bad-looking man, with thick, curly hair and skin that wasn't pockmarked or creased. He wore a checked sport jacket when he came to their house, and sometimes a silk scarf tied around his neck.

For Sera's mother, Manuel was salvation. When her husband died, Josephina had withered like a grape picked from the vine. In less than a year, her hair turned from coal black to gray, her once proud figure stooped and thickened, and her sparkling eyes sank into dark circles that advertised her sadness. She had been a pretty woman, and proud of her beauty, before she aged ten years in one.

That was before Manuel began calling.

He was always polite, bringing flowers or candy for Josephina, and sometimes a small package for Sera. He asked Paul to fish ·with him, as mate. "I have no son," he said.

Paul had known Manuel from the docks, and never liked him. "You can't fish with a man you don't trust," he said to his mother. "On a boat, another man can drop six tons of fish on you."

"Did he ever drop a load of fish on anyone?" Josephina asked.

"Maybe not. But he's rimwracked boats that don't know his tricks. He goes out over a foul bottom and drags with his nets a few fathoms down. Another boat sees him, comes in with a deep drag, and wrecks a net. They say Manuel laughs when he hears about it. He doesn't even fish with the men on his boat. He sits in the cabin like a king. Look at his hands. They aren't the hands of a fisherman."

"He's a kind man," Josephina said. "He earns a good living. He likes both of you. He has said that someday you could be captain of his boat."

Manuel had the biggest boat in the Stonington fleet, a fifty-five-foot dragger with a diesel engine that he had bought with insurance money after his first boat burned. He had been the only fisherman with insurance then, and bragged that he had been smart enough to be covered against fire. The other fishermen quietly snickered at the fortuity of his timing.

He could always pull a roll of bills from his pocket, and was quick to pick up tabs in a bar. "The fishing's been good," he would say, as he paid for a round of drinks. Despite his generosity, he wasn't liked. Offshore fishing is a dangerous business, and trust is the bottom line for any man who risks his life each day. Fishermen are careful in choosing their friends.

Josephina knew that Paul and Manuel didn't get on, but she begged Paul to fish on Manuel's boat, at least for a few months. "After the marriage he will change," she said. "Give him time."

"Marriage?" Paul and Sera said it together.

"We need a man at home," said Josephina.

That man? thought Sera.

Manuel and Josephina were married in the church. Manuel moved in that day. Overnight, his timid gentility evaporated as he became the lord of his new castle.

Every afternoon Josephina made sure she was home when Manuel came in, waiting for him with slippers, a fresh cheroot cigar, and a glass of wine. She would do anything for him. And every afternoon, Sera watched his eyes, the way he raked over her, his gaze lingering, his smile sly.

"You could bring him his slippers once," Josephina said to Sera. "He would like that."

"Never."

"Sera, he's your father."

"My father is dead."

Josephina crossed herself, a reflex, like when she went into the church. "May he rest in peace. Manuel is your father now. He loves you. He's good to us. Why can't you be kind to him?"

Sera hated her mother's pleas. Josephina's eyes drooped when she pleaded, like a dog begging for food. The sad eyes made her seem weak and vulnerable.

"I hate it when he touches me," Sera said. "It gives me the shivers."

"Sera! You shouldn't talk like that. Manuel's a good man. He likes you. What's so terrible about that? Your father, may he rest in peace, used to hug you every night when he came home. Was that so terrible? Has Manuel ever hit you?"

"You know what I'm talking about, Mama. Why do you pretend?"

"Sera—" Josephina's voice held for an instant, then broke off as she turned back to the table where she was cutting vegetables.

"There are things that happen with men," she said. "It's the way men are."

"Men? My father wasn't like that."

Josephina didn't answer. There were things she would not talk about with her daughter, questions she could not answer. Time and again, Sera had asked her, "What's it like to be with a man? To . . . you know what I mean. What does it feel like?"

Josephina hid from the question. "What do you ask me a question like that for?" she would say. "You're too young to talk of such things."

One day Sera pressed. "I'm not too young, Mama, tell me. What's it like with a man?"

Josephina turned her head from the sink. "Every girl worries about it, Sera," she said. "But it's not to worry. It's something you do. Not so bad as you think."

It was only a week and a day after Manuel moved in that he and Paul had their first fight. Paul fished on Manuel's boat as a regular, working alongside the other men. When money was paid out after the catch was sold at the dock, he got the same share as every other hand. Saturday night, Manuel pulled out his bankroll and peeled off more bills that he put on the table in front of Paul.

"What's that for?" Paul asked.

"Family is different."

"The men got short shares. You said that's all the catch brought."

"The *men* aren't family. They aren't going to be captain of Manuel Gomes's boat someday."

Paul shook his head. "It's not the way we fish," he said. "How can a man go offshore if he doesn't trust the other men on the boat? You send a man home with a short share, he takes out a little shack, and there's nothing left for his family."

"You talk like that, and you'll be working donkey engines and filet knives your whole life."

Paul pushed the money back to Manuel. "I don't want it."

"Suit yourself."

"I'm not fishing with you next week," said Paul.

"Suit yourself. There's plenty of men on the docks."

"Which is why you can cheat them out of their shares."

Manuel grabbed Paul by the collar. "I don't cheat nobody," he said. He was bigger than Paul, but not as fast. Paul twisted free and cocked a fist. Josephina shrieked, covering her face with her hands. As Paul and Manuel jostled, the table tipped. Dishes went flying. Sera grabbed Paul's hands in hers and stood between the two men.

Paul tried to fish other boats, but even a week with Manuel had tainted him. Every skipper on the dock knew Paul, and no one had been more respected than Paul's father. But once he fished with Manuel, the skippers of other boats assumed Paul was spying to find the good fishing grounds for his stepfather. "Blood is thick," they would say when Paul asked to fish with them. "Even new blood."

"You want to come back with me?" Manuel asked after Paul hadn't fished for two weeks. "I'll give you a regular share like everyone else if that's all you want."

Paul stared at Manuel for a long time. Then he turned to his mother, who was looking up at Manuel with her deep, sad eyes. Without saying a word, Paul walked out of the house. He slept that night on the floor at Jake's cottage. The next day he hitchhiked to Boston, drew seaman's papers, and signed onto a general cargo freighter bound for the Pacific. Jake Werth drove Sera to say goodbye to Paul in Boston.

Josephina cried when Paul left, but she didn't go to Boston. She wanted to be home when Manuel got back from fishing that night.

The first time Manuel came up the front steps with that light bouncy tread was two weeks after Paul left. Sera was home alone after the seven-to-three shift at the velvet mill. She had gone up to the roof to sit in the afternoon sun, to let the warmth bake the soreness out of her fingers. Seven and a half hours on the looms left her with cramps from her shoulders to her fingertips.

Tending looms at the velvet mill was a good job; at least that was what everybody said. Only two years before the workers had been paid $35 per week to run three looms. They went out on strike for sixteen months to resist the demand that they each work four looms. In the end they got brighter lights and wooden platforms to stand on, and $24 per week to work four looms. If she had a choice, Sera thought, she wouldn't work the looms for $24,000 per week.

Manuel came straight up the two flights of stairs and sat on the railing of the widow's walk next to her.

"Why are you home?" she asked.

"Weather like this, the men don't need me every day. Carlos is driving the boat. It's good for him. Someday he'll be a captain." Carlos was Manuel's cousin from Newport.

Manuel looked around the rooftops, like a skipper scanning the horizon. "I don't want you to sit out here," he said. "The neighbor boys will watch you."

"So?"

Manuel put his hand on her shoulder. His hands were big but surprisingly soft for a fisherman. "I don't want one of them to spoil you," he said.

Sera tried to sit up, shrugging her shoulder to shake off the big hand, but Manuel held his grip, slowly moving his fingers across her back, toward her neck.

"Manuel, don't." As she tried to roll out from under his hand, he put his other hand on her waist.

"Sera, you're a woman now," he said.

"Manuel!" She tried to twist away, but the big hands held her. When she tried turning the other way, she ended up in his arms.

He pulled her against him. "Sera, I just want to be sure no one hurts you. . . ." The rest of his words were lost as he nuzzled her neck.

She thought of screaming, then remembered the neighbors on all sides. The village was small, the houses all but on top of one another. All day, every day, Mrs. DaCunha sat in her kitchen with the window open, watching and listening. Whatever happened, anywhere in the village, she knew. Sera's mother trembled in fear of what Mrs. DaCunha would say, the chinks she suspected and explored in families.

Reaching around with her free hand, Sera dug her fingernails into Manuel's arm. He recoiled, then caught her hand in his, pulling it up to the middle of her back, high enough that it hurt. His other hand reached up under her halter, cupping her breast, fingering the hard nipple.

"Never trust a man with coarse hands," he said. "A man should be gentle."

"No!" Her shout was muffled as he pressed her against his shoulder.

"Sera, you know I won't hurt you." Manuel spoke softly, as if he could not or would not recognize that she was struggling. He kissed her throat as his hand ran over her breasts, stroking and caressing. The insistent fingers slid down to her shorts.

"You listen to what your body is telling you," he whispered. His fingers lifted the waistband of her shorts as he pressed one knee between her thighs. "The boys will try to do things that you don't want. But you can tell when your body is like this. Then you'll know. . . ."

Sera brought her knee up, trying to push into Manuel's groin. It was the wrong move, letting him pin her leg with his. She could feel him between her legs, thick, pressing against her. She pushed with her hands against his shoulders, tried to bite his face and neck. But it was no use. He was strong, and the weight of his body held her.

"I'll kill you," she said. "Someday I'll kill you."

"No," he said, in a soft, uncomprehending voice. "You'll thank me."

Sera fought for an idea, a weapon, anything. If only Josephina would come home. If only Paul were there.

"No!" she said again, less to Manuel than to the thought that she needed Paul or her mother. With a strength she didn't know she had, she pushed him back, pressing with her fingers on his throat, then getting her free foot under him and kicking. She knew her foot had found a vulnerable spot from his eyes. For a moment he stood over her, stunned.

"Sera!" He said it as a reprimand. She feared what would come next.

"Sera?" Another voice echoed from downstairs. Josephina.

"I'm here, Mama."

She heard the footsteps on the stairs, coming up to the roof.

Manuel composed himself, and opened the door to the roof with his best smile. "Josephina, my sweet. I was just telling Sera that she's too old to sit out here on the roof dressed like this. Don't you think so?"

Sera's mother looked at her, as if she were seeing Sera as a woman for the first time. "Yes," she said. "It isn't right." Her eyes found Manuel and thanked him for the wisdom.

"Mama!"

"Manuel is right," Josephina said. "You shouldn't sit out here like that. Come, you can help me rinse the *bacalao*."

Alone in the kitchen with her mother, Sera said, "On the roof today. Manuel didn't tell you what really. . . ."

Her mother looked at her with wide, sad eyes, like a dog about to be whipped. Sera said no more. She wished Paul still lived at home.

Sera had heard that light, almost gay footfall only once before, but she recognized it immediately. She was alone in the house after a day at the mill. Josephina had gone to the Holy Name Society to work on the food for the festival. Before Sera could think of where to go or what to do, Manuel was in the kitchen, wearing clean trousers and a white shirt, with a scarf tied around his neck.

"Carlos took the boat today," Manuel said. "He's a good fisherman. He understands how to get a trip that will bring a good price. Most of them think only about how much fish they catch. They forget that it is money that buys things. Not fish. *Money.* Your brother wouldn't understand that."

Sera didn't answer. There hadn't been an incident since that day on the roof, but she was terrified to be alone with Manuel.

"A boy like Carlos would make a good husband. He works hard, handles the boat well. Maybe I'll give him the boat in a few years. Then he would be rich enough even for you with your fancy ideas."

Still she didn't answer. There were two doors in the kitchen, the regular door leading to the front hall, and a back door that led to the trash can and the coal bin. She glanced from one to the other.

Manuel saw her eyes flicker toward the back door.

"You think you're too fancy for Carlos?" He moved quickly, putting himself between her and the door. "I watched you at the harbor, looking at the sailboats. I know why you go with that Werth. You think that you can show those legs and get a rich boy." She watched his eyes rake down her body. "You think those legs are too good for a fisherman?" he said. "Or is that Werth already . . . ?"

Manuel's arms were long enough to reach over the kitchen table. But Sera was quick on her feet, moving around the table so that he had to follow. It was a dance step for her, like the festival dancing.

"Is it Werth? Is that what your brother wanted for you?" Manuel tried to match her agility as she circled the table. "You think I married Josephina for her cooking?" As he tried to keep up with her, he stubbed a shin on a table leg.

"Damn!" He looked down at his shin.

It was just long enough for Sera to make it to the hallway, then down the front steps. She could hear her feet pounding on the planks as she ran. Once in the street, she was safe.

Where? she wondered. To the Holy Name? What could she tell Josephina?

"Trust Jake," Paul had said. "Whatever happens, you can trust Jake."

She walked quickly up Water Street, past the familiar shops in the arcade, Camacho's, the Portuguese grocery store in the basement on Water Street, and Johnny Bindloss's coal company, where the old-time whalers sat outside on their rockers, hawking, spitting, and God-damning everything in sight as they retold tales of their days of glory on the whaling grounds. When a woman tried to avoid the mud by skipping through the high ground where they drew sketches with their sticks, the men on the rockers would shout "Tha' she blows! She's aspoutin' high, wide, and beautiful!" and laugh.

Sera ran by the bakery, with the smell of sweet Portuguese bread wafting from the vents on the side. Three or four afternoons a week she would come there to pick up sweet bread.

The village was small. Every shopkeeper had known her since she was born. They had seen her smile, seen her cry, heard her laugh. They could read her face. She walked quickly, afraid that her face would tell too much.

Why am I ashamed? she asked herself. I did nothing.

Why was it that women who had done nothing were ashamed? She remembered her mother before Manuel started coming to the house. Josephina was a proud woman when Sera's father was alive. You could see it in her eyes, in the way she carried her head. The pride made her beautiful. Where was that pride now? She had been a woman who would have spit on a man like Manuel. Now, she was always afraid—of being alone, of what others in the village would say, of Manuel, of shame.

Sera stopped at the top of the gravel road that led down to the boatyard. A dragger was on the railway, with the bare wood and red primed seams of a new plank showing at the turn of the bilge.

She ran down the steep driveway, enjoying the breeze in her hair and the familiar smells of the harbor and the boatyard, of pine tar, turpentine, linseed oil and fresh-sawn wood.

Jake came out from behind the boat on the railway, smiled when he saw her, then looked out over the water. As he turned his head, the breeze blew her hair across her face.

"Southwest," he said.

Sailing was magic for Jake. On a boat, he was always at peace, no matter what the wind and waves did. It was as if he and the boat became one. Sera had hardly ever sailed with anyone else, but she was aware that what was so easy and natural for Jake was a challenge for most people. Paul was good at every sport he tried, but when he sailed he would get flustered when the breeze was too light, and white-knuckle tense when it piped up.

Not Jake. In a breeze, he loved the excitement, the flush of speed, the challenge of sailing on the edge. When the air was light, he loved the concentration, the ability to pick up each little zephyr. He had sailed everywhere, on big boats and small, yet he never seemed to tire of the beauty of boats and the sea: a hull knifing through a calm sea, the necklace of shore lights around the Sound on a clear night, the curve of a perfectly trimmed sail, or the choreography of a well-executed maneuver.

"Could we?" she said, nodding toward the Monohull. The small boat was hardly big enough for two of them, but it was fast and wet and exciting.

Jake glanced up at the dragger on the railway. "Joe Costa's waiting for his boat. I don't think there's much on his table these days."

Sera wondered what Jake would do if she told him how much it mattered. "Maybe I'll come back later," she said.

"Do. If I can finish, the breeze will be perfect."

As she started back up the drive, Sera watched Jake putting away his caulking tools. She loved to watch him work. His hands were strong and callused from working with tools and wood, but his touch was incredibly gentle. Once, when they were sailing, Sera had gotten a splinter in her finger from the centerboard casing. "This will hurt," Jake told her before he pulled it out. And it did hurt. But his fingers were so sure, the hands so gentle and steady, that she was sure no one could have made it hurt less.

Jake was different, and not just because he wasn't Portuguese. The men from the village tried to act strong all the time. Not just on the fishing boats or at work, but at home, even when they said hello to someone on the street. Paul, her own brother, was afraid of his feelings. When he was angry, even when he sulked after he had fought with Manuel, Paul wouldn't talk about it. He was like her father when he came home after a bad day on the boat. He would never admit that it had been a bad day.

For the men and women of the village, life was deliberate and controlled. It was as if their lives had been planned. If you were a man and your father or your uncle or a cousin had a boat, you fished. If you were a woman, you worked at the velvet mill, or maybe at Atwoods where they built equipment for spooling silk and rayon, at least until you were married and ready to have a baby. It was as if someone had written it all down in a big book. Where you would go, how you were supposed to feel. Nothing just happened.

Except Jake. Jake was the only man she had ever known who wasn't afraid to say that a sky was beautiful. He would admit when he was sad or angry. He had gone to college, worked in California, sailed everywhere. With any other man, you could picture him in five years or ten years or fifty years. But what would Jake be doing in five years? Sera couldn't even guess.

From the top of the drive, she could see the wind on the water beyond the breakwater. She remembered when Jake had taught her how to feel the zephyrs on her cheek, even when the water was as smooth as glass. He had twisted her hair up on top of her head and blown softly against the back of her neck, raising goose bumps and sending chills down her back.

"The breeze kisses you," he said. "Even if you can't see it, you can find it if you know what it feels like."

She had loved every minute of the races in Newport, especially when Jake took the second race by sailing fast and smart. He had the third race too, almost. Sera remembered how much she had wanted to go to the Yacht Club after the race, to see the faces of the girls from the spectator boats who had been laughing. And she had wanted to see the tall, gold-haired man who sailed right under the dragger. She had laughed at him, and cheered when Jake beat him to the mark, but it had been hard turning her eyes away when he sailed up close. He was long and lean, with skin like gold. His skin wasn't sunburned like a fisherman, but golden, and so smooth it glistened.

She turned back up the gravel walk, and ran up toward the viaduct that led over the railroad tracks and out of the Borough. It would be wonderful if Jake could understand, but he was still a man. Sera was sure, just then, that there was only one person she could talk to.

It took forty minutes to walk past the cemeteries and the big houses, across the Post Road, and up into the low hills where stone walls and tree-lined roads framed a world that seemed hundreds of miles from the village. The sun was low in the western sky. She could hear the rustling of small animals in the underbrush.

Rosa's farm was little more than a shack and a patch of hillside. The mailbox was nailed to a tree, without a name or a number. From the bottom of the dirt drive, Sera could hear the sheep making a racket, *maa*-ing in choruses. Halfway up the drive she saw the ewes bunched up close to a wall at the edge of the field; the pasture behind them was rough, most of it eaten down, but with tufts of odd grasses and weeds sticking up like patches on a blanket. The stone walls had tumbled in places, and the openings were filled with makeshift fencing made from saplings, lengths of wire, and an old bedframe. It wasn't a pretty farm, not at all like the pictures on calendars. It was the only farm Sera had ever seen.

As Sera reached the head of the path, Rosa came to the door, wearing a short-sleeved blouse, a long, colorful skirt, and boots. Her hair was short and thick, with streaks of gray, and there were crow's-foot wrinkles around her eyes and mouth. But she looked vibrant, smiling easily, jaunty in her steps. Sera had never thought about Rosa's age. She always seemed more mature than the women in the village—she had to be to live alone out there—and at the same time, so much younger than the women who wore black and seemed to lose their figures, their love of fun, and their smiles as soon as they got married.

"Sera!" Rosa hugged her, kissing her on both cheeks. "I learned that in France," she said. She always kissed Sera on both cheeks, and always said she learned it in France. Someday, Sera promised herself, she would get Rosa to tell her about France.

As long as she could remember, Sera had heard stories about Rosa, not told to her, but whispered among the women of the village. The men talked about her too, though never within earshot of young girls. Whenever Sera asked about Rosa, the answer was snickers from the men and hush-ups from the women. It had taken Sera a long time to put the snickers and whispers together with the nice woman who sold vegetables and wool yarn from a cart under the viaduct, and delivered lambs for Easter to half the families in the village.

Rosa was from the village, at least she had been born there. When she was still in school, she had disappeared to New York City, and from there to Europe. Ten years later she had come back with a small child and no husband and moved outside the village to the little run-down farm, far enough away that she didn't have to listen to the gossip and stories.

They sat down on a bench made out of a log, looking out toward the hills to the west, where the sun was sliding down toward the treetops. They had hardly sat when little Jean-Claude scurried out, followed by two dogs that were almost as big as he was. Jean-Claude looked up at Sera with a dirty-faced smile and a wave, before he and the dogs ran off toward the pasture.

Rosa laughed as the boy tripped over one of the dogs and ended up on his back with both dogs licking his face.

"You're always happy," Sera said.

Rosa nodded. "Why shouldn't I be happy? Life is good."

Sera watched Rosa's eyes take in the field and the sky. She had been brimming to tell Rosa about Manuel, about how she couldn't stand another day living in that house. Out in the fresh air, with Jean-Claude and the dogs running through the fields and the sheep munching the grass, the peace of the countryside and Rosa's easy smile made the big problems seem far away.

As they sat, the two dogs began a chase along the stone wall. Rosa watched with rapt attention.

"Did you see him?" Rosa said.

"See who?"

"Dinner." Rosa went through the screen door and came out with an old single-barreled shotgun and a handful of shells.

Sera pulled back. The only guns she had ever seen, except in the movies, were on the swordfishermen's boats. "What are you going to shoot?" she asked.

Rosa nodded toward the wall. "The rabbit."

Sera's eyes widened. "You know how to shoot a gun?"

"Anyone can shoot. Want to try?"

"Really?"

"Sure." Rosa said it with a broad smile, as if nothing were impossible. "Just wait until Jean-Claude is on the porch."

When Rosa held the gun out, Sera hesitated, not sure where to put her hands.

"It won't bite you," said Rosa. She held the shotgun up to Sera's shoulder, the stock against her cheek, positioning Rosa's fingers on the grip and forestock. "Keep your eyes open and point. The way you would point your finger. Hold the little dot at the end of the barrel on the rabbit and swing so the gun follows him. Then go ahead of him a little, keep moving, and shoot." She swung Sera's shoulders, following an imaginary rabbit. A minute later, another rabbit popped out from the stone wall, with the dogs in hot pursuit. Sera swung the gun by herself to follow the rabbit.

"That's right," Rosa said. "Eyes open and point. Move with him. When it feels right, pull the trigger."

"You really think I can shoot it?"

"Try."

Sera swung the gun again, at a make-believe rabbit. This time she pulled the trigger. The explosion so close to her ear, and the recoil of the gun against her shoulder, surprised her. "Oh!" she said, "is that shooting?" She rubbed her ear with the back of her hand.

"Almost." Rosa took the gun, broke it open, and put in another shell. "Remember to move ahead of the rabbit before you pull the trigger."

"You really think I can shoot one?"

"Of course you can."

Sera tried and missed. The puff of dirt from the pasture told her what she had done wrong, leading too far ahead of the rabbit. She reloaded herself and waited until the dogs flushed another rabbit. She pulled the trigger just before the rabbit got to a hole in the wall. The rabbit flew up a foot off the ground before collapsing into a pile of fluff.

"Wonderful!" shouted Rosa, as one of the dogs brought the rabbit.

"I shot him?" said Sera.

"A perfect shot. See, it's not hard. Most things aren't."

"How did you learn to shoot a gun?" Sera asked, as she watched Rosa cut the fur around the legs and down the belly and pull the skin off the rabbit.

"A friend taught me. In France."

"You know everything. You do what you want. Tell me about France."

Rosa smiled, first openly, then a sly grin. "That was another life, Sera. I was young, in love. When you're in love, the sun shines every day. Even when it rains, the sun shines. How is Jake?"

"Why do you ask about Jake?"

"Because we were talking about love."

Sera looked away, suddenly shy. "Jake holds me like a fancy china plate, as if he were afraid to break something. I thought love would be a man who—"

"A prince on a white horse? I had a prince once, Sera. It was a silver car instead of a white horse, but his hair was gold, and his teeth were like stars, and he smelled like the trees."

"What happened?"

"It was like reading a story you've read before. I knew what the ending would be before the story started. This is the ending. Me and Jean-Claude. I'm not sorry. Not for anything. I'm good at reading people, Sera. Jake seems more than a friend to me."

"He thinks I'm a little girl."

"Maybe he respects you. Jake's not like other men."

"Sometimes I wish he was."

Inside, at the kitchen table, Rosa cut the rabbit into pieces, and poured wine over them in a bowl. "Did you ever eat rabbit?" she asked.

"I don't think so."

"We ate it all the time in France." Rosa started to smile again, that same sly grin, when a terrible racket began outside, loud thumps, followed by a chorus of *maas* from the sheep.

Rosa ran to the doorway, then stopped, put her hands on her hips, and threw her head back to laugh. "Now you've really got yourself in a fix," she said to some stranger outside.

Sera ran for the door. Rosa's outstretched hand pointed to a big sheep stuck on top of a stone wall, with two legs on one side of the wall, and two legs on the other. The sheep looked absurd. Sera couldn't help laughing.

"It's Rimbaud," Rosa said. "The ram. He just couldn't control himself, I guess."

Sera looked puzzled. "Why is he on top of the wall?"

Rosa grinned. "I don't like to breed the ewes until September. Christmas lambs are no good. But Rimbaud doesn't think he can wait."

"You mean he wants to get to the sheep?"

"The ladies. He's like every man, I guess."

Sera stopped laughing. "What's it like with a man, Rosa?"

"What's it like?" Rosa laughed. "It isn't like anything, Sera. It isn't like anything else in the world."

5

J ake had no phone at the boatyard.

To the fishermen, phones were like telegrams, harbingers of bad news. A phone call usually meant an accident, or trouble with the police. Wives at home dreaded a phone ringing during the night, fearing it would be the Coast Guard or another fisherman telling them that a boat was missing, or that a son or husband had been in an accident or drowned.

The village was small enough that people could still do everything in person. If a fisherman needed supplies for his boat, he went to Bindloss's or one of the little shops in the village. Fuel, ice, repairs, food, the fish buyers—all were right there. The working language on many of the boats was still Portuguese, and many of the shopkeepers were swamp Yankees with accents as thick as the autumn fogs, but body language and facial expressions could fill in when words failed.

Even for calls from outside the village, a phone wouldn't have done Jake Werth much good. He was almost never in the office. If he wasn't working in the yard, he was off on the workboat or the truck. He was accustomed to getting mail from people who discovered he had no phone, asking that he get in touch with them. Still, he was surprised by the note that was waiting for him in his box at the new post office on the square.

It was from William L. Langer, written not on his Harvard history department letterhead, but on a personal note card. The message was terse, an invitation for Jake to visit at the house in Cambridge at his earliest convenience. "Call first, but almost any evening is fine," Langer wrote in his tiny, neat hand.

Jake had taken two seminars with Langer. He had officially been a student in the naval architecture program at MIT, but after a year of learning how to design ships that had already been built a thousand times, and having every effort to explore a new direction dismissed as inefficient, impractical, or unproved, he drifted to the other end of Cambridge and Langer's seminars on diplomatic history. He had done well in Langer's courses, to the surprise of the Harvard students who wondered about this fellow who showed up in work clothes and spent his afternoons working at a boatyard on the north shore.

Langer had encouraged Jake, inviting him to sit in on a graduate seminar, and urging him to transfer and continue his study of history. Jake, his finances stretched by the two years of naval architecture, quit school for his first love. "I need to be near boats," he told Langer.

Jake had left Cambridge so long ago, with no intervening communication except a passing wave when he had seen Langer in the cockpit of a sailboat in a Massachusetts anchorage, that the easy friendliness of Langer's note was jarring.

He remembered the Langer house on the corner of Raymond Street and Huron Avenue in Cambridge. The history seminars met in Langer's attic study, a narrow room furnished mostly with books. After a student had been grilled for the evening— the seminars were more interrogation than discussion—Mrs. Langer would bring up hot chocolate and the professor would hold court, plumbing his deep knowledge on some arcane topic in a command performance. Langer's incredible ability to make connections between apparently unrelated events drew students who sought a respite from the cynicism and skepticism that were the usual style in Cambridge.

Later, Jake had been invited to Friday night musical soirées at the Langer house. Langer played the viola, his wife played a cello, and they would recruit student or faculty violin players to make up a quartet. The audience would squirm as the quartet scraped and screeched their way through a piece. Polite applause would prompt an encore, sometimes two, until the guests learned to temper their applause and spare themselves further cacophony. A visiting professor from Princeton once whispered to Jake that until that evening he hadn't believed violin music could be even worse than what he had heard at Albert Einstein's house.

Jake had no idea what to expect when he called from the phone at Camacho's. A housekeeper answered, told him the Mrs. Langer he remembered was no longer Mrs. Langer, and that the professor was expecting him. Jake agreed to drive up that Thursday afternoon, stopping on the way to finish his survey on James Putnam's motorsailer in Newport.

He found little wrong with Putnam's boat. It was a heavily built English design, a boat for a man who liked the image of sailing but never really sailed. The teak decks, varnished brightwork, and commodious engine room were meticulously maintained. The rigging and sails were an afterthought. There were some lightly corroded areas in the galvanized shrouds, but the rigging had plenty of life left, even if it didn't look right next to the brass fittings that Putnam's boat man polished every day. From the yard payphone, Jake explained that the only the problems were cosmetic, but Putnam wanted new rigging installed *as soon as possible*. He also asked if Jake would strip and revarnish the hatches and rebuild the companionway. Jake pointed out that there was really nothing that couldn't wait until a winter fitting. Putnam was insistent that the work be done immediately.

Jake agreed to do the work—he had no other work lined up—but he couldn't help contrasting the fishermen who couldn't afford the time or money for much-needed repairs, and a man like Putnam who insisted on having unnecessary work done on his boat *as soon as possible*. Jake wasn't surprised. He had always wondered if powerful men found a refuge from the vagaries of business and personal relationships in a boat. Was it because unlike business or personal relationships, a boat seemed perfectable? The exaggerated and obsessive love for a boat was something wives and business associates rarely understood.

In Cambridge, Langer answered the door of the clapboard corner house himself, still as tall and erect as Jake remembered. He said "Hello" and "Let's go up to my study where we can talk" in the same sentence, brushing away any possibility of light conversation. Jake recalled that the graduate students used to tell jokes about Langer, imagining a student coming to Langer in office hours to explain that his parents and wife had just been killed in a terrible accident, that he had lost all of his funds, and now had four starving children and wasn't sure where he would get their next meal. As the anecdote had it, without looking up from papers on his desk, Langer would ask, "How is your seminar report coming along?"

The attic study was crowded with even more books than Jake remembered. Horizontal volumes were stuffed into every available space above the shelved books, and more books and issues of journals were stacked on the floor in front of the dormer windows, like barricades against the outside world. Langer closed the door and offered Jake a seat at his worktable.

"It's been a long time, Jake," he said. "How have you kept out of trouble?"

"Mostly sailing. And building boats."

"You know my soft spot for sailing, so I certainly understand. You never regretted not continuing with history?"

"School and the world were too far apart for me."

"That's our loss. I take it you've been successful in your boatbuilding?"

"Mostly repairs. I wouldn't turn down a commission."

"And I'd love to give you one. But that isn't why I invited you here tonight." Langer glanced down at an index card. "Despite the demands of the boatyard, I'll wager that you've found time to follow the newspapers."

"I try to keep up."

"What do you think of Britain's chances?"

"Better than they were a year ago."

"Do you think they can defeat Germany without American intervention?"

"I guess that depends on how deep the mud is in Russia. Hitler seems not to have read up on Napoleon."

"Well put. Are you still keen on naval history?"

"There hasn't been much to follow. I'm not sure we'll ever see the likes of Jutland or the Straits of Tsushima again."

"Why not?"

"The weapons have changed too much. Between the threats of aerial bombardment, highly maneuverable small attack boats, and submarines, I wonder if any navy is willing to risk their battleships in a head-on battle."

"You're probably right, Jake, although I'm not sure our Navy would agree with you. That's why I invited you here to talk." Langer looked and spoke like a patrician. His words weren't rushed, and rarely betrayed excitement. Jake had heard a rumor that Langer—who had been a brilliant lecturer—was fighting a battle against stage fright, but it didn't show. Years in the lecture hall, seminar room, and senior common rooms had accustomed him to being listened to and understood. "We may be in the unenviable situation of having to formulate policy in spite of our own naval strategies."

"We?" said Jake.

Langer got up and walked to the door. It was already shut, but he fiddled with the doorknob before sitting down again. "Do you know the name William Donovan?"

"No."

"Donovan is a highly respected lawyer and an adviser of presidents, a superb man. Last month he was asked by the President, very quietly, to head an Office of Coordinator of Information. Donovan's core staff includes James Phinney Baxter, a fine American historian and the president of Williams College. Baxter has organized what we call a 'lunch group' here in Boston, and asked me to chair a Board of Analysts. I am in the midst of writing two books now, and I'd give almost anything to spend my time in the Annisquam house finishing up. But when my president calls, I have no choice."

Jake smiled as he realized that Langer was talking not about the president of Harvard, but of the United States. Langer went over to a file cabinet and pulled out a manila envelope, carefully undid the string tie, and spread the contents—photographs and a marine chart—on the table.

"Does the name Taranto ring a bell?" he asked.

"Italian naval port, inside the heel of the boot."

"What do you know about Taranto?"

"Not much. It's well-protected, commands the approaches to the Eastern Mediterranean, shallow anchorage—the sort of port that makes admirals cocky."

"Exactly. It's been a port since the Greeks were out colonizing whatever they could grab. Pliny the Elder wrote that Tarentum was the finest natural harbor in the world, and that the Tarentum sheep had the best wool. I don't know about the sheep, but that port seems to have lulled the Italians into complacency. The Brits attacked last year and took out half of the Italian fleet."

Langer picked out some of the pictures he had spread out on the table. "The damage is remarkable: three battleships sunk or out of commission, a slew of smaller ships damaged." He offered the photographs and a magnifier to Jake. "What I don't understand, Jake, is how the Brits did this much damage."

Jake looked up from the photographs. "Last time I looked we were friends with the Brits. Couldn't you ask them?"

"They won't share their aerial reconnaissance. We only got these photos because the British recently received some Martin Marylands for long-range reconnaissance. They needed an American technician to do some work on the planes. He flew on a couple of missions and took these with a Leica."

The photographs were remarkably clear. With the magnifier, Jake could make out a battleship that had been beached, another listing, a third sunk in shallow water. In the inner harbor oil slicks spread around heavy cruisers at moorings and another tied stern-to at the wharves.

"The Germans make good cameras," said Jake.

"How could the Brits sneak into a harbor like Taranto and bomb those ships?" said Langer. "The Italians supposedly have listening devices to detect airplanes at long range. They had barrage balloons, heavy guns on shore and on barges, the guns on the ships."

"I don't think this damage was done by bombs," said Jake. He handed the glass to Langer. "It's easier to sink a ship by letting water into the bottom than by letting air into the top. Look at the oil slicks around the ships. Slicks are from hits below the waterline, which probably means torpedoes."

"Isn't a harbor like that too shallow for a submarine?"

"For a conventional submarine. There are miniature submarines, or a torpedo can be dropped from the air."

Langer shook his head. "Toy submarines are not the Royal Navy style. We know the Italians have human-steered torpedoes, but again I don't think the Brits would use them. And the Brits are notoriously behind in naval aviation. They're still flying biplanes off whatever passes for a carrier. Even if they had modern naval aviation, how is a torpedo attack from the air possible in a harbor?"

Jake picked up the chart from the table and traced through the anchorage with a fingertip.

"It wouldn't be easy. When you drop a torpedo from an aircraft, the torpedo sinks deep before it rises to operating depth." Jake saw a quizzical look on Langer's face and reached for a sheet of paper and a pencil.

"Remember your high school physics? When the aircraft releases the torpedo, the torpedo is moving forward at the speed of the aircraft. Add the acceleration downward, and by the time the torpedo hits the water its entry vector is close to optimum for achieving maximum depth—exactly what you don't want in a shallow anchorage. Your torpedoes end up stuck in the mud on the bottom."

"How much depth would they need to launch torpedoes?"

"That's not a back-of-the-envelope problem."

"The answer is important," Langer said.

"Why? Are you worried about Narragansett Bay?"

Langer forced a quick laugh. "No, the ladies of Newport would never allow that. But there are some major naval facilities where the Navy is, well, a bit complacent. If the Brits could accomplish this"—he pointed at the photographs—"with their biplanes, we have to ask what could be done with more sophisticated equipment and experience."

"The Germans?" Jake said.

"I've said all I can say for now," said Langer. "Except to pose the big question, the reason I invited you here. Could you pull something together on this? We're not looking for you to develop a new weapon or new tactics, just a 'what-if' to see what kind of attack is possible on a shallow harbor. Conduct any tests or experiments you need, keep track of your time and any expenses, and submit a bill as if it were repair work on a boat. We have special accounts for work like this. Needless to say, it is all very hush-hush."

"Why not let the Navy do it? They probably have analysts who are specialists in stuff like this."

"The Navy has a bad habit," said Langer. "They know the answers they want before they ask the question. We need an independent checkpoint."

Jake looked at the photographs and chart again. "I hope you aren't in a rush. I agreed to do some repair work on a motorsailer in Newport. The fellow is pretty impatient about my getting to it. I can't afford to turn down good work these days."

Langer smiled. "I know. Your bill for this work will also go to Mr. Putnam."

Jake shook his head, as if he were clearing a cobweb. "You mean Putnam is part of this?"

"James Putnam is a friend of Mr. Donovan. I knew we would need a block of your time."

"How did you know I'd be in Newport?"

Langer smiled again.

"And what made you so sure I'd say yes?"

"That's a good question. I know you say no more often than yes lately."

"What's that mean?"

"You didn't want to build attack boats for Steven Biddle."

"You know about that too?"

"Biddle is a security agent. Sending him wasn't my decision. Indeed, I don't like the whole security nonsense. We're required to have a check run on anyone involved in this work. I'm sorry it has to be this way, Jake. But this isn't a history seminar. It looks like we'll be at war before the year is out."

"What happens to the information?"

"That depends on what you find."

"I may need to do some experiments. I don't think your security agents would like me launching model torpedoes in Newport harbor."

"Worried about spies? We can get you access to a laboratory or a towing tank if you need it. We have people with connections at MIT."

"A quiet anchorage would do the trick. The mast on Putnam's motorsailer is all the the height I'd need, and that beamy motorsailer is a stable enough platform. You picked well, Professor Langer." He winked.

"I doubt you'll believe me, but the choice of Putnam's boat is coincidence. But I will find you a quiet anchorage with a private dock."

"Just like that?"

"It shouldn't be difficult. I think I know of a house with a private dock on the backside of Jamestown where you could work. I'll arrange it."

"Sounds like you can do just about anything you want."

"If the information we need is important enough, I suppose we can. I find it as surprising as you do. Call it the power of war."

Patriotism is the last refuge of a scoundrel. Jake was thinking of the quote and trying to remember who had said it when he stopped at a filling station on the way home.

"Might as well fill 'er up now," the pumpman said. "While you still can. Once FDR sits down to dinner with Mr. Ford, that'll be the end of gas for the rest of us."

"Henry Ford and FDR?"

"Mr. Ford ain't no dummy. When he figures he can make more money building tanks than selling cars, he'll have dinner with FDR and we'll be in a shooting war. And once we're in a war, there ain't goin' to be no Sunday drives 'cause there ain't goin' to be no gas or tires for anyone but the soldiers. The rich'll get richer, and the rest of us dumb fools'll be cannon fodder."

Everyone had an opinion. In a way, Jake thought, America was already at war, a civil war. Lindbergh and the America

Firsters said the President, the Brits, and the Jews were trying
to drag the nation into war, that Lend-Lease was the beginning
of the end, the slippery slide that would lead to American boys
dying on foreign soil, fighting battles that were none of our business. Others watched the newsreel images of German troops
parading through Paris, the nightly bombing and rocket raids on
London, the footage of titanic battles on the Russian front, the
weekly maps with the dark blob that represented Nazi Germany
growing ever larger—and concluded that we had to join the
effort to stop the spread of fascism, to restore order and sanity
to a world gone mad. The two positions split America. In bars,
in truckstops, at dinner parties, any place people of different
minds gathered, people either consciously avoided the question
in the interest of social peace, or fell to ferocious arguments on
a subject that offered no middle ground.

He tried to picture the village when war came. Even if the
Coast Guard didn't restrict fishing grounds, the fishermen would
have a hard time getting enough fuel. And before long, the Navy
and Coast Guard would begin requisitioning fishing boats for
patrol duty. When Sera's brother Paul had gone off to join the
merchant marine, men in the village had questioned why anyone would leave. What would the same men say when their
boats were requisitioned, when they were called up? Was a draft
notice any different from Langer's invitation?

Either way, who would be left to dance with Sera?

6

The hallway outside the bridge offices smelled of strong, sweet tobacco. The heady scent made Mr. Raymond faintly dizzy, reminding him how much he hated these visits to New Haven.

The reaction always surprised him. Raymond expected to feel superior on a college campus. When he parked his dark green V-12 Packard convertible, undergraduates in their argyle sweaters and bowties would crowd around to gawk at the car. In his natty linen suit, with a bright silk tie and matching handkerchief in his pocket, Raymond felt sartorially splendid alongside the shabby tweeds of the professors and the dirty corduroys of the undergraduates. He knew he didn't have the education or easy money of the students, who even dressed-down had the swagger and stylized slang that came from growing up with wealth. But he told himself that if he hadn't grown up on the North Shore of Long Island or in the Back Bay of Boston, he had at least seen the world, or a chunk of it, and not from the deck of a merchant ship as an ordinary seaman. On "business," a term he had resolved to stop using because it sounded too lower-class, he had been to Lisbon, Panama City, and Havana. And it hadn't been only business. He allowed himself a smile as he remembered that he had been to private clubs that these undergraduates could never imagine.

But once he went up the steps of Street Hall to the bridge that spanned High Street, and caught the waft of Balkan Sobranie tobacco from under the door of the office of Professor J. Bradford Alden, Mr. Raymond suddenly felt uneducated, unmannered, and ignorant. He despised the feeling.

Alden was tall and slim, with thinning dark brown hair that he combed straight back. He wore bespoke-tailored tweed suits even in the summertime, and spoke with a faint but recognizable English accent. In his handwritten notes, Alden favored spellings like "colour" and "manoeuvre," crossed his 7s, and wrote a 1 so it looked like an inverted V. A student waiting outside the office once told Raymond that Alden's accent and writing were affectations picked up during the two years he spent as a Rhodes scholar, that in fact the man was born and raised in Brookline, Massachusetts, from less than patrician stock. But Alden wore the mannerisms so gracefully, and radiated such self-confidence, that Mr. Raymond found it hard to believe he wasn't the scion of generations of wealth.

Alden's specialty was Japanese art history. Raymond had asked once in a gallery in New York, and was told that Alden's catalogue raisonné of early Japanese landscapes was the definitive text. The dealer in New York, like everyone Raymond had asked in New Haven, thought that in addition to his professorship at the university, Alden ran a lucrative business as an art consultant, importing valuable artworks for private clients on his frequent trips to Japan. Alden made no secret of the extra income, and seemed to have no qualms about living in a style that other faculty at the university could only envy.

"How good to see you," Raymond said, as he closed the office door behind him.

Alden was sitting crosslegged on a woven floor mat in a corner of his office, facing the low wooden benches where he kept an ornate tea service and the brushes and pens he used to practice Japanese calligraphy. He didn't look up or acknowledge Raymond for several minutes, then slowly rose from the floor, and very deliberately took off the short robe he wore over his vest.

"Pull down the curtains," he said.

By 1941, with travel to Japan difficult for an American, Alden had begun doing much of his work from glass plates that were kept in metal cabinets in his office. To accommodate his research, the much-sought office on the bridge, with its tall windows that offered a splendid view over the rest of the campus, was fitted with blackout curtains. A pulldown projection screen stood in front of the bookshelves.

Raymond settled into a chair. Alden selected a meerschaum pipe with an amber stem from a burled walnut rack on his desk. He kept his tobacco in a buttery-soft leather pouch, and used a hand-chased silver and ivory pipe tool. It seemed to Mr. Raymond that there was no item in the office that hadn't been selected with exacting care, and probably no detail of Alden's life that hadn't been thought through with the same precision.

Raymond found himself increasingly nervous as Alden clicked on the projector. The first slide was a Japanese landscape, soft colors on creamy paper.

"Lovely, isn't it?" Alden said. "Have you ever seen anything so restful and serene?" Alden took his time lighting the meerschaum pipe. The heavy, sweet redolence of the Balkan Sobranie tobacco smoke filled the office, making Raymond light-headed and nervous.

Raymond, who knew nothing of Japanese art, said, "Nice." It was the part of these interviews he hated most of all, questions that seemed to have no purpose except to make him feel ignorant. Alden once asked him if realized that the bridge offices were modeled after the Bridge of Sighs in Venice. Raymond, who had never heard of the Bridge of Sighs, pretended he hadn't heard the question. Why, he wondered, can't we just get down to the job at hand?

"I have more information," Raymond said, filling the uncomfortable silence. "There have been more failures in test firings. The engineers blame the submarine captains, say they miss the targets. The captains blame the design and construction of the torpedoes."

Alden held up his pipe, stopping Raymond in midsentence. "Raymond, we have a new area of investigation. We would like you to make some inquiries about naval aviation."

"Flying boats?"

"Torpedo-launching airplanes and bombers. Particularly those launched from aircraft carriers."

"I thought torpedoes were the problem. Isn't that why I'm in Newport?"

"That was a building block, Raymond."

"Why airplanes?"

"*Why* isn't your question Raymond. Usually you ask *How much?* We haven't scrimped. You've lived well in Newport for many months now."

"It's just that Newport isn't the place to snoop naval aviation. They have a few planes at Quonset, and they're expanding the field there, but there are no aircraft carriers."

"It isn't the planes or carriers that interest us. Our concern is plans."

"Plans? If they don't have planes or carriers here, what plans would they have?"

"Raymond, for our purposes the Atlantic Fleet and the torpedo factory on Goat Island are far less important than another Newport institution. The American Navy is famous for exploring strategy and tactics at the Naval War College in what they call war games."

"That's Newport, fun and games."

With an exasperated expression, Alden retamped and relit the pipe. "These are not children's games, Raymond. They are simulations of fleet engagements. The research that goes into the games is painstaking. They fire naval guns at slabs of armor plate, and use measurements of the damage to estimate how many hits from a certain sized gun it takes to sink each ship. The fleet and tactical plans of the Navy are born and refined in those simulations. Your job is to learn whether they have dealt with naval aviation in recent games."

"Why?"

Alden blew a series of smoke rings, watching them dissipate. "I don't like your questions," he said.

"I'm asking because what you want me to do is impossible."

"How is that?"

"Obviously, the games are secret."

"No doubt they are stamped 'secret.' So are the results of torpedo tests. Did you have to slink around in a trenchcoat, meeting in dark alleys, to get information on torpedoes? I doubt it. You bought a few rounds of drinks, or maybe paid for a brothel for a couple of workers from Goat Island, and they were more than delighted to have an audience. And once they realized you would listen, you flattered them for being smart, agreed that the Navy was stupid, and they told you everything you wanted to hear.

"Your *profession*—ironic, isn't it, that we also call prostitutes professionals?—is not as exacting as you like to pretend. In an open society like America, secrets are there for the asking. How about the movements of capital ships? Can there be any secret more important or revealing of war plans? Look at this"—he held out an issue of the Honolulu *Star-Bulletin*—"an ordinary daily newspaper, available at any newstand. Because Honolulu is a port, the paper also includes shipping schedules. And because wives want to know when to start behaving and the Honolulu whorehouses want to know when their customers will arrive, the printed schedules aren't just for merchant ships. There are notices of every sortie and return of naval ships. This issue, from a week ago, announces that two battleships and a group of destroyers have left Pearl Harbor. Watch and their return will also be noted in the newspaper. It hardly takes a sophisticated spy to ferret out that sort of information."

Mr. Raymond watched Alden tamp and relight the pipe. He waited uncomfortably for the heady tobacco smoke. "The newspapers in Newport don't exactly publish war games," he said.

"No. But then the people you're dealing with in Newport aren't exactly Albert Einstein either."

"And what if no one is willing to come up with this information?"

"That looks like an expensive suit you're wearing. A bit flashy, but good quality linen. That Packard convertible of yours is very nice too."

"Okay, I get the point. If I come up with a useful contact, what exactly do you want?"

"We'll talk again, Raymond. If not here, in the gallery in New York."

Raymond got up, straightened his trouser pleats, and buttoned his jacket. He started for the door, then turned back. "Do you really expect me to find out what they're doing at the Naval War College? If those games are as important as you say, that's probably the best kept secret they have."

Alden puffed slowly, then tipped the pipe into an ashtray and ran his silver tool around the inside of the bowl, scraping out the core of burned tobacco. He pushed the smelly ashtray away from him, across the desk toward Raymond.

"That is exactly what I expect," he said.

Part Two

7

There was a lot of idle talk in Newport that summer, murmurs that with the blitzkrieg on in Europe, the teas and balls and riding and yacht racing of a Newport season were somehow inappropriate. Appearances, after all, mattered, and those fortunate enough to be part of society had an obligation to bear themselves in a manner befitting their stations.

The talk meant little to Sybil Westcott, who spent most of her afternoons that summer of 1941 planning a ball with her daughter Lisa. What Sybil had in mind wasn't an ordinary party, but a full-dress ball of the sort that no one had seen in Newport for a long time. She even had a theme—"Damn the Torpedoes, Full Speed Ahead!"—meant to appeal to those who were properly irked by the boredom of the season, and to echo those rakish balls of the past that were so admired by the grandes dames of Bellevue Avenue.

There hadn't been a party at the Westcott residence for a long time, and for this one Sybil had determined to go all out, with handsome young War College officers as escorts—at least Russell could help there—and liveried waiters standing behind the guests. Whenever Sybil thought of the waiters, she laughed. "If those slope-nosed Bellevue Avenue bitches try the snub on me," she said gleefully, "they'll end up with roast duck on their boobs."

The party was important because, as in so many families, the genetic inheritances among the Westcotts hadn't come out according to plan. Lisa's older brother Russell inherited their father's good looks and easy charm. His Navy career—the Navy was the one option that both his mother and father had urged him not to choose, which meant that it was a certain choice for the headstrong young man—held little promise, but Russell could get by on the strength of his prowess among the ladies, his charm, and the famed Westcott smile that would break down any barrier.

Lisa, unfortunately, was a plain girl. If she had an interesting face, with the borderline homely features that people call hand-some in a society woman, there might have been hope. But no one called Lisa handsome. Indeed, except when her shrill voice announced her outrage with the world, no one noticed her at all. The right schools and the right clothes, including a summer in Switzerland to learn the graces, had accomplished little.

By the summer of 1941, when Lisa was nineteen years old and had never been on a date that hadn't been arranged for her, Sybil concluded that it was time to launch a major offensive on Newport society. First, they needed to establish a beachhead with an eligible young man in Newport. In the fall, they could consolidate the position and negotiate a marriage. After all, Sybil reminded herself, a variation of the same plan had worked, years before, for her.

Although she could hold her head as high as anyone on Belle-vue Avenue, and had mastered all the fine points of the snub, that turning of the back and askance look of swiveling eyes that is the keynote of the grand ladies of Newport, Sybil Westcott was not a Newport lady. Before she adopted monogrammed sta-tionery with Newport and New York addresses, Sybil's address had been Port Chester, New York, where her father, Herman Fortzman, had made a substantial fortune supplying cigarettes and "other merchandise," as Sybil described it, to private clubs in the Bronx and Westchester.

Sybil's mother died when Sybil was twelve. The death cer-tificate gave the cause as consumption, but Sybil had seen enough empty bottles around their house to know that self-prescribed, pre-Prohibition "medicine" had done most of the damage.

As a widower, Herman Fortzman was lost. His wife had been

in charge of raising Sybil, and Herman didn't know where to begin. He did know how to write checks, so he sent Sybil away to private schools, and gave her anything money could buy. In 1913, when Sybil was seventeen, and Herman had run out of schools to send her to, he agreed to her long-standing request that they spend a holiday in Newport. Sybil announced to her friends in Port Chester that they would be "summering" in Newport. Later, she corrected her diction to say that they had spent "the Season" in Newport.

In Newport, Sybil discovered, Herman Fortzman's money meant next to nothing. To be part of the society that counted, it took an ineffable something else that, depending on the most recent snub she had received, Sybil variously identified as a name, family, style, manners, or connections—none of which could easily be bought, even with Herman's ready checkbook. In 1914 and 1915, Sybil begged her father to buy a house on Bellevue Avenue, or a yacht, or at least to rent a bigger house for the Season. If they looked the role, Sybil told herself, they could belong. "Otherwise," she told Herman, "no one will ever know we're here."

Herman was oblivious to the subtleties of society, but he had enough business sense to know the difference between money and show. "What do you care if they notice you?" he said. "Those ladies can stick their noses up so high they'll stab themselves in the back. They still don't have anything."

"What do you mean they don't have anything?" asked Sybil.

"People like that have enough to put on a show. It's what they call 'maintaining appearances.' When the crunch comes, they'll be in the street."

"Really?"

"I know what I'm telling you, Sybil."

Sybil thought Herman a barbarian, but since making money was the one thing he did well, money was one subject on which she trusted him. She had also heard enough business talk—with her father there was no other kind of talk—to know that when two parties each had something the other wanted, it was only a matter of time and careful negotiation before they made a deal. Herman Fortzman had money. If he was right, there were undoubtedly lots of attractive young men in Newport who had the name and connections that seemed to open doors, but who lacked the money to sustain the style to which they were accustomed. Thus was born a plan.

Sybil's plan was perfect, except for one thing: she hadn't counted on falling in love. But then in Port Chester, New York, Sybil had never met anyone like Russell Westcott, Jr.

They met by accident, at least Sybil thought it an accident. Sybil was sunning herself ("Exposing herself," Herman called it) on the dock of the cottage she had persuaded Herman to rent, watching boats scurry about Newport harbor before a Sunday afternoon race. The Fortzmans didn't belong to the Ida Lewis Yacht Club, of course, and neither Herman nor Sybil could sail or even drive the launch that bobbed on a conveniently sited mooring outside their cottage. As Sybil watched the handsome skippers maneuver their sailboats around the harbor, a mahogany runabout came alongside the dock, the man driving the boat smiled at Sybil with a smile that could have lit up the midnight sky, and right there, she fell madly, insanely, uncontrollably in love.

Russell Westcott, Jr.—everyone called him Wes—was born with all the virtues a man needed to thrive in Newport: he was handsome, athletic, and charming; he never talked about politics or business; he could ride, sail, and shoot; and, while the Newport ladies wouldn't have used the term in proper conversation, he was devastatingly sexy, especially when he smiled. It was the kind of smile—his bright blue eyes never wavered, but didn't press either—that made you feel as though you were the only other person in the world.

Wes had gone to the right schools, gotten the right grades (what later generations would call "gentleman Cs"), belonged to the right clubs, and had developed an attitude toward money so regal that he would have been genuinely surprised to be told that when he charged clothing or a fine shotgun in a store, a bill was later sent, or that when he wrote checks, someone had to deposit money into his account to cover the drafts. And whatever the situation, he had that smile that made problems disappear.

Within a week, Wes was taking Sybil everywhere. Never in her sheltered life, even in her wildest fantasies, had Sybil Fortzman dreamed of a man so dashing, or the possibility that so many hours of the day could be devoted to sheer pleasure. Riding and sailing were Wes's favorites, along with fast driving in open cars, parties, and endless hours on any reasonably private, reasonably flat surface—a bed, meadow, beach, or deck would do—where he introduced Sybil Fortzman to a range of activities she had scarcely dared to imagine from the protected Victorian house in Port Chester, New York.

Herman wasn't too sure about this blade with the fancy clothes and no answer beyond a faintly condescending smile when asked what he did for a living. When Herman suggested that he have someone make inquiries into the Westcott family, Sybil was horrified. "The Westcotts are society," she said. "Beyond question." Sybil, deliriously happy, leaped into marriage. Big weddings, Wes told her, were definitely out. They were married in a quiet ceremony at a small church in Rye, New York, which at least avoided the opprobrium of Port Chester. An Episcopal priest officiated. Herman, knowing there was no use protesting, wrote the newlyweds one big check after another.

In short order, Sybil and Wes bought an eight-room cottage on Coggeshill Avenue that had been remodeled from the stable house of an estate, a Duesenberg roadster, two Arabian geldings that even Sybil, who knew nothing about horses, thought the most beautiful animals she had ever seen, and so much clothing that Sybil was never aware of any laundry being done. The buying spree took place without a single discussion of money. When Sybil once questioned whether they could afford for Wes to order shirts in batches of a dozen and a half, he dismissed the discussion of money as "the trades," an activity for which he admitted, indeed boasted, having no inclination or talent whatsoever.

Sybil forgot her question in another whirl of riding, shooting, sailing, and bed. The pleasures, it seemed, were without end. Even the haughty ladies of Newport found Sybil a delight, just rakish enough with her colorful language and traces of a Bronx accent to inspire peals of giggles. There was no secret about her background, but as she had assured Herman, the Westcotts were society, *beyond question*. Barring the truly outrageous, marriage to a Westcott was Sybil's green card to Newport society. Within a week of the marriage, there was no shortage of calling cards on the silver tray that sat like a beggar's hand on the butler's tray in the foyer of what Sybil had already learned to call their "cozy" cottage.

Dazzled at her good fortune, Sybil moved slowly that first year, cautiously making the rounds and accepting invitations before she tried a party of her own. Sometimes she had to pinch herself to make sure that Wes and Newport weren't a dream.

She and Wes had been married for thirteen months, and Sybil was seven months pregnant, when she got an unexpected phone call from the bank advising her that their account did not have sufficient funds to honor a check Wes had written.

"There must be a mistake," Sybil said. She hadn't thought about money since she had gotten married. Wes's money—anyone who carried himself as Wes did had to have money—together with the steady flow of checks from Herman, was certainly enough for whatever they might do. She discreetly drove to the bank, where she was escorted into a private office to review twelve months of bank statements.

Sybil had never looked at a bank statement before, but she quickly caught on to what the numbers meant. Wes had never had any money of his own, and after he had written a remarkable series of checks drawn to "cash," neither did she. The banker, accustomed to Newport and the ways of its wealthy, was discreetly euphemistic. "Wes," he said, "has always enjoyed games and wagers."

When she got home, Sybil went out to the stable to find Wes. The horses were there. He wasn't. Then she heard voices from the stable apartment upstairs. She found Wes on the bed with an attractive young woman, engaged in quasi-athletic pursuits to which Sybil—despite her year of tutoring by Wes—hadn't yet been introduced.

Wes, ever a gentleman, made no excuses about the gambling or the woman. If Sybil didn't like it, he said, he would understand if she chose to leave. He would give her a divorce if she wanted it.

"No," Sybil said, she wouldn't leave. She would stay. Obviously he had learned his lessons and was sorry.

Wes smiled, the easy, broad grin with which she had fallen so helplessly in love. "I finished school a long time ago," he said. "There are no lessons I need to learn."

Sybil looked around, at the house, the view of the water in the distance, the stables with the horses, and at Russell Westcott, Jr., with his million-dollar smile. The decision was an easy one. Right then and there, she and Wes made a truce, a new marriage contract that would govern their lives together.

In a way, Sybil told herself, it was like taking a new set of vows. They sealed these with a handshake instead of a kiss, but if less romantic, they were more thoughtful, and certainly more likely to be observed than the automatic vows they had said before the Episcopal priest. She and Wes agreed to stay together, through thick and thin, sickness and health, transgressions and trials. Sybil and any children would get the good name of Russell Westcott, Jr., their entry ticket to the right clubs, the right schools, and the right parties. Wes would get a steady source of spending money, not what he had briefly enjoyed, but enough to maintain a respectable collection of horses and boats. Herman, she warned, would put strings on the checks. But even with strings, there wouldn't be wolves at the door.

In outward appearances, nothing had changed. Sybil could still go to Bailey's or the Casino or the Skeet Club as Mrs. Russell Westcott, Jr. She could leave her cards in any foyer, and expect cards from callers. But overnight, something didn't feel right. One afternoon, as a test, she dressed to the nines, drove to the Casino, and strolled down the stairs to the circle around the lawn court. There were conversations all around her, and while no one stopped to talk to her, no one looked askance either. She paraded around the court, holding her head high, then started up the stairs. It was then that she noticed that every woman had turned just enough that Sybil was walking through a gauntlet of backs. It was like the horrible ceremony she had

once read about when Captain Dreyfus had been drummed out
of the French army.

Afterward, she tried telling herself that it had only been her
imagination, but from that day Sybil was convinced that she
could recognize every woman in Newport from the back, since
it seemed that it was only their backs that she ever saw.

Before that fateful day, Sybil felt that she was on the verge
of belonging, that a few more weeks or perhaps months of good
behavior, of putting up with the snooty looks and haughty talk,
and she would finally be accepted. Now, she still had Wes, after
a fashion—she was convinced that she couldn't live without
Wes—but she knew she would never really belong to society,
that she would forever be on the fringes, a tolerated outsider.
She was miserable.

Herman died in 1923 from a gunshot wound. The newspapers
called it a hunting accident, although he had never been
known to go hunting before. The day after the funeral, which
Wes declined to attend, Sybil went to Herman's office in a run-
down building on the Post Road in downtown Port Chester.

The furniture was cheap, a few old desks and chairs crowded
into a shabby second-floor office. There was no view, no fine art
on the walls, no rack for pipes or tray for cut-glass bottles, none
of the accoutrements which Sybil had seen in the offices at the
bank. Herman's secretary and bookkeeper had shared the office
with him. The secretary wore her hair in a tight bun and a
terribly out-of-fashion long skirt, and the bookkeeper wore a
green visor and sleeve protectors over his shirtsleeves. They
were old and dowdy, but they both accorded Sybil the courtesies
and deferences due to the owner of a thriving business, including
a proper display of foot shuffling and a deferential "Yes, Mrs.
Westcott" that even her maid in Newport wouldn't grant her.

Cleaning out Herman's desk seemed the logical first chore,
so Sybil rolled up her sleeves and pulled out the drawers, which
were stuffed with scraps of papers scribbled with Herman's
cramped handwriting. It took her most of the morning to read
through the mishmash of papers, and to discover that the estate
Herman had left to her included several large, fast boats, a fleet

of trucks, a warehouse in Port Chester with a considerable inventory of bottled goods, and a collection of rakish business connections that promised both profit and excitement.

Then she asked to see the account books. It took her until after dark to parse her way through a thick general ledger which was in its own fashion a brilliant work of fiction. The secretary and bookkeeper stayed as long as she was there, and by the time she finished with the ledger book and asked some questions, the tone of their "Yes, Mrs. Westcott" replies had assumed an almost military snap. The respect for her intelligence and her position was an unexpected and welcome reward, a far cry from the snubs of the Newport ladies.

Before that day, Sybil had never even balanced a checkbook herself. She was smart enough to know that recognizing falsified records was only a first step toward actually understanding how Herman's business worked. But the chance to be away from the oppressive ladies of Bellevue Avenue and the challenge of keeping the complex business running was irresistible. Instead of coming home after the funeral, she decided to stay in Port Chester to, as she told Wes, "tidy up" Herman's business affairs.

What Sybil had to learn those first shaky weeks had not been covered in her private-school curricula or at afternoon tea parties in Newport. But it didn't take her long to realize that she had a talent for business, especially for Herman's business: Sybil found that she had an uncanny knack for judging whether a potential supplier or customer could be trusted. When anyone in the business commented on her seemingly unerring sense of people, she told them that the years in Newport had given her the ability to sniff out a phony. Under her direction, the "import" business thrived, picking up goods from mother ships in Long Island Sound and truck runs to Canada for resale to the speakeasies of the Bronx and Westchester.

Once Sybil had the business organized, a day a week in Port Chester was enough to keep things rolling. To acquaintances in Newport, she described her regular trips out of town by saying that she was going to the City for the day to shop. Wes asked about the funeral and her trips to New York only once, in his most circumspect fashion. She snapped back, "Don't worry, you'll still get your allowance." She heard the bitterness and sarcasm in her voice, and realized that their relationship, and her life in Newport, had taken another turn for the worse.

In time, Sybil's "import" business allowed her to buy a fine townhouse on Sixty-eighth Street in Manhattan, where for a few hours or days at a time she could forget the pains of Newport. Although it was immensely profitable and kept her busy, the business, even the birth of Russell, and later, the birth of his sister Lisa, did little to assuage Sybil's unhappiness. In Port Chester or the New York townhouse, she could sometimes forget the snubs and the humiliation of her relationship with Wes. With the end of Prohibition, she had to sell the townhouse. Living full time in Newport, there was no escape. She was resigned to her misery.

Sybil and Lisa were spending yet another afternoon in the library, quibbling over the guest list for the ball, from which Lisa wanted to expunge all young women who would in any way compete with her, when a pale-skinned, dark-haired woman in a riding habit came through the French doors from the terrace. The woman walked straight toward a telephone on the desk, without noticing them.

"Been riding?" Sybil asked. In the Newport house, her tone, no matter how she tried to control it, was combative.

The young woman froze, as if she had been caught in flagrante delicto. "I just wanted to use the phone," she said. "I had no idea someone was in here."

"Someone?" Sybil snapped. "Is Wes according me the dignity of being *someone* these days?"

"Hello, Sybil." Wes beamed his smile as he slid through the door, forever all innocence. He was fifty-one years old, and as handsome—no, more handsome—than the day Sybil had met him. His body was still trim, and the hint of silver at his temples and crow's-feet around his eyes added an aura of maturity and elegance. "The trails are marvelous today. You've met Melissa Adams, haven't you? She's quite an accomplished horsewoman. You know, Lisa, you should take up riding again. It's wonderful for your. . . ."

"We can see what it's wonderful for," said Sybil, staring at Melissa Adams, whose riding breeches looked as though they had been sprayed onto her. Sybil paused only long enough to let the words sink in before she said, "Tell me, Melissa, has Wes shown you his sword collection yet?"

"Sword?" Melissa's innocence made her the perfect foil. "I didn't know you collected swords, Wes."

"Sybil!" Wes tried to steer the girl back through the French doors, but Sybil's tongue was faster than his most adroit steps.

"Really," said Sybil. "I'm surprised he hasn't shown it to you yet. Wes's sword is his favorite plaything."

His answering look was withering, or would have been if Sybil hadn't steeled herself. "Let's go, Melissa," he said. "We should get back to the stable."

"Good day, Melissa," said Sybil. "You know, I think you may get to see that sword yet. I ought to warn you, though. It might be blunter than you expect. Even a good sword wears down with too much use."

From the sudden arch of her eyebrows and the slackness in her jaw, the gist of the conversation had just dawned on Melissa Adams as Wes escorted her off in the direction of the stables.

For a long time after they left, Lisa stared at her mother, watching Sybil's lips alternately purse and quiver. "Mommy," she asked, "why are you and Daddy so vulgar?"

"Vulgar? We aren't vulgar. Not in the least. The word you want is honest. Brutally honest sometimes, but nonetheless honest. That's more than I can say for most of the couples in Newport."

"How can you let him parade in here with a tramp like that? Did you see her riding breeches? They didn't leave much to the imagination."

"Don't be naïve, Lisa. She used what she had, led with her strong suit. If you could wear breeches like that, you would."

"Why? To be led off to the stable house by a cad like Daddy? Or Russell? Do you know why Russell left the club after the race on Saturday? He was chasing after some tramp on one of those Portuguese fishing boats. Probably some round-heeled, greasy hag."

"Knowing your brother, I doubt she was a hag. Whatever their foibles, your father and brother have splendid taste in women."

Lisa jumped up, covering her face. "How can you sit there so calmly, talking about them like they were gods?"

Sybil smiled, her face suddenly soft and warm. "You'll fall in love someday, Lisa. When you do, you'll understand."

"Love? Sitting here with a grin on your face while he's out in the stable house with a tart? If that's love, I'll pass."

Sybil got up to pour herself a drink from a glass decanter on a side table. The bottles looked like sherry and port, proper drinks. The one she chose, from the back of the table, could have been water. It was vodka.

"Love isn't something you 'pass,' " said Sybil. "The day I met your father, he was wearing a shirt so soft it was like a cloud. He had the collar unbuttoned so that the hair from his chest peeked through—twenty years before Clark Gable did it. Wes wore white slacks and his hair hung down over his forehead in a curl that made you want to straighten it with your fingers, or maybe just play with it. When I sat up as he pulled alongside in that beautiful launch, he handed me a single long-stemmed rose, smiled that incredible smile of his, and rode off across the harbor. I didn't even know his name, but I knew that I would never want to look at another man."

Lisa nodded, begrudgingly acknowledging the romantic appeal of the story.

"By the time I saw him again, I was head over heels in love with the man."

"Couldn't you tell that he would . . . I mean, Daddy has always. . . ."

"Lisa, when I was with him, I felt like the only woman in the world."

"You think that's what Russell does to women too? I listen to girls talk about him, and I can't believe it's my brother they're talking about. At the club Saturday, Nicole Breedlove practically peeled the clothes off Russell. And of course Russell took off to chase some tramp. Like father, like son."

"What tramp?"

"How am I supposed to know? The last anyone saw Russell,

he was down at the fishing boats looking for some Portuguese girl."

"Those disgusting wrecks?"

Lisa shrugged. "As long as he doesn't bring her to the ball."

By late afternoon, after two more glasses of vodka, and with what Lisa promised was the last review of the guest list out of the way, Sybil was feeling mellow and relaxed. She lay down on the bed in the room she and Wes hadn't shared for fifteen years and closed her eyes, letting her mind wander back to those first wonderful days in Newport, when she was deliciously in love. She was so lost in the memories that she couldn't tell whether it was a dream or real.

When she opened her eyes, Wes was standing there, the curly blond hairs of his chest peeking through his open shirt.

"You looked so peaceful," he said. "I didn't mean to wake you."

"It's all right. I was remembering." She watched his face, looking for the softness and the smile that had always been enough to make the hurt go away. "You look very handsome, Wes. You know I've never been able to resist that smile."

He sat on the edge of the bed, resting a hand on her arm.

"Do you ever wish we could turn the clock back, Wes? Back to those first days?"

He didn't answer.

"Wes . . . ?"

"It was very nice, Sybil."

"Very nice? Is that what it was?" She sat up, shaking off his hand. "Is that what you say to the tarts, too? 'It was very nice.' How unimaginative of you! At least you could say something like 'Did the earth move for you?' "

"Sybil! Why do you do this to yourself?"

"Oh, Wes, how thoughtful of you to worry about me. Did you worry about me when you brought Miss Tight Breeches into the library today?"

He bolted off the bed. "What's wrong with you, Sybil, is that you have no sense of time or place. You refuse to restrain that vulgar mind and mouth."

"My vulgar mind? My God, Wes. Are the standards for the Westcotts really so different? A barb or two from me is vulgar, but for you to parade in with a tramp when I am talking with our daughter is just fine. Or what about the time your son walked into the stable house and found you wearing nothing but your silk socks and garters, with your ass in the air humping away at some floozy? Russell was what, eight? That, I suppose, was your sense of an exquisite time and place for a lesson on life for your son.

"The lesson seems to have set in just fine. Now he's chasing around after some Portuguese tramp. I just hope that you can teach him how to find a rich wife, because he won't get far on the great Westcott fortune."

Wes backed toward the door. "I wouldn't worry about Russell. He's more a Westcott than a Fortzman."

"A Westcott? Is that all it takes? War, depression, crashes, hurricanes—it can all come and go, and Russell is safe because he's a Westcott. When the war comes, we should make certain that Russell paints his name on the side of his ship. Surely, the Germans won't sink a ship when they see that Westcott name."

"You wanted the name enough."

"Did I?"

"Why else would you put up with our arrangement?"

Sybil hesitated, letting her face soften. "I wanted you, Wes. If only you would, or could, understand that."

The words caught him. He stood in the doorway, without an answer, smiling his irresistible smile. For an instant, she saw a streak of tenderness in his eyes.

But it was only an instant.

8

No one, including Russell, disputed that Russell Westcott III was the least qualified officer appointed to the junior class of 1941 at the Naval War College. He had not graduated from Annapolis, had no fleet experience or advanced training, and his service record was, to put a fine point on it, undistinguished.

Even worse, Russell had gotten his commission outside the usual path through Annapolis. At Annapolis, cadets learned to pass a senior officer on a walkway with a brisk "By your leave, Sir," and to yield the position of honor on the right-hand side of the walkway. By the time they were junior officers, they knew that senior officers would make social calls to appraise the "cut of the jib" of a junior officer, and that it behooved a young officer who wanted to get ahead to show that he was made of the right stuff, that he could conduct himself accordingly. They learned to quote with approval a remark allegedly once said to the famed Admiral Mahan about a fellow officer, "He's the sort of man, you know, who would wear a frock coat unbuttoned."

Instead, Russell had gone from St. George's, a prep school in Newport, where his father was on the board of trustees and Sybil had hosted fund-raising functions, to Brown University, where gentleman Cs were the most distinguished grades he received. On the eve of his graduation, the dean concluded that even Russell's athletic contributions and his mother's annual gifts to the school were not sufficient to compensate for his dismal academic record. Only half facetiously, the dean suggested that perhaps a stint in officer's candidate school would bring about a much needed change in attitude. Sybil and Wes were horrified: the Navy was hardly the career they had in mind for Russell. Russell, who had no other plans, quickly concluded that any career they both opposed was worth a try, and signed the papers and swore the solemn oath. He didn't take the idea of a commission or the commitment it represented any more seriously than the schedules of exams or athletic competitions at Brown.

Russell's classmates and the staff of the college were left in the dark, wondering what screw-up in the Bureau of Navigation, then in charge of personnel appointments, had allowed the irreverent blond lieutenant into the elite Naval War College. Russell didn't have to wonder. He knew he had gotten his appointment the same way he had "earned" so many of the accomplishments in his life: his father happened to have gone to St. George's with the Assistant Secretary of the Navy, and Wes thought it a good idea for Russell to be in Newport, around the right sort of people, rather than at some wretched outpost like Norfolk. At his previous billet, in Cavite, he had been involved in enough fistfights at the officers' club and on the streets of Manila to earn three reprimands and a brush with an admiral's mast, but friends in high places kept those blemishes off his record and smoothed the way to the plum appointment in Newport.

From his first day back in Newport, Russell was convinced that he would suffocate under the smugness of the War College. Whenever he walked into Mahan Hall, he would remember the blatant self-congratulations of the welcoming lecture from Admiral Kalbfus when the classes gathered on July 1.

"Gentlemen," the admiral had said, "I don't have to tell you the traditions you have inherited and that you have the privilege of carrying to future generations. There is a reason that the Navy is the only service branch mentioned by name in the constitution. Ultimately, it is on the Navy, and the Navy alone, that the defense of the nation rests. It is the Navy which can—and soon, no doubt, *will*—be expected to project the power and authority of the nation to the furthest corners of the globe. You, gentle-men, the select officers who have been chosen to prepare for possible fleet command, represent the hopes and aspirations of the Navy and the nation. You are the future of America! Wel-come to the Naval War College!"

Most of the class clapped, applauding themselves and the good fortune that had gotten them appointments to the War College. Russell sat low in his chair, not quite asleep, but not really listening either. From the age of ten, he had overheard the mighty men of Newport discuss politics and war in tight-jawed pronouncements:

"Hitler is a ludicrous joke, an unemployed paperhanger. It's a measure of British decline—the same thing we see with their faltering efforts at the America's Cup—that they can't handle this Hitler."

"The Japanese hardly matter, at least not to us. Let those yellow races fight it out amongst themselves."

"That damn socialist Roosevelt is one of our own, even if he and that ugly wife of his spout off like a couple of union organ-izers."

The men who made those pronouncements were scions of wealth and breeding, heirs of fortunes that sometimes went back as far as the history of America. They harbored no doubts that *they* were the future of America, as they had been its past. How was Russell Westcott III supposed to believe the theorists of the War College, with their scenarios of make-believe war and Jap-anese imperialist aspirations, over the wisdom of the men whose fortunes and wills had built America?

Remarkably, despite his skepticism and the predictions of those who had seen his naval record, Russell thrived at the col-lege. In classes, no matter what the subject, he was a mediocre student, carrying on the gentleman C tradition of the Westcott family. But then the classes on global strategy, engagement tac-tics, international politics, and racial character hardly mattered. The professors lectured and the junior officers took notes, but the note-taking was a courtesy, an expected gesture to show respect for the lecturers. The important exercise at the college, indeed, the only activity that mattered when it was time to name graduates to new billets, including fleet commands, was the famed war games.

Whoever named the exercises war *games* had a finely-tuned sense of irony. The games were deadly serious. Men would stay up for ninety-six hours at a stretch, with no more than occasional catnaps, working through hours of supply and firepower calculations before they ordered a single move of the metal model ships that were pushed around the tile floors of the game room with long wooden sticks. The pressure cooker atmosphere of the game room, with senior officers lolling around the balcony, monitoring the successes and the demeanor under stress of the participants on the gaming floor, was enough to drive junior officers into hysterics or tears. When the annual fleet game was over, the Naval Hospital in Newport would be flooded with cases of physical and mental exhaustion.

The experiences on the gaming floor would stay with men throughout their careers. Naval historians could list every flag officer who had been promoted from the ranks of the War College classes; biographies never failed to mention their advanced training at the college. No one kept count of how many careers ended on that floor.

Few admitted it, but most officers in the junior class dreaded the games. At the mention of the word, many would flee to the officers' club, driving away the thought of the brain-wracking demands of juggling so much information and so many options with the comfort of a drink and unthreatening stories of the Philippines or the South China Sea.

Not Russell. To Russell Westcott III, the war games were just that, a *game*. He took one look at the game room, with its black and white tile checkerboard floor and the spectator galleries for onlookers, and immediately grasped what most of the officers would never figure out: that despite the repeated assurances to the contrary by lecturers and senior officers, the real object of the war games was not to understand the consequences of a complex exercise, the logistics and firepower constraints of a fleet assault, but to *win*, to annihilate the opposition, to triumph totally and absolutely. Winning was one thing Russell Westcott III understood.

Even as a child, Russell had played every game the same way—all out, tenacious, totally bent on victory. When he got into a competition, whether it was a junior class steeplechase at prep school, a game of checkers, a skeet match, or a summer fleet exercise, something came over him, a transformation so sudden and so complete that other competitors, even spectators, were amazed, or frightened.

In Russell's first try at the war games, he was hopelessly unprepared, unable even to complete his firepower calculations. He stared at the tiny model boats on the tile floor, the pads of maneuvering sheets and the complex maneuvering board, the shelves of tables and charts, and the faces of eager officers around the room, some engaged, others watching. The conversations everywhere were logistics, trajectories, and damage assessment. People rattled off figures from homework and calculations he had never done. Behind him he heard kibitzers whispering that his situation was hopeless.

Russell spun around, glaring at the officers in summer whites. "I'm going to win this fucking game," he said.

"The object isn't to *win*, Westcott."

"Fuck you. I play to win." Without even a pause to glance at the firepower tables, he called for a tactical aircraft strike from a carrier in his task force.

"An air strike?" he heard from behind him. "Ludicrous."

By every measure of conventional wisdom it *was* ludicrous. The textbooks said that tactical air strikes were not used as an offensive weapon once the opposing fleets had spotted and engaged one another. The purpose of aircraft was reconaissance, or spotting for the big guns of the battleships. But, whether it was brilliance or beginner's luck, Russell's aircraft met unprepared ships. Within three hours he had crippled the opposing fleet.

Soon, the staff at the War College were talking about the remarkable competitive spirit of the young officer. Privately, Horatio Breedlove said he had never seen anything like it. In class, it was all Russell could do to keep his eyes open. More often than not in lectures he would be asleep in his chair, holding his head off the table by sheer willpower. A day, sometimes even an hour later, he would be in the tile-floored game room, his concentration so intense that if a real air or sea attack had come instead of the maneuvers on the floor, he probably wouldn't have noticed.

Once, after Russell had made an outrageously bold flanking maneuver in a tactical game, a move that had transformed a desperate situation for Blue into a colossal victory, Breedlove asked Russell why he had done it, when the odds of success were so slim.

"It was the only way to win."

"There was no way it would work unless your opponent were a fool. What made you so sure that Orange wouldn't call your bluff?"

Russell's answer, a nonchalant shrug, enraged Breedlove.

"Lieutenant, these aren't games of poker. You risked an entire battle squadron of ships, men, and matériel. If Orange hadn't been so trusting and conventional in their reaction, you would have lost it all. In a real-life situation, your tactics were unsupportable."

Russell grinned, the famous Westcott smile. "But we won," he said.

That day, he became Breedlove's prodigy.

From the day he reported for duty in Newport, Russell had stayed away from the officers' club that had been established in a room upstairs at the Reading Room, the most distinguished of Newport's private men's clubs. There was a condescending tinge of noblesse oblige in the original invitation offering the use of the upstairs room to the War College, but most of the naval officers were so thankful for even a hint of recognition from Newport society that they closed their eyes to the subtle snubs of the real members downstairs. Russell had already inherited a proper membership at the Reading Room, which he had never used. For him, the place was doubly damned: upstairs were the officers he wanted to escape; downstairs were the friends of his father and mother, the natty swells who used the club as a home away from home, watching the world parade by from the security of the club piazza, and for the sake of the cachet of the

Reading Room, putting up with the indignities of a menu of canned soup and crackers.

His own choice for a hangout was the White Horse Tavern, an ancient shambles of a place, billing itself as the oldest tavern in America, so that it was sometimes overrun with tourists. At least, he reminded himself, the talk was about something other than fleet tactics, the racial characteristics of the Japanese, and the tedious Navy gossip about rank, promotions, and billets. He had tried some of the bars close to the harbor, but they were the preserve of the enlisted seamen who had come to Newport for training, and the workers from the torpedo station on Goat Island. The vocabulary in the harbor bars was saltier than what he heard at the officers' club, if you even found an enlisted man who was willing to talk with an officer around, but it was still Navy talk.

The last Saturday in July, like many Saturdays, Russell was sitting alone at a table at the White Horse, nursing a whiskey and soda and halfheartedly watching the traffic. Women came to the White Horse in the late afternoons, usually in pairs, but he wasn't looking for women. It had been only six days since the Sunday regatta in the harbor, and for those six days he hadn't thought about anything except the long-legged, dark-haired girl on the fishing boat.

He couldn't stop thinking about her. He had looked up Stonington on a map and planned a dozen ways to get there, but the War College would never give him the time, and he would somehow have to borrow both a car and money for gas.

Russell had been at the White Horse for almost an hour, nursing the drink he didn't really want, when Mr. Raymond came in. Russell knew Mr. Raymond had seen him from the doorway, and he watched the man walk to the other end of the bar to order a drink alone. Mr. Raymond was wearing cream-colored slacks and a blue blazer, with an ascot at his neck.

No one was quite like the mysterious Mr. Raymond. He was an outsider, but not like most outsiders. Usually, people who didn't belong in a cliquish society like Newport were so eager to be seen with the right people, so anxious to hear their own names from the right lips, that they lingered too close, imposing themselves, trying by proximity to draw the aura of the rich and famous, as if it were some perfume that stuck to the clothes and skin. Mr. Raymond was self-effacing and undemanding; he never forced himself on anyone. He was content to wait for scraps of conversation or company that were thrown his way.

Who is he? Russell wondered. Why would anyone be content to hover in the background, to grasp at the meager company of people like Russell. Allow him, and Raymond would pick up checks, spring for bar bills, dinner, clubs. Shortly after they met, he saw that Russell had no money one evening and discreetly offered him two fifty-dollar bills.

"A gentleman shouldn't go around with empty pockets," said Mr. Raymond. "You never know what may happen."

"And you never know when I might get around to paying you back," said Russell.

"I hardly need worry. A gentleman is always a gentleman."

Not long after, Russell had mentioned that his boat was tired, with worn sheets and a sail that was just about falling apart because he was too busy to dry it properly after the races.

"You ought to have a new sail," said Mr. Raymond. "You shouldn't compete with substandard equipment."

"I should have a lot of things, but neither the Navy nor the Commanders-in-Chief think it is of the highest priority for Russell Westcott to race with a new sail on his Monohull."

"Commanders-in-Chief?" With his hollow, forced diction, Mr. Raymond put the emphasis on the plural. His Adam's apple bounced as he spoke. His cheeks were shaved so closely Russell could scarcely see the roots of the whiskers.

"Sybil and Wes," Russell explained. "The Joint Command. They may never agree on anything, but that doesn't keep either of them from commanding their forces."

Mr. Raymond looked down, as if the conversation were embarrassing. "At your age, and with your ability and background," he said, "I should think you ought to be quite independent."

"Agreed. Why don't we tell the Commanders?"

"I'm not sure you need to do that," said Mr. Raymond, still looking down at the table. "I could take care of the sail. What are friends for, after all?"

The sail Mr. Raymond bought had gotten Russell three firsts so far.

What was in it for the man? Russell wondered. A little hob-nobbing with the rich? A chance to be seen in the right places? A few stories to take home to his friends? Russell didn't even know where Mr. Raymond was from. How could anyone tell you so little about themselves? And he had never asked for a favor. Not a ticket to the Casino, not an entry to the Clambake Club or Bailey's, not even an introduction or an invitation to a party.

Was he a faggot? He had never asked about women, never shown the slightest interest in the attractive women who some-times paraded into the White Horse. Russell remembered once when a homosexual had approached him in the men's room of a movie theater in Washington. A spin-kick to the gut and two swift punches to the face had left the queer sprawled out on the tile floor. If there had been a scrap of cardboard nearby, Russell would have left a note behind: *This is what happens to faggots!*

It had been a full week since he had noticed a woman, except for the girl on the fishing boat. Is there something wrong with me? he wondered. Am I a latent? Is that why Mr. Raymond hangs around, because he picked up those signals?

He watched Mr. Raymond turn toward him, ever reserved, hinting a smile, obviously reluctant to seem pushy. Russell lifted his eyebrows, and watched Mr. Raymond's smile broaden as he straightened his jacket and brought his drink down the bar. No, Russell concluded, the man wasn't a homosexual. He was gen-uine, and not the first person Russell had met who was fasci-nated by people like Russell. Athletes and movie stars had their fans for the same reasons.

Russell! I didn't get a chance to tell you how terrific you were last Sunday, especially in the last race. I've never enjoyed a race more."

Russell smiled. Mr. Raymond knew nothing about yacht rac-ing, but even uninformed adulation felt good.

"You look gloomy. The college still got you down?"

"It's like going to church. They know everything. Breedlove is so fucking cocksure that if the Japanese ever did something other than what he's predicted he'd declare that they were acting against their own best interests. You'd think they call him for permission every time they send a fleet somewhere."

"Remind me again, who's Breedlove?"

"Professor of strategy. The self-appointed W.F.E. on the Japanese, with auxiliary expertise on all other subjects."

"W.F.E.?"

"World's Foremost Expert."

Mr. Raymond laughed, a hearty, easy laugh that puffed his cheeks and squinted his eyes. He was a welcome relief from the stuffiness of the college and Newport.

"And why do they care about the Japanese?"

"Because, according to the W.F.E., we're going to have a war against Japan. He—they—have been planning it for twenty years, and no one is going to cheat them out of it. It's like a script. The whole war has been planned and rehearsed. All that's left is the performance."

"And that's really what you do at the college? I thought it was literature and history and that sort of thing. In fact, I could never really understand how you could have a 'war' college unless it was to read about Athens and Sparta or Lord Nelson at Trafalgar."

Russell shook his head, signaling his lack of interest in the subject. More than a quip or two about the college usually bored him.

"Mr. Raymond, what do you do?" The question burst out, and a residue of manners that had been drummed in from childhood told Russell it was wrong to ask.

"I thought I told you. I'm self-employed, Russell. A bit of a coupon-clipper. I know it's fashionable to be ambitious these days, at least in some circles, but I've got more than enough to tide me along. So I read the newspaper, put in a call to my stockbroker every so often, clip off the coupons when they're due, and the rest of my time is free to enjoy life."

"What about those trips you told me about?"

"Ah, the pleasures of the idle not-so-rich. When I have the inclination, I charter a boat and go sportfishing. This is the place for it, you know. The sword and tuna fishing off Montauk and Block Island is the best I've found anywhere."

"Fishing?" Russell lit up. "Do you know anything about the Portuguese fishing boats?"

"Not a thing. Mine is strictly sportfishing. I never even keep the catch. Fact is, I don't like fish." Mr. Raymond had an admirable habit of never probing, never asking the obvious question that followed. He seemed to know that Russell was anxious to talk, and he listened eagerly to Russell's description of the girl on the dragger.

"She sounds eye-popping," said Mr. Raymond. "It doesn't surprise me one bit. Before the war started in Europe, I was in Lisbon on business. Some of the Portuguese women were spectacularly beautiful. Their dark skins are wondrously sensuous."

Wondrously sensuous. Exactly the words for her, thought Russell. "Around here, the Portuguese are fishermen, or they work in the shipyards. The women wear black dresses shaped like sacks, and most of them are fat. You don't expect to see someone like her."

Mr. Raymond smiled, stretching the skin of his cheeks and forehead. "Beautiful women are always a surprise. Why don't you go find this spectacular lady?"

Russell pointed his finger at Mr. Raymond, the thumb cocked as if his hand were a pistol. "Perfect idea, except that I've got no wheels, no gas, and no leave. A pair of fishermen down at the docks told me she's from Stonington. It's a little fishing village in Connecticut. With the ferry it's probably three hours."

"Well, you're certainly welcome to the Packard. But if I were going to see a Portuguese lady who lived in a fishing village, I wouldn't go by car. I'd go by boat. The Portuguese are people of the sea. I don't really understand what they teach in that college of yours, but my strategy would be to use every weapon. Frontal attack, I think it's called." He laughed.

Russell shared the laugh. "Actually, I had the same idea. But

Wes keeps the tank on the commuter empty to make sure no
one (that means 'yours truly') borrows it."

"So all you need is gasoline? Russell, you surprise me." Mr.
Raymond reached inside his breast pocket. "What are friends
for?"

9

Just west of Watch Hill with its grand Victorian hotels, a thin peninsula of sandy beach stretches out toward Fishers Island. Not so long ago, the beach curved back on itself, connected at Napatree Point to a thirty-five-acre patch of dunes named Sandy Point. Three states laid claim to the dunes: Connecticut and Rhode Island because the cartographers had drawn their border through the center of the spit, and New York because Fishers Island was only a short hop away. During Prohibition, an enterprising bootlegger took advantage of the muddled jurisdictions by building a warehouse over the intersection of the state lines. When state agents raided, workers would roll the cases across the floor to the safety of another state.

The only other buildings on Sandy Point were a row of summer cottages along Fort Road and the ruins of Fort Mansfield, which had once boasted a three-gun coastal battery. A developer had plans for house lots on the point, along with a yacht basin amidst the ruins of the fort. The houses would have enjoyed spectacular views over Fishers Island Sound, and out through Watch Hill Passage to the open sea.

The great hurricane of 1938 put an abrupt end to the plans. Within hours, waves as high as the lighthouse at Watch Hill broke over the spit, sweeping away the cottages and the ruins of the fort. Through the afternoon and evening, the wind and waves hammered relentlessly until they finally cut a channel through the sands of Napatree Point, leaving what had been a spit as an island. When the wind and rain ceased, sandy beaches on all sides and a freshwater pond made the new island a splendid natural habitat for ducks and seabirds. With no residents except the gulls and terns, the beaches remained pristine, the fine sand washed daily by the tides. Anyone enterprising enough to sail or row out could find a private beach, the kind of retreat the rich would pay untold sums to own.

The first time Sera swam across the channel to Sandy Point was on a dare. She was fourteen. Until then she had swum in the calm water at the foot of Wall Street in the village, where the sea swirled in bright colors from the dyes at the velvet mill, and the streaks of purple or crimson on her skin were an undeniable admission that she had been swimming. The untouched island across the channel, with its promise of private swimming, was a constant invitation.

Her brother Paul had swum across the tide-swept channel to Sandy Point, first, strutting like a peacock afterward. That had been enough to goad Sera into taking up the challenge. Her crawl stroke, learned by imitation and experiment, was peculiar, and Paul and his friends told her she did it wrong, that she was supposed to take a breath on every stroke, instead of waiting four or sometimes six strokes. But by the end of the summer, after she had beaten most of them in makeshift races, they stopped both the criticism and the challenges. The next spring, with Paul crewing on the draggers, the island was hers, a private retreat. One day, she peeled off her swimsuit and swam naked, a lady's privilege on her own island.

Jake had given Sera an old pulling boat that she kept tied to a tree close to the water on the backside of the village. But usually she didn't bother with the boat. It was more fun to swim, even though the current could be rough when the tides were running strong. Swimming made the hideaway that much more private, a club with a secret initiation rite.

She needed that one place to be alone. The village was too small for secrets. The draggers had no sooner tied up at the dock than everyone knew how well each boat had done. Before the fishermen had reached their homes, at every dinner table in the village there would be talk about how big each man's share had been and where he spent his *shack*, the sum a fisherman set aside from the money he brought home. If a man decided to court a woman, Mrs. DaCunha and the other gossips knew his plans before he reached her house. If he kissed the woman, or walked to the end of the point with her, it would be the talk of the docks, the mills, and the streets before she got home.

In the village, Sera felt eyes always watching her. Not only Mrs. DaCunha, but her mother, Manuel, other neighbors, the shopkeepers, even the old fishermen who patched nets and readied lobster baits on the dock. If she wore her hair tied up with a ribbon some evening, the next day three people who hadn't even seen her with the ribbon would say, "I like it better down." Sometimes she wondered if even her own thoughts were secret— or did Mrs. DaCunha and the other ladies have a way of reading her mind? Sandy Point was one of the few secrets she had.

Sometimes she fantasied having a house on the island, with glass doors that would open so the breeze could come in off the sea. Jake had told her about houses on Fishers Island with rooms that could be opened on three sides, and cupolas and widow's walks high enough to see boats far out at sea. One night when they were sailing she told him her fantasy about Sandy Point. When they got back to the boatyard, he sketched a house with broad verandas on three sides and a grove of trees behind. She kept the sheet of drafting paper with his sketches rolled up in her bureau drawer, a concrete image to refuel her dreams.

After Paul went to sea, Josephina said it was wrong for Sera to swim alone at Sandy Point.

"I can swim better than Paul. It was all right for him."

"It's not the swimming, Sera. You know that."

"What is it then?"

"What if someone came by in a boat and saw you alone there?"

"What if they did?"

"Sera! It's enough. You don't want me to have to tell Manuel that you swim there."

The warning didn't stop Sera from going to Sandy Point. It only stopped her from talking about it. Josephina was wise enough not to ask.

On Sunday morning, after church, Sera had done what she had to do, helping her mother clean the house, airing the bed linen, adding to the soup on the stove, kneading dough for the sweet bread, cutting vegetables, and picking up clams for dinner. In most houses of the village, young women did the identical chores, adding the same vegetables to their soup pots, making their sweet bread with the same recipe.

Sera worked quickly, without dallying, knowing she could be free once she finished the chores. She had long before noticed that Josephina and the other women in the village slowed the pace of whatever work they had until it filled the whole day. They seemed to fear having an hour with nothing to do. It was as though there were some law that said women should be busy until their men came home.

By the time Sera reached Sandy Point, the beginnings of a southwesterly had set in, stirring the still late morning air with the refreshing scent of the open sea. The water and air were warm, the only clouds wisps of frail cirrus, the tide close to full flood. She stretched out on her back on the beach, breathing in chest-filling gasps from the hard swim, before she turned over and hiked up on her elbows.

There was a faint haze over Fishers Island. Jake had taught her that when there was haze to the southwest, the sea breeze would build. "A reefing breeze," he called it. "If you know it's coming, you've got the race."

Out in the harbor, a lone oysterman poled over the flats. Behind him, a dragger steamed toward Watch Hill Passage, its slow-turning engine chugging like the locomotive sounds on a radio show. The dragger was already too distant to identify. Sera watched until the outline faded on the horizon, the faint image wavering in the heat until it could have been a sailboat or a marker or a mirage. She could remember watching her father sailing off on fishing trips, out through the breakwater and Watch Hill Passage to the open ocean. When he said goodbye at the dock, he would say, "Next stop, Portugal."

"You're coming back, aren't you?" Sera would ask.

Her father would wait a few seconds, straight-faced, before he hugged her and tickled her under the ear with his nose. "Of course I'm coming back. How could I stay away from my Seraphina?"

Sera had no idea how long she had been daydreaming when she heard the engine of a motorboat. The sound came on abruptly, like a balky car that suddenly roars to life. Once she heard it, the roar of the engine was insistent. Sera had spent long enough around the harbor to know the sounds of boats the way Rosa knew the sounds of animals in the grass. This one wasn't a fishing boat. The pitch was too high and powerful, like the cries of a caged beast. She watched the end of the island, waiting.

The sound grew louder, then faded. She thought it had turned away until she remembered that the islands and rocks in Fishers Island Sound did strange things to echoes and sounds. Jake and Paul used to fool one another by finding passageways that would make the sound of an engine seem to come from somewhere else.

Twice, the roar grew closer and faded. She found herself hanging on the sound of the engine, thinking of nothing else. She remembered walking in the woods with Rosa, and how Rosa would stop to listen to the faint sounds of birds or animals.

Suddenly, a bright varnished hull rounded the end of Sandy Point. The mahogany planking was deep reddish-brown, reflecting the sunlight in swirls. The trim pieces around the cockpit were bright chrome. She had seen fancy runabouts in Newport, but this wasn't an ordinary speedboat. The hull was easily forty feet long, with a flaring bow, and a huge hatch cover over the engines. Sera had never before seen a boat like it, except in the drawings in Jake's cabin. And even the drawing on Jake's wall, his father's huge speedboat knifing through heavy swells, didn't seem as powerful as the lean mahogany hull in front of her. Throttled down, its bow cutting the water instead of skimming the surface, the boat was like a big cat, stalking its prey, ready to pounce.

The boat kept a steady distance offshore, not more than a hundred yards off the beach. With the sunlight in her eyes, Sera couldn't tell whether the man at the helm, scanning the shore, was alone. She remembered her mother's warnings.

"It's not safe out there alone."

"You never cared if Paul went."

"It's different for a man."

As the boat traced along the shore, a patch of thin cirrus clouds drifted in front of the sun, cutting the harsh glare of the backlight. She could see the blond hair of the man at the helm. She felt a twinge of recognition before she connected the man to the race two weeks before. There was no one else on the boat.

He motored to the head of the island, where the narrow channel led to Watch Hill, then turned back, tracing the shore, this time only fifty yards off the beach. He was wearing a white shirt, open at the neck. His blond hair blew back from his face as his eyes scanned the shore. She could tell he was looking at her, but he was far enough away that neither of them had to acknowledge the gaze of the other.

When the boat was abeam of her, it turned into the wind. She heard the engine throttle down, and watched him scamper out of the cockpit and over the foredeck to toss in an anchor. The boat rocked in the cross current, but he never reached for a handhold.

Sera suddenly felt warm. Her face was flushed, and dewdrops of sweat beaded on her lip and forehead. The sun alternately peeked out from behind the wispy cirrus clouds, but she knew it wasn't the sunshine that made her flush.

The man on the boat went back to the cockpit, reversed the engine against the anchor, then killed it. The boat pitched and rolled in the wavelets, but he stood easily on one leg, then the other, as he stripped off his shirt and trousers until he was wearing only a white swimsuit. He kept his eyes on her the whole time, right up until he dove off the stern of the boat and began swimming toward the beach with long, steady strokes. He swam like a swordfish, just below the surface, with no splashing. She watched him correct his course as the current swept him in an arc toward the south end of the island.

Sera felt very alone. She wished she had a real swimsuit, like the taffeta one-piece suits on the cover of *Life* magazine, or one of the stylish two-piece suits she had seen in a store in New London, instead of shorts and a halter top. She wasn't really afraid, but she had never been alone with a strange man, especially not on the lonely beach of Sandy Point.

Then she remembered the wrecked house, a topsy-turvy relic that stood precariously over the beach, the timbers sun-bleached, the shakes and sheathing gone, leaving only a weathered frame that was gradually losing its battle with the wind and waves. The stairs were long gone, but Paul had hung a rope ladder from the second floor, where what had once been a terrace was now a raised platform over the beach. Sera ran to the house and pulled herself up the rope. She had learned the trick by watching Paul and Jake.

When she looked down from her perch to the water below, the man was halfway to the beach. Below her, she watched a wave recede, leaving wet sand below the end of the beam.

For almost a whole year, Paul and Jake had dared one another to dive off the beam into the shallow water, only a foot deep when the waves were out. It took Jake to figure out that you had to wait until the water was just starting in before you dove. Then the water would be at its deepest when you hit the surface. If you didn't know the trick, you ended up, like Paul the first time, with a broken wrist, which meant the doctor and dire warnings from Josephina.

When Sera looked back toward the boat, she saw the man treading water, looking up toward her. She cocked her legs, waited for the wave below to recede, and dove.

The water was layered, warm at the surface, cold underneath. Her fingers and palms dug into the sandy bottom from the force of her dive. When she pushed off the bottom, she was careful not to break the surface.

She swam underwater as long as she could, peeking up only long enough for a deep breath and a quick bearing from the church steeple in the village. Even underwater, her skin tingled.

When she surfaced the second time, she looked toward the beach, expecting to see the man. He had anchored only forty yards offshore, and with his steady stroke, he should have made it to the beach.

She scanned up and down the beach, but he wasn't there. Treading water, she turned to look behind her at the boat. The light glistened off the topsides as the varnished planking took on the color of the sun. There was no sign of the man.

She turned back toward the beach again, then to the boat, and back to the beach. It was such a short swim, and he had looked like such a strong swimmer, with his easy, deliberate strokes. What could have happened?

She started to swim toward the boat. Maybe he had gone back and was on board? Then she caught herself, treading water while she tried to think. If he was at the boat, he didn't need help. She tried to remember whether a drowning man floats or sinks. The fishermen never talked about it. Even to mention drowning was bad luck. Jake had explained it to her once, the reasons a body would sink or float, but she couldn't remember which it was.

It was by chance that she looked up toward the wrecked house, and saw the man, standing tall on the overhanging beam. He stepped to the end, drew his arms back, and cocked his legs. His skin glowed like the topsides of the boat in the afternoon sunlight.

He was going to dive. But how could he know when to leap? He would kill himself. "No!" she shouted.

He looked down toward her, and she thought she saw a smile. Then his cocked legs sprung, launching him high over the water. For an excruciatingly long moment he soared, his arms like wings, before he tucked his head and arms at the last moment to plunge into the water. He looked like a fabulous golden bird.

There was almost no splash. She waited a long time for him to surface, but there was nothing, not even a ripple amidst the wavelets. She wanted to shout, but what was there to shout? She didn't even know his name.

She remembered her father's stories about the mermaids who

lured mariners to their deaths. "They were so beautiful that the sailors couldn't stay away," he said. Sometimes he called Sera "my little mermaid."

"I wouldn't lure a seaman," she protested.

"A pretty girl can't help it."

She swam to the beach with slow, cadenced strokes. The sun was warm, but she shivered as she lay on the sand, her chin on her hands so she could look out at the water. She could feel her wet hair against her back, and rivulets of water running across her back and down her sides as she watched the water.

"Hello!" The voice came from behind her.

She twisted her head around. The man was taller than she expected. And blonder. His eyes were pale blue. She could feel her heart thumping.

"You shouldn't have tried to dive off the beam," she said. "You could have broken your neck."

"You did it."

"But I knew how."

"I guess I did too."

"How? How did you know?"

His smile was soft, a grin more than a laugh. "Navy men are supposed to be resourceful."

"Navy? My father said there are no real sailors in the Navy. Only boys who dress up in pretty uniforms."

"And where does he say the real sailors are?"

She sat up, clutching her arms around her knees. "On Portuguese boats."

He knelt on the sand. "So you really are Portuguese?"

"Of course."

"Of course?"

"In the village everyone is Portuguese. Almost."

"The village is Stonington?"

"Of course."

"You say 'of course' a lot. Do you think everything can only happen a certain way?"

Sera smiled, caught herself, and turned away, looking down at her feet in the sand. She wished she had polish for her toenails. "Why did you come here?" she asked.

"To find you."

"Me? Why?"

"I almost lost that race because of you."

"You were losing. I don't understand how you won."

"I sailed better."

"Did you?"

He didn't answer, just turned to glance out at the Sound and Fishers Island in the distance. "We haven't even met," he said. "I'm Russell Westcott."

"My name is Sera. It's short for Seraphina."

"Like an angel."

"What's like an angel?"

"Your name. The dictionary said it means 'like an angel.' "

"You looked it up in the dictionary? How did you even know my name?"

He smiled again. "A one-legged fisherman told me."

She thought for a moment. It was so strange for this man to have spoken to someone about her. Then she remembered that it must have been in Newport. "With gray hair?" She waited for a nod. "That's Georgio. He fished the banks with my father. It was in the old days, with handlines. Why did you ask him my name?"

"To find you."

"And why did you want to find me?"

"Because—" His smile broadened. It was a lovely smile, bright white teeth resting on his lower lip. "You're the most beautiful woman I've ever seen."

Sera felt the flush explode in her face. All her life, people had told her she was pretty. Not just Josephina and her father and aunts and uncles, but neighbors and friends in the village. She had grown accustomed to the compliments. Some had even called her beautiful. But never had a man looked into her eyes and called her a "beautiful woman." The words seemed overwhelmingly intimate.

He sat down on the sand next to her, stretching out his legs. His body was long and lean, the muscles low ripples in his silken skin. "Who taught you to swim like that?" he asked.

"No one. I watched my brother, jumped in, and started to swim."

"Maybe you're a mermaid."

"My father used to say that."

"Is your father a fisherman?"

"He was. He's dead."

"I'm sorry."

Sera leaned up on one elbow, so she could look at him without craning her neck. Rivulets of water from her wet hair tickled her shoulders. "Why are you sorry? You didn't even know him."

"No, but I'm sorry something bad happened to you."

"But you don't know me."

"I'm working on that. How did he die?"

"He fell off a boat, at night in a storm. He was on deck alone, tying down a loose otter board. If he hadn't gotten it, it would have smashed a hole in the side of the boat."

"Didn't his shipmates try to rescue him?"

"Rescue? At sea?" Sera squinted into the sun. "Have you ever been on a dragger?"

"No."

"I think my father was right about the Navy." Sera watched the man's eyes wander to her legs, then slowly back to her face. The caress of his gaze was so distracting that she lost her train of thought. "What do you do in those pretty uniforms anyway?" she asked.

He laughed. "If you're trying to get me to defend the Navy, you have the wrong man."

"Is that a Navy boat?" She rolled onto her side to point out toward the mahogany hull. When she turned back toward him, he was lying on the sand next to her.

"It belongs to the Commanders-in-Chief."

"Really?"

Russell laughed again. "It's a private joke. The Commanders-in-Chief are my parents. They've had the boat for as long as I can remember. Wes keeps it on a mooring with no gasoline in the tanks. I have to steal it to use it."

"Did you steal it today?"

"In fact"—he let his grin broaden, slowly—"I did. All part of a carefully planned maneuver to sweep you off your feet."

Sera turned away to conceal her blush.

"Why do you look away?" he asked.

She turned and looked right at him. "How can you spend a whole day swimming at the beach?" she asked. "Don't you have to work?"

Russell laughed. "Be careful—you'll sound like my mother. Actually, I'm supposed to be working right now. As far as anyone knows, I am in the library, boning up on Pacific fleet supply routes and the geo-economics of the East Asia basin."

"What's that mean?"

"Nothing, at least to the real world. I'm posted at the Naval War College, the last refuge of absolute knowledge and total confidence—with the possible exception of Portuguese fishermen's daughters."

Sera laughed, more from his breezy inflection than from the words. "Is what you do really work?"

"It's what I don't want to do. To me, that's work."

"Work is what you don't want to do? I never thought of it that way." How different this man was! In the village, everyone was always busy. If it wasn't work on the draggers or in the mills, it was women at home, cleaning, cooking, mending, making work if they didn't have work, as if it were sinful not to be busy. Father Loftus had once said to her, "You're too old for frivolity." When she asked what frivolity meant, the priest said, "Fun at the wrong time."

"Do you want to see the boat?" he asked.

She looked out at the anchored boat, rocking gently in the breeze. The planking was so even and tight that the hull looked seamless. Jake had talked sometimes about fitting planks. "It's one of those things that can be perfect," he said. "When they're right, they belong together."

"It looks fast," said Sera.

"Come on, we'll go for a ride."

Sera looked at the sharp bow and raked topsides. All her life she had grown up around working boats. This one seemed frivolous and menacing at the same time. "No," she said.

"I thought Portuguese fishermen were brave."

"They are."

"Then why are you afraid?"

"I'm not afraid. Maybe I'd go on the boat with a Portuguese captain."

"How about Saturday?"

"What about Saturday?"

"Will you go out on the boat with me Saturday?"

His smile was so open, the curls of hair on his forehead so childlike, that it was hard to say no. "Maybe. But if Manuel—"

"Who's Manuel?"

She thought a minute, then her smile fell. "It doesn't matter. Saturday is the Feast."

"Feast?"

"The Holy Ghost. Everyone in the village goes. It's a festival each summer."

"A festival?" His smile was genuine, pure enthusiasm.

"I don't think you'd like it. Portuguese dancing and food, and a parade to the church."

He beamed. "I love a parade. I'll be there."

"You go anyplace whenever you want? Don't you have to work?" she asked.

"I'm supposed to be boning up for the tactical game, but a festival sounds like more fun."

"Game?" She turned toward him, her eyes wide in interest. "I guess my father was right about sailors."

He laughed. "I seem to be having a rough time with your father. They aren't really games. At least not what you think."

"What aren't really games?"

"They're called war games. We read a mountain of technical material, work out calculations until we can't see anymore, and finally move some tin ships around on a tile floor. Captains galore stand around in the gallery with disapproving looks, and when it's all over, the judges announce that the Blue fleet sunk eight Orange ships, or that Orange trounced Blue. Sometimes it's Red against Blue or Black against Blue."

"Black and Blue?"

"Blue is the U.S., the good guys. Black is Germany. Orange

is Japan. War College Rules: never call anything by its own name."

Sera listened intently, trying to understand. All the men she had ever known went out on boats, or worked in a mill. Jake was almost an exception, but as much time as he spent on designs and plans and sailing, when a boat needed repairs in the yard, he would work until he was dripping with sweat. Labor—sweat and muscles—was what men did. "Is that really all you do?" she asked. "Swim and play games?"

"Don't forget tennis, riding, skeet, sailing, scheming on how to avoid classes, and at least for the last week, an inordinate amount of time planning how I was going to get myself to Stonington to meet you."

Sera couldn't help laughing at the cascade of words.

"And now, since I can't even get you to go for a ride on the boat, I'm going to have to start scheming all over again to get back here Saturday for your festival."

"Tell me more about the games you play."

"I can't."

"Why not? Is it all something you made up?"

"Even Russell Westcott the Third at his most fiendish couldn't make up anything quite like a Naval War College game. The reason I can't tell you about them is that the games are secret. We have to sign for the material, it's all stamped SECRET, and when the game is over every page of the game books has to be turned back in. The people who draw up those games think they are planning what will happen in a real war. Actually, that isn't quite right. People like Captain Horatio Breedlove are too sure about the future to say this or that *might* happen. He *knows* what will happen."

Sera shook her head, letting the mane of almost dry hair tumble around her face before she brushed it back with her hands. "It sounds like the games my brother used to play on the beach. He and Jake built model boats and took them down to the harbor so they could throw rocks to try to sink each other's boats. One day Jake would be England and Paul would be Germany, and the next week they would swap. Whenever I wanted to play they would tell me I didn't understand naval battles."

"Where's your brother now?"

"Hawaii. Or maybe it's Australia already. He shipped out on a freighter. He's in a different place every week."

Russell smiled. "A Portuguese sailor who can't stay away from the sea?"

"It's in our blood," said Sera. "That's why Portuguese men are the best sailors in the world."

"And will all these splendid Portuguese sailors be at the festival Saturday?"

"Of course."

"Including the fellow who was sailing that other Monohull Saturday?"

"Jake? He isn't Portuguese."

"Will he be at the festival?"

"Probably."

Russell grinned, with his lovely teeth flashing above his lip. "So will I."

10

From the end of the drive, Jake looked back at the expanse of empty gravel. Costa's boat had been the last repair, and repairs were the only work he had, except for Langer's job in Newport. The fishermen couldn't afford to buy new boats, and yachtsmen commissioning new designs went to the sure and safe naval architects who belonged to their clubs, like Olin Stephens and John Alden.

For two years, between repair jobs, Jake had worked on line drawings of a sloop he was sure would sail circles around the New York 40s, then the dominant class in the New York Yacht Club. The NYYC was still sailing old-fashioned gaff rigs. Jake's design was a Marconi-rigged sloop that would be faster, handier to sail, and easier to maintain. He had gone over the materials and labor calculations a dozen times, until he was sure he could build the design out of first-class lumber and fittings, with a first-class finish, for three-fourths of what Herreschoff charged for a New York 40.

But just because a design was faster, more comfortable, better finished, and cheaper, didn't mean anyone would buy it. Down at the Larchmont Yacht Club, a crowd gathered one day for the commissioning of *Gesture*, a 57-foot cutter that Olin Stephens had designed. The festivities were bigger than usual; the talk was that with war coming this might be the last big yacht for a long time.

Jake had been called in at the last minute to do some rigging work on the boat, and he was still there when the fancy-dressed crowd showed up for the ceremonies that a *Life* magazine photographer captured in a full-page spread. When everyone retreated to the tables inside for canapés and drinks, Jake caught up with H. J. Callahan, who had won half the races on the Sound schedule in his New York 40, and asked him to look at the drawings of Jake's new design.

Callahan seemed fascinated. "She looks fast," he said. "Where can I look at one?"

"In my yard," said Jake. "Four months after you place the order."

Callahan winked mischievously. "You show me one. If it's good as those drawings, I'll order it."

It was a vicious circle: Until he built a boat, he couldn't sell a boat. And until he sold a boat, he couldn't build a boat. He was left with repairs and crazy jobs for former professors.

Sera was waiting for him at the point. The fading seabreeze swirled her skirt around her knees.

Jake had never asked Sera out on a proper date. Their friendship went back to the days when Jake and Paul were pals and Sera tagged along. The old pattern was hard to change. Sometimes he offered to meet Sera at her house on School Street before they went sailing or off on the workboat to Newport or Fishers Island, but she always said no, insisting that she would meet him at the boatyard, or somewhere else in the village.

It was because she was Portuguese, he told himself. The Portuguese families were conservative. The mothers insisted that young girls be chaperoned when they went out with young men, even with friends of their older brothers. And, Jake reminded himself, he was an outsider.

The Portuguese hadn't been there that much longer than Jake's father. Sam Werth had come down from Montreal at the beginning of Prohibition when the Man sent him to look at a boatyard that was supposed to be able to build fast, reliable boats. Sam, who until that day had been a bookkeeper and jack-of-all-trades, took one look at the piles of mahogany timbers and the perfectly cut planks and ribs and keel timbers that workmen in the yard were fitting together into boats, and knew that he had found what most men only dream of encountering, his calling. All he wanted to do for the rest of his life was to build swift boats. To his astonishment, he didn't have to convince the Man to buy the yard and put him in charge. "We got enough goods to ship that we can use our own navy," the Man said.

Sam learned boatbuilding faster than anyone could imagine. Before long half the fisherman in Stonington were bringing their boats to him for repairs. A few were surprised that he had learned so much so fast. Others said, "It's in his blood." But he and Jake were still outsiders.

If the Portuguese hadn't come that much earlier than Sam Werth, they came in numbers and built a tight-knit little community. Whole families came, filling blocks of the narrow streets in the village. They brought their music, their language, their food, and their festivals. And even as Jake went to school with Portuguese kids, and the fishermen had brought their boats to Sam Werth for repairs, there was always a gap, bridged by politeness, between their worlds.

Jake lived in the village until he went off to MIT to study naval architecture. For the next five years he lived to sail and sailed to live, moving from one boat and port to another, working as what the yacht owners called a B.N. or "boat nigger." He sailed in Marblehead and Long Island Sound, crewed on big ocean racers and an America's Cup defender, hitchhiked to California and spent two years working there with an uncle, his father's younger brother. He had repaired and sailed more boats than he could count. He had been back in the village for three years, trying to rebuild a yard that had been leveled by the hurricane of '38. In those three short years, he had become part of the village again, at least to a point. He had patched together almost every fishing boat in the fleet, waited to be paid when the fish weren't coming in, and celebrated with the fishermen when the catches were good. He went to their festivals, shopped at the village market where they bought supplies for their boats, could say hello by name to everyone he saw on the street. Still, after twenty years, to the Portuguese, Jake was an outsider.

But there was more to Sera's no. No matter how many evenings they sailed together under dusky blue skies, no matter how many times their bodies touched, whether an accidental, grazing caress when they swam or lay on their backs in a drifting sailboat to watch the first stars appear, or an exuberant hug after a victorious race—there was a hesitance in their relationship. They were the best of friends, and that itself was odd in the village, where women didn't have *friendships* with men. But whatever others might have thought, stirred by the tales of the village gossips, Jake and Sera were only friends. Sometimes, Jake felt as though Paul were still there, watching over his little sister. He wondered if Sera held back for the same reason.

As they walked down Water Street, Sera batted down her skirt, letting the breeze tumble her hair across her face.

"You've been so busy," she said. "I thought Joe Costa's boat was your last repair."

"It was. Except for a job in Newport."

"Newport?"

"A guy with a motorsailer. Not much wrong with the boat, but he wants it fixed yesterday."

"What about the man who came to your yard?"

"How did you hear about him?"

"At the dock. They talk. Manuel says that someone came with jobs for everyone, and you turned him down."

"He wanted to build disposable boats. Nobody should have to go to sea in a boat like that, and nobody should have to work in a factory building boats like that."

"Who was he going to sell them to?"

"The Navy."

"No wonder. You hate the Navy and Coast Guard."

Jake smiled. "That's an old grudge, Sera."

"How can you have a grudge against the whole Navy? People have grudges against people, not the world."

"I'm not angry at the world," said Jake. "Just a few men in uniform who went too far."

"You may all be in uniform before long. The newspaper said that a hundred and fifty-two men from Stonington have already enlisted."

"Maybe."

"What will happen to the village?"

"Some of us will go and fight. A few will stay behind and make fortunes."

"Is war always that way?"

"Only for the last three thousand years."

Sera laughed and took his hand. "Mama wanted me to wear an embroidered skirt tonight. You know, with a design from some village in the Azores. I guess that's a uniform too. 'Not tonight,' I told her. Tonight I'm going to dance until the band goes home, and then more. No one can stop me."

Jake smiled. He knew Sera was never as happy as when she danced.

They walked to the rocky point at the tip of the village. They could look out at three states: Connecticut behind them, Watch Hill and a strip of Rhode Island shore off to the left, and Fishers Island, New York, across the harbor. Sera seemed never to tire of the view.

"You know why I love it here?" she said. "My father used to walk me down here at night and point out toward Block Island. 'The whole world is right there,' he would say. He was right. Just turn your back on the village and the whole world is there."

"Maybe it's the other way around. When you're out there, it's nice to know there's home to come back to."

"You can say that, Jake. You've been out there. You went away to college in Boston. You worked in New York and Newport and California. You sailed at those fancy clubs, on big yachts. Like Rosa. She lived in France. She's seen all kinds of things. I've never been anywhere. I'm a prisoner here. When I was at school, I would look out the window and see the mill and tell myself that the one thing I didn't want was to end up working there. Now, during breaks at the mill I come out and look up at the Borough School and think my whole life is right there, trapped between those two brick buildings."

"You won't be here always, Sera."

"No?" She turned toward him. Her lower lip jutted. "Why not? Everyone from the village is here. They're born here. They live here. They work here. And they die here. Who ever left, besides you and Paul? As soon as they can leave school the boys go on the boats. If they can't get on a boat, they work in the mill. Girls get married or work at the mill. Then what?"

"You're different, Sera. Who can stop you from getting what you want?"

"How about Manuel?"

"You've never been afraid of him."

"No? Do you know that he has forbidden me to see you?"

"Why?"

"Manuel never explains anything. He thinks he is a king, or the bishop. He likes to say something that he knows will make us angry, and then watch Mama or me try to fight him. He probably thinks that if I don't see you I'll marry someone like Carlos and wear a black dress and wait home every day until the boat comes in, and then bring Carlos his slippers and a glass of wine. And when Manuel visits I'm supposed to bring him slippers and wine too."

"Who's Carlos?"

"Manuel's cousin, from Newport. Manuel lets him drive the boat. He probably promised it to him. Carlos is stupid enough to believe a promise from Manuel."

"Is Manuel really that bad?"

She turned toward Jake. "It's because of Manuel that Paul left. I wish he would fall overboard." She laughed, a hard, vicious laugh. "It's no use. He'll never fall overboard. He's so lazy he never goes on deck. His clothes aren't even dirty when he comes back from a day of fishing."

"Is he going to be at the dance?"

"Who, Manuel?"

"Carlos."

"Maybe."

"Are you going to dance with him?"

Sera laughed, taking his arm and pressing it against her. "Only if you can't keep up with me."

The dancing didn't start until nine o'clock, after the crowd at the Holy Ghost Society had stuffed themselves from the buffet tables of lobster, corn, linguiça, sweet bread, and wine. Around the open dance area young girls smoothed their skirts and fingered their hair as they glanced shyly at the men. The girls called out songs they wanted the band to play, mostly from radio greats like Glenn Miller and Harry James. The band, from New Bedford, stuck to familiar music, old Portuguese tunes from the Azores and the mainland.

At the edges of the dance floor, young men in white shirts and black trousers looked over the girls like livestock dealers checking the stock before an auction. Jake watched eyes turn toward Sera, as they always did—Sera the unapproachable, the beautiful, the proud girl who could run and swim faster, sail better, and drive a boat as hard as any young man in the village. There were girls who danced better than Sera, who knew more steps, or who could move more gracefully. But there was no woman at the festival that men wanted to dance with more than Sera.

She stood close to Jake, humming along with the music.

"I don't care if we're the first ones," she said.

Jake led her toward the floor. The band had paused for a moment, and Jake wondered whether they would play more Portuguese music, or maybe one of the popular radio tunes, like "Chattanooga Choo Choo," or "The Hut Sut Song," or "Why Don't We Do This More Often?"

He was still waiting for the music, holding both of Sera's hands in his own, when he saw Johnny Cravinho come toward him from the dock, wearing oilskins and heavy boots. Jake knew something was wrong. No fisherman worked on the day of the festival. Most of the boats would be decorated, or at least scrubbed down and left open for all to visit. The fishermen would have spent the morning scrubbing and polishing, not at sea. A lobsterman like Cravinho would have repaired traps, or washed down his boat. It was a day for Sunday best.

"Johnny?"

The band started to play a Portuguese song, the familiar dance called the *chamarita*.

Cravinho's eyes were gray. His hands were covered with grease.

"Jake!" The salutation was as much a signal as the long face. "It's the stuffing box," he said. "I saw it was more than a regular drip, so I tightened her down. I guess I musta tightened too hard. Feels like the packing's gone, and she's takin' water. Pretty stupid of me."

Sera's hand was on Jake's arm, her fingers pulsing to the beat of the drummer.

"It's probably not anything you did, Johnny. The wood around that stuffing box was punky years ago. Can your pump keep up?"

"I got Bindloss's big pump on her. She'll be all right, I guess. I'm just worried about next week. I'm behind on my payments and if I go a week without hauling traps, I could lose her."

From the corner of his eye Jake saw Sera's foot tapping to the music. She smiled at Cravinho.

"We'll haul her on the high tide in the morning," said Jake. "With any luck at all I'll have her back in the water Tuesday afternoon. Just make sure she stays dry enough to get up there tomorrow."

Cravinho reached toward Jake's hand, then hesitated, waving his greasy hand instead. "Thanks. Tide's high at eight-thirty. I'll be at the yard at seven." His shuffle lightened to a skip as he ran back toward the dock.

Jake led Sera out onto the floor.

"You'd do just about anything for those fishermen, wouldn't you?" she said.

"Johnny's a good man. That boat matters to him. She's an old girl, but all he's got now."

"Why do men always call boats 'she'? It's like you think they're alive."

"For a man like Johnny, the boat is alive. When the boat's happy, he's happy; when the boat hurts, he hurts. It was the same for your father. When you're at sea, and it blows up, you're taking green water over the deck, waves breaking over the stern, you have to trust the boat. That kind of trust is too special for an *it*."

"I don't think it's trust. I think it's love. If I—?" Sera didn't finish the question. The band started playing a Harry James tune. "Come on," she said. "Let's dance."

Dancing transformed Sera. Minutes before she had been pen-

sive, her foot tapping nervously as she watched the crowd.
When she began to dance, even a slow foxtrot under the eyes
of the fishermen, her eyes lit up and her skin glowed with a
flush of excitement. Jake could smell a scent on her skin, not
from a bottle, but like an afternoon seabreeze.

Jake could see men watching them from the sides of the
open-air dance floor. He had grown accustomed to other men
staring at Sera. Sera too, he knew, was used to the eyes. All her
life, men had looked at her. The attention was so constant that
she took it for granted. When she smiled back, her smile was
familiar, an acknowledgment of friendship that no one in the
village would misinterpret.

They danced three dances in a row. Sometimes Sera hummed
a few notes of the music.

Jake had never taken a dance lesson. In college, he remembered the stories of boys who had gone to cotillions and dancing
academies. The years when they were learning to dance, Jake
had hung around the boatyard, learning the ways of wood. Sera
too had never really learned to dance, except the Portuguese
folk dances that mothers taught their daughters. But they had
seen dancing in the movies, and the rhythms came easily to both
of them. An expert would have said they were doing it all
wrong, but they moved gracefully together, neither really leading, the touches of their bodies enough to keep them moving
as one.

After the foxtrot, Sera said, "You know why I like dancing?
It's like sailing. The music's like the wind. Once you feel it, your
legs and feet know what to do."

The second dance was a fast lindy that left both of them
sweating. They barely had time to catch their breaths when the
band started another foxtrot.

With each dance, Sera pressed herself closer to Jake, her
cheek against his, her body touching his from their shoulders to
their thighs. He could feel her breath on his neck. The smell of
his own sweat and the splash of aftershave he had slapped onto
his cheeks mingled with her sea-air perfume.

During the third dance, Jake gradually became aware that
Sera's gaze was lost somewhere in the crowd behind him. He

pulled his cheek back from hers, and saw her lost in a mask of concentration.

Manuel? he wondered. Even Manuel wouldn't make a scene at the festival.

Sera's lips were parted. For a moment, Jake thought she was daydreaming, like the times when she would stare off at the open sea or at the sky, and he knew her thoughts were miles away. Then he turned his head to follow her eyes. The dance area was crowded, people in Portuguese native dress, party clothes, working clothes. The faces were familiar. Stonington was a small village. He knew everyone.

The band paused only long enough to change some instruments before the music started again, a quick scale from the accordion, followed by a riff of chords from the bass.

"Come on," said Sera. "Remember? We're going to dance all night." She took both of Jake's hands in her own as the band started up another lindy.

"Not even time-out for a Coke?"

"Not yet."

In minutes they were caught up in the music. Whirling under Jake's arm, her skirt flaring as she turned, Sera was carefree again, her eyes smiling, her hair flying, her lips parted in a broad smile. "Until the band goes home," she shouted. "I love it."

They danced until the last note. The band, rested after their break, segued immediately into a slow foxtrot. Sera pressed close against Jake, her arm around his shoulders, her breasts against this chest, her thighs grazing his with each step.

He couldn't remember being happier.

11

J ake!"
Jake heard the voice, but with Sera so close to him, her perfume and touch filling his senses, it took him a moment to react, to swing first his eyes, then his head.

It was Johnny Cravinho. His overalls were wet up to the knees, his sleeves were rolled up over the elbows, and his arms were covered with grease. His face was longer than before.

Jake kept dancing. Whatever it was could wait to the end of the dance. But as he and Sera whirled around again, he saw the gray panic in Cravinho's eyes, the desperation of a man who fears he is about to lose it all.

Jake danced to the edge of the floor.

Cravinho didn't speak until they were next to him. "I'm sorry, Jake. I don't want to bother you here."

Sera, her face misted with fine beads of sweat, pulled back, away from Jake.

"It's no good," said Cravinho. "The pump can't keep up."

"How much water?"

Cravinho drew a line with his palm, slicing across his knees. "I tried to start the engine to use the water intake as a pump, but she won't catch. Points must be wet. I was hoping maybe you got a pump up at the yard that would help."

"If Bindloss's big pump won't do it, nothing I have will help."

Cravinho shook his head. "It didn't seem that serious before."

Jake looked out over the crowd toward the harbor, waiting for his eyes to adjust to the dimness of the light. In a few seconds, his night vision came back enough to make out the wavelets lapping against the pilings, inches below the bleached wood of the high-water mark. "Tide's still high," he said, speaking as much to himself as to Cravinho. "How fast is she taking water?"

"It was here when I left." Cravinho sliced across his knees again with his palm. "Started coming pretty fast. I can beach her, Jake. I'll rig lines to the winch."

Jake shook his head. "We'd have to float her off in the morning. If she's leaking that bad now, dragging her off the beach isn't going to do her any good." He turned to Sera, looking down at the hands he still held in his own, waiting for her eyes to meet his.

"I don't want to take you away from the dance, Jake," Cravinho said.

"I don't want to leave. But I'm no good at underwater salvage. We better get her up on the rails now.

"It won't take long," he said to Sera. "I'll be back before you've had a chance to dance with that line of men who've been giving you the eye all night. I promise."

"You have to go?"

"Johnny's boat's in trouble. Real trouble."

"A lady in distress?" Sera's inflection was halfway between a question and a statement. She squeezed his hands in her own, and kissed his lips lightly. Her lips were moist. Strands of hair stuck to her forehead. "It's okay. I'm not supposed to be with you anyway. Remember?"

"Wait for me?" he said.

"As long as there's music, I'll be here."

N̲o thanks, Georgio. I think I'll sit this one out." It was the third dance Sera had sat out, and the fifth man who had asked her. From her perch on a bench at the head of the dock, she could look out over the harbor to Fishers Island in the distance. She thought of Rosa sailing to France, all alone. And she thought about the lieutenant.

Along the dock, the draggers and lobster boats were lined up, most with streamers and banners in the rigging. There was a gap in the line where Cravinho's boat had been. Up at the head of the harbor she could see the loom of the lights in Jake's yard.

She remembered festivals when her father had been alive. Sera and Paul would spend the whole day before helping him scrub and paint the boat and put up streamers. On Sunday afternoon, when families motored around the harbor on their boats, taking along guests, Sera and Paul would take turns at the wheel while their father beamed. Later, they would have an open house for their friends, with wine and cakes. That day, her father was a king.

"Hello there." The voice came from behind her.

The golden hair reflected the lights of the dock. Sera was so startled that she spoke without thinking. "You look like a saint," she said.

"I know a lot of people who would argue with that. But then coming from a Seraphina, it must be true."

"The lights make your hair glow," she explained quickly, "like a halo."

"You don't need a light."

The lieutenant's white trousers and light wool blazer stood out in the crowd like a flasher buoy on a dark night. He was bareheaded, and his blond hair contrasted with the black hair around him. His skin was tanned, his hair barbered and combed, swept back in a low wave, with a stray curl over his forehead.

Sera couldn't help smiling back at the lieutenant's easy grin, the flash of white teeth, the pale blue eyes so waggish and confident. "I didn't think you would come. You shouldn't have."

"I couldn't help myself."

She wanted to tell him to leave, that he didn't belong, that it was only a matter of time before trouble started if he stayed, but the words didn't come out. Instead, she asked, "Why don't you wear a uniform?"

"Because I don't have to. One of the few privileges of the Naval War College."

"Did you come in the boat?"

"Over there." He nodded toward the lobstermen's dock, close

to the breakwater. "They wouldn't let me tie up here because I didn't have fishnets on deck."

"Don't joke about the fishermen," she said. "This is their festival. It's important."

"Any party is important."

"It's more than a party. There's an old story."

"Tell me. I love a good story."

"You're teasing me."

"If I could come this far, at least you can tell me a story."

Sera looked around to make sure they were alone. "A long time ago floods ruined all the crops, and there was nothing to eat in all of Portugal. It was so terrible that Queen Isabella offered prayers to the Holy Ghost. She promised to sell her jewels to feed the people if only the rains would stop. Her prayers worked, and when the rain stopped she ordered a procession in honor of the Holy Ghost. So every year we have a parade and carry her crown. One family gets to keep the crown for the whole year."

"Good story," said Russell, nodding at the sky. "And obviously true. Not a drop of rain. Perfect weather for our boat ride."

"What boat ride?"

Russell took her hand in his. "We're going for a boat ride tonight, remember?"

"I can't."

"Why not?"

Sera hesitated, aware of the fingers around her own. "I'm waiting for someone. Anyway, my stepfather would kill me."

"Is he one of the fishermen?"

"Yes."

"And he won't let you go anywhere?"

She nodded. "He's strict."

"What does he want you to do with your life, wear a black dress and cook codfish while you wait for the boats to come home?"

Sera turned toward the dance floor. The men who had asked her to dance after Jake left were standing in a circle on the edge of the floor, drinking beer, glancing over at her, barking the loud laughs that men use to assert their camaraderie. Behind them,

Mrs. DaCunha was chattering to a group of women in black dresses. The voices and the Portuguese music were too loud to make out Mrs. DaCunha's words, but Sera could imagine what she was saying. Some of the women around her were no older than Sera, but already they were in black dresses, with big bellies announcing their recent marriages. *How does he know?* she thought.

When she turned back to Russell, he was smiling.

There were no surprises on Cravinho's boat. Just two rotten plank ends at the stuffing box and a floor timber too punky to hold fastenings.

"Big job?" asked Cravinho, as soon as the boat was up on the rails. His tentative smile was apprehensive. Jake had seen the same smile on the faces of men in storms at sea, and on the faces of men waiting in line at the bank. It was the smile that wondered if this time was the last time.

"She'll fish again," said Jake.

"How long is it gonna take?"

"To do the job right?"

Cravinho shook his head. "I'm at the bottom, Jake. I got to haul pots Tuesday, Wednesday the latest."

Jake knew wood boats well enough to do a quick estimate of the job. It would take hours just to cut away the waterlogged, rotten wood, then days to dry the soaked planking and frames, to let the wood stabilize before a new floor timber was fitted and new planks were cut to replace the old. Even rushed, a proper repair would take a week.

But Tuesday was less than three days away. Two fishermen had already lost their boats to the bank. Jake had watched the dejected men go off to mill work that would take them away from the sea. In better times, they might have fished on other boats, and at least stayed at sea. Now, a man who lost his boat lost everything.

"I don't like to do it," Jake said, "but if I cut the punky wood out, sister the floor timber instead of replacing it, and scarf onto those plank ends, I could probably get you back in the water Wednesday morning."

"I'll come first thing tomorrow to help," Cravinho said.

Jake shook his head. "The punky wood has to come out now. Otherwise, the plank ends won't dry. Could you go back to the dance and tell Sera I'll be a while?"

Jake didn't change to work clothes. He planned to do only what had to be done that night.

But as usual, he lost all track of time as he worked. Cutting away rotten wood is a delicate operation, like a surgeon excising a tumor. Cut too little and the rot comes back; lean too heavy with the saw or chisel and you've damaged good wood, maybe enough to compromise the integrity and weaken the hull. It is not a job you can do while watching the clock. A man's livelihood and his life depended on the boat being fixed right.

He worked flat on his back under the boat, trimming the plank ends by hand in carefully tapered scarfs. He had no idea how long he had been working when he heard an engine on the water behind him.

It can't be time for boats to go out already, he thought.

As he backsawed the plank end, the boat drew closer, until the sound of the big engines was unmistakable. Most boat engines rumbled or throbbed. Even with the throttle backed off, these engines let out a high-pitched, powerful whine. What were engines like that doing in Stonington? he wondered.

He wanted to look up, but he couldn't stop in the middle of the saw cut and leave an unfair surface on the plank. For a short eternity, while he worked through the plank with the fine-toothed backsaw, his ears traced the progress of the engines, motoring up the harbor and around in a slow turn. The powerful engines were throttled down, held in check like a skittish horse on a short halter.

He could remember when his father had built boats with Liberty aircraft engines. The newspapers called them "rum-runners," and celebrated each time the Coast Guard destroyed or captured one. To a boatbuilder, they were the biggest, fastest, most beautiful boats ever put together. The people who ordered them would pay any price, and for Sam Werth that meant that he could finally build the kind of boat he wanted to build, a boat with no compromises, a boat as good as a boat could be.

Jake remembered his father setting off that last evening, in the last boat he built. Before he got into the boat, Sam Werth stood alone with Jake on the dock. "You know, Jake," he said, "everyone thinks I'm crazy. 'It's only a boat,' they say. 'It doesn't have to be perfect.' But just once, I had to build a boat right. You understand, Jake? Not just good enough. *Right*. Maybe nobody will ever know. Maybe nobody will ever see the stringers in the bilge or the ceilings in the cargo compartment. Maybe to everyone else it just doesn't matter. But I know. And you know. And someday you'll remember."

Jake never saw his father again. And he never forgot.

The plank end came off square, so smooth it hardly needed sanding. Out on the water, the engines had turned back from the head of the harbor. They were still throttled down, whining in protest because the big air-gulping aircraft engines wanted to race at high rpms. Jake slid out from under the boat, stretching his legs and rubbing his neck before he looked out over the water.

There was just enough moonlight to silhouette the boat, a late 1920s launch with a bright mahogany hull. It was a common design; Sam Werth's last boats had been just like it. Most had been built with large cargo areas forward, for the liquor trade. The few that survived were usually set up as commuters, with covered bench seats for the swells who would be driven from fancy Long Island homes to their offices in Manhattan. In the moonlight, Jake couldn't tell who had built this one.

The boat was tracing along the ends of the docks. Jake watched as it pulled abeam the boatyard railway, steering a course down the middle of the channel. Even throttled down, the boat threw off a wake that lapped up onto the beach and the railway.

When the boat was just past the railway, with the moonlight shining over the cockpit, Jake could make out the face of the man at the wheel, on Jake's side of the cockpit. It was the lieutenant he had raced against in Newport. An instant later, he saw a mane of black hair behind the man's head. It was all he needed to see.

It didn't really surprise him. As long as he could remember,

Jake had come up against men like the lieutenant. When he played club soccer at MIT, the heavies of the teams were men like the lieutenant. They weren't really better players, but they came on the first day as though they had been born to play. The coaches, in awe of their names and money, named them captains, gave them the chance to play forward and score.

On the big J-Boats in the America's Cup, the afterguard were men like the lieutenant, sons of commodores at the Yacht Club. No one ever asked how well they could sail. They had the helm by right. And in the Olympic trials, when Jake had been turned away because he didn't belong to a proper yacht club, the winners had been men like the lieutenant, men who had spent their lives in the right clubs, with brand new boats in the racks, dockboys to carry them to the water, and crash boats to bring the sailors in after a day of practice.

It didn't surprise him to see Sera in the boat, because he had seen enough of men like that lieutenant to know what those uniforms, and the boats and homes and cars, did to women. Not just women. To anyone. Jake could remember working on boats in Newport and watching as tourists walked by, their jaws agape and eyes popping. He had heard snippets of their conversations as they pondered wealth and beauty beyond their wildest dreams.

But, he told himself, Sera was no fool. She would see through a man like the lieutenant.

He knew what was happening, could explain it all. He still felt as though someone had just kicked him in the stomach. When he looked down at his hands, his knuckles were white. He was clutching the backsaw as if it were a gun.

Go faster," Sera said. The deep, masculine throb of the engines was exciting—more than dancing, more even than the thrill of a hard breeze in a small boat. She could feel the rumble of power through the quilted leather seat.

Russell turned toward her, shrugging his shoulders to say "Which way?"

"Straight down the channel, between the markers. Watch out for the end of the breakwater." Sera slouched low in the cockpit, her shoulders barely even with the tucked and rolled seatback. She didn't sit up until they were clear of the harbor.

Russell opened the throttles when they cleared the breakwater. The boat sat back in the water, the bow lifting until it just kissed the surface. Sera had to shout to be heard over the roar of the engines. "Have you really been to Portugal?"

"Only once. A place called Estoril. A bunch of deposed kings and queens hang out there. People like my mother love to say they saw the Queen of Romania at lunch."

"Where does she live?"

"The Queen of Romania?"

"No, silly. Your mother?"

"She'd like to say New York."

"In one of those big buildings with an elevator?"

"They had a house on East Sixty-eighth Street."

"A whole house? I thought everybody in New York lived in apartments. If they have a house in New York, why are they in Newport?"

"They summer in Newport."

"In a hotel?"

"A house."

"Their own?"

Russell nodded.

"So they have two houses?"

"It was all they could afford."

From the breakwater Russell turned southwest, into Fishers Island Sound. Sera had sailed through the sound dozens of times, but at six or seven knots, the speed of a sailboat or a workboat. Now, the markers hurtled by at twenty knots, so quickly that she could scarcely identify the rocks and reefs that had turned Fishers Island Sound into a graveyard for so many boats.

"You're crazy," she shouted, aware of the excitement in her voice. "There are rocks out here that would rip this boat open."

He smiled. "Only if we hit them. Want to drive?"

"Me? You're teasing!"

"You keep telling me the Portuguese are such great seamen. Let's see." Russell throttled down as he slid toward Sera. Keeping one hand on the wheel, he traced from her shoulder down her arm with his other hand, grazing her hip as he nudged her across his lap. For an instant, he held her on his lap, with his arms around her, before she slid onto the seat in front of the wheel.

"Got the wheel?" he said. "The throttles are here." He pointed to a pair of chrome levers with varnished wooden balls on top.

She held the wheel tentatively, until she saw that he had taken his own hands off. It wasn't like any wheel she had ever seen on a boat. There were no spokes, and it was tilted instead of vertical, more like a car than a boat. But then it wasn't like a car either. At least no car she had ever been in. The throb of the engines pulsed through the wheel and the seat like a heartbeat, incessant and exciting.

He put his fingers over her right hand, letting her grasp the throttle levers before he eased her hand forward. The response of the boat was instantaneous. The pitch of the engines went up an octave and the roar filled her ears. She felt the acceleration in the small of her back as the bow of the boat lifted onto a plane.

For an instant she was frightened. The boat steered too easily, the bow jerking to one side then the other at the slightest motion of the wheel. She saw Russell start to move his hand toward the wheel, then stop as she caught on to the rhythm of steering. The boat skipped from one wave to another, dancing on the water. The sensation of speed and freedom was unlike anything she had ever known.

"Hey!" he said. "You do know boats."

Sera smiled, then laughed, loud enough to be heard over the roar of the engines. Loud enough, she thought, to be heard across the ocean.

12

Bernardinho watched Jake look up as Sera walked by the boatyard. It was a few minutes before seven o'clock in the morning.

Sera was in the midst of the troop of women and men who trudged up the street to the morning shift at the velvet factory. She was on the opposite side of Water Street, and walking quickly, but her stride was unmistakable, a proud, head-high strut that stood out from the belabored shuffles of the men and women around her. Her hair blew back from her head, loose. She would have to wear a scarf in the mill, but for now she was the familiar Sera.

Jake had been working since early that morning on Johnny Cravinho's lobster boat. He looked up, then quickly back at the plank of oak he had clamped onto a pair of sawhorses. He shaped the piece that he would sister onto the frame with short, choppy cuts of the plane.

"Your father used to say a man can't work wood right when he's mad," said Bernardinho. "You can maybe fool a man. The wood knows."

Jake didn't answer. He slowed the angry plane strokes.

Bernardinho waited for Jake to look up. "I know I'm just an old Portuguese with wine on my breath and hands that don't hold steady except when I'm working the wood. But I been around long enough to know some things. You were right to be a hard-head with that fellow Biddle. Man like that don't know what it is to build an honest boat. No way to convince a man like that except with the cold shoulder.

"But I'll tell you something else that's true. It's no good bein' a hardhead with a woman. I watch your eyes when she walks by—" He waited for Jake's begrudging grin before going on.

"I'm not so old or so wine-soaked that I don't see. Even a man with a face that don't show more than a codfish, when there's a woman in it, his eyes tell you everything. Bein' a hardhead won't fix it."

"Hold the frame steady," said Jake.

Bernardinho's trembling hands steadied as he held the oak. "Your father was the same. After your mother died, he never looked at another woman. We used to joke that the boats he built were his ladies, that he poured so much into them there was nothing left for a woman. But it wasn't that. He was just a hardhead. He was so mad when the influenza took your mother back in '19 that he wouldn't forgive the world. Trying to talk to him about it was like shouting at the sea. He wouldn't hear a word. You going to be the same?"

Jake stifled a flash of anger, partly at the gossip that made private life public, mostly at himself.

"Let's get these ends fitted," Jake said. "Cravinho will be chomping for his boat by tomorrow. And I've got to get up to Newport to work on that motorsailer."

Bernardinho waited for Jake's eyes to meet his. "Why do you have to go to Newport? You runnin' away? Or just bein' a hardhead like your father?"

It was less than a week after the festival that Russell Westcott showed up on Water Street in Stonington, driving a long, shiny Packard convertible. The car was dark green, with chrome bumpers, a spotlight, a leather strap across the hood, and a bold insignia proclaiming the twelve cylinders to anyone who couldn't hear them.

Sera met him on the street in midmorning. It had taken elaborate scheming and promises to get Rosalie Esposito to fill in for her shift at the velvet mill, and to make sure word didn't get back to Manuel. Manuel had already asked where she had disappeared to during the dance. Sera lied, saying she had taken a walk along the beach.

She admired the car for a moment as Russell opened the door for her from inside. She slid in and slumped low in the leather seat.

"Afraid to be seen?" he asked.

"I'll get murdered if I'm seen."

Instead of a uniform, Russell wore khaki slacks made of fine wool and a tweed jacket with a patch on the shoulder. Sera studied his jacket as they drove. The back of the jacket was vented with extra material in a bellows along the side. The slanted jacket pockets were edged with a thin bead of suede. Men in the village wore suit jackets for weddings and funerals. Their suits were utilitarian, never rich fabrics like these, or with trim beyond the minimum.

"Your car?" she asked.

"A friend's."

"Nice friend. Where are we going?"

"Have you ever been to a skeet shoot?"

"What's a skeet?"

"A clay pigeon."

"Do you like to eat clay?" Sera asked.

Russell drove fast. Between the roar of the engine and the whoosh of wind past the open top, they couldn't talk until they were over the Jamestown bridge and on the ferry to Newport. Sera watched him drive, watched the golden hair dance in the breeze. When he noticed her gaze, he flashed that incredible smile, his upper teeth just touching his lower lip. She felt like she was in a movie, that it couldn't all be true.

From the ferry landing in Newport they drove around Ocean Drive with its fabulous mansions perched up over the water.

"Do people really live in these houses?" Sera asked. She had seen the mansions from the deck of Jake's workboat, but never up close.

"Cottages," said Russell. He pointed out a pretty farm. "That one, with the chocolate cows, belonged to Arthur James. It's supposed to look like a Swiss farm. For parties he would have his staff dress up like Swiss farmers. Then the guests wear silly hats with feathers and pretend it's a cottage in Switzerland."

"I thought a cottage was a little house."

Russell laughed. "You've just learned the first rule of Newport: always pretend opposites. If you've bought the biggest yacht anyone has ever seen, you say you've picked up a nice little sailboat. If a woman is a real bowwow, you say, 'Isn't she lovely?' The more rooms and the bigger a house is, the more they insist on calling it a cottage."

"So when you said all those nice things to me, that just meant I'm a bowwow."

Russell squeezed her hand, then gently brushed the hair from her face. "No. I'm not like them."

He pointed out the lawns of an estate, and explained that the owner used them to play golf by himself, with a caddy. "He likes to play without a ball," Russell said. "That way every drive and every putt is perfect. That's Newport."

Russell drove past Bailey's Beach, then down Bellevue Avenue and around Easton's Point, beyond a development of small houses, to a clubhouse perched on a cliffside. The clubhouse was rustic, built like a log cabin. There was no sign, but Russell explained that it was the Clambake Club. "It's another pretend, like calling a house a cottage. They have servants wrap clams and lobsters and other goodies in seaweed, and bake it in those pits. The waiters serve it with fancy napkins draped over their arms, and everyone pretends they're having a casual picnic."

The rows of parked cars, long and black or very dark blue, looked like the sedans she remembered from movie newsreels of the coronation of the king in England. Chauffeurs in tall boots and caps stood outside some of the cars. The dark green Packard convertible, which had looked so out of place in Stonington, didn't seem special there.

The men and women milling around the manicured lawn outside the clubhouse were dressed in tweed jackets as fancy as Russell's, with suede patches at the shoulders. Some carried matching soft leather pouches over their shoulders. The women wore thin leather gloves, and low shoes of tooled brown leather. Sera was self-conscious in her saddle shoes.

She watched men take beautifully engraved shotguns out of
fitted leather cases, and custom-fitted picnic baskets out of the
trunks of the cars. Everyone seemed relaxed and chatty, as if it
were perfectly normal to be out there in the middle of the week
with no work to do. The women kissed one another with little
pecks on the cheek and the men shook hands, the way men in
Stonington did after they made an agreement about shares from
fishing. Sera had to keep reminding herself that it was a workday. She had never known anyone who didn't have to work.
Even Jake.

Only a few hours before, she had gotten up as though it were
any other workday, and trudged off toward the velvet factory so
Manuel wouldn't find out where she was really going. By now,
she thought, her friends, including Rosalie Esposito, had already
been on the looms for four hours.

Sera watched the carefree men and women, wondering what
that kind of freedom was like, until Russell called out to her.
He was holding matched shotguns, with scenes of pheasants and
dogs engraved on the blue metal of the receivers. He handed
her one and she carried it the way he carried his, over his shoulder. It was much lighter than Rosa's shotgun. She noticed that
the other women carried their shotguns over their arms, like a
woman holding a baby. But then they had special shoes and hats
and gloves too.

At a grassy area overlooking the water, Russell put his shotgun
on a stand and stood behind Sera, his cheek alongside hers as
he wrapped his arms around her and lifted the gun in her hands.
His smell was sweet, not like the strong bay rum she was used
to men slapping on their faces for parties. His body was so close
to hers that they moved as one person when he swung the shotgun, sweeping the end of the barrel up from a small house on
the edge of the cliff and across the sky. She followed his body
easily, so mesmerized by his smell and closeness that she heard
nothing he said.

"Ready to try?" he asked

"Sure."

"Pull!" Russell said. A target exploded from the little house,
whirling low and then lifting and soaring like the flat stones that

Sera and her brother used to sail across the tops of waves off the point.

Sera swung the shotgun, trying to remember what Rosa had told her. She missed the first clay, and the second. Russell handed her the other shotgun.

"Pull!" he said again.

Eyes open and point. Keep moving with him, then a little ahead. When it feels right, pull the trigger. For an instant the whirling clay was a rabbit running along the wall of Rosa's pasture. Sera swung the gun—it was easier to handle and better balanced than Rosa's long shotgun—moved ahead of the clay, and squeezed. The clay exploded.

"Fantastic!" Russell said.

Sera basked in the praise. It didn't seem that much of an accomplishment, but Russell's enthusiasm, and his smile, were hard to resist. Stonington seemed a million miles away.

After a few more practice clays, they walked over to one of the ranges. Sera couldn't help noticing the looks she got as they took turns in the queue. People would watch her and smile politely, mechanical smiles. No one spoke to her. Russell would cheer each time she hit a clay. From the others, she got the same hollow smiles whether she broke the clay or missed.

Before long she was hitting more than she was missing. It wasn't really fun after a while—the noise and the pounding on her shoulder bothered her—but it felt good to be doing well, and she adored Russell's praise.

As the group moved on to a second range, Russell turned to a woman who was strutting toward him in a bold black and white checked jacket. "Mother!" he said. "What a surprise?"

"I doubt that you're surprised," Sybil said. She was wearing a skirt and shoes like the other women, but wasn't carrying a shotgun. "You certainly didn't come up here today by accident. Well, aren't you going to introduce me?"

Russell introduced Sera with no last name. And his mother as "Sybil."

Sybil said, "I understand you've done some nice shooting today. Perhaps this isn't your first time? I always thought your people favored fishing."

"A friend taught me," said Sera. "With a rabbit."

"Rabbit?" said Russell. "That's a thought. How about lunch?"

"Won't you be joining us for the clambake, Russell?" said his mother.

"I think we'll go into town."

"Suit yourself," said Sybil. "There are some shops with Portuguese signs over by the fishing boats in Oldport."

As they got into the Packard, Sera asked, "Why does your mother dislike me?"

"Why does the sun rise?"

"Did I say the wrong thing? Is it because I'm not dressed right?"

"It wouldn't matter what you wore or said. You committed the ultimate sin."

Sera questioned with her eyebrows.

"Lisa—my sister—and Sybil like to buy things. This summer Lisa is planning for Sybil to buy her a husband. Neither of them likes the thought that there are some things, like your beauty, that money can't buy."

Usually compliments didn't make Sera blush, but Russell looked right into her eyes as he spoke. He wasn't embarrassed to say things she could only imagine hearing from a man. His steady blue eyes and easy smile made Sera laugh and flush bright red at the same time.

From the skeet club they drove to a tiny restaurant, dim inside, with checked red tablecloths and flowers on each table. The waiters greeted Russell as Mr. Westcott.

"Why don't they call you lieutenant?" Sera asked.

"I came here long before I joined the Navy. And I hope to keep coming long after."

"I thought being an officer was a career."

Russell laughed. "I'm not sure I could make a career of anything, except maybe pursuing lovely Portuguese ladies."

"Are there others?"

"Not yet."

The menus were handwritten in French, with no prices. Russell ordered for both of them, including wine. "No rabbit today," he said. "The veal is usually good."

She couldn't stop watching him. Even the way he ate was different. He would tear off small pieces of the crusty bread and eat it without butter, following each bite with a sip of wine. The thin slices of veal, tiny roasted potatoes, and long thin spears of asparagus were delicious, but he didn't finish everything on the plate. She tried to imagine Manuel or her brother not finishing everything on a plate.

From the restaurant he drove her to a huge house with trees and bushes shaped like animals. "Topiary gardens," he called them. From there they walked along a hilltop, overlooking the harbor. Below them, the fishing boats were specks, dwarfed by the lines of gray warships. They sat on a wooden bench under a tree, then lay down on the grass. She noticed the time on an outdoor clock and realized that it was time to be walking home from work. The whole afternoon felt like a dream.

"Tell me about the Portuguese," he said.

"What's to tell?"

"Why do the women wear black?"

"It means they're married. They also wear their hair up, in a knot, so others will know. Widows cover their hair, to show they still mourn their husband. There are always widows, because so many fishermen die at sea."

"Is everyone a fishermen?"

"Men fish if they can. It's good money, and on a boat, a man is free. If a man can't get on a boat, he ends up in the mill. The men say the mill is women's work. I have an uncle who works on a farm. It's hard work, and a farmer is never boss like a captain on his own boat. On a boat, a man has a good sunrise haul, and the rest doesn't matter."

"What's a sunrise haul?"

"The first time you lower your drag in the morning. That's almost always the biggest take of the day. At least for a good captain who knows the bottom and doesn't lose a net to the wrecks in Hell Hole or the horse mussels on the Mussel Bed."

Sera watched Russell as she spoke. He listened, looking right at her, hearing every word. She had grown up in a world where men rarely listened to women. It was exciting to be heard.

The first kiss came easily. Sera wanted his hands to touch her, to feel him close to her, to breathe in his delicious sweet smell. His touch on her back and neck excited her. She was surprised that he held back.

Russell came to Stonington again only four days later, this time to take her to a beach club in Newport.

She had tried not to talk about Russell at the velvet factory, but it was so unusual to get someone to fill a shift that everyone wanted to know all about Russell.

"Where will he take you?" the girls in the shop asked.

"He said the beach."

"The beach? You could go to the point."

"It's supposed to be a famous beach."

"Does your stepfather know?"

"He'd murder me."

Russell drove her down Bellevue Avenue, past the sharp turn and down to the Spouting Rock Beach Club. They changed in an inside cabana.

"We're only Class B members," said Russell. "To my mother's eternal chagrin."

When they walked out onto the beach, people stared at Sera. She asked Russell if she had done something wrong. "Is it this?" She was wearing shorts and a halter instead of the one-piece bathing suits of the other girls on the beach chairs and under the umbrellas. Some of the older women wore cover-up suits with full skirts. One woman wore dark-colored stockings.

"No," he said, with another of his wonderful smiles. "Can you blame them for looking at a beautiful woman?"

She and Russell sat under an umbrella and later swam, but the beach wasn't really attractive. Seaweed and banana peels dotted the sand, and the water felt oily. Sera thought the little beach on the point in Stonington, and especially her private beach on Sandy Point, were cleaner and nicer for swimming. What she couldn't believe was the fancy umbrellas and chairs at Bailey's Beach, and the outside cabanas, each with two dressing rooms. There were houses in Stonington where entire families lived all year long smaller than those cabanas.

The younger women who sat in front of the cabanas didn't even swim. Some of the older members went out into the water and frolicked, splashing themselves with water, but the younger ladies would sit for a while in one of the ornate chairs, then walk over to another cabana and visit with someone, then walk back. Servants circulated, bringing drinks on trays.

Russell watched Sera gazing in every direction. "Hungry?" he asked.

"Sure."

"I have a plan. When you get dressed, leave your suit on underneath."

They drove from Bailey's around to a desolate rocky shore. Just offshore was an island, with the wreckage of a building.

"There used to be a private club out there," Russell explained. "Before the hurricane. The Gooseberry Island Fishing Club. Fourteen old codgers would take a special little ferry out and swim in the buff. Then they would have a private lunch with their lady friends."

Sera wondered if he would invite her to swim in the nude—the thought was exciting—but he didn't. They ate a picnic on the beach, from a basket that had been prepared by a restaurant. The basket was lined with a checked cloth like a restaurant tablecloth. They ate chicken with their fingers, and Russell licked her fingertips. Before long they were kissing. Russell kissed the corners of her lips, slowly and teasingly. It seemed so natural to Sera. She kept thinking how wickedly delicious it was to be on the beach with this beautiful man, and then she would have a passing thought about how hard it would be to pay Rosalie Esposito back for filling in, and the risk that the foreman would find out and tell someone who would get word back to Manuel. She wondered what would happen when she came home with a short pay envelope. And then as easily as the thoughts came, she would forget about work and Stonington, and think only about what it felt like to be with him, how arroused she became from his kisses and caresses.

And yet he held back.

Sera said, "Why did you stop?"

He said, with his lovely smile, "Some things are worth waiting for."

The days turned into a whirl. Russell was back again the next weekend, and again in the middle of the week. Sera could no longer keep track of how many times they had gone out. One afternoon they drove around Newport Harbor in the big motorboat. Another time he took her riding, her first time on a horse. And always they would find a quiet spot and before long the idle chatter would turn to kisses and caresses. Each time it surprised Sera that Russell didn't expect or demand more.

Late one afternoon, when she was dressing in her only good dress to go out to dinner, Josephina said, "This boy you are seeing—?"

"How did you know?"

"Everyone knows, Sera."

"Does Manuel?"

"I hope not. This boy, Sera, has he tried—?"

"Tried what, Mama?"

"You know what I mean, Seraphina. Men are men."

"He's a gentleman, Mama. He's not like the boys in the village."

"Men are men, Seraphina. You be careful. Men like that want only one thing."

Seraphina hid her grin from her mother. It wasn't Russell who wanted. He was a perfect gentleman. There was nothing Sera wanted more.

Josephina lied again to Manuel, saying Sera was at a meeting of the Daughters of Isabella and then going to a friend's house. The night they went out she and Russell ate at the fanciest restaurant Sera had ever seen, with candles and flowers on the tables. Each place was set with two wineglasses and a water glass, and there were silver plates under the dinner plates. Russell didn't even ask for a menu.

"What's good?" he said to the waiter. The waiter knew his name.

The waiter brought plate after plate of food, oysters in their

shells, thin slices of salmon with capers, roasted pheasants
served with a clay covering that had the feathers stuck into it,
and tiny potatoes that puffed up into balls. Sera asked about the
different wines and forks, and Russell made silly jokes about
each. He never took his eyes off her. She felt like they were the
only two people in the world.

"Do you think we'll be in the war soon?" she asked. The
commotion in Europe and China had seemed too distant for
worry until Paul left. Now, that question had begun to come up
everywhere, even among the girls at the mill.

"At the War College they can't wait," he said. "They're excited because everyone assumes advancements in rank will come
twice as fast in wartime."

"What do you think?" Sera asked.

"I think I'd rather be with you."

Sera smiled. She no longer blushed at each compliment. She
found the evasion annoying. "My brother is on a freighter. He
was in Hawaii, then the Dutch Indies, Australia, and back to
Hawaii. He says that we're all silly to think war won't come to
the U.S. I keep wondering what it will be like?"

"More wine?" Russell asked. He never took his eyes off Sera,
but seemed not to hear what she was saying.

"What will you do when war comes?" Sera asked.

Russell shrugged. "The Navy has been playing war games for
so long I'm not sure a real war will be any different."

"Some of the girls in the village are starting to talk about
marriage. They're afraid that there will be no time once the men
are called up. Where do you think you'll be sent?"

Russell, still looking straight into her eyes, smiled a shy, beguiling smile. "I haven't thought about it."

"It could be someplace exciting, couldn't it? Like Hawaii, or
Europe?"

"Exciting for me would be a posting right here. Or no posting
at all."

"I don't believe you," said Sera. "I remember when my
brother and . . . his friend used to play games with toy ships.
They would set up their ships, little models made of scraps of

wood, and argue about which ships would win the battle. Then they read about someone named Billy Mitchell and started dropping pebbles on each other's ships."

"You know about Billy Mitchell?" said Russell.

"He sunk a battleship with bombs from planes."

"You're amazing," said Russell. "You know more than half of the admirals."

"Do you use airplanes and bombs in your war games? Or is that one of those secrets I'm not supposed to ask about?"

"You're not supposed to ask anything. Just be you. And let me keep staring at that wonderful lower lip." He leaned toward her, his hand holding hers as he gently kissed her lip.

A waiter hovered behind the table, waiting before he cleared the dinner plates and scraped the crumbs into a silver container with a special knife. When he finished, Sera was about to ask Russell another question when a man with thinning hair and a brightly colored handkerchief in the breast pocket of his white dinner jacket walked toward their table. The man stood obsequiously, some distance from their table, until Russell nodded to him.

"Russell," the man said. "You weren't exaggerating at all."

The man turned to Sera and bowed deeply. When his face was close to hers, she saw that his dark beard had been closely shaved. His fingernails were long and manicured. Clear polish made them shine.

"You, no doubt," he said, "are the fabulous Seraphina. When Russell said you were the most beautiful woman he had ever seen, I was foolish enough to raise my eyebrows in skepticism. If anything his compliments were gross understatements." The man reached for her hand, kissed her fingers, and clicked his heels together as if it were some sort of salute.

"Hello, Raymond," said Russell. He introduced them.

"I didn't mean to disturb your dinner," said Raymond. "But surely you wouldn't be so selfish as to deprive a man of a close glimpse of this lovely lady. Truly, I am transported."

"Who was that?" Sera asked, after Raymond went back to his own table.

"His name is Raymond. That's about as much as I know about him. He likes to show up at races, or the Casino. The Packard is his."

"Must be a good friend if he lets you drive it that often."

"Friend? Raymond is a hanger-on, one of those people who likes to watch."

"I'm not sure I liked the way he looked at me."

"You must be used to it by now."

She sipped at the wine. "Do you ever dream of going off somewhere, just escaping from everything and everyone?"

"Sure. Where do you want to go?"

"I don't mean like to a movie or dinner. I mean *away*."

"Name the place. If I can get leave, we're there."

"How can I even know when I haven't been anywhere?"

He reached for her hand. "I guess we'll just have to try everywhere. How about starting with a dance?" He nodded toward the dance floor, where a band had begun to play a muted foxtrot.

Dancing with Russell was unlike any dancing she had ever done. The music was slow, and he held her in the formal positions she had seen in movies. His hand was strong in the small of her back, and following his steps was easy. He was close enough to smell and feel, yet they were just far enough apart that their bodies grazed, like tiny kisses. The touches and teases excited her. She couldn't believe it when the music ended. "That was heavenly," she said.

They stood by the edge of the dance floor, waiting for the band to start again. Sera was aware of eyes watching her, and could hear fragments of conversations, people talking about "the handsome couple" and the "lovely girl with the dashing lieutenant."

After dancing a whole set, including some dances Sera had never done before, like a tango that left her alternately swooning and laughing, they sat down to dessert and another bottle of wine, this one white and sweet.

Russell said, "My mother is having a ball for my sister Lisa. They've spent the whole summer planning it. They've probably even ordered a full moon for that night. Will you come?"

"I don't think your mother would like that."

"She isn't the one inviting you."

"Are you using me to fight with her?"

Russell laughed. His laugh was infectious, not loud but giggly and boyish. "I don't need help to fight with my mother."

"She doesn't like me. Remember?"

"But I do."

"Why are you so distant from your mother and father?"

"I rather think I'm the prodigal son, come back from the far reaches of Cavite to the ancestral home."

"I'm serious. You never talk about them."

"What is there to say? My mother is obsessed with being *somebody*, whatever that means. My father has devoted his life to his own pleasure. I was like him, actually. Until I met you."

"It's so strange. You talk about them as if they were people you just met. Weren't you ever close to them? Like when you stubbed your toe and were little, didn't you run to your mother? My brother would never cry, even when he cut his leg open on a rock in the harbor and the water was red with his blood. He was so scared until my mother was holding him. It was the same with my father. I would have a terrible fight with someone at school and be so angry I couldn't think of anything else. And then my father would come home, and I'd hear his footsteps on the porch, and whatever was bothering me didn't matter. I can't imagine life without having family close."

"If I had been close to my father, I would have had an early education in the sort of life that belongs in bad books. Being close to my mother would be like swimming with sharks."

"But they're your own mother and father. I don't get along with my stepfather, but that's different. He's not family."

"Will you come to the ball, Sera? I would adore dancing at a ball with you."

Sera stared at him, looking at those wonderful eyes and the curl of hair that drooped over his forehead, and the hint of a smile tucked into the corners of his lips. She found the twists and turns and dead ends of the conversation troubling. It was as if they were not talking to one another. She found it hard to understand, because he always seemed to be listening so intently, his eyes fixed on hers as if there were no one else in the room. The earlier talk of the war must have upset him, she thought.

She tried to picture a ball. All she could remember was her old storybooks, with pictures of carriages and footmen opening the doors for ladies in long gowns. "I've never been to a ball," she said.

"Did you ever read *Cinderella*? That's all you need to know."

The music started again. Russell lightly stroked her hair with his fingertips. She couldn't wait to dance again. Their bodies, thought Sera, fit together perfectly. As she walked to the dance floor she thought of pumpkin coaches.

13

As much time as he had spent there, in Newport Jake Werth was an outsider. In the years that he had crewed on America's Cup yachts, he had been what the owners liked to call *professional* crew, living apart in a boardinghouse, on a pay scale that bordered on indentured servitude. The afterguard in their blue wool jackets and straw boaters called themselves *Corinthians* to distinguish their amateur status from the paid hands. They would show up only for the races, and quickly leave for dinner at fine restaurants and private houses. They talked to the crew the way they would talk to the servants at their mansions in New York and on the North Shore of Long Island.

James Putnam was considerably more hospitable. He offered Jake the forward cabin in his motorsailer for as long as Jake was working on the boat, and guest privileges at the New York Yacht Club station. Jake used the berth, but passed on the yacht club. Instead he ate in cafés and diners on Long Wharf and Thames Street where workers from the torpedo factory on Goat Island gathered, and showered at the YMCA. Newport was a YMCA town: there was even Robinson House, a special Army-Navy YMCA up among the mansions on Bellevue Avenue.

It was easy to find a routine in Newport. Mornings, when his mind was sharpest, he worked in the main cabin of Putnam's motorsailer, using notes and textbooks from his naval architecture days and a slide rule to play the deadly serious what-if games for

Langer. The limits of the problem Langer posed were easy: a dropped object always accelerates at 32 feet/second/second, and an object launched from an airplane starts out with the same forward speed as the airplane. The challenge, and the fun of the project, came when he played with the variables. What if the torpedo were dropped with a parachute? Could a parachuted torpedo be aimed? Was there a way to slow the fall and still preserve the aim? How much would the entry angle affect the depth? How much could that angle be changed? Like most good problems, each small question expanded into new sets of questions.

After a morning of brainstorming, he would work on Putnam's boat to clear his mind. In the evening, he would eat dinner at one of the cafés, then pass an hour or two over a beer in one of the Oldport bars, listening to the chatter and trying not to think of Sera.

By the late summer of 1941, the incessant snobbery that was Newport's bastion against social revolution had hardly abated. Only the talk of war in every bar and café seemed to cut across the class lines that divided Newport like formal boundaries. On Thames Street, off-duty sailors in pressed whites and shiny black shoes wandered between shops and bars, deciding which would get the hard-earned two-dollar bills the Navy doled out in pay envelopes to track where sailors spent their money. The Navy scheme might have provided useful information if the bars and whorehouses hadn't used bundles of two-dollar bills for their unrecorded cash transactions.

There were long lines in the street outside some of the bawdy houses. As intent as the sailors were on spending a fifth of their monthly pay for five minutes with a woman, in the street queues, as in the waterfront cafés and bars where the torpedo factory workers relaxed after a hard shift, the talk was of war.

Everyone had an opinion. When Jake tried to relax with a beer in a tavern on Thames Street, a burly fellow just off a night shift at the torpedo factory badgered anyone who would listen: "You can't guess what the Navy's up to? Look at the barge traffic and the stockpiles up on Gould Island. You ever check out the heavy construction at Melville, or over at Quonset? You don't need to read an admiral's mind to know there's something going on up there."

Before long a sailor would wander in, listen for a few minutes, and voice his own opinion. When someone had too much to drink, or when a group of sailors decided to blow off the steam that built up in a peacetime navy, fights would break out. If the fights got too rowdy, the Shore Patrol would come around with their white nightsticks.

Even when it didn't come to a fight, the talk in the bars was in that knowing insider voice of people who had a fragment of information that wasn't in the newspapers or on the radio. Sailors had seen ship movements, sometimes just from one anchorage to another. With war waging in half the world, the transfer of two destroyers took on a weighty significance. Torpedo factory workers counted the output and calculated when the U.S. would be ready to go to war.

Jake wondered how different the talk was at the other end of Newport, where young Naval War College officers mixed with the fringes of Newport society, taking advantage of bright white uniforms to dazzle the unwary. Maybe I am a hardhead, he thought.

Jake was in Newport ten days before he spotted the boat.

One afternoon, after a morning lost in the thicket of equations and calculations, he decided to clear his mind by taking Putnam's sailing dinghy out in the harbor. As he poked around the moored fleet in Brenton Cove, he recognized many of the big cutters and ketches, boats he had raced against. He made mental notes, picking up details of boats that were well-rigged and well-maintained, and others that could use some help. He could tell what shape the boats had underwater by how skittish they were on a mooring.

He spotted the commuter at the edge of the anchorage, close to the beach, riding uncomfortably in the swells that rolled through the anchorage as a pair of frigates steamed out of the harbor. The bright varnished topsides and powerful shape of the hull stood out even in an anchorage of big yachts, but the deep-V hull that gave the boat formidable power in a seaway left it

vulnerable to even the smallest swell at anchor. Jake recognized
the boat immediately, and couldn't stop the intertwined memories—the last time he had seen his father, and Sera with the
lieutenant behind the wheel.

Even from a distance he knew it was one of his father's boats.
The deck fittings were polished to a high shine, but age and
some sloppy boat handling had taken a toll. There were telltale
dark streaks under the varnish: whoever had done the refinishing
hadn't taken the time to strip the mahogany bare. The design
had been modified too. What had once been the forward cargo
hold was now covered with a peaked skylight, probably for a
cabin below. But it was still an incredibly beautiful boat, powerful on its lines, with that solid, balanced look of a boat that
has been designed and built right.

As he sailed in close, he could see the details that marked a
Sam Werth boat. In the stern was the trademark samson post,
the chamfers that a workman had cut with a drawknife as crisp
and sharp as the day the boat left the yard. Whatever it had
done in the last twelve years, this boat had never been relegated
to towboat duty.

Jake found it hard to adjust to the look of the peaked skylight
forward. The multiple panes of glass broke the flow of the boat's
lines, and the skylight seemed too delicate and fragile for a hull
as powerful as this one. These boats had been built to be sea-
worthy, able to take the tidal currents of the Race or open sea
swells even when the big Liberty aircraft engines had them up
over 30 knots, fast enough to outrun any other boat they might
meet. Sam had modified the design to beef up the keelson and
floors so the boats could take the roughest seas, accidental collisions, even groundings. The one thing he hadn't beefed up was
the deck. Why would a boat need a strong deck? That had been
Sam's undoing.

Jake tried not to remember the last time he had seen the boat,
the night of the festival in the village. Fighting the memory was
like the joke he and Paul used to play with one another as children. "A dime says you can't go ten seconds without thinking
of a hippopotamus," one would say, followed immediately by,
"You lose."

Jake pushed the tiller of the dinghy down, jibed around, and sailed back toward his tie-up on the work dock.

Sam's boat deserves better, thought Jake. He remembered when his father lavished incredible workmanship on boats like that one. They were the pride of his yard. The newspapers called them "rumrunners," because the only people who could afford them were buying the powerful hulls for their speed and cargo capacity, as contact boats that would go offshore to meet the big supply ships for loads of Prohibition goods. The newspapers wrote up their exploits, cheering when a Coast Guard cutter managed to haul one in. Bernardinho would come to the yard with a different story from a fisherman who had seen the powerful runners speed away, leaving the Coast Guard cutters in their wake.

When he heard the stories, Sam pretended he didn't care. "Does an artist pay attention to who buys his painting?" he would ask. But he, and Jake, and everyone in the yard would feel a twinge of pride when they heard another story of a bright, varnished hull outrunning the Coast Guard boats off the Race or outside Watch Hill. Who wouldn't be proud of a boat like that?

Sam Werth didn't question what his customers did with the boats. In return, they didn't quibble when he built them far more than they asked for. His boats could easily outrun a Coast Guard 75, even the fast, new Coast Guard 36s. The public watching the *Île de France* set off from New York for her celebrated transatlantic record noticed a mahogany-hulled boat dancing in and out of the liner's wake, doing pirouettes around the liner at 50 knots. The Coast Guard watched and wept. Sam Werth read the reports and smiled.

For speed alone the liquor importers would pay a premium. What most of the buyers never realized was that Sam Werth had built more than speed and strength into the hulls. He had given them the finest boats ever built, frames and floor timbers that would take anything the sea had to offer, hulls planked with wood from a single tree, the planking matched and fitted so carefully that even up close the varnished wood appeared seamless.

Other builders followed roughly the same design, a deep V-hull for power in a seaway, low freeboard amidships and aft, the cargo hold forward of the cockpit, two big Liberty aircraft engines aft of the cockpit. A few builders put together even bigger boats, like the infamous *Goose* and *Gander* out of Greenport, 59-footers with three big Liberty engines. But other builders never picked through stacks of carefully dried wood the way Sam did, insisting on quarter-sawn lumber, hand-selecting every plank to find the grain he wanted. The customers only knew his boats were tough, without realizing the care that had gone into fitting laminated floor timbers to stiffen the hull, extra ribs sandwiched in to provide rigidity to the straight sections of the planking. Even buyers who appreciated the beauty of the varnished hulls rarely noticed details like the bilge stringers inside the engine compartment and the cargo hold that were varnished to the same standard as the exposed planking. Asked why he bothered to finish an engine compartment to that level, Sam always had a ready answer: "Why make it good enough if you can make it right?"

Sam insisted on putting a samson post in the stern of every big boat he built, anchored soundly to the keel so it would take any load, but raked to match the lines of the hull and tapered above the deck with chamfered edges and an elegant brass fitting on top, so it bore no resemblance to the heavy samson posts of a workboat. It took a man three days to cut and fit that samson post. "She's powerful enough to work," Sam said. "No reason she shouldn't be ready."

Other builders, even men in Sam's yard, snickered. "The only towing those boats will see will be after a Coast Guard cutter blasts them out of the water."

"Those boats will be around long after Prohibition," Sam would say.

He was right. He built those boats so well that many had survived. Except for his last boat, the best of all. A Coast Guard cutter had rammed that one in the Race the night of sea trials, not even hailing first to see if it carried contraband cargo. The heavy bow of the cutter came down on the deck just aft of the cockpit, breaking the boat in half. The only one aboard was

Sam, a boatbuilder putting his masterpiece through sea tests on a beautiful evening. Jake was sixteen when it happened. The Coast Guard inquiry ruled the ramming a "justifiable error."

Jake had been angry at the world ever since.

Two days after he spotted the boat, Jake was wiring in some deck lamps up on the starboard shrouds of Putnam's motorsailer. From his perch in a bosun's chair twenty feet above the deck, he watched a midnight-blue Buick sedan pull up to the head of the dock. A woman got out of the backseat, dressed in a dark suit and a white blouse with a frilly collar. From her wobble down the dock, Jake thought she was drunk, until he realized that she was wearing shoes with pointed heels that were awkward on the loosely fitted dock planking.

After a few more steps she took off her shoes and walked in her stockings. She had the elegant, understated clothes and confident, no-nonsense, horsewoman's strut that in Newport shouted *money*.

"You are Jake Werth, aren't you?" the woman said when she was abreast Putnam's boat. She was in her early fifties and attractive, less from good features than from careful grooming and fine clothes worn well. Every detail, from the broad-brimmed hat to the leather handbag and gloves, radiated easy wealth.

Jake answered with a smile and a nod.

"Do you expect me to shout, or are you coming down?"

Jake laughed. "I don't expect anything. What do *you* expect?"

The woman shaded her eyes from the sun. "I'm certainly not coming up there."

Jake tied off some loose wires and lowered himself to the deck. "Want to come aboard?" he asked. "It's James Putnam's motorsailer. I'm sure he won't mind."

"I'm Sybil Westcott. I know Putnam. He undoubtedly *would* mind if he knew it was me."

Jake was shirtless in the warm sun, wearing only dungarees and a pair of canvas shoes. He noticed Sybil Westcott's eyes lingering on his chest and arms.

"How do you know my name?" Jake asked. It felt awkward to shout from the deck to the dock, so he climbed over the rail and stood next to her on the dock. He wished he had a shirt.

"Actually, I believe we met once. You were a schoolboy then, hanging around your father's yard. I still remember when I first saw the boat there. It was marvelous. The—what do you call it?—varnish glowed like the sun itself. Your father was a splendid craftsman. I was very sorry when I heard he died."

"Westcott? I spent some time with his records. I don't recall the name."

"The boat was bought under a different name. It was a business purchase."

Jake smiled. "Those were rather specialized boats, for a specialized business."

"The boat was big and fast and beautiful. I still think it's as lovely as any boat in the harbor. Don't you?"

Jake shrugged.

"Mr. Werth, I saw you taking in our boat the other day. You weren't subtle."

"I wasn't trying to be subtle. There's a lot to learn from the way my father built those boats. He built an honest boat."

"Indeed. And I ran an honest business."

"That's an odd word to choose for bootlegging, Mrs. Westcott."

"Not really. People wanted a product, it was difficult to come by, and we supplied it, the very best quality too. Is that so different from what your father did? People wanted big, fast boats, and your father gave them what they wanted. He had a reputation for building the best boats money could buy. Our product had the same reputation. I guess you could say we were in the same business."

"That might be stretching things a bit."

Sybil Westcott's mouth tightened before she caught herself and forced a quick smile. Jake noticed tiny wrinkles around the corners of her eyes and mouth.

"Do I hear contempt in your voice? I do hope I won't have to listen to a speech about honest boatbuilders and dirty accountants. After all, is that really what we're talking about? Or could it be something else? Tell me about your lady friend. She's a very attractive young woman."

Jake watched Sybil's eyes rove again to his chest and arms. It was an obvious gesture that made him as uncomfortable as the question.

When Jake didn't answer, Sybil looked back at his eyes and said, "It seems that my son has taken a fancy to your friend. That's unfortunate. You perhaps don't know him, at least not well, but I worry about Russell. He is so wasteful. He always has been.

"Some men are careful. I'd be willing to wager that you're a careful man. When you finish a sailboat race, you wash your sails, dry and fold them, put them away with loving care. It's an admirable trait. You'll go far on your carefulness, as your father did.

"Unfortunately, that isn't Russell's way. He finishes a race and just walks away. The sail that served him so well is left in a wet heap. It can lose its shape, even rot for all he cares. I wish it weren't so, but he's always been that way. With everything. No doubt I share part of the blame for spoiling him.

"Sad to say, but that's the way he is with women too. And that is truly a shame. Your friend is so young, and she seems so innocent and pure, so vulnerable to those flashy white uniforms and that Westcott smile."

"Why are you telling me this, Mrs. Westcott?"

He watched the subtle smile cross her face, a gesture as quick as the tightening of her mouth when he brought up rum-running.

"As lovely as your young friend is, Jake—and I hope you won't misunderstand this—I don't want Russell to get in trouble with a girl like that. It's nothing personal, mind you. I'm sure she's a very nice young lady. But there are distinctions. And here, perhaps more than anywhere, we observe those distinctions. The young men in Newport have an expression, odious in the way young men are, but honest. They say that some girls are for practice."

14

R ussell was broke.

To those he hit up regularly for what he casually dismissed as "pocket money," Russell seemed always to be in debt. There had been plenty of ready sources for quick funds when the junior class at the War College first assembled. Russell was friendly, charming, and seemed well-fixed enough to pay off any debt. And he had a manner so easy, a bearing so obviously upper class, that it was hard to imagine that he didn't periodically come into substantial sums of money. A rich young officer like Russell might be resented for the connections that got him billets and promotions that others struggled to achieve. If nothing else, his classmates assumed, he was responsible.

Those who had readily reached for their wallets soon learned that Russell Westcott III's notion of responsibility was different from theirs. It didn't take long before no fellow officer—around the War College that summer, the term "fellow officer of Russell Westcott" had come to be regarded as an oxymoron—would loan him money.

In fact, Russell would never willingly cheat anyone. He simply had no regard for money, no sense that it was the product of hard work, that it was not limitless, that there were times when desire had to be put aside so money could be husbanded. He had inherited his father's naïve trust that there was no need to account this green stuff as everyone else seemed to do, that more would somehow miraculously appear when it was needed.

Sybil had conscientiously tried not to spoil Russell as a child. When his father would promise the boy a pony or a boat, it was Sybil who stepped in, said "No," and took the rap as the stingy mother. Whenever it came to a loggerhead she could have her way, since she controlled the family purse strings, but more times than not, she too had given in, charmed by her son's smile and manner, and realizing that whatever her intentions, and no matter how many times she had tried to put her foot down, Russell had never shown the slightest indication of learning the lessons of responsibility and diligence that her exercises in arbitrary penuriousness were supposed to instill. In school, and later in the Navy, he spent as he had always spent, recklessly.

The weeks of squiring Sera had been even more expensive than Russell's usual flagrant disregard for cost, and he had soon exhausted every source of ready cash, even the soft touches who found it easier to give him money, despite the odds against being paid back, than to listen to the entreaties.

Sybil would not help. After the encounter at the Clambake Club, Sybil was determined not to support a habit of which she resolutely disapproved. Russell's father, though always sympathetic, rarely had cash to offer. "Women are an expensive habit," he would say with a grin. "What choice have we?"

There had been a time when Russell could run up tabs in Newport restaurants and shops. He had never established a formal account anywhere, but Russell was known by name in the better shops and restaurants, and when he was a young man about town it was silently understood that tabs he signed would be honored. Shortly before Russell returned to Newport from his year at Cavite, in the Philippines, Sybil had gone around to the shops and restaurants and explained that in the future bills signed by Russell Westcott III, like bills signed by his father, were not to be sent to her. Afterward, restaurants didn't turn Russell away, but when his orders were extravagant, the wine steward would politely report that they did not have the expensive wine he had ordered and suggest a more modest selection.

In the last weeks, while Russell had spent every spare moment, and more than a little time the War College was unwilling to classify as spare, with Sera, Mr. Raymond had not only allowed Russell to use the Packard on short notice, but had kept it gassed up. On several occasions Raymond had discreetly slipped Russell a few bills, always with an obsequious manner that avoided an ostentatious show of generosity. Yet as generous as Mr. Raymond was, Russell resented the time he needed to cultivate Raymond. The man was a bore, forever asking for tidbits of gossip, and time spent with Raymond was time he could not spend with Sera.

Russell was hooked on Sera as he had never been hooked before. The more he saw her, the more he fell in love. There had been many women before, from the easy pickings of Newport and the debutante balls in New York to the ready women of Manila and Hong Kong. This was the first time he cared.

It wasn't just Sera's alluring beauty, although he found himself constantly surprised and enraptured by her sheer loveliness. She had no fancy clothes. Compared to the young women of Newport, she dressed rather shabbily, without the pointed bras and fancy shoes and silk stockings with seams up the back that were the fashion. She wore no makeup except for lipstick, and never had her hair styled in the fashionable and overly controlled waves that had become a uniform. Yet whenever he looked at Sera, as he did almost every minute they were together, Russell could hardly take his eyes away. He concluded that she was the first woman he had ever really seen.

He loved to listen to her, to marvel at how knowledgeable she was about the oddest topics. Was it because she was the first woman he had ever listened to? he wondered. Or was she just different from the girls of Newport and New York, who seemed to have nothing on their minds except fashion, society, and their endless calendars of events? When he spoke, Sera was interested, a genuine listener. The women he had known were expert at feigning attention, but they never really heard anything. They would stare at him, as if they had learned from cotillion class or a book that they were supposed to hold a man's eyes, and wait for a pause to nod or say yes. Even when she occasionally teased him, there was a sincerity and simplicity in Sera's attention that made the deliberate and arch manners he had met so often seem the height of phoniness.

And Sera was refreshingly open and enthusiastic. At a restaurant, she would admit she had never before tasted escargots and openly enjoy the new experience. At the beach, instead of pretending delicacy and gingerly poking at the water, she would swim as far as he did, and ride the waves back in to the beach. When they sailed, she took the helm when a stiff afternoon seabreeze was capsizing small boats all around the harbor entrance. Nothing put her off. At Bailey's or the Clambake Club, she would notice the foibles of the rich, and wasn't afraid to laugh at them. It was as if a sudden gust of fresh air had come into his life, blowing away the phony affectations that had seemed so inevitable in Newport.

He had toyed with inviting Sera on the sort of date he had sometimes fantasized, a walk on the beach or on the pathways around Fort Adams, without a stop at a club or restaurant first. But Russell had grown up in a world where pleasure was synonymous with money; if it wasn't expensive or exclusive, it wasn't desirable. He wondered whether a girl like Sera would even want to be with him if he couldn't take her to the sorts of places everyone expected him to frequent.

He had sometimes seen young couples sharing a bench alongside the harbor, nuzzling one another. Sometimes he watched couples walking on Ocean Walk, holding hands. He envied their simple pleasures. Did they wish they could go to Bailey's or the Casino? he wondered. Maybe we're equally trapped.

Any problem with my using the Packard Saturday?" Russell had met Mr. Raymond for yet another drink at the White Horse. They never actually agreed to meet. Russell just knew that if he showed up after nine on a weeknight he had a good chance of finding Mr. Raymond at the bar.

"For that heavenly lady?" Raymond asked.

"No, it's to take the Secretary of the Navy out on a picnic." Russell regretted his sarcasm before he finished the sentence. I've been around Sybil too much, he thought.

"She really is splendid, Russell. Are you taking her to that ball your mother is having?"

"How do you know about the ball?"

"Newport talks. I listen."

"They talk about Sybil's ball?"

"Word has it that it's the first real ball in quite a while. In fact, Russell, I was rather hoping you might arrange an invitation for me."

"You're kidding. It'll be nothing but phonies, Raymond. Sybil will drag in every desk admiral and two-bit former diplomat she can find, anything to have plenty of dress uniforms and sashes with medals."

"I doubt anyone would notice me amidst all that glitter."

"Guess again. Sybil and Lisa have gone over that guest list with a nit comb. They'd notice an uninvited flea. Frankly, Raymond, you'll have a better time here. Lisa has devoted the summer to weeding every good-looking woman out of the guest list so she doesn't have to compete."

"All except one. It would be worth the price of admission to see the eyes in the room pop out when that lovely lady of yours walks in."

Russell sipped at his drink. "I'm sorry, Raymond. As they say on shipboard, no can do. Really—why on earth you would you want to go?"

Raymond finished his drink, a fancy rum concoction that he had taught the bartender at the White Horse to make, then ordered two more with a wave of his fingers. "Because, Russell, I am a man who appreciates pleasures, any pleasures, whenever and wherever they might be found. In Lisbon I spent hours in dark, smoky clubs, listening to the most wonderful lady singers. They sang songs that make you weep without understanding a word. In Havana I watched dancing that is beyond description, women in the most extraordinary costumes, wild concoctions of fantasy on their heads, with little of the rest left to imagination. A fancy-dress Newport ball is one pleasure I have never seen. I suppose I'm a—what's the word for it, a man who lives for pleasure?—sybarite, I think."

"Aren't we all?"

"Not really. Most people pretend. They live in circumscribed little worlds, pretending that a movie or a tame nightclub is the height of pleasure. They never allow themselves to enjoy what the world offers."

Russell thought of the dates he had dreamed of, walks along the bluffs or the beach. What would Raymond think of that? he wondered.

Raymond finished his rum concoction and said, "Come with me, Russell. I'll show you something you've almost certainly never seen."

They drove north in the Packard, up into Portsmouth, past warehouses and low factory buildings, and finally onto a side street of two-story brick buildings. The doorway where they stopped could have been the entrance to offices or a storeroom. An interior staircase led to what looked like the second floor of an apartment building.

When they got to the landing, Russell could hear sorry jazz from a trio, sour and slow. The doorway at the head of the stairs reminded him of a speakeasy, made of heavy wood with a sliding port. Raymond knocked, the port slid open a crack, and Raymond said something in a low voice before the door opened.

The doorway led straight into a good-sized room that looked like it had been converted from a warehouse or loft. Small round tables, arranged around a stage area, were crowded with groups of men and a few couples. Most of the people were fairly well-dressed, with jackets and ties. A dense cloud of cigarette smoke hung low in the still air. There was no talk, not even the low, indecipherable murmur of an upscale bar. A heavyset man in a tired, shiny tuxedo stood by the door.

The stage in the middle of the room was covered with pale gold carpeting. A pallet of mattresses in the center was draped with satin sheets. Colored overhead spotlights focused on the bed. The sorry jazz trio played in the corner.

On the bed two women were making love. One, with henna-dyed black hair, was lying on her back, moaning. The other, with long legs, erect breasts, bright red hair, and long fingernails to match, had an enormous tongue that she flashed at the audience as much as she applied it to the woman on the bed. Mr. Ray-

mond was instantly fascinated, even before they found their way
to a table. When a waiter came to their table, Raymond didn't
look up. He raised his index finger in a circular motion which
the waiter seemed to understand.

For Russell the women on the mattress were interesting for
a moment, only because he had always been curious about
women making love. The black-haired woman writhed in exaggerated motions while the redhead with the enormous tongue
tied her ankles and wrists with silky golden ropes to white posts
at the corners of the bed. Russell thought of the waiting lines
outside theaters, the only place he had ever seen those golden
ropes before.

The waiter brought a bottle of champagne in a bucket and
two glasses. Russell poured a glass only to find that it tasted like
ginger ale mixed with cheap wine. Mr. Raymond, absorbed in
watching the two women, never reached for his glass.

When the black-haired woman was tied to the posts, the silky
cords slack enough to allow her to roll her shoulders and hips,
the redhead flashed her huge tongue at the audience again, then
hunched over the black-haired woman, and begin licking her
legs with long strokes of her tongue. The moans of the black-
haired woman escalated, and her body began to pump and twist,
as if she were trying to pull the other woman into her. Russell
found himself alternately fascinated and repulsed, wondering if
the gestures and moans were real or feigned.

The music grew louder, the slow syncopated beat fading into
a heavy, pulsing bassline. Russell could hear Raymond breathing,
his long breaths drawn through open lips, followed by quick,
syncopated exhales, the rhythm so erratic it seemed he had to
remember to breathe.

The writhing women had reached a feverish pitch when without warning the saxophone broke into a riff that segued into a
brassy fanfare. The drummer dropped his insistent bass beat for
a roll on the snare drum. Eyes at every table turned to a far
corner of the room, as if they all knew what to expect.

A tall black man walked from behind a curtain toward the
carpeted pit, wearing a white toga over his shoulders. His steps
were slow, like the paced oars of an admiral's gig. The two

women feigned fear at each step with the exaggerated gestures
of a silent movie. The redhead got off the bed, approached the
black man, and dropped to her knees. She lifted the toga,
peeked underneath, and gestured fear with exaggerated wide-
open eyes. With a regal gesture, he motioned for her to rise and
undo the clasps on the toga. The rituals were stretched into a
long pantomime, with the trio playing a burlesque riff, until the
toga finally fell to the floor.

The black man's skin was oiled so it glistened. He was tall,
and well-muscled—like an oarsman on an eight-man shell, Russell thought. He had the largest member Russell had ever seen.
The redhead fell to her knees, grasped the black man around
the knees, until he gestured again, and she slowly began to
stroke him with her hands, then with her tongue.

For Russell, after a few moments of curiosity, the performance had all the appeal of watching a sweaty workout in a
gym. As he looked down at the table and poured himself another glass of the wretched champagne, he saw Mr. Raymond
slide forward to the edge of his chair, totally engrossed as the
man and woman, then the man and both women, went through
their paces.

The act dragged on. Russell was amazed by the staying power
of the black man, and the variety of activities, though before
long, as the silent-movie pantomimes gave way to a sweaty,
gymnastic performance on the bed, the coupling began to seem
ever more forced and awkward. When he looked closely, the
sheets on the pallet and the togas were stained and gray.

Raymond didn't look away until the spotlights and the music
faded. A moment later the lights came up as the man and two
women draped themselves in togas, took bows as if they had
just danced *Swan Lake*, and walked from the arena. The audience responded with polite applause, as if they had just heard
a chamber music concert.

"Beautiful, isn't it?" said Mr. Raymond. His voice broke from
the dryness of his mouth, and his Adam's apple bounced with
each word. He reached for the champagne, gulped down a glass,
then poured another. "It's remarkable to me that there are men
and women who pretend to be cultured and to have limitless

admiration for art. Yet they deny themselves the most sensuous of all art. They will go to a ballet, which is only teasing, and rave, applauding for a dozen curtain calls. And yet they will never allow themselves the opportunity to appreciate beautiful bodies engaged in the most beautiful of all acts."

"What do you pay for a club like this?" Russell asked.

Raymond waved the question away, as if he were sweeping crumbs off a table. "Money is only good for the pleasures it brings. I have a simple rule of life, Russell, which is never to deny myself or my friends genuine pleasure."

He filled his own glass, and Russell's, with champagne. "You said you had plans for this Saturday? You're welcome to the Packard. Let me know if you need spending money. I understand how—shall we say *parsimonious?*—the Commanders-in-Chief can be."

15

Off and on, for twenty years, Sybil Westcott had tried to establish a salon in Newport. She didn't call it that. No one she knew in Newport would have known what a *salon* was. Her society friends knew everything there was to know about teas, balls, shooting parties, Marie Antoinette play-farm parties, the hunt, yacht races, tennis matches, dinner parties, cocktail parties, debutante parties, and garden parties. Had they heard her idea, most of them would have looked down their noses at the notion. Even a book club would have been frowned upon as insufferably boring. Still, Sybil had never abandoned the idea, and she was ever on the lookout for writers, musicians, artists, or architects who would add spice and substance to the dreary intellectual life in Newport. For a while she had teamed up with her artist friend Caroline Fiske, until Sybil realized that Caroline, who had a different sort of activity in mind, had seduced Russell and almost every other man she met through the tentative salon efforts.

It was then that Sybil realized that it wasn't really a salon that she craved. What she wanted was a man friend. Not a lover. Wes, as tenuous as their marriage ties remained, was all the lover she had ever needed. Even when he had brazenly paraded trollops before her, Sybil had never desired another man. But after the years of business talk with her father, and the years after his death when boat captains, heads of truck fleets, bootleg suppliers, and owners of well-known and fabulously profitable speakeasies had respected and dealt with her—not with the namby-pamby chitchat of the Newport ladies, but in frank, straight talk—Sybil craved a man friend, an intelligent man who would listen to her and talk to her as an equal. In Newport, it had never happened.

For all his infinite charms, Wes was a child at heart. When he first met a woman, he was all ears, hanging on her every word, drawing out conversation with his incomparable smile. Women thought him a wonderful listener, but Wes was only listening for cues, for signals that a woman was susceptible. For Wes, every conversation with a woman was the first step in a seduction. Every relationship, even those that went no further than a quick conversation or a dance at a ball, was an affair. When he no longer wanted to seduce Sybil, he stopped talking to her. After a year of marriage, their conversation had descended to quips and banalities, mean-spirited and ungracious digs at one another followed by civilities that might have been exchanged by strangers. Each time, Sybil regretted the bitter sarcasm in her voice—she would wince inside when she heard herself—but the hurt of what had become of their relationship was so deep that she was powerless to stop herself.

Russell was afraid of her. Even as a boy, long before he discovered his marvelous good looks and charm, he had been wary and standoffish, as if he were afraid his mother's probing mind would discover his secrets. Other little boys instinctively ran to their mothers when they skinned a knee. Russell would choke back tears, his eyes defiant.

When he was thirteen he answered a question about his father's whereabouts by saying "He's down in the stable house, boffing some babe."

Sybil reached out to slap his face. He caught her wrists, holding them tightly in his hands until she stopped struggling. When he finally let go, Sybil forced herself not to rub the reddened wrists. "I hoped for a gentleman as a son," she said. "And I got a copy of a cad."

After that, she never tried to talk to Russell.

Driving back from the dock at the Newport Ship Yard, hidden behind the tinted glass windows of the backseat, Sybil West-

cott imagined a serious conversation with a man like Jake Werth.
She knew, from a few quiet inquiries in Newport, that he was
exactly the kind of man friend she craved. He was quiet, had
studied naval architecture at a serious university, had traveled
off the beaten path. On the dock, he had not been afraid to
speak his mind, and hadn't been afraid of her. He seemed the
kind of man who wouldn't automatically avoid serious subjects
or reduce a conversation to frivolous chatter about the weather
or the Season because she was a woman. She was sorry she had
been so short and cruel with him, regretting that years of bitterness had allowed her to build a shell of sarcasm that fended
off the very people she sought.

With the end of Prohibition, and her full-time return to Newport, Sybil had almost forgotten the years of excitement when
her quick mind and quicker tongue had risen to the challenge
of business. It wasn't until she began making the arrangements
for Lisa's ball that she suddenly remembered the charged aura
of those grand days in Port Chester, when with a telephone call,
a hand-delivered note, or a quick visit in the car that one of the
warehouse men drove for her, she could make things happen.
Dealing with caterers, an orchestra for the ballroom and a quartet for the entryway, hired footmen and waiters, the tent service,
landscapers, and stationers lacked the excitement of the old days
of furtive meetings and briefcases bulging with cash, but at least
she felt useful and competent.

Manuel was supposed to be in the dark about the ball. After
the evening when Sera went out for dinner and dancing
with Russell, and once when he caught her sneaking back into
the house after a date, Manuel had stormed and shouted, ac-
cusing Sera of "throwing herself at fancy boys." Sera, with no
appetite for Manuel's ultimatums, and even less for his leering
eyes and roaming hands, ran out of the house.

The next afternoon, when Sera walked home from the velvet
factory, Josephina was waiting on the porch. "Tell me about this
boy," Josephina said.

"What boy?" said Sera.

"It's all right, Sera. You can tell me."

"He's very nice. We have fun together."

"I'm sure he is nice, Sera. And that you have fun. But sometimes it isn't enough for a boy to be nice. You're old enough that you have to think about what it means when you see a boy like this."

"What does it mean, Mama?"

"They say he's a Navy officer with a fancy car, and that he is from Newport."

"*They* say?"

"It's a small village, Sera. People aren't blind."

"What else have they been saying?"

"I don't listen to the talk."

"Really?"

"Sera, I don't want you to be hurt. These rich boys, they don't respect a girl. Oh, I'm sure they can seem nice and take you to fancy places. But what happens when they're done?"

"Done?"

"It will happen, Sera."

"What happens when a boy from Stonington is done?"

"Boys here know that if they don't respect a girl, there are consequences. They grow up with a sense of honor."

"Mama, it's not like that. It's fun to be with him. We went for a picnic. We had dinner in a restaurant. We talk. We laugh. It's the boys here that think of only one thing."

"All boys think of only one thing."

Later, when Sera came down to the kitchen to help with dinner, Josephina said, "Tell me about this ball."

"How do you know about the ball?"

"I don't remember who told me. Maybe Mrs. Esposito."

"It's for his sister. There will be an orchestra, and the men will wear suits with tails like in the movies. The women wear long dresses."

"Long dresses?" Josephina went into the other room and came out with two dresses that she had stored under sheets in an armoire. She held one, then the other, up to Sera. They were impossibly old-fashioned, with puffy sleeves and lace-trimmed bodices.

"Not right?" she said. "I could make you a dress."

"A dress for what?" came the voice from the other room.

Manuel strutted in. He wasn't wearing fishing clothes. He stood with one hand on his hip, blocking the doorway, as he pointed first at Sera, then at Josephina.

"You think you pull the wool over Manuel Gomes's eyes," he said. "I know what you're thinking. You think you'll go to some big party and then next it will be off to some big city. Well, that Werth can go all he wants. You're not going. I know what he wants, and he's not getting it."

"Manuel," Josephina said, "she isn't going anywhere with Jake. It's just a party. There's no harm if Sera goes."

"No harm?" said Manuel. "I have a reputation to protect."

"What harm is there in a party?" Josephina said. "They dance here, in the village. So she dances at another party. What is the harm?"

Sera watched her mother's eyes drop. She hated when her mother pleaded with Manuel. It wasn't just her eyes that reached out. Her whole body seemed to beg for mercy, like a dog rolling on its back to expose its throat.

"Never mind," Sera said. She was close enough to the back door to slip out before anyone could stop her.

"Where do you think you're going?" Manuel shouted. "I said—" The rest of his words were lost behind the slammed door.

Sera ran up the street, past the shops, past the boatyard, quiet since Jake had begun working in Newport. In all her trips to Newport, she had never seen him. She was glad. She thought how impossible it would be to try to explain to Jake.

She found Rosa in the enclosed porch behind the farmhouse kitchen, washing and trimming vegetables and arranging them in baskets. The carrots, tomatoes, and greens she had harvested from the garden were covered with soil, and most had bad spots from worms and bugs. When Rosa finished washing and trimming with quick slashes of her knife and arranged the vegetables in baskets, they looked like pictures. The women in the village gossiped about Rosa behind her back, but they ran for her stall in the market near the rail tracks.

When she saw Sera, Rosa put down her knife, wiped her

hands on her apron, and hugged Sera with the familiar kisses on both cheeks. "Well," said Rosa, "tell me about him."

"Him?"

"When a woman looks like she is ready to explode inside, it can only be a man."

"How come you're so smart?" Sera asked.

Rosa laughed. "I'm not smart, Sera. I just say what everyone else is afraid to say."

"He's—actually, Russell isn't like anybody. He's very handsome, with gold hair and blue eyes and a smile that is just wonderful. Sometimes I can't stop looking at him. But it's not just that. And it's not that he's from Newport and a Navy officer and drives a convertible. He's not like other men.

"He doesn't work. His hands are soft and smooth. All he does is play games. Really. He calls them games, but they're more than games. He laughs about it and about the war, but he must be very good at it. He's good at everything he does. He never has to try hard; everything is easy for him.

"One day I watched him play tennis against another officer. He let the other man score a few points, and kept looking up at me. I thought I was distracting him. I even wanted to hide. Then all of a sudden, without any warning, he started playing with a fury. He would rush to the net and run to the back of the court and reach out to get a ball. He won points one right after another. A few minutes later he was smiling at me the way he does and the game was nothing."

Rosa answered with only a smile.

"When I'm with him," Sera said, "he listens and looks right at me. It's like he doesn't care about anything or anyone else in the world."

"I know. It happened to me too," said Rosa.

"In France? Tell me."

"I don't have to tell you, Sera. I always waited to tell you about France because it was something I knew you would only understand when you were in love. Now, I don't have to tell you. Jean-Claude's father was a man like the man you met. When I was with him, I forgot the rest of the world."

"Like you were the only woman in the world?"

"When I was with him, I *was* the only woman in the world."

Sera's eyes danced with excitement as she described the times she had spent with Russell. Rosa, still cleaning the vegetables, nodded at each story. Her laughing eyes made Sera want to go on and on.

"He sounds like Jean-Claude's father," Rosa said, with a wistful sigh. "Just remember that men are not always what they seem. Or maybe they are."

"What do you mean?" Sera asked. She had already begun to scrape and trim some of the radishes and carrots with a knife. Working was instinctive.

"Nothing, really. Tell me about the ball."

"It's so his sister can meet a husband. It sounds like a fairy tale. Russell and the other Navy officers will wear uniforms with swords. Other men wear tails and sashes with medals. The women wear gowns down to the floor."

Rosa said, "I had a ball gown once. White peau de soie, with a red silk sash. I wore it with nothing underneath and felt wicked. Every step I took the gown rubbed against my skin. The feel of the dress was as exciting as anything else."

Sera started to blush, then laughed. "That's what it's like when I dance with Russell. We touch, and then we don't touch, and I can't wait until we touch again."

"What will you wear?" asked Rosa.

Sera shrugged. "Mama said she would make me a dress. Then Manuel heard her and started shouting."

"I have some cloth I brought back from France. If I don't make something soon, the moths will eat it." She stepped back from the table and measured Sera with her eyes, then went to the sink, pumped enough water to wash her hands, and wiped them on her apron.

Rosa wrapped a cloth tape measure around Sera, measuring her hips and waist and bust and across her shoulders. When she measured Rosa's arm, she took Rosa's hand and held it up and they started dancing, a whirling waltz that took them around the kitchen and out to the porch. They hummed and danced and laughed.

"You'll be lovely," said Rosa.

The motorsailer didn't steady up until Jake got around the tip of Jamestown and into the open water of the West Passage. Even without the short chop of the Newport side of the bay, the boat was awkward to handle—he had to motor instead of putting up a sail—but at least it stopped pitching on every swell.

James Putnam's house was secluded behind a stand of craggy pines. The landscape was stony, the rough shale shoreline broken only by gnarled pines, stunted and twisted from their endless battle against the prevailing winds. Patches of wild grasses filled the pockets of soil in the outcroppings. The house was a shingled cape with huge picture windows looking out at unspoiled bay. Jake could imagine the view at sunset, the open water punctuated with the occasional barge on its way up to Providence or sailboats backlit by the setting sun.

A dock led out into deep water. There was no sign of anyone living at the house, but discarded cigarette butts and disturbed moss on the paths suggested that someone had been down to the dock recently. Probably agents making sure it was a secure location, Jake thought. He smiled at his easy familiarity with the idea of agents.

As he tied Putnam's motorsailer up, it was hard not to imagine sharing the incredible beauty of the spot. The wind on this side of Narragansett Bay was almost as reliable as Buzzards Bay. Jake could imagine Sera's excitement at the setting and the breeze. She would adore the spartan landscape, so different from the houses piled on top of one another in the village at home.

He got ready to enjoy a quiet evening, missing only the newspapers he would normally pick up when he went up to one of the cafés on Thames Street for dinner.

All the news was Europe: German troops plunging ever deeper into Russia, and the British waging a desperate war with the Italians to keep the sea lanes in the Mediterranean open. Yet the problem Langer had posed made no sense in Europe. The Germans had no naval aviation capability, at least not the ability to mount an air attack on a fleet. The only powers that did were the U.S., Britain, and Japan. Was Langer thinking about an attack on a major German naval facility like Kiel? Or the Japanese attacking the U.S. in the Phillipines or the British in Singapore? Or were Langer's worries defensive? Jake had been facetious when he suggested Narragansett Bay: there was nothing to fear from the Germans. Did he think the Japanese would attack San Diego or Pearl Harbor?

16

Russell wasn't surprised by the summons to Horatio Breedlove's office.

He had spent the day before with Sera. They had gone for a sail around the harbor, until a sudden thunderstorm forced them back to the Yacht Club. When they toweled off and peeked into the dining room of the club, they turned to one another and laughed. Everyone else in the dining room was old enough to be a grandparent.

"Let's just go to a bar," Russell said. "Anyplace dry and quiet." They drove from Brenton Cove to the row of bars on Long Wharf. Russell picked a place called the Blue Moon, with a sign that promised dancing and dinner. The bar was dim inside from dirty windows blocked with neon signs and the bartop was stained and sticky. They sat at a booth, alone except for two petty officers drinking beer at the bar.

"It's a Navy bar," said Russell, nodding at the long counter.

"You should be right at home."

Russell shook his head. "Not my Navy."

"Why do you never talk about the Navy?"

"What's to say? As long as they give me time for you, it's fine."

"It must be an exciting time at the War College now."

"Sera, the only exciting thing is being with you. The college is like the rest of the Navy. There are guys there who would drive over their own mothers to get a good billet. They're the ones who are excited

about the war. They figure they'll bump up the ranks faster in
wartime."

"It doesn't have to be that way, does it?"

Russell saw Sera glance up, behind him. As he turned to look
over his shoulder, two men stepped from behind him to the end
of the table.

"Mind if we join you?" said one. He was tall and muscular,
with greasy blond hair. The sleeve of his T-shirt was rolled
around a package of cigarettes. The other man was shorter and
heavier, with cropped dark hair.

"Actually, we do," said Russell. "Looks like there are plenty
of tables free."

"We like this one."

"It's yours." Russell said, taking Sera's hand across the table
as he slid out of the booth.

"You leave," said the tall man. "She stays."

It was impossible to lead Sera from the booth without pushing the tall man aside.

The tall man pushed Russell back against the table. "You trying to start something?"

"No," Russell said. "I don't want a fight." He craned to look
for the bartender, but the shorter man blocked his view of the
bar.

The tall man reached for Sera's arm. "You better just leave,"
he said to Russell.

Russell let go of Sera's hand, and took a step back. His hands
dropped to his sides, his fingers curled and elbows half-bent. "I
don't want to fight you," he said.

"*I don't want to fight you,*" mocked the shorter man.

The tall man took a step toward Russell. His fists were halfway raised, as if he weren't sure whether he would punch or
wrestle. He seemed not to notice the intenseness of Russell's
concentration or the deliberate, relaxed crouch as Russell rocked
back and snapped off a spin-kick with his right foot. The sole
of his shoe smashed into the tall man's lip and nose, and the
man fell back hard against the side of the booth. His hands
covered his face as he slumped to the floor.

The shorter man looked down at his friend and hesitated before he squared off in a boxing crouch, bouncing heavily on his feet. Russell spun to face him, flaring with a quick left, drawing the man's eyes. A side-kick with his right foot caught the shorter man in the gut, doubling him over. Russell brought the edge of his right hand down on the back of the man's neck, sprawling him on the floor. Russell jumped to stand astride the man, but it was all over. The fight had lasted less than a minute.

"Come on," said Russell, leading Sera by the arm as she stepped over the two men on the floor.

The shorter man brought himself up to his knees, gasping for breath. The taller man was lying on his side, holding his hands over his nose and mouth. A trickle of blood ran down his chin. "You fucking broke my nose," he said.

Russell put a five-dollar bill on the bar. "Sorry," he said to the bartender. "I wasn't looking for trouble."

The bartender and the two petty officers were staring at the two men on the floor. "Never seen anything like that," the bartender said.

"I should have known we would run into creeps," Russell said as he helped Sera into the car.

"How did you learn to fight like that?" she asked.

"In Cavite. If you didn't want to listen to stories about the South China Sea, there was nothing to do. One night I saw a little guy—he weighed about a hundred and twenty pounds—take on three drunk sailors outside a bar. I followed him home, persuaded him that I wasn't the Shore Patrol, and got him to teach me kick-boxing. Once I learned a few moves, word got around and guys off the ships would challenge me to fights. I thought it was all just fun, but some guys start baiting and won't stop."

"What did you you do?"

"Mostly, I tried not to fight. But I guess I had reputation, so there was always some guy who would jump me in an alleyway or a dark corner of a dock. I left one sailor's nose looking like a plate of mashed potatoes. Another time two guys jumped me outside a bar. One ended up in the hospital. I went to see him and the nurses told me that he would be drinking through a straw for weeks. The only good thing is that it helped me get transferred out of Cavite. And that meant I could come here and meet you."

Sera said, "I wish I could figure you out."

The summons from Breedlove came the next morning.

"Well, Russell?" Breedlove was sitting behind his desk, with open texts piled around him.

"I'm sorry, sir. I tried to avoid it."

"Avoid? What are you talking about, Russell?"

"The fight yesterday. In town."

"Did you win?"

"I don't think anyone wins street fights. They got hurt and I didn't."

"Good. Actually, that's not the reason I called you in. I want to talk about the fleet game. Are your studies going well?"

"All right, sir."

"Russell, I don't think I'm the only one to notice that you seem off of late."

Russell knew exactly what Breedlove meant. Before he met Sera, Russell had been lackadaisical in his work at the War College, rarely doing the reading assignments, but at least he could concentrate enough to snap off a quick answer when called upon. Now, he was missing classes—the trips to Stonington and the hours he spent humoring Raymond for the Packard and spending money took a toll. Even when he was in class he was so preoccupied daydreaming about Sera, planning how and when he would see her next, that he had begun answering questions with a blank-faced stare and a tiresome "Beg your pardon, sir." His plummeting performance had occasioned rumors and talk at the college.

"It's nothing, sir," he said.

"Are you well rested?"

Was this sarcasm? Jake wondered. It wasn't like Breedlove. "Yes, sir."

"Sit down, Russell. You needn't be formal."

"Yes, sir."

"I'm not asking these questions out of politeness. Are you ready for the fleet exercise?"

"As ready as I ever am, sir."

"I don't think so. You know, Russell, that I've taken a personal interest in your work here. I pride myself as a judge of men, and I don't like to think I'm wrong this time. The fleet exercise isn't like other war games. I don't just mean the length and complexity. From long experience, we know that these fleet games are the ultimate measure of men, separating ordinary, competent officers from those who can legitimately expect to rise to fleet commands. In the challenge and pressure of the fleet games we—both staff and visiting fleet officers—get a true sense of. . . ."

Russell, lost in daydream about Sera, missed the rest of what Breedlove said. He snapped alert with the silence at the end of Breedlove's speech. "Yes, sir."

"Russell! I just asked what your plans were for the game? *Yes* is hardly an appropriate response."

"Sorry, sir."

"Russell, I say this not only as your instructor but as a friend: You are facing what may be the most important watershed in your career. Don't you think it would be wise to have some plans at the ready?"

Russell didn't answer. He looked at Breedlove, and then up at a photograph of Admiral Mahan, in his long coat and full beard, on the wall behind the desk. Breedlove's full face and balding head didn't look at all like the stiffly posed admiral. The juxtaposition seemed so ludicrous that Russell smiled.

"This is not a time for mirth, Russell. You're losing focus precisely when your concentration should be most honed. For an officer of your talents, this is the opportunity of a lifetime."

"Frankly, sir, I haven't given a thought to the game."

"That is unwise, Russell. These are not ordinary times. An era of glory is upon us. In the next months, a year at the most, we will be called upon for the most sacred mission of mankind. The fleets, and the men who command them, will be called upon to defend our civilization."

"And if I don't want to defend our civilization?"

"I'll ignore that. It's obvious that you're distracted. Suffice it to say that success in the fleet exercise is your ticket to a command."

"What if I don't want a command?"

"Isn't that a bit like saying, 'What if I don't want to breathe?' We each have a purpose on this earth. It is no coincidence that a man of your caliber and talents has found his way here."

"What if all I want is an easy billet? Or no billet, just out of the Navy?"

"Russell, listen to me. The peacetime Navy that you so obviously detest is governed by privilege and persistence. It is an institution with no respect for panache; an organization that lends itself to the triumph of the ordinary, men who by sheer hard work get ahead of the position to which their birth, breeding, and talents would normally entitle them. Today we stand on the cusp of peace and war, at the dawn of an historic era. The gray line stands ready, awaiting the call to battle. A few will know the highest destiny of man, to command men and ships, to stand on the bridge of a flagship, at the head of a line of men of war."

"Breedlove, it's bunk."

"Pretend cynicism if you must. But natural talents like yours cannot be concealed. If we've learned nothing else, we surely know the differences of races, and within races, of classes. That's why you're here, Russell. Success in the fleet game is your ticket. Do well and you can write your future."

Russell started to drift again, until the last phrase caught him short.

"Sir, what did you just say?"

"Russell, this absentminded drifting ill becomes you. What I said is that if you do well in the fleet game you can write your future."

"I thought you said that, sir. I agree."

"Good. I want you to know that I consider you an important ally for the game."

"Ally, sir?"

"Russell, here at the War College, the war has already begun. The traditionalists still believe that the inevitable war with Japan will culminate in a massive strike by our battleships deep in

Japanese waters. They are wrong. The truth is that the battleships will never reach Japan. The weapon of today is no longer
the battleship. I hardly need to tell you this. You understand
the effectiveness of naval aircraft. Your employment of aircraft
as an offensive weapon in the tactical exercise was brilliant. It
was one more proof of the superiority of naval aviation over the
battleship."

"Thank you, sir."

"But they ignored it, Russell. As they've ignored every other
demonstration of the superiority of naval aviation. When General Mitchell's aircraft sunk the *Ostfriesland* in twenty minutes,
there were admirals watching who wept. Instead of accepting
naval aviation, they turned their backs. They came back here
and reshaped the curriculum to emphasize battleships. Think
about your training: the maneuvering board exercises, firepower
tables, damage tables, fire control exercises—everything is done
in terms of the battleship. Damage is measured by how many
hits of a sixteen-inch battleship gun a ship can withstand. Tactics
are dominated by the question of maneuvering close enough to
bring the sixteen-inch guns to bear on the enemy. They refuse
to accept that long before the battleships are close enough to
use those guns, enemy naval aircraft will have launched a deadly
hailstorm of torpedoes and bombs. They ignore even the reality
of our own fleet exercises."

Russell was already thinking about Sera, and whether he
would have a chance to see her before the ball.

Breedlove picked up a manila folder from his desk. "In Fleet
Problem IX, twelve years ago, the carriers *Saratoga* and *Lexington* simulated an attack on the Panama Canal. *Saratoga* broke
from her escort of slower battleships and launched her aircraft
in two bombing runs on the canal. Both were successful. It was
a brilliant maneuver, and a staggering victory for naval aviation.
What did the traditionalists do? They argued that the fleet exercise was actually a defeat of naval aviation because later in the
exercise the *Saratoga* was sunk. Do you know why she sunk?
Because she was following fleet orders to return to her escort.
It was as if they were trying to sabotage her.

"They set up another test two years later, Fleet Problem XII.

Two aircraft carriers were supposed to prevent a force composed of almost the entire battle fleet from executing a landing. The traditionalists got what they wanted that time. The carriers failed—what else would happen if you put two carriers against the entire battle fleet?—and aviation was relegated to scout duty and spotting for fire control.

"Fortunately, there was one more test. Fleet Problem XIX, in 1938, simulated an attack against Pearl Harbor. Admiral King was in command of the *Saratoga*, and allowed to operate independently of his battleship escort. He took cover behind a weather front, approached Pearl Harbor undetected from the northwest—where no one would expect an enemy force—and launched a successful strike without losing a single plane. I did an analysis of the exercise"—he pointed to a report, sitting on top of the stack of manila folders—"but with the exception of the few carrier skippers, like Spruance and Fletcher, it has been ignored. They refuse to accept the truth."

Breedlove noticed Russell daydreaming again. "Russell!"

Russell smiled, almost sheepish.

"This is important material, Russell."

"They're exercises, sir. Games."

"They are more than games. You know that as well as I do. Read the lessons right and these exercises will determine the outcome of the next war. I want you to take this material—no one else at the War College has paid attention to it—and study it."

Russell looked at the stack of folders that Breedlove pushed across the desk. "Don't get me wrong, sir, but an attack on Pearl Harbor? Isn't that stretching things a bit?"

"You're sounding like the traditionalists, Russell. The real lesson of that exercise is the value of naval aviation. If our carriers were caught and sunk in an attack like that we could very well *lose* the war. The next game may be may be the last we will play here. If we can make a show of the effectiveness of naval aviation, we may not only turn the tide of naval warfare but the outcome of the war."

"To the Breedlove doctrine?"

"Call it that if you want." He handed the documents to Russell. "These analyses are highly secret material. Exercise the usual cautions."

Sera walked by Jake's boatyard every morning and every after-noon. She thought about Jake each time, remembering the afternoon sails on the sound, the times when she would watch his hands working on a boat. On her way home from the mill, she would watch the sky and the breeze on the trees, and think about how much she had looked forward to seeing Jake.

How was he? she wondered. And then just as quickly she pushed the thought away and hurried past the boatyard.

Rosa was excited to see her, and held up the dress. Rosa had tried it once earlier, but then the panels of fabric were basted together with long loops of white thread and it seemed more costume than gown.

"Take off your underwear too," said Rosa, as Sera slipped off her shift.

"Really?"

Rosa laughed. "The way I made the dress, there might not be room for anything but you."

As Sera slipped off her bra and half-slip, Rosa stepped back, as if she were looking at a statue in a museum. "You are a beau-tiful woman, Sera." Her tone was more matter-of-fact than sur-prised.

Sera shrugged. "I know, I know. 'Such a pretty girl.' "

"I didn't say *pretty*. Every mother tells her little girl she is pretty. Beautiful is different. It is special, a gift. Like being able to sing opera." She held out the dress.

Sera had to wriggle to get into the dress. The thin black fabric tingled her skin.

Rosa hooked the tiny hooks at the back, then stood back. "Oh, my," she said. "Oh, my."

"Is it okay?"

Rosa brushed Sera's hair back with her fingers, twisting and piling it up into a soft roll. "More than okay."

The dress was a simple sheath, slit up the right side to above the knee. The bodice was fitted, with straps as thin as spaghetti over the shoulders. There was no decoration on the dress, not a single ribbon or bow. The stark but lush black fabric—Rosa said it was a blend of silk and fine wool—accented the shine of Sera's hair.

Rosa stood as far back as she could, still holding Sera's hair in the loose roll. "Almost perfect. There's just one thing missing." She let Rosa's hair tumble as she went into her bedroom and came back with a small lacquered box. She opened it carefully, and held out a pair of long silver earrings. "Wear these," she said.

Sera took the earrings in her open palm. Tiny diamonds glittered at the tips of the pendants. "Are they real?" Sera asked.

"Yes."

"They're beautiful. Where did you get them?"

"In France." Before the words left her mouth they were both laughing.

"It's not a mystery, Sera. Nothing that happened in France is the mystery that people here make it. Jean-Claude's father gave those to me."

"What happened to him?"

Rosa closed her eyes and shook her head. "He used to write. Then the letters stopped. It didn't matter when he stopped writing. The letters were sweet, but they aren't the man I knew. Those"—she pointed to the earrings—"are."

She swept Sera's hair up again, this time pinning it. Sera put the earrings on without a mirror, then spun on her bare feet, as if she were dancing. But for her long neck, the earrings would have grazed her shoulders. "Well?" she said.

Rosa held out a hand mirror.

Sera looked at the mirror, tilting her head so the earrings glittered in the light. She twisted back and forth, holding the mirror as far as she could reach. With a smile spreading across her face, she put the mirror down and danced across the room.

"I feel beautiful," she said.

Bull Langer—outside of class the students had all called him that—showed up at Putnam's Jamestown house with no advance warning. "I wish I could have come by boat," he said, meeting Jake on the dock. "What a delight it would be to get out on the water for a few weeks. I haven't even been out on a daysail lately."

Langer held out two loaves of bread. "They call it Vienna bread, but it's really Portuguese. A bit of a hobby for me, you know. Jewish caraway rye, Italian, French, sourdough. Anything but that blotter paper that passes for American bread."

Jake led him into the salon of the Putnam's boat, where the table was cluttered with models and sheets of gray-ruled graph paper. They ate the bread while they talked.

"Any progress?" asked Langer. The calm, assured voice reminded Jake of the seminars.

"It's an interesting problem," said Jake. "Torpedoes are sort of like Br'er Rabbit and Br'er Fox in the briar patch. Every time the fox comes up with a new trick, the rabbit has to find a new defense."

Langer grinned as he sat down on the cushioned salon bench.

Jake handed him sketches on sheets of graph paper. "A torpedo dropped from an aircraft is moving as fast as the plane. The trick is to control the drop, limit the depth that the torpedo dives below the surface of the water. I tried a lot of options. A parachute would destroy the aim and make the torpedo an easy target for gunners. Bigger control fins on the back of the torpedo, extended and angled just right, could cut the sink depth in half. The problem is that in the water oversized fins overwhelm the depth-control system and the torpedo ends up porpoising on the surface of the water." Jake waved his hand to illustrate what he meant.

"I tried attaching oversized fins with water-soluble glue so they would fall off on entry." He showed Langer a wooden model, less than two feet long. "It didn't work—the glue won't dissolve fast enough—but while I was testing, the fins on one model snapped off by accident, and I realized that it wouldn't take much engineering to do it by design. Use wooden extensions like these on the fins and you have a torpedo that can be launched from an airplane in shallow harbors."

"That simple?" said Langer.

"I came up with an even simpler version. It might not work with a fast launch plane, but it would work fine with slow biplanes like the Brits use. You could attach a wire to the front of the torpedo, and reel it out from the airplane as the torpedo falls. If the strength of the wire is just right, the wire will break when the torpedo enters the water. I used thread for tests; on a real torpedo a single-strand wire should work. It took even less fiddling than the fins to get it to work."

"How shallow a harbor would be vulnerable? Could these torpedoes be used in eight or ten fathoms?"

"Any anchorage deep enough to moor a battleship."

"Why hasn't anyone used them before?"

"For every trick of the fox, the rabbit has a new defense. If you surround the ships with barrage balloons holding up steel cables, an attacking plane will think twice about trying a low attack. Steel nets around the ships can protect them from torpedoes. Look closely at this photograph of Taranto you left here, and you can see tiny floats around the battleships, probably for torpedo nets."

Langer found a magnifying glass on the crowded salon table. "I see what you mean. If the Italians had torpedo nets, how did the Brits sink those ships?"

"The nets probably only extend as deep as the draft of the ships. The waterline is the area you try to protect. The Italians even have a special feature called a Pughliese bulge that they build into their ships, sort of a double hull at the waterline that absorbs the shock of explosions. The Brits could defeat that by sending their torpedoes under the nets."

"Wouldn't the torpedoes go under the ship too?"

"Right. And a magnetic trigger could fire them off. A few thousand turns of fine wire around a heavy core would generate enough current when it passed near a large steel hull."

Langer wrote some notes in a tiny memo book. "Is there a defense against that?"

"Extend the nets to the bottom, or wrap them under the ships. The problem is that a ship trapped in a net like that takes a long time to sortie, and that makes the ship a good target for bombs. You would probably need the equivalent of a direct hit with a sixteen-inch shell to do much damage to the deck armor on a battleship, but if you have enough time, bombs will do the job. The bottom line is that ships in a shallow anchorage could be vulnerable to air attack."

Langer sat back, closing his notebook. He picked up Jake's crude torpedo models, holding them up and turning them from side to side. "Are you sure?"

"Yes."

"You should know that the Navy disagrees with you. The CNO claims that seventy-five feet is the minimum depth for a torpedo attack. Admiral Stark won't hear of torpedo nets; he says they're absolutely unnecessary and that they would impede a sortie by the fleet."

"He's the admiral. But I'll stand by what I found."

"The Navy made a big mistake not grabbing you, Jake. I'm hoping their loss is our gain. Will you take on another problem for us?"

"More toy torpedoes?"

"No. Do you recall FDR leaving for a holiday on the presidential yacht? He sailed from New London with a bit of fanfare. Like he was going to view the Harvard-Yale races on the Thames, but with no destination. He told the reporters he needed a long fishing trip for quiet and rest."

Jake nodded.

"It isn't a holiday, and he won't be fishing. He's being transferred at sea to the cruiser *Augusta*. The ship will take him to Argentia, in Newfoundland. He's meeting Winston Churchill there, and they're going to divide up the world."

"Like Spain and Portugal in the sixteenth century?"

"Close. The formal statement will probably read like Woodrow Wilson. The crux is going to be what isn't announced: We and the Brits are going to agree to defend one another in the Pacific. When the Japanese figure that out, it means war."

"Expecting torpedoes?"

"Maybe. I know we're going to want you to spend more time in Newport."

"Why?"

"We don't exactly know yet."

17

A baby-faced sailor in a dark blue uniform was behind the wheel of the Packard convertible. The car had been washed and polished; the paint and chrome glistened against the late summer brown of Rosa's yard. Russell emerged from the backseat in a slim jacket that came only to his waist. Gold braid hung from his shoulder. A sleek cummerbund and the high-waisted trousers made him seem very tall and slim.

Rosa, watching through the window as she finished Sera's hair, whispered, "He's a prince, Sera."

When Sera walked down the steps of the farmhouse, Russell never took his eyes off her. All he said was, "Hmmm."

"Is that a good hmmm?" she asked.

Russell seemed totally relaxed in his fancy-dress uniform, as if he were unaware of the jarring oddity of a man holding an inlaid scabbard, with gold braid on the shoulder of his uniform, and a woman in a sleek floor-length black gown, standing on the rickety wooden steps of a hardscrabble farm. "No, it's not a good hmmm." He let the pause hang before the easy smile lit up his face. "It's a *great* hmmm. You're dazzling."

"That's really a uniform?" Sera asked.

"For now. They're scrapping evening dress next month. They say we can't afford them with war coming. No doubt Sybil persuaded the Navy to wait until after her ball."

Sera had to hike up her skirt, and Russell had to twist his
sword to one side for the two of them to climb into the backseat
of the convertible. They had hardly gotten to the bottom of
Rosa's drive before tendrils fell loose from the elegant roll Rosa
had made of Sera's hair. Sera reached up to try to tuck the first
stray hairs back, then gave up the battle. Before long, she welcomed the noise of the slipstream of wind blowing past the open
top of the car. She was too beguiled to talk.

Russell held her hands, kissed her cheek and neck, and joked
with the young sailor at the wheel, telling him to keep his eyes
on the road.

When they drove off the ferry in Newport, Russell told the
driver to drive up to Bellevue Avenue, then over to Coggeshill.
Sera tried to fix her hair, realized she could never re-create the
fancy braided roll, and instead combed her hair down with her
fingers and piled it on her head in the simplest of rolls, holding
it up with the tortoiseshell hairpin Rosa had given her.

"Is this okay?" she asked. "Rosa worked so hard to make it
perfect."

Russell looked at her with mock sternness, then leaned close
to her, nuzzling her cheek. "No matter what you do, it's perfect."

They stopped in a line of cars that backed up in the circular
driveway of a house. It wasn't an especially large house, at least
not compared to the mansions on either side, but the long queue
of cars, the footmen with gold braid on their jackets opening
the doors, and the men in tails and women in long gowns under
the portico made the whole scene gala. Sera watched other
women get out of the sedans and limousines in long white or
pastel gowns, covered with sequins and embroidery. She wondered if her dress was wildly inappropriate.

"Wow!" said Sera.

"It was a stable. The ballroom was where they stored carriages."

"I wish I lived as well as those horses."

When the Packard reached the head of the line, footmen on
either side of the car bowed and opened the doors. Men standing

under the portico smiled when Russell climbed out of the backseat, and watched silently as Sera emerged from the other side of the car.

"Russell!" one man said. "Is that a seaman driving? Nice perk." He made no effort to introduce the woman with him, and stared at Sera.

Russell smiled and nodded to greetings from every side as he led Sera up the few steps and into a large entry hall decorated with huge vases of flowers. To one side she could see a wide hallway, crowded with couples on their way to the ballroom. In front of them was a porch with a view over a lawn, leading down to the water. There were flowers everywhere, in tall vases, floor stands, shorter vases on tables, and immense, ornate centerpieces. A string quartet played in the entryway. A fountain bubbled. Flowers were floating in the water. Orchestra music drifted up from the end of the hallway.

Sera felt a tinge of dizziness from the whirl of sounds and sights. In every direction men were standing in stark black tails and bright white shirts, the uniformity punctuated only here and there by the glitter of a uniform like Russell's, or an occasional bemedaled sash. The gowns of the women consumed acres of fabric and millions of sequins. Most of the women wore heavy jewelry on their necks and wrists, and had their hair arranged in ornate creations with jeweled tiaras or draped strings of tiny pearls.

As they walked down the hall, Russell nodded to people he passed. He held Sera close, his arm around her waist so he could nuzzle her ear. "There are two secrets to survival at Newport parties," he whispered. "Keep moving and don't ask questions."

"Why no questions?"

"Because you can't trust the answers."

They stopped at the entryway to the ballroom, where another footman carrying a silver tray stood next to a a man wearing an even more elaborate uniform. The man took cards from the tray and announced the names of guests.

"It's really a ballroom," said Sera.

"Remember, it was a stable. Sybil hopes no one else will remember."

As they waited their turn in the short line, Sera watched Russell's mother walk toward them. Sybil wore a pale yellow gown with slender sleeves and a high collar. It was simpler than most of the dresses in the room, and she wore only a double strand of pearls around her neck. She leaned toward Russell and gave him a quick kiss on the cheek.

The handsome man with her looked exactly like Russell, except for a hint of fullness in his face and neck and a tinge of silver in the hair at his temples. He seemed as relaxed in his tails as Fred Astaire in a movie.

"You remember Sera?" Russell said.

"Indeed." Sybil lifted her head in a subdued version of the classic Newport snub. Her eyes raked down the length of Sera's plain dress and then back up, stopping on the diamond earrings.

"Your earrings are interesting," said Sybil. Crow's-feet appeared around her eyes and mouth and her lips pursed.

"Your young lady is striking," she said to Russell.

Russell started to smile, until Sybil added, in a whisper just loud enough for Sera to hear, "Sirens always are, you know."

Wes, oblivious to the exchange, said. "Well, well, Russell. You *must* introduce me."

"This is Sera," Russell said. "My father."

Wes had already taken Sera's hand, holding it in both of his for a moment before raising it to his lips. He held the kiss a bit too long. "You simply must promise me a dance, Sera. With all this war talk, I don't know how many more balls we'll see in Newport. I would never forgive myself if I were to miss an opportunity to dance with a young woman as lovely as you."

Sera felt his eyes looking right through her dress, but he was so obvious and cheerful in his lechery that she couldn't help smiling back at his easy grin. It was the same beguiling smile she found irresistible from Russell.

Sera tried hard not to stare.

There were women whose bodies had been forced into heavily sequined gowns, their fleshy arms and necks bulging from the hand-stitched edges of the fabric. Many wore layered makeup so heavy they looked ghoulish. Even younger women wore so many jewels around their necks and arms that they seemed uncomfortable. Huge brooches and necklaces accented the fleshy expanses of shoulders and necks. Portly, middle-aged men looked like penguins in their white ties and tails.

Tables at the corners of the room were decorated with huge swans carved out of ice. Smaller swans, with tiny dishes set into the ice, lined up behind the big ones. Reeds and flowers were arranged around the tables to make it seem as though the swans were floating on a pond.

In the middle of the dance floor, a young woman in a full-skirted white gown stood regally with a cluster of men around her.

"My sister," said Russell. "You'll wish you had a bulletproof vest under that dress, but we might as well get it over with."

As they wound their way through the crowd, Sera saw the young men around Russell's sister turn their heads toward her. They were all younger than Russell, and their gawking gestures—holding their eyes wide and staring directly at Sera—made them seem bratty schoolboys.

"Russell!" Lisa called out in a gay voice. Her gown had a deeply cut bodice and puffy sleeves off the shoulders. The white fabric was woven with glittering gold threads. Tiny diamonds on golden strings were laced through her straw-colored hair.

She was laughing and holding her fingers to the mouth of one of the young men, until she saw Sera. She froze in place while her eyes scanned up and down Sera's dress. All she said was "Black?"

"Nice contrast, isn't it?" said Russell. "This is Sera. My sister, Lisa."

"Hello," Sera said.

Lisa glared at Sera, then looked at the young men around her, as if searching for words. When she fixed Sera again she said, "I hope you didn't expect a funeral."

Russell leaned close to Sera's ear and whispered, "Remember, keep moving and no questions."

At one side of the dance floor a cluster of young women gathered. Their dresses, all pastel and strapless, were remarkably similar. Sera watched one of the girls eye Russell, winking when she thought she had his eye, and running her tongue over her lip.

"You have a fan club," Sera said.

"It doesn't match yours. The men on the far wall are all staring at you."

A moment later the orchestra started to play a waltz. Russell's father walked slowly across the floor, nodding to friends on either side. He bowed to Lisa, then led her to the center of the floor. They waltzed dramatically, spinning in a pattern that took up much of the floor. Lisa seemed to have difficulty following her father but he was sure enough for both of them. Polite applause broke out from around the room.

"If I don't do a son's duty, I'll never hear the end," said Russell. "Will you excuse me?" Sera watched Russell walk toward his mother, bow, and lead her to the floor. Sybil was awkward on her feet, but she forced a gracious smile as they danced. A few moments later other couples joined them.

"Sera, may I?"

Sera took her eyes off the dance floor to see Russell's father bowing. He took both of her hands in his, and didn't wait for an answer. The orchestra had just finished the waltz.

"Do you like the rumba?"

"I don't know. I've never tried."

"Just stay close to me."

She had no choice. Wes held her in his arms, her breasts pressed against his jacket. His right hand was splayed on her back, two of his fingers high enough to touch the skin of her back above the line of the dress. He grazed those fingertips back and forth on her skin, and pressed his cheek against hers. He was easy on his feet, and while the rhythm and the steps were unfamiliar, he was easy to follow. There were only a few other couples dancing. Sera noticed eyes on them, including Sybil's.

When the music stopped, Wes bowed, holding her hands. In her ear he said, "I could dance with you forever in that dress. But I suspect Russell has the same idea."

She watched Russell's face burst into a smile as he approached her.

"Was my father his usual lascivious self?" he asked.

"He's a very sexy man."

"That opinion seems to be widely shared among the ladies of Newport."

The orchestra started a slow foxtrot. The orchestra sounded exactly like the music Sera had so often heard on the radio. She was used to the little music groups at the festivals in the village, with their violins, bells, mandolins, and guitars. This was a real orchestra. The trombone players stood together for a solo, holding mutes in their instruments.

"My turn?" said Russell.

He didn't wait for an answer. He held Sera as he always did, their stance seemingly formal, but close enough that her body grazed his. With nothing under her thin dress, she could feel the buttons of his uniform jacket and the edges of his cummerbund. The grazing touches were exciting.

"I made a real hit with your sister," Sera said. "I seem to have a magic touch with your family."

"Actually," said Russell, "you've made quite a splash. People are staring at you."

"Am I that strange?"

"No, that beautiful."

She looked up at him and caught an utterly magic smile. The orchestra segued to a lindy, and the older couples who had been dancing drifted to the edges of the floor.

"Game?" he asked.

"If I can kick off these shoes."

Before they could get back to the dance floor, two couples approached them. The conversations were vapid: "Well, Russell, missed you at the skeet shoot" or "Haven't seen you on the hunt of late" or "Word has it you've been entirely too busy up at that War College."

No one said a word to Sera. Russell barely got free of the first couples when more people appeared, pushing to get close, as if they had something terribly important to say, only to recite the same pleasantries about Bailey's Beach or the Casino or the yacht races. While they waited to say hello to Russell, they would glance over at Sera, looking her up and down as if she were an exhibit in a zoo or a painting on a museum wall. The men stared, their eyes raking the long lines of her dress. The women tilted their heads back, as if they were looking through the bottoms of nonexistent bifocals.

Sera wondered what it was that made her so exotic. Was it the black dress, so simple in the midst of the overdone gowns? Was it just that she was a stranger? Had Russell's mother and sister spread stories about her?

A waiter appeared with a platter of tall, fluted glasses. Russell took two, offering one to Sera. The champagne tickled her throat as it went down. She hadn't eaten all day, and the first few sips left her light-headed.

"Now's our chance," said Russell, putting his glass and hers down. They had missed two dances amidst the long line of greetings. The band was back to another swing number, and Russell led her out to the floor.

She found herself quickly wrapped up in the dance. Russell was a strong, if slightly too exhibitionistic dancer. He used the floor aggressively, and they were soon alone. Lights seemed to sparkle all over the room, tiny bulbs in the chandeliers, glistening glassware on tables and in hands, jewels on earrings, bracelets, necklaces, and brooches. The colorful gowns and flowers flowed into a dizzying palette. Voices and stiff laughter syncopated the music. She could feel the drums and the bass with her stockinged feet on the polished wooden floor. The overpowering sensations merged until she forgot the snubs and stares of a few minutes before as they whirled on what had become a private dance floor.

At times they were close enough for Sera to feel Russell's uniform through her dress, then far enough apart that only the touch of fingertips connected them. Sera had all but forgotten the crowd around the floor, until she gradually became aware of the dozens of eyes watching them. The rest of the ball, the chatter and quick kisses and small talk, seemed to pause as couples gathered at the edges of the dance floor, watching Sera and Russell. Conversations tailed away, and the music seemed louder and more insistent, focusing ever more attention on Sera and Russell. She forgot the crowd again in the dizzying sounds and glitter, and the whirling steps, until Russell's smile and the light flashing off his hair and uniform was all she could see.

When the music ended, people at the edge of the dance floor clapped. It was quiet, polite applause, like after a particularly good return in a match at the Casino. Lisa, surrounded by a retinue of young men who took their cues from her, withheld her accolade. With no effort to conceal a smirk, she turned abruptly and walked away.

"That was wonderful," said Sera, breathless from the dance and the whirl of colors and light.

"You were wonderful." Russell took two more glasses of champagne from a platter. He led her to one of the tables with swans, and offered her a round of thin toast smeared with tiny black beads and covered with what looked like grated hard-boiled egg.

"What is it?"

"Caviar."

"Is it good?"

"Try it."

She bit into the round of toast. "It's salty."

Russell laughed. "Then drink more champagne."

Dinner was served at buffet tables. Waiters in white dinner jackets put anything she pointed at onto the plate for her.

"What is it called?" she asked the waiter.

"Beef Wellington."

Sera marveled at the ingenuity that had gone into getting the meat cooked inside the layer of pastry. She noticed glances from all sides. People averted their eyes when she caught them looking at her.

"Why do so many people stare at us?" she asked.

"They're jealous."

"It's something else, Russell. They look angry."

"Well, you've stolen the ball."

"What does that mean?"

"You asked about the war before. Well, a ball is war. People don't come for a good time. Maybe they did once, a long time ago, but now it's desperation. All the effort that goes into those gowns and the hairdressers, the trips to the bank to bring jewels home from the safe deposit box, arranging limousines and drivers if they don't have proper livery—it's all to keep up a strong defense, a show of force to cut off a potential flanking attack. Families that have seen their fortunes slide have to put on an especially good show, lest anyone think the rumors are true.

"And then along you come. With what looks like no effort at all you're spectacularly beautiful. Whatever they did was for nought. That's called stealing the ball."

"Could we go outside?" Sera said. "It's hot in here."

18

As Russell had predicted a month before, the moon was bright over the water. He hadn't seen Sybil or Lisa consult a nautical almanac, but it was one of those details that never got overlooked. The moonlight reflected off the calm water in the harbor. A half-dozen launches were tied up along the sides of the dock.

"People come by boat?" Sera asked.

"If they have what they think is the right boat."

They walked out onto the dock.

"The air feels good," said Sera. "Maybe it's the champagne, or just those cold stares, but I started to feel claustrophobic."

From the dock they could look out over the harbor. Lights on ships at anchor were like low stars.

"Are balls always like this?" she asked. "I remember stories about balls when I was a little girl. They sounded so wonderful. The princess would dance all night with handsome men."

"I could dance all night with you," he said.

She stood very close to him. He put his arms around her, and she could feel his fingertips through her dress. The air was warm, but she felt a sudden tingle when his fingers touched her. She ran her finger around the edge of the champagne glass and touched it to his lips. They kissed, and the kisses lingered. Russell seemed as aroused as she was. She found herself pulling him closer. Her dress and his uniform, so beautiful on the dance floor, seemed in the way.

"Is there any place we could be alone?" she asked.

"The launch." The boat was tied at the T of the dock. The companionway was open, and the cabin was fresh, without the musty smells of a closed boat. She had only once been below in the launch, and that was in the daytime when she had gone into the locker for an oilskin to wear against the spray.

At night, with moonlight flooding in through the peaked skylight, the mahogany paneling glowed. The quilted plush of the benches was soft. Russell slipped off his shoes and jacket, and her shoes tumbled off onto his as she nestled into his arms.

"I love the feel of you through this dress," he said.

"It works both ways," she said.

She had thought about making love with Russell ever since the day he arrived unexpected on the beach at Sandy Point. It had always been a tumbled thought. Russell, with his beautiful smile and laugh and easy compliments and wonderful smell, seemed the perfect man. Yet he was sometimes so obtuse, seeming to listen yet not responding with anything but compliments that grew tiresome with repetition. The thoughts of making love with him were always shadowed by flitting memories of dire warnings from Father Loftus and Josephina, Manuel's raging and his own filthy assaults. Manuel and Josephina and the Father had made her body something so special, so valued and negotiated, that she wondered if it was really hers.

She had thought sometimes of Jake, and wondered if she was burning her bridges, trading away a predictable future for a world that had no future.

In the warm glow of the cabin of the boat, with the moonlight bright through the semiopaque glass of the skylight, the qualms and thoughts that had once tumbled uncontrolled in her mind were strangely quiet. Russell stood up, loosening his cummerbund and tie. He lifted the edges of the peaked skylight, holding it up with a shiny brass brace. By twisting her head, Sera could see a few bright stars and a corner of the moon through the opening. The outside air was refreshing, warm with the heavy balm of summer.

He kissed the back of her neck and her shoulders. Her dress, which had taken so long to button up, came off effortlessly. She remembered for a moment the questions she had always wanted to ask Rosa, questions that seemed too silly to ask. And then the questions seemed not to need answers. He caressed her neck and shoulders gently and ever so slowly. Their clothes disappeared, as if they had been waved away by a magic wand.

She was astonished at the smoothness of Russell's body, the long muscles, the skin without blemishes or scars. Most men in the village rarely went to the beach or wore bathing suits, but she had seen her father and brother without shirts, showing off the bulging muscles of their arms and backs. Russell's long, lean muscles seemed nothing like them. She ran her fingertips from his lips down his neck and across his chest, amazed at the way his body reacted to her touch. When he touched her, her skin and tiny muscles she couldn't control responded extravagantly, surprising her with the intensity of reactions that had only hinted themselves when she had explored her own body.

She had anticipated that there would be moments of awkwardness, but their bodies found one another as easily as their lips had in those early exploring kisses. It surprised her that every inch of his skin had the same sweet smell and taste, even as arousal brought out a fine film of sweat, tiny beads on his upper lip and a sheen that glinted on his skin in the moonlight through the propped opening of the skylights.

She could hear faint music from the house up on the hill. As their bodies came together, she heard him whisper to her. The words were lost as his breath, the smell and feel of his skin, even the beat of his heart and pulse were so close that she could no longer tell his breath and smell and heartbeat from her own. For a moment she wondered if there was something else she was supposed to do, something he wanted. Before she could ask, she heard a tiny sound from his throat, not a word and not an animal sound. And even as she tried to parse what it could mean, she felt him inside her, and felt herself on a mad roller coaster, her body responding in ways she had only imagined.

"Yes," she said. "Oh, yes."

What she had thought would be only a fleeting moment of pleasure went on and on. She had no sense of how long it lasted. Her eyes were shut, and she had lost all sense of place and time.

Then she heard a faint sound, a cough. The sound was muffled and different. The only thing she was sure of was that it wasn't Russell.

"Russell, I hear someone."

"There's no one," he said. "We're the only people on this earth."

She looked beyond him, to the peaked skylight. The moonlight was so bright that after having her eyes closed she could see nothing else. She tried to forget what she had heard, tried to let herself slide back into the interrupted rhythms. Instead she found herself listening intently and watching the skylight. She remembered that Jake had once taught her how to look near a bright light, even the sun, by using her peripheral vision.

She heard another muffled cough. From the corner of her eye she caught a glimpse of a face. It was visible for only an instant through the opening where the skylight had been raised. Backlit by the moonlight it was hard to make out features, but something about the face seemed familiar.

"Russell!" She pointed with one hand, and pushed him away with the other, reaching for clothes, grabbing his shirt. "Someone is watching us."

He looked up at the skylight. "I don't see anyone."

She had felt no self-consciousness when they were alone. Now, she was consumed with shame. She wrapped his shirt tightly around her and looked at the clothes scattered on the sole of the cabin. The dress that had felt so sensuous before seemed tawdry. Russell's uniform, in a heap on the cabin sole, looked vulgar.

Russell pulled on his trousers and went up on the deck. She saw him talk to someone on the dock, and recognized the man she had met in a Newport restaurant.

Before he came down the companionway, she had pulled on the dress. The fabric against her skin, exciting before, seemed wicked.

"It was a misunderstanding," he said. "The fool was lost."

"He was watching us."

"Sera, it was an accident." Russell reached toward her.

She backed away. "I don't want anything to do with you and

your perverted friends!" She wrapped her arms around herself, as if she were hugging a coat.

"He's gone. It was an accident, Sera. Have some champagne."

She looked over at the two glasses on a shelf, and the bottle of champagne in a silver bucket. Russell opened the bottle easily. His hair glistened in the moonlight. His smile was as easy and inviting as the first time she had ever seen him. He was a shockingly beautiful man.

Only now she hated the smile. When he held out a glass she punched it back at him. Champagne splashed his chest. The glass broke on the cabin sole.

Reaching down for her shoes, she ran past Russell, up the companionway and out onto the dock. Her hair was tumbled down onto her shoulders. She held her shoes in one hand, and hitched up her skirt with the other so she could run on the dock.

Russell scrambled after her, wearing only the high-waisted trousers of his uniform and an unbuttoned shirt. She heard a burst of laughter from couples who had strolled down the hillside toward the dock.

He caught her at the head of the dock, and held her firmly with both hands.

"Sera!"

"I hate you," she said.

"It was a stupid accident. He's a fool."

"No."

He kissed the edges of her lip, and the tears on her cheek. His kisses were tiny and gentle. He seemed oblivious to the people in gowns and tails on the grassy hill behind them.

"I love you," he said.

She felt his lips and his arms around her. She noticed his smell, that easy sweet scent like no other man she had ever known.

Then, his hands still around her, he tipped his head back. A curl of blond hair was in the middle of his forehead. His smile was dazzling.

That's all it is, she thought.

"I hate you," she said again, pushing him away and running up the lawn.

When she looked back, she saw him standing on the dock, watching as she ran across the lawn. The dew on the grass felt clean on her bare feet.

Three cars stopped to offer her rides. She waved the first two off. When the driver of the third car saw her hesitate, he snubbed his cigarette out in the ashtray and opened the door. "I'm not the big bad wolf," he said. "Looks like you already met him."

Sera got in, huddling close to the passenger door. The driver wore a sailor's uniform.

"Where are you heading?"

"The trolley terminal."

"You're a little late."

"I'll wait."

"Last trolley ran about fifteen years ago."

"Is there a bus?"

"Where to?"

"Stonington?"

"Where's that?"

"Connecticut. On the shore."

He looked over. "There used to be a bus in the summer. Left from the Viking Hotel and met the train. That's gone too. I think you have to take a bus to Providence and catch the train there. They leave around six or six-thirty in the morning. Maybe you want to go someplace. I know a decent bar, no drunken sailors or torpedo workers. I'll listen to your woes and you can listen to mine."

"Could you just take me to the bus terminal? Or let me out?"

"Hey, whatever someone else did, don't blame me."

"I'm sorry. I just—" She felt tears coming, thought about trying to stop them, and realized that she didn't care.

"Guess it must not have been much of a party. I always wondered about the people in those houses."

"Don't wonder," Sera said. "They're horrible."

The Newport streets were quiet until they reached the waterfront at Long Wharf. On Thames Street, men in disheveled uniforms wobbled down the street, singing loudly until they saw

the white leggings and nightsticks of the Shore Patrol. On one
side street she saw sailors in a line, waiting to get into what
looked like an apartment building. She wondered what they
were waiting for.

"Your party couldn't have been worse than this," the sailor
said. "Those guys are trying to pack three months of fun into
one night. They're counting days until the war. What do they
say about the war at the big houses?"

"Nothing," said Sera.

"If anyone ought to know, it's the admirals and swells."

"They don't care. Not about the war, or about anything else."

"You really got a dose, didn't you?"

The bus station was quiet. One bus was standing empty.

"Thanks for the ride."

"You have money for the bus?"

Sera realized that she didn't have the tiny bag Rosa had given
her. She had nothing but her dress and shoes. She looked up
sheepishly, then laughed. "I was with the richest people I've ever
seen, drinking champagne, dancing to a real orchestra. It looked
like a movie. And I don't have a dime."

"Here." He reached into his pocket and held out a handful of
change, then changed his mind, reached into another pocket and
offered her two dollar bills. "Take it. I'll give you some advice
too. You seem like a nice girl. Stay away from that bunch. Officers and bosses and rich guys are all the same. They don't give
a damn."

"Thanks." Sera smiled, then leaned over and kissed the sailor
on the cheek.

The door of the bus was open. She sat on the front seat for
what seemed a long time before a voice said, "I s'pose you can
set there if you want, but this bus ain't goin' noplace. Actually
it's goin', but nobody goes on it. Called a deadhead." It was a
black man, wearing a gray uniform and cap, and carrying a
whiskbroom and a sack for rubbish.

"Where does the bus go?"

"Providence. Driver takes it up empty."

"I'll pay a fare."

"You could buy the bus and they wouldn't take you. Some kind of rule."

"When can I ride?"

"Six-ten in the morning is the first run. You got no place to go?"

Sera nodded.

The black man brushed off seats. "Newport ain't a real nice town for a girl with no place to go. Those sailors see a woman in a dress like that . . . I don't mean it ain't pretty. It's real pretty, but those sailors, they're out on a ship so long and they're afraid they're going to war and never comin' back and they get crazy. You watch out for yo'self, okay?"

"Thanks."

She watched the man dust his way back. Then he came to the front of the bus and said, "In 'bout twenty minutes this bus'll be leavin'. You sit in the back, curl up on a seat so the driver don't see you. You ain't supposed to ride on the deadhead, but I don't think a nice girl oughta sit around the bus station in the middle of the night neither."

Sera smiled and walked to the back, tucking herself into a ball on the seat. A few minutes later the driver, wearing a short dark blue jacket and cap, and stroking his mustache with his fingers, climbed up into the bus. She heard the engine start, and felt a clunk as the driver shifted into reverse.

She wished the bus was a trolley. She remembered once, when she was little and they had ridden the trolley to New London late at night. She had watched the cascades of sparks as the pantograph jumped from one overhead wire to another. The sparks had been as pretty as the glittering light off the glasses and chandeliers at the ball.

Outside the windows, she watched quiet farms without a single light showing. She could see cows lying in the fields, roads without a car or truck. The driver discovered her when they drove under the lights on the approach to the Mount Hope Bridge.

"Nobody is supposed to ride on a deadhead run," he said.

"I know," Sera said. "I'm sorry. I didn't know any other way to get home. I never knew how beautiful it could be out here at night."

The driver's frown softened at her smile. "Well, it is nice," he said. "Just don't tell anyone it was my bus."

They wound through tiny hamlets, slowing for grade crossings but never quite stopping. In the outskirts of Providence, the fields gave way to warehouses, small factories, and rows of tiny houses. On the streets she saw graveyard shift workers outside the gates of a factory, smoking cigarettes and talking. One worker waved. When she waved back, the whole group of workers waved at her.

At the Providence station, the mechanics, surprised to find a passenger on a deadhead bus, invited her to have coffee with them. They joked about how she must have convinced the driver to let her ride. When she asked when she could get a train to Stonington, they laughed.

"Better get one quick," said one worker. "These trains might not survive the war, even for ladies in fancy dresses. Once they start moving war freight and troops, they're going to want highways and trucks. Be a different world."

A different world. All the way home on the New Haven train, she couldn't get those words out of her head. Better than thinking about him, she thought.

The pale loom of the dawn was already visible in the east when she got off the train and started the walk down Water Street. Before she reached the boatyard, she crossed the street to the side away from the water. It was silly when no one was awake, she told herself, but she had instinctively avoided the yard for months now.

She couldn't help turning to look. The yard was quiet and empty. The Monohull was on the rack, where it had been for months.

She ran the rest of the way home.

19

Langer led Jake up the stairs of Widener Library. Undergraduates on the steps wearing corduroys and sleeveless sweaters reminded him of his own days on the campus. It seemed an eternity ago.

Outside the door of the third-floor study, a man in a double-breasted suit and fedora stood with a small notebook.

"Nothing strange?" Langer asked.

"Just the men on your list," said the man.

"This is Jake Werth," said Langer.

The man in the gray suit checked off a name on his notebook.

"We're the last," said Langer. "There shouldn't be any interruptions."

"The price of rank," Langer explained to Jake in a low voice. "He isn't the worst either. They put a safe in my office, where I'm supposed to keep papers. So much for our vaunted ivy walls and academic freedom."

Inside the tall-ceilinged room, three men sat at a table. Sunlight poured in through the open blinds on the west windows.

"Gentlemen," said Langer, "this is Jake Werth. You've seen his report."

The three men at the table nodded.

Langer pointed to the man at the far end of the table, with short reddish hair. "The man sitting like a Navy captain, is. Captain Leslie Topham, U.S. Navy, *retired*, now vice president for long-range planning at Westinghouse. I'm told Leslie's Navy colleagues were dumbfounded when he left the Bureau of Ships and what must have been a sure shot at flag rank. I like to attribute his decision to the triumph of skepticism. Westing-house, I might add, is no fool in allowing us to borrow Leslie; no doubt they're already adding up the war business they antic-ipate coming their way."

Topham said, "Nice report, Werth."

"The gaunt fellow to Leslie's left is Max Bishop. Max read Japanese history here before going to BIA, the State Depart-ment's own little nest of snoops. Until a few months ago he was in the Tokyo Embassy as third secretary. Their loss is our gain. Max is the only person I've ever known who breaks the clichés about the allegedly inscrutable Japanese."

Topham and Bishop both laughed. The ex-Navy captain had an easy, open laugh.

"Finally, the smug look belongs to a man who despite his youth has earned it. Meet A. Whitley Griswold, Yale's man of all seasons. He's been an instructor in English, an assistant pro-fessor of government and international relations, an associate professor of political science, and a professor of history. He's just completed a survey of our policy in the Far East."

Griswold nodded. "I have the feeling that my survey is going to need a few more chapters," he said.

"We will have no minutes of this meeting," said Langer. "Lest the question ever arise, let me say my interest in this area is not accepted by higher-ups. At least not so far. The Navy has an official position on these matters, and as you know, the President trusts the Navy. We're not supposed to use the word *strategy*, lest we offend the Navy or the War Department, and the word *policy* is off-limits because it would offend the State Depart-ment. So officially, this meeting is not happening. Incidentally, the Navy is aware of our group. They see us—Donovan and especially our assessment group—as the worst possible combi-nation of Wall Street and Ivory Tower."

"Hard to disagree with that assessment," said Leslie Topham. His deadpan delivery prompted laughter.

Jake sat down at an empty chair. Langer took the chair at the head of the table.

"You've all read Jake's report. If Jake is right, any navy with the will and the right aircraft could attack ships in a shallow anchorage. The obvious question is why doesn't our Navy believe it's possible?"

Leslie Topham squared his shoulders. "I'll speak to that," he said. "There's an old saying about admirals: They believe that Neptune is God, Mahan is his prophet, and the United States Navy the only true church."

Everyone laughed. Topham went on. "Trouble is, it's not a joke. The Navy has been planning the next war for almost half a century. Teddy Roosevelt told them to plan for a war against Japan. They liked Teddy, because he showed the great white fleet around the world, and they've followed his orders to the letter. They've asked every question a thousand times, including the question about torpedo attacks. The difference is that the Navy doesn't ask a question until they know the answers they want.

"The sad truth is that fleet admirals don't want to believe in airplanes. They've been nurtured on the Mahan doctrine, that wars are won in the battles of great ships. Admirals have waited entire careers for the glorious moment when an enemy fleet is sighted and they can give the command 'Form battle line!' to a fleet of battleships. The Navy hasn't been in a battle like that in anyone's memory, but the dream won't die. Admirals don't want to hear that the battleships may never see that battle, that they could be sunk by a cheap, noisy little airplane dropping bombs or torpedoes."

"There's no gainsaying the power of myth," Langer said. "It might even be harmless if it weren't for the other collection of papers in your packet, the one that starts with a report written by Commander Arthur McCollum, Chief of the Far Eastern Section of Naval Intelligence. The McCollum document is the official Navy response to Ambassador Grew's report that Tokyo is rife with rumors of a sneak attack on Pearl Harbor. McCollum and the Navy have no doubts: 'Naval intelligence *confirms*'—his word—'that there is no evidence the Japanese are planning an attack on Hawaii or any other American installation.' He also dismisses the speculation about Japanese attacks in books like

Bywater's *The Great Pacific War* and George Fielding's article in
the *Mercury*. Do we know anything about this McCollum?"

"I've heard of him," said Topham.

"Would you trust his report?"

"I trust he would follow SOP."

"In other words, he subscribes to the myth."

"What we're calling myth is official Navy policy."

"Maybe it's time to look at the other side," said Langer. He
turned toward Max Bishop. "Max wrote Ambassador Grew's
report."

"Is that why you're here instead of there?" asked Topham.

Bishop said, "State isn't big on explanations these days. All I
was told is that there was to be a cutback of staff in Tokyo, and
that I would be reassigned in Foggy Bottom. When I got back
to Washington, there was a note to call Professor Langer."

"Still stand by the report you wrote for Ambassador Grew,
about the rumors of an attack?"

Bishop said, "The Japanese aren't gossips, and of course there
was no public discussion. But it was impossible to avoid the
tension in the streets. People were worried. It's not surprising;
they have more to lose in a war than we do.

"I had no way to research the rumor directly, so I started on
the edges. Our embassy in Rome reported that the Japanese sent
a naval delegation to Taranto after the British attack. It was more
than a courtesy call. A group of officers and technical personnel
stayed in Taranto for days. That interest in an air attack made
me wonder about the Japanese admirals.

"Historically, their admirals are traditionalists, even more than
what Captain Topham said about American admirals. The victory of Tsushima Straits, when the Japanese fleet destroyed the
Russians, is their model, the pinnacle of naval glory. They've
been on a binge of battleship building ever since they announced
they wouldn't adhere to the Naval Treaty limitations, and their
official war plan is that the U.S. fleet will be lured to the western
Pacific; that they will harass and weaken the fleet, like the Russians nibbling away at Napoleon when he got deep into Russia;
and when the American supply lines are stretched to the limit
and the American fleet is weakened, the Combined Fleet will

attack and defeat the Americans in the naval battle to end all naval battles. The Japanese believe they will win because their ships and admirals are better, and because they think the Americans lack the will to pursue the struggle to victory. I found only one admiral who openly disagreed with the official plan."

He fumbled in his papers and brought out two photographs. One was a stern man, with short hair and an emotionless gaze, posed in the uniform of a Japanese admiral. The other photograph was of the same man, but much younger, wearing Western civilian clothes. The younger man forced the same stern expression, but there was a hint of mirth in his eyes.

"The man in the photographs is Admiral Isoroku Yamamoto. Ten years ago he was in charge of the technical division of the Imperial Navy Air Office. He's an outspoken advocate of naval aviation, he's strong-headed, and he's unpopular in the Navy and in Japanese industry: the Japanese don't admire troublemakers. Despite the opposition, or maybe because of it, he's gotten the Japanese air industry to develop superb aircraft. He's also risen through the ranks rather spectacularly. I suspect he's too brilliant to ignore. He's now Commander-in-Chief of the Combined Fleet, roughly their CNO. Yamamoto is the man who would have to approve any plans for a naval offensive."

When the photos were passed around the table, Langer commented on the stern expression.

"He's more interesting than that photo lets on," said Bishop. "I knew about him before I went to Tokyo. In fact, he's one of the reasons I got interested in Japan. From 1919 to '21 he was right here, at Harvard. Later he went to Washington as a naval attaché at their embassy. He also visited the Naval War College in Newport at least once."

Topham said, "Sounds like SOP for a rising sun. Don't the Japanese ape American innovations like the War College?"

"They do. But Yamamoto isn't the sort of man to ape anything. Most attachés stay in Washington, go to a few receptions, visit the Navy yard, buy some souvenirs, and go home with another kudo on the résumé. Yamamoto was different. He traveled around the U.S. on his own, in civilian clothes. He was seen in Texas and Mexico photographing oil wells. It could be

because he's from Kyushu—the only Japanese island with oil—
but from everything else we know I doubt he's the kind of man
who suffered sudden bouts of nostalgia for his hometown oil
wells."

Topham said, "Watch out for an admiral who is thinking
about oil supplies."

"There's more," said Bishop. "He was attaché in Washington
when *The New York Times* reviewed *The Great Pacific War*. I
can't determine that he saw it, but it was a front-page review,
and very clear on Bywater's theory that the Pacific war will begin with a sneak attack by Japan on Pearl Harbor."

Langer jotted some notes as Bishop went on. "I tracked down
people who remembered Yamamoto at Harvard and in Washington. He wasn't unfriendly, and spoke quite good English. People who remember him all use the same words to describe him:
quiet, studious, private. A few added smart, or brilliant. It took
me a long time to find a common thread connecting his friends.
They weren't all Japanese, weren't all from farms or small towns
or big cities or the seashore or mountains. They don't share a
religion, aren't homosexual, don't all like pornographic movies
or Chinese food, they weren't regulars at speakeasies or strip
clubs. I went through these reports a dozen times before I found
the one thing they had in common."

Eyebrows went up around the table.

"Everyone who spent any time with Yamamoto was a gam-
bler."

Langer laughed. "Every Asian I've ever met has been a gam-
bler."

"I'm not talking about Monday night poker players. Yamamoto's friends were serious gamblers. He was willing to play
any game for money: bridge, gin, poker, twenty-one. He is especially good at a Japanese game called go. In 1923, he stopped
off in Monte Carlo on the way home from his assignment in
Washington, and got himself kicked out of the casino for winning too much."

Langer said, "What strategy should we expect from a gam-
bler?"

"There's something else," said Bishop. "People report that

sometimes Yamamoto wouldn't join a game. I asked over at the psychology department, and they say that's actually odd. Most compulsive gamblers can't say no. They play anytime, anyplace, even games that aren't their favorites. Yamamato wasn't like that at all. He would ask questions about who was playing, details about the game. Depending on the answers he'd often turn down a game."

"I'm not sure I get it," said Leslie Topham.

Langer grinned. "I've known men like that. Their compulsion isn't gambling. It's winning. It sounds as though Admiral Yamamoto only gambles when he's sure of the odds."

Griswold, who had been quiet, said, "I'm not sure how much credibility I'd put on Yamamoto's willingness to gamble on a surprise attack. Lots of Asians are gamblers. I have trouble imagining a Japanese admiral, even an admiral as unusual in his predilections as Yamamoto, ordering a surprise attack. Certainly, the idea of a single decisive blow is very Japanese. Look at judo or sumo wrestling: much preparation, then a single decisive blow decides the match. But in one respect war is different. The warrior tradition is important to the Japanese, and the tradition stresses honor. A surprise attack is not honorable."

"Is defeat honorable?" asked Topham. "Anyone with enough strategic sense to study our oil reserves knows that Japan cannot win a long war against the U.S. It comes down to simple arithmetic: we can sustain losses of ships and matériel; they can't. Yamamoto may have concluded that an attack that takes out major elements of the Pacific Fleet is their only hope to get the U.S. to sue for peace."

Bishop pointed his index finger at Topham. "I came to the same conclusion. Especially after I saw these."

He brought two more 8 × 10 black and white photographs out of his envelope. "These were taken at a place called Kagoshima Bay, on the south shore of Kyushu. The images are blurry because the film speed was too slow. These are very fast planes, and the photographer was inexperienced."

With the photographs he passed around a magnifier. The photos showed a line of single-engine aircraft flying low over a ridge, then diving down toward the water. Under magnification, it was just possible to make out torpedoes, or dummy torpedoes, under the airplanes.

"Who took these?" asked Leslie Topham.

"They were taken by a farmer. The ridge the planes are flying over is in the Iwasaki Valley. I'm not sure we need to talk about how a rice farmer got hold of a Contax camera, but I can assure you that they are authentic. The planes had been practicing these maneuvers for a full week when the photographs were taken. For what it is worth, the farmer thinks the Imperial Navy is insane."

The room was quiet while the photographs and magnifier were passed around.

"If I hadn't read Jake's report," said Langer, "I'd have thought the Imperial Navy insane too. Could they be practicing something other than torpedo attacks?"

"You don't use torpedoes for offshore rescue missions," said Topham.

"Looks like you were right on target, Jake, if you'll forgive the pun."

Langer looked toward the open window, then back to the group. "As an historian, this is the point where I get a queasy feeling. I'm trained to put evidence together, to create a credible explanation of what *has* happened. Most of all, as an historian I'm supposed to stop with what I know. Unfortunately, we don't have that luxury. Our job now is to to extrapolate from what we know to what might happen.

"I think we can agree that war is inevitable. The embargo has the Japanese backed into a corner. They need petroleum and rubber. Their only sources are the Dutch East Indies and Malaya, and it's only a matter of time before they move on one or both. Either means war.

"The real question is when and where it will start. Given their strategic concerns with the U.S., they may conclude that the war can only begin elsewhere, with the goal of achieving an early advantage. Since our own Navy is—let's be charitable and say—*reluctant* to consider the possibility of a surprise attack on the Pacific fleet, I think it behooves us to extrapolate from what we

know. I'd like to ask Leslie some hypotheticals. If you were planning an attack, what would you want?"

Topham said, "It looks like Yamamoto already has trained pilots, we know he has carriers and capable aircraft, and from
Jake's report a working torpedo design is within their grasp. My
first priority would be the obvious: a man in Hawaii. I think we
can assume they have that base covered. We certainly make it
easy enough. The water at Pearl is so clear that a few rides on
a tourist glass-bottom boat is as good as having a detailed chart
of the anchorage with depths marked. The departures and arrivals of warships are announced in the shipping columns in the
Honolulu *Star-Bulletin*. A drive on the roads along the ridge
around the harbor with a sketchpad would probably be enough
to compile a grid map of the anchorage with the position of
every ship. Incidentally, the hills around Pearl Harbor look very
much like the ridge in those photos."

"Sounds too easy," said Langer.

"That part *is* easy. Planning an attack isn't. The Japanese
would have to assume we're listening and watching the sea
lanes, so an attacking force would have to sail a long northern
route to avoid being seen. That means refueling at sea, not an
easy job, at least not in winter in the North Pacific. They would
have also have to maintain radio silence, which means sailing
with stale intelligence. Once they leave port, their only addi-
tional intelligence would be from carrier-based reconnaissance
planes; that sort of information isn't very reliable with typical
midwinter cloud cover.

"The tricky part of planning an attack like that is that they
would have have no recent intelligence on what ships were at
Pearl. They wouldn't know if a fast cruiser force was out on
maneuvers. Attacking in the face of something like that would
be suicide. The cruisers could engage an attacking carrier force,
block a retreat, and give our main battle force time to sortie
from Pearl and butcher the attackers. And what if our carriers
weren't at Pearl? Yamamoto's planes would end up banging up
a few battlewagons that probably won't matter much, and leave
us with an intact carrier force. If that happens, Yamamoto will

have signed a death warrant for his fleet and Japan. His only hope is a knockout blow, and that means getting our carriers."

"Is there any way Yamamoto could know the Navy's plans for those carriers?" asked Langer.

Topham said, "Sometimes I'm not sure our own Navy knows what they're planning for the carriers. We've got a few admirals—King, Halsey, Fletcher, Spruance—who understand carriers and naval aviation. They've all spent time at the Naval War College, and I'd be willing to bet they've gamed Japanese attacks in a fleet exercise. Probably more than once. War games aren't plans, but that's where strategic and tactical ideas are born. The Japanese have already copied our war college, so they understand the importance of war gaming. If I were Yamamoto, I'd want a look at those war games."

Griswold said, "A Japanese agent would sure stand out in Newport."

Max Bishop said, "Would he? I think they may already have someone there. I learned in Tokyo that the Imperial Navy is confident that American torpedoes are no good. There is open talk that either the American sub skippers can't hit their targets or their torpedoes are no good."

Topham looked at Langer, then at Bishop. "You heard that in Japan? I don't think anyone beyond BuShips knows about it."

"Wouldn't the subs be in New London?" asked Langer.

"The Atlantic sub base in New London. The torpedoes are made in Newport, and the test range is off Newport."

"Sounds like the FBI should be looking around Newport," said Topham.

Langer picked up a pencil, twirled it in his fingers, then held it up like a pointer. "Newport is a small and cliquish town. Strangers stick out. An FBI agent would be about as inconspicuous as Admiral Yamamoto photographing oil fields in Texas."

"Then it sounds like our work is cut out," said Topham. "Who's going to be our man in Newport?"

Langer turned slowly to Jake, making no effort to hide a smile.

When the others left, Jake said, "I know how to fix boats. I don't know anything about spies."

"We're not asking you to spy," said Langer. "Just stay on in Newport for a while and do what you're doing. You know the waterfront. You can talk to the hired men who chamois the dew off the brightwork of those gold-platers every morning and not look out of place. If you walk into those Oldport bars where the sailors and torpedo factory workers hang out, no one notices. You can talk to yacht owners or officers from the War College or fishermen off those draggers and never get an odd look.

"All we want is for you to keep your eyes and ears open. Go to the Sunday races. Bring your boat down and enter. Get yourself invited to a society ball. If you need a tuxedo, put it on the repair bill for whatever boat you're working on. If you don't like the boats we've found for repair jobs, I'll find others."

"The boats are fine. Best work I've seen in months. But I've got qualms about the rest."

"Qualms?"

"It's personal."

"We'll be at war before the end of the year, Jake. The world will turn upside down. Whatever you're calling *personal* won't be worth a cup of bilgewater."

"It's not just that. I'm not sure I like the idea of spying."

"Jake, you're sounding like Secretary Stimson back in the twenties, when he closed down the code-breaking department in the State Department. 'Gentleman don't read one another's mail,' he said. Nice, lofty sentiment. Stimson was good at lofty talk. But tell me, what consolation is lofty talk to a mother whose son is killed in a battle that wouldn't have happened if we had our eyes open?"

"Am I the only one who can do it?"

"You have someone else to nominate?"

"What am I looking for?"

"Anyone who is too curious."

"And if I find someone?"

"Tell me."

Part Three

20

R ussell moped for weeks.

With the fleet game approaching, there were no leaves for junior class officers at the War College. Even Breedlove, who usually could be counted on to intervene when Russell came up with a reason for a personal leave, wouldn't hear of a leave now. It hardly mattered. Russell had no way to get to Stonington. He wasn't about to ask Raymond for the car.

He was supposed to be studying. The entire Naval War College had turned into a study hall as students from the junior and senior classes pored over fire and damage tables, ship profiles, armor and armament charts, and the specifications of the new radar devices that were now going to be used on the Blue fleet in the games. They had all done every procedure before, but the pressure during the game made men forget even the simplest ideas. In the library and empty classrooms, men practiced with the maneuvering boards and fire control tables, going through sample exercises to duplicate the multiple calculations of trajectories, fire angles, and damage assessment for each salvo in a battle.

Russell found an empty seat in the library. Every time he looked at the books and tables his mind drifted. He saw Sera standing on the old fishing boat in dungarees, on the beach in a halter and shorts, at the ball in that wondrous black dress. He couldn't shake the images.

Every effort to reach Sera had failed. His first phone call to the velvet factory had gotten through, but he never even heard Sera's voice before she hung up. When he tried again, they said she wasn't available. He wrote letters every day for a week and every other day for another week, and hadn't gotten an answer. She just needs some time, he told himself.

He thought of the officers' club, but watching others come in for a quick beer would only be a reminder that he should be studying. He tried walking Thames Street, where at least he wouldn't see another officer. The street was thick with off-duty sailors and town boys. He couldn't take a step without bumping into someone. He was afraid he would end up in another fight. He retreated to the White Horse, thinking that at least he could find anonymity.

It didn't surprise him to see Raymond at a corner table, looking down at a drink. Raymond waited a long time before walking over to Russell's table.

"You've been studying too hard," Raymond said. He waved to the bartender with his usual gesture of two fingers.

"Fuck off," said Russell.

"That's no way to treat a friend."

"Listen, Raymond, you pay for your perversions in your sick little clubs. Not on my dock."

"Russell, you're not angry because of that little accident? Remember, it was you who told me to come by boat. I tied up at the side of the T, exactly as you suggested, wandered up the dock, heard a bit of noise from your launch, and came over to investigate."

"Raymond, you asshole, you got me in some serious trouble. I haven't seen Sera in weeks."

"You're overreacting, Russell. Really. I say this as a friend, and as someone with a bit of experience. I can't imagine it will be hard to win her back. Frankly, she seemed to be enjoying things quite as much as you."

Russell jumped up, his fingers instinctively curled, his elbows loose but ready. He stepped away from the table, shifting his weight to the back foot, smiling at the thought of Raymond with a wired jaw, sucking rum punch through a straw. "You aren't worth the reprimand," he said. He reached for his hat to leave.

"Russell, we've hardly had a chance to talk. We do have some unfinished business."

"We have no business."

"I wish you would avoid this unfriendly tone. As for business, I don't like to cheapen a friendship by putting numbers on it, but I'd say the numbers are starting to add up."

"What numbers?"

"In round terms, $2,200. Cash mostly, and some tabs you signed with my name. I'll be friendly and call it two grand."

"You did me some favors and I did you some. I'd call it even."

"Would your commandant call it even?"

"What are you talking about?"

"Russell, I don't have to tell you that the Navy is strict about indebtedness of officers. The charge is 'conduct unbecoming.' Interesting that they use the same term for an officer in debt as for an officer suspected of homosexual inclinations. Of course, once the notation goes on your service record, it looks the same. They tell me it's a guaranteed one-way ticket to Panama."

Raymond was right. The Navy was paranoid about officers in debt and subject to blackmail. During their first week at the War College, the junior class had gotten a lecture about the sensitivity of their assignment, and a warning about the temptations of Newport. One word to the commandant and Russell would be lucky to end up on a supply ship in the Canal Zone.

"Is this some kind of shakedown, Raymond? What are you threatening? Are you going to report that I borrowed your car a few times?"

Raymond took out a pocket notebook, flipped past the first few pages, and started reading. "July 2, $100. July 15, new sail, $210. July 27, car and $50. July 29, $150. It's a long list, Russell." His Adam's apple bobbed as he spoke.

"They were gifts. 'Between friends,' you called it. Or don't you remember? What were some of your other lines? 'Friends don't keep tally.' I never signed an IOU."

"Really Russell, I don't think this discussion is necessary. But if you force me, I assure you, it would not be difficult to find corroboration of your indebtedness. Some of your fellow officers have been in here from time to time. From what they tell me, you've been unfriendly to them too. That's unfortunate. Perhaps as a friend I should have warned you that what goes round, comes round. Don't misunderstand me. The last thing I want to do is go to your commanding officer. It's just that after so many months of friendship, your sudden coldness is deeply disappointing."

Russell didn't answer. He found every word and gesture—the unctuous voice, the sweet cologne, the foppish ascot, the cloying language—grating. It was hard to imagine that he had put up with Raymond for as long as he had.

"Russell, worrying about this young lady is no good for your studies or your spirits. Why don't you borrow the Packard and visit her?"

"I don't want the Packard, Raymond. The rent is too high."

Raymond drove to New York. At least he wasn't going back to the office at the university, he thought, as he drove through New Haven on the Post Road before picking up the new parkway. Alden could be just as haughty and condescending at the gallery, but there were diversions in New York. Raymond had the name of a new club on the edge of Harlem with an after-midnight act they called "The Tsarina and the Stallion."

Alden's gallery was on a second floor in Chelsea. The open loft was broken up into smaller display areas by translucent screens painted with stylized landscapes. Polished chests of ornate gnarly wood and woven mats were the only furniture. At the back of the gallery, behind a doorway discreetly hidden by a screen, were the offices: a workroom with a fiberboard barrel of shredded paper and a worktable used to wrap parcels; and beyond that a private office with space only for Alden's desk, an extra chair, and bookcases of black portfolios, tied with neat knots and lying on their sides.

Alden met Raymond in the front room, and led him back to the office. Sunlight through a double column of glass bricks illuminated the cramped office.

"Well?" Alden said.

"Everyone in Newport thinks war is close," said Raymond.

"We *know* war is close, Raymond."

"They've been testing aerial torpedoes in Newport. They have some old flying boats up at Gould Island."

"What about the games?"

"They've done games against Japan at the War College."

"Who do you think they would do games against—Mexico? Did any of the games involve naval aviation?"

"Don't get your hopes up. The games are ridiculous."

"Are you sure your information is good?"

"No one could make this up. They did a joint Army-Navy war game with carrier-based planes attacking the Panama Canal. And they did another game in 1938 with a carrier, the *Saratoga*, launching a sneak attack on Pearl Harbor."

"Pearl Harbor?"

"That was my reaction. If that's what they do in their games, you haven't got much to worry about."

"Save the editorial comments, Raymond. You aren't being paid for your skills as a naval analyst. Tell me more, specifics."

"How much more specific can it get?"

"Where did you get that information?"

"I asked."

"Whom did you ask?"

"Hey, I get paid for information. Giving you the source is like the dairy turning over the cows."

"Nice analogy. But let's not pretend that your information is the product of some profound investment of time and effort. Who did you meet, what did you ask, and *exactly* what did he say?"

"What do you think he said? I gave him a song and dance about my insatiable curiosity. Once he told me what the games were about it was hard to imagine why anyone would bother to make them secret. When I pressed he looked at me as if I were a lunatic. 'Why do you want to know this shit?' he asked."

Alden got up from the desk, took off his suit jacket, and put on a short robe painted with red and black calligraphy. "This is excellent, Raymond."

It was the first time Alden had ever complimented Raymond. Raymond found it more frightening than the usual sarcasm.

"Now, tell me about your source," said Alden.

"He's young, an officer at the Naval War College. And he's connected in Newport. Real Society."

"What is his name?"

"He's a contact," Raymond said.

"I need to know. This is a critical moment, Raymond. That secret meeting of Roosevelt and Winston Churchill in New-foundland was not about the platitudes in the newspaper; they have made a pact. And there is information from a captured courier document that the British will not defend Singapore. Do you have any idea what that means?"

Raymond shrugged. At least it wasn't questions about Japanese paintings.

"Singapore is one of the most heavily guarded naval facilities in the world. There are over one hundred thousand crack troops there, along with a substantial British fleet. If the British were to resist, it would take a main force to capture Singapore. Those resources can now be reassigned. This makes the information I've asked you to get vital."

"I got you what you wanted."

"No, Raymond, you confirmed that it exists."

"Why does it matter so much?"

"Your problem, Raymond, is that you have never had the faintest loyalty to anything above your belt."

"I meant why do *you* care so much? I don't get it. I make no bones about what I'm doing: It's all just business to me. How else is a guy like me going to live well? But you, between the professor business and the rich ladies, you've got more than you can spend. So what's in it for you? Do you really like the Japanese that much?"

Alden took a pipe and a soft leather tobacco pouch from a drawer, and filled and lit the pipe with painstakingly slow movements. Raymond found himself uncomfortable as he anticipated the cloyingly sweet smoke.

"I do admire Japanese culture," Alden said. "And I mean much more than just the art. I admire their sublime sense of serenity and beauty. Our culture has abandoned standards; they have not. Something as simple as a tea ceremony is done with grace and dignity and precision. Instead of the scribbles of West-

ern handwriting, they cherish the beauty and perfection of calligraphy." He puffed the pipe, slowly and deliberately. The smell
of Balkan Sobranie filled the tiny office. "But to answer your
question, I don't care which side wins."

"Then why all the speeches about how important it is to get
the information? You can't be in it for the money. You have
everything you'd ever want, the pipes, the ivory tamper, the
fancy offices. What difference does it make?"

Alden blew out a smoke ring, letting the smoke linger between them. "Do you find ordinary life that engrossing, Raymond? Yes, we have art and other distractions, and you have
your silly pornographic shows, but are we ever really engaged?
Is anything you ever do as enthralling as a game like go or chess,
a pursuit which involves all of your mental capacities toward a
single goal? War is the same game, pursued to the ultimate limits. What could be more engaging?"

"*Games* again? Are you crazy, Alden?"

"No, Raymond, I am not crazy. The outcome of the game
intrigues me."

Raymond heard horns and shouts from the street below the
window. He watched Alden make a face at the intrusion of vulgar sounds into the regulated privacy of the gallery before he
slowly retamped and relit the pipe.

"It is quite clear to me," Alden said, "that the scope of this
matter is out of your realm. To carry on in Newport, you would
need to pursue these questions among proper people. I don't
think that is possible."

"Think again. They had a formal ball, and yours truly went."

"And?"

"Quite a show."

"*Quite a show?* That banal remark more than proves my
point. I'll take over from here."

"Look, they're phonies. About as deep as a rain puddle. At
least I get invited to their balls. Anyway, without me, you're no
place."

"Is that a threat? I dislike threatening language."

"So do I. And I resent your tone. Remember, I know enough
to. . . ."

"To?"

"I could embarrass a lot of people, especially you."

"Could you? How is that? What embarrassing secret do you think you know?"

Raymond looked shocked. "I know you're helping plan some kind of Japanese attack."

"What, exactly, is your threat? You could write a letter to the newspapers chronicling our discussions and it would not harm our efforts. There have been books and magazine articles written about the possibility of a Japanese attack. The American ambassador to Japan has already told Washington that Tokyo is full of talk of a sneak attack. Care to guess what the official reaction was? A Navy expert declared that there is no possibility of a surprise attack. What makes you think they would suddenly believe you?"

Raymond tried to think of something to say. When he looked up, Alden had already turned away behind a cloud of sickly sweet pipe smoke.

Raymond had always felt little when he left the bridge office at Yale. Walking out through the gates of an Ivy League university, brushing against the lounging swells with their carefully dirtied cords and sport jackets from good stores with the elbows deliberately worn through and patched, the snide young men with their arcane slang and arrogant expressions, carefully dressed down in a mockery of everything he aspired toward— just seeing them made him angry and cowed at the same time. Those rich kids could thumb their noses at poor slobs like him because they knew they would someday wear bespoke suits, work cushy jobs in banks with paneled offices and private dining rooms, eat lunch in Fifth Avenue clubs where he couldn't peek in the door, be driven home by chauffeurs, and let into the house by butlers who would look down their noses at Mr. Raymond. By the time he left the bridge office, he would be so intimidated, not just by Alden's condescensions, but by the ubiquitous privilege of the students and the clubby privacy of the campus, that he would find himself feeling small and awkward, so eager to escape that awful feeling that he would eagerly give in to Alden's demands just to escape the condescension.

As he walked down the stairs from the gallery to the street, Raymond smiled at the thought *This isn't Yale*. If Alden had his clients in New York, overdressed, ugly, rich old ladies and faggots who came in to fawn over the stupid Japanese pictures, Raymond had his own connections. And he had read enough upside-down scraps of paper on the desk to know what Alden did with the information. He might not have a gallery with blond wood floors and landscape paintings on the walls, but he could sell information.

No, he told himself, he didn't have to be afraid of Alden in New York.

Russell knew what Wes would say. There was really no point asking him.

It was only after he had heard other men talk about their fathers with feelings of awe and respect and fear that Russell realized how strange his relationship with his father was. He had sometimes admired his father's poise and charm, his suave style around women of any age, and his devil-take-the-hindmost attitude toward the cares of the world. But it was always a distant admiration, more like the reaction he had toward a Fred Astaire dance number or Clark Gable in a film role than the respect he heard other men voice toward their fathers.

His first reaction when he discovered his father with women had been surprise mixed with a sense of betrayal. It was later, when his father would wink and smile as if to bring Russell into his conspiracy, that Russell's reaction turned to a sharp revulsion, followed by a growing sense that his father had to be treated as a permanent child who was incapable of staying away from the cookie jar. If anything, Wes seemed to delight in being caught in his transgressions, as if he were proving his prowess to himself and the world. To Russell, his father's endless affairs were worse than the compulsive shoplifting of his prep school roommates, who never lacked for money but couldn't resist the thrill of getting away with their petty heists of stationery they didn't need and clothes they never wore.

Although he never made the connection in his own mind, it

was after he joined the Navy that Russell's feelings toward his father changed. Each year, the women his father chased were getting younger and less capable of even a polite conversation. Russell found his sense of betrayal mixed with fear. Will I become like him? he wondered. Will I also be incapable of feelings, a Don Juan compelled to prove myself while the world looks down with a pity concealed behind knowing smiles?

Still, as Sybil liked to say, blood was thicker than water. How many times had he fulfilled a strange and stretched filial duty by covering for his father? Maybe, he thought against all reason, Wes would feel a reciprocal need to help his son.

"Two thousand dollars?" Wes answered. "I can't say she isn't worth it, and I'd love to help, but you know me and money."

"How about part of it?"

"Bad time, son. I've had a few scrapes myself recently, bets that have gone sour, that sort of thing." Wes winked, that conspiratorial wink that angered Russell even more than his father's amorality. "I'll give you a bit of advice about situations like this: It's never as bad as it seems. A lot of these people *like* to be owed money."

"I don't think so. Not from what he's said."

"I know it sounds strange, Russell, but it's true. Men with money are like beautiful women: they know how to use their assets to get what they want. It's unfashionable to talk about classes, but the fact is the world has just come out that way. And for someone in the trades, a debt owed them is their tie to a life they know they can never live themselves. They tag along, come to a chukker or two of polo, watch a yacht race—how else would they be part of that world? Trust me, most of the time, they aren't really in it for the money. What they really want is to be close. That's why they'll accept a handshake and a smile for interest."

"He wants more than a smile."

"Well, explain that you're paying only interest now. After all, what can he do?"

Russell found Sybil in the living room, sipping at a heavy glass. He knew from the time of day that it was vodka. She seemed to be waiting for him. He dreaded this even more than talking to Wes.

She pursed her lips when he named the sum. "I was right, wasn't I?" she said.

"You're always right, Mother."

"Russell, I'm trying to be sympathetic. I wasn't surprised when your vamp left Lisa's ball. She is lovely in a way, but her kind is never comfortable in circumstances like that. I tried to warn you then."

"Warn me?"

"Not to get her in trouble."

"I didn't *get her in trouble*. I borrowed money from a guy. Carfare, a dinner or two."

"A tacky motel room or two? It sounds like you've made your bed, Russell—oh, how the expression fits!—and now you're going to have to sleep in it. You know those tawdry married officers' housing units up in Portsmouth, the ones with the laundry hanging on clotheslines and dirty-faced children playing out in front? You better get used to the idea. Do you think your vamp will wear her slinky black dress and diamond earrings there?"

"God, you really are vulgar. If you could only hear yourself."

"I'm not the one asking for two thousand dollars for a tramp."

"It's not for her. And she's not a tramp."

"Russell, I'm not naïve. She had nothing on under that dress. Oh it was effective: you should have seen the look in your father's eyes, or did you? And just about every other man there had the same thought. What's the expression? Easy on, easy off. I guess it doesn't surprise me that you're as foolish and childish as your father. At least he has been careful enough not to get his floozies in trouble.

"I've spoiled you for too long, paid for your peccadillos, cleaned up your messes. I thought you would learn. I was obviously wrong. I don't know when you'll ever understand this, but it's for your own good. I am not bailing you out this time. You made your bed; now you can lie in it. Or is it lay in it?"

"Thanks."

Russell walked back to the War College. He couldn't keep his head clear. He would picture Sera and think of what he would say to her, and then picture Raymond, and then think about a billet on a supply ship in the Canal Zone. For the first time in his life, the future mattered. So this is what love is all about, he thought.

He kept replaying the last meeting in Breedlove's office. Breedlove, in his pompous way, had prattled on about duty and fleet commands and destiny. Russell daydreamed through three-fourths of what Breedlove said, but he had heard the bottom line loud and clear: if Russell did well in the fleet game, he could choose his future. Let the eager beavers like Robert Butler, the overambitious round-faced lieutenant from the Midwest, go for executive officer slots on frigates and destroyers. A guy like Butler had a whole Navy career mapped out in his head: from exec on a frigate he'd hope for a destroyer or light cruiser, then a first command on a frigate, and on up the ladder. Russell wanted no part of it. He'd already decided to bid for Melville, the fuel depot up the harbor from Newport, for his next billet. The Navy was building a training facility for small attack boats at Melville. Small boats had no prestige. They were a stepping stone to nowhere. But Sera would be a quick drive away.

She just needs time, he told himself. And he needed to make sure his next billet was right there, in convenient driving distance, and not in some hellhole like Cavite or the Canal Zone.

21

It was three weeks before Sera knew something was wrong.

At the factory the other girls had finally stopped asking questions about the ball. The phone calls from Newport had stopped. The first call was the Monday after the ball. A secretary from the office came out on the loom floor, looking for Sera as if there had been an emergency. Why else would anyone call? In the village, a phone call meant bad news, a fisherman hurt, or a boat that didn't come home.

She heard Russell's voice and shivered. She closed her eyes and could see his face. It was as if the smile and the curl over his forehead were right there, so close she could smell him. She said nothing and hung up the phone. He called again the next day. She told the office it was a wrong number. After a few days the calls stopped.

She had gotten the first letter on Tuesday. One or two arrived almost every day for a week. More came after those. Josephina would say, "It isn't good, Sera" when she handed the envelopes to Sera. "You know it isn't right. If Manuel found one of those letters, I don't know what he would do."

The letters were written on expensive blue monogrammed paper, with a watermark of Russell's initials. Russell wrote with a loose, sprawling hand. Put next to one another the messages seemed all the same: "I'm sorry," "It was a mistake," "I need to see you," "I love you." After the third letter she stopped reading them, and just put the envelopes into a cigar box she kept in her closet.

When the letters and phone calls finally stopped, she had almost stopped thinking about Russell, until the day, three weeks after the ball, when she realized that she had missed her period.

Sera had missed her period before. She had often been irregular, missing a month now and again for no reason. In the summers, when she went swimming almost every day, she sometimes missed two periods in a row.

This time it felt different. Her body wasn't the same. Her skin was hypersensitive to her touch. Her breasts looked larger, and they were tender. Her mouth tasted different. She thought she even smelled different. One night before bed she stood for the longest time, staring at herself in a mirror, trying to see what had changed. She stroked her skin with her fingertips. She remembered dancing, and the feel of the ball dress against her skin. She took a few tentative dance steps.

She heard a noise in the hallway. Manuel loved to barge into her room and catch her undressed. She wrapped herself in a robe, hugging it tightly around her.

After work the next day, a Friday, she swam to Sandy Point and back, stopping only long enough to catch her breath. The fall currents were strong, the water was cold, and she found herself exhausted from the swim. For the first time in weeks, her mind was clear. She thought that the hard swim would wash all the strange feelings in her body away. But the sense that something was changed wouldn't go away.

She thought to herself that feelings like that were something you were supposed to talk about with your mother, but she couldn't imagine talking to Josephina. Josephina would make a tsk-tsk sound and shake her head and pretend it was something only for the two of them. And almost certainly she would tell Manuel.

Sera knew there was only one person she could tell. Saturday afternoon, after work, she ran up over the railroad tracks to Rosa's farm. Rosa smiled and kissed her on both cheeks and listened as Sera described the changes she had noticed. "Does that happen to everyone the first time they . . . I don't even know a nice word to use."

"Call it making love."

"Does it happen to everyone?"

"No. Sera, you know what it is, don't you?

"What do you mean?"

"Sera, it sounds like you're pregnant."

"We were together once. One night. One time. It wasn't really finished even."

"It only takes once."

"Rosaria and her husband have been trying for almost a year. What do I do?"

Rosa took her hands. "Have you told anyone? Your mother?"

"No."

"How about Jake?"

"It's not Jake."

"I know it's not Jake. But he's a real friend."

"This is none of Jake's business. He's not even around."

"Why do you think he went to Newport? You and Jake were friends. Being friends can make it hard to recognize real feelings when they come. Love isn't always a prince in a carriage, Sera."

"It's still none of Jake's business."

"And what about your lieutenant?"

"What about him."

"Have you told him?"

"What is there to tell?"

"If you're going to have a baby, you can't keep it a secret from him."

"I hate him. Why would I tell him?"

"Because a child is something special. You can't take that away from him."

"Does Jean-Claude's father know about him?"

"Of course."

"Then where is he?"

"Sera, real life doesn't always end like a story in a book. Jean-Claude is a love child. His father used to send him presents and letters on his birthday and Christmas. I read the letters to Jean-Claude, and I've told him about his father. Then the letters stopped. Now, all I have is Jean-Claude and some memories. I think they're memories, but sometimes I don't know where the memories end and fantasies begin. It doesn't matter for me. When I came home with Jean-Claude, I knew I'd be alone. It's different for you. You have family. You have friends like Jake. I didn't.

"You have to tell the father, Sera. You owe it to him. If you don't tell him, there will come a time when you will be filled with regrets."

"What could he do? I don't want him. I don't want to ever see him again."

"There was something between you, Sera. It has to come to an end. Otherwise, you will think of him a thousand times."

"I finally stopped thinking about him. It was a mistake. Everything that happened was a mistake."

"People make mistakes."

"I know. That's why I'm afraid to see him."

"Are you afraid he'll be angry? I don't think he's that kind of man."

"No. I'm afraid I'll still be in love with him."

22

For the first time since the junior course began, months before, Russell seemed to belong at the War College. For three weeks he had been at the college every day, not just in classes, but at the library, even out on the lawn where pickup games of kitten ball, an indoor version of baseball, passed the time. Stories about his problems with a girl had gotten around. The tales, embellished by a few cycles through the gossip mill, were rakish and fallible enough to make him seem one of the gang. Fellow officers smiled at him. Men who had once turned their backs and checked their wallets when they saw Russell coming were suddenly friendly.

Except Robert Butler. Butler had grown up on a farm in Indiana, worked hard to earn an appointment to Annapolis, and even harder to get the coveted appointment to the War College. He never let up, and from the first day he had expected to be the golden boy of the junior class. He studied hard, aped the manners and style he thought would be admired by senior officers, and starred in every classroom, offering quick answers to questions that left no doubts that he had done the work. He made no effort to conceal his resentment of Horatio Breedlove's patronage of Russell.

"Breedlove's looking for an in to Newport Society," Butler told anyone who would listen. "Kalbfus gets an honorary membership over at their fancy Spouting Rock Beach Club and downstairs at the Reading Room because he's the head of the War Col-

lege, which pretty much makes him head of the Navy in Newport. Poor slobs like Breedlove have to grab at whatever crumbs
they can get. He must figure that if he takes care of Westcott,
Westcott will open some doors for him."

Whatever Russell did, Butler had a comment. When Russell
played in the pickup ball games on the lawn outside Mahan
Hall, Butler made snide comments from the sidelines. When
Russell went to the library, Butler would sit two tables away,
conspicuously piling tomes on the table next to him when he
saw Russell daydreaming or staring out the window. Russell had
heard about the psychological warfare that went on before the
fleet games, how some men stole material so others couldn't use
it. Butler seemed to be a master of the art.

On a rare trip to the officers' club, Russell saw Butler playing
an aggressive game of Ping-Pong, polishing off a lanky lieutenant
who seemed delighted to have the game over so he could get
to the bar.

"Game?" Butler asked Russell.

As good a way as any to forget everything for a while, thought
Russell.

Butler let Russell win the rally for serve. From Butler's stance
far back from the table, and his backhand grip with his thumb
and forefinger on one side of the paddle, it was obvious that
Butler prided himself in his play. He won the first point by
charging the table and smashing the ball across Russell's court.

Russell lost a string of points. He was playing lackadaisically,
his mind drifting.

"Point game!" Butler said, as he backed up to serve.

Russell saw two officers wander over to watch. He returned
the serve with enough spin that the ball took a weird bounce.
Butler missed by a foot.

The lead went back and forth three more times, until Butler
won with a shot that just cleared the net. When Russell put
down the paddle, Butler said, "Two out of three? How about a
little money on the game to make it interesting?"

"Sorry. I'm broke."

"Russell Westcott the Third of Newport is broke? Couldn't
you have the butler bring over a few crisp new bills?"

"I'll play you for a beer," said Russell.

"Beer money? Losing your confidence, Westcott?"

Butler quickly ran up a string of points. Russell was drifting, playing mechanically.

"Point game!"

A crowd gathered again, larger than after the first game. Butler's rivalry with Russell was no secret; this was the first time they had met head on at anything. Russell overheard enough sidelines talk to realize that Butler was considered the officers' club champion at Ping-Pong.

Russell shook his head, as if clearing a cobweb. He answered Butler's lobbing serve with an overhand smash. His own serve, with a wicked spin, caught the corner of Butler's court. The crowd on the sidelines commented on each play. Russell realized that Butler was trying scripted plays, as if he had studied a game book telling him what to do in every situation. Once he could predict Butler's moves, Russell won a string of points and the game in quick succession.

On the third game, Butler again ran up a streak of points. Russell wasn't drifting this time. He was making bets with himself that he could predict Butler's next move. Butler used set sequences of three or four shots, following a deep lob to a corner with a rush for the table and then a predictable smash. His winning streak went to 14–0. Butler nodded toward the bar. "I'm getting thirsty," he said.

Butler set up his lob and rushed the table. Russell, waiting for it, dropped a tiny shot over the net. Butler sprawled awkwardly on the table as he missed. On his serve, Russell put enough English on the ball to make it spin in place, dancing above the table. Butler missed awkwardly again. Russell placed lobs on the corners, blocked smashes, dropped little shots just over the net when Butler was set for a deep smash. It quickly became apparent to the crowd, and finally to Butler, that Russell was toying with him, allowing and scoring points at will.

Butler kept trying his sequenced plays, waiting deep with his feet braced to charge the table. On the last point, he reached up as if to smash a long driving shot, then watched helplessly as his racket smashed empty air. The crowd burst into laughter.

"You owe me a beer," Russell said.

Butler threw down his paddle and scrambled around the table, his face scarlet.

Russell backed away, letting the crowd of fellow officers defuse the situation. He walked to the bar and ordered a beer. "Put it on Lieutenant Butler's tab," he said.

The next day, Butler came up to Russell outside Mahan Hall.

"Looking for a rematch?" Russell said.

"The only game I've got time for now," said Butler, "is the fleet exercise."

Russell grinned. "Let's call that the rematch."

"What are you talking about?"

"How do you think you'll do?"

"I'm ready. This isn't a tactical exercise where you can impress a farthead like Breedlove with some flashy move. Fleet games are the whole show: logistics, firepower, damage tables, maneuvering. And leadership. On this one, the game goes to the prepared."

"I guess you're prepared?"

"Let me tell you something, Westcott. Guys like me, we start out with nothing. No friends in high places, no rich daddies with connections and deep pockets. Most of the time we don't have a chance. We work harder, play by the rules, and watch a lazy do-nothing with the right name grab the kudos. Not this time. The fleet game is when the work pays off."

"Confident enough to bet?"

"I thought you were broke. What happened, you send for the butler?"

"For a sure bet, I'll find the money."

"What did you have in mind? Ready to risk a hundred dollars?"

"You must be more confident than that? I was thinking of two thousand."

"Two grand? You gotta be kidding. I don't have a butler I can call."

"This is between gentlemen, Butler. Only the loser needs to pay up. Sounds like you have nothing to worry about."

Butler turned away for a moment, then punched one palm with the other fist. "You know something, Westcott. It wouldn't surprise me if the rumors are true, that you don't have the bucks. That makes a bet too tempting to pass up. But as much as I'd like to watch you squirm, I'm not going to risk a 'conduct unbecoming.' It's enough to just watch you go down in flames. I'll pass."

Russell toyed with trying to persuade Butler, but didn't. On the way into Mahan Hall he couldn't control a smile. It would work out, he told himself. It always did. Everyone loves a victor. Raymond wouldn't call in his chits. Sera would forgive and forget. As Breedlove had said, the fleet game could write his future.

23

J ake went from one job to another, never even taking time out for a trip back to Stonington. He spent weeks working on a beautiful bright-finished yawl that belonged to Elkins Weatherby, a banker. She wouldn't sail well to windward, because the keel was too short and the long ends, elegant at anchor in a harbor, would pitch in any kind of sea, but she was built of good Honduras mahogany, filled to get the color even, and finished with coat after coat of well-brushed spar varnish. Like the Sam Werth boat he forced himself to avoid on the other side of the harbor, Weatherby's yawl was a builder's boat, with dozens of little details that only someone who had worked wood and understood what wind and water do to boats would notice.

As with most of the boats Langer sent Jake's way, Weatherby wanted cosmetic patches: a new extending table in the galley area and changes to the navigation station. Jake had gotten Bernardinho to drive up a load of mahogany off the racks at the boatyard, so he could pick through the planks to get the grain he wanted. The whole job would have been easier with the boat in the Stonington yard. Jake had to remind himself that the jobs were coming his way only because they wanted him in Newport. And he didn't want to be in Stonington.

He spent evenings in the Long Wharf bars, stretching a beer while he listened and watched. Men in bars loved to complain. Feed the complaints with an occasional grunt of agreement and the stories would ramble and escalate. A torpedo worker would start with the incompetence of his foreman and the design mistakes in the torpedoes, segue to the narrow-mindedness of the plant manager, and before long be questioning the nincompoops in the Bureau of Ships for ordering the torpedoes and the moron of a Secretary of the Navy for letting fools run BuShips. There were enough bars on Long Wharf and Thames Street, and enough lonely men willing to talk to a stranger, that Jake could have gone on for months. Except that he never heard anything useful.

The assignment Langer had given him wasn't like fixing a boat. With a boat you could isolate the problem, cut away rotten wood until you found the cause, and then do whatever it took to make the hull sound. This was like fishing off a pier, throwing out a line and waiting for a nibble. Worse, in a way, since he didn't know what he expected.

"What's your story?" a heavyset drinker who had seen him in another bar asked one evening. "I see you around a lot."

"I fix boats. Mostly yachts."

"Yachts?" The other man wore a blue workshirt and dark trousers, like a merchant mariner. He explained that he was a civilian worker at the torpedo factory on Goat Island. "Sounds like good money."

"It is, when they pay."

"Ain't that just it? They got enough money to buy a gold-plated yacht, and they won't cough up the repair bills to a working stiff. To tell you the truth, buddy, I've seen you around a couple of places. I was kind of hoping you were the sort who pays for answers. My luck."

"See many like that around?"

"Not me. But I know a guy who got himself one helluva run of drinks from a guy asking questions. Told me he never figured the guy out. Fancy clothes; you know, like a jacket with a crest on the pocket, one of them little doohickey scarves tucked inside his shirt, enough cologne so he stunk like an old whore. And a blue streak of questions. When I saw him hanging around the bar I thought he was maybe a homo or something. My buddy was smart enough to string him along. The guy told him he needed to know stuff because he goes to bars and makes bets.

You know, how fast one of those new torpedoes can go. What's the range of the deck guns on the new frigates? I couldn't believe the guy. Maybe people in the swell bars have nothing else to do, so they make bets on bullshit questions like that. I wouldn't know."

"Seen him recently?"

"My buddy?"

"The guy who's asking questions."

"Nah. Not here anyway. I seen him once near the docks on a Sunday. Looked like he was going out to watch the sailboat races. Must have won one of those bar bets and moved on to richer pickings."

"You know a name?"

"Why, you planning on selling him something?"

"Beats trying to collect from deadbeats."

"I never remember names. Wait, no, there was something weird about his name. Yeah. He only used one name. Raymond, something like that. He never said whether it was his first name or last. Weird guy, that one. But I guess he had a thick wallet."

For almost two months Sera had avoided the boatyard. Even when the workboat was missing from its familiar tie-up on the dock, and she was sure she wouldn't see Jake, she stayed on the opposite sidewalk, across from the yard. With Jake in Newport, with no boat up on the ways, with no others awaiting repairs or painting, the boatyard was dead. It was as if the heartbeat had been taken from the village.

One afternoon when she had stayed late at the mill so she could walk home alone, the yard looked so abandoned that she crossed the street and ventured down past Jake's cottage and the woodshed toward the harbor edge. The yard felt forlorn. Even the sawdust and paint stains on the gravel had washed away. As she wandered past a stack of the heavy timbers that had been used to prop up hulls, she remembered the days when she would come to the yard to watch Jake working, the hours she had spent staring at his hands as he shaped wood or caulked a seam or stroked patiently with a brush. Sometimes he would let her help, with the promise that they could sail later. Usually she watched quietly, knowing he was concentrating too much to talk.

She walked as far as the empty railway that led down into the water. She had always found the harbor shore comforting. The low stone breakwater outside made the harbor a refuge. From the pebbly beach, she could watch boats swing quietly on their moorings. Tiny wavelets that lapped the pebbles were the only reminders of the open sea outside.

She wondered how many times she had stood on these exact pebbles, staring over the breakwater at the low shape of Fishers Island, imagining the world beyond. Whenever she had fantasized a world beyond the village, there was always a boat in the image. Sometimes it was a steamer, like the old side-wheelers that used to bring passengers from New York to Stonington to catch the trains to Boston, or a big steamer like the Fall River Line boats that even a few years before had made the run from Newport to New York. Sometimes she had fantasized big sailboats, like the yachts from the New York Yacht Club that sometimes pulled into the harbor on their summer cruises. She remembered asking Jake about sailing to Portugal. How big a boat would you need? How long would it take?

She had loved the escape of those fantasies. Now, she couldn't force the old dreams back. She had no idea where she would go, what she would do. She told herself she should think through the choices and decide. But there were no choices. As much as she admired Rosa, she knew she couldn't live that life. Rosa had lived first, seen the world and then chosen to come home. Rosa had no family, no constant reminders of what Sera knew they would all call her *mistake*.

She felt tears coming. She looked up at the afternoon sun, hoping the sun would dry the tears, but it only hurt her eyes. She kicked the pebbles, and tried to remember the dreams that had once come so easily, like when Jake had sketched a house for Sandy Point, and she had imagined living there with wide open porches, and windows without curtains. The house would be private, on its own island. Mrs. DaCunha couldn't watch her every move. She had never told anyone about the dream house, not even Paul. Now, she knew it would never happen. Was that why the tears came?

She heard footsteps behind her, stepping hard on the gravel, trying to be heard. When she turned around, Bernardinho was holding scraps of wood. His face was gray with a three-day-old stubble.

"Sera," he said. "You okay?"

"No."

"That don't sound so good. You want to talk?"

"No."

He walked toward her slowly, as if he were afraid to frighten her.

"I'm a pretty good listener, Sera. Lord knows, I done enough listening in my day."

"Oh, Bernardinho. I've been foolish."

"Ain't no one around who hasn't been a fool sometime. Jake's father was the smartest man I ever knew, and he was plenty stupid sometimes. Jake, he's smart as they come and he's done some damn fool things. Your father was one smart fisherman, and he made mistakes. I heard even that Einstein gets it wrong sometimes."

Sera couldn't help smiling at the flood of words. It was a joke in the village that if you asked Bernardinho the time he'd tell you about every watch he'd ever owned.

"Thing is, there ain't many mistakes that can't be fixed, unless it's something like your father reaching for that otter board in a storm. Me, I don't call that a mistake anyhow. Leaving a wife and two kids is no good, but there's another side, like savin' a boat and four good men."

"Tell me more about my father."

"Don't have much to tell that you don't know. He was a man who did what was right."

"It isn't easy to know what's right."

"For some people it's easy to know and hard to do. A man like your father, he didn't think so much; he just did what was right. Then there's men like Jake. I been working for Jake since he came back to Stonington. Damn hardhead, that one. He's stubbed his own toe plenty o' times. Still does it. Why do you think I'm haulin' planks up to him in Newport? He don't really need the work up there. He's just hardheaded, that's why."

Bernardinho looked up at Sera as if he expected her to say something. "You want to know how Jake is?" he said.

Sera smiled. "How is he?"

"Well, as long as you're asking, not good, I'd say. Goin' to Newport for work ain't right for Jake. I'm not so dumb as people think. Jake's father used to say that tools don't lie. Well, eyes don't lie neither, and I look in Jake's eyes and he don't seem right. They might pay real well up there, but that boy, he don't work for the money. Mostly he does a job because it's good work, an interesting job, or different enough to be a challenge. Or he does it because a man needs the work done. Jake's funny that way, but that's the way he is. I go up to Newport and see what he's doing, and it's nothing but boats that some rich guy needs a little doodad on. I say the only explanation is that Jake's a hardhead.

"He's like his father. You probably don't remember Sam. He could build a boat like nobody could build a boat. He'd pick up a piece of mahogany, eye it, run his fingers down the grain, and tell you what would happen to that wood when it was fitted as a plank. 'Bout wood, he knew everything there was to know. But he was a real hardhead. All those years he held a candle for Jake's mother. Ten years after she died, Sam wouldn't look at another woman. Raised Jake by himself.

"Well, Jake's the same, maybe worse. All those years with no mother changes a man. A mother makes the soft side for a man, teaches him about people. When Sam died, Jake was on his own. He did good, went to college and all, but he was too young to be on his own. Growing up fast like that hardens a man, makes him wary. Sometimes that's a good thing. Jake says it woulda done me some good, because I'll believe anything and anyone, and Jake has to be the one to say it isn't what it looks like. But the other side is that sometimes he's just a hardhead instead of doing what he knows is right. You have to understand him when he's like that."

When Bernardinho looked over to see if Sera was still listening, tears were running down her cheeks.

Bernardinho touched her hand gently, like a child reaching out toward a big dog. "Hey, world ain't right when a pretty girl cries. I know it ain't none of my business, and I'm not pokin', but there's just nothin' that could happen to you that couldn't be fixed."

"I wish that were true, Bernardinho. Oh, how I wish that were true."

Manuel had become a village busybody. He was spending fewer days on his boat each week, instead letting his cousin Carlos skipper while he stayed in the village. In his baggy pale green slacks, with a silk scarf tied around his neck, he would make daily rounds of Bindloss's fish dock, Wilcox's chandlery and net loft over in Mystic, and the fishermen's bars. Sometimes he went over to Noank to listen for gossip in the bars there. He said he was looking for investments.

Manuel was always on the lookout for what he called "opportunities," but there were a few places he avoided, like Jake's boatyard. Things had never been good between Jake and Manuel. No one could explain when it began, but Manuel had little kind to say about Jake or his father. He liked to start or spread rumors about Jake, always with a passing remark, like when he said he would never let a Jew fix his boat. Most of his rumors were ignored; a few split opinions among the fishermen in the fleet.

Jake generally ignored the spats of nastiness, and the two men hadn't spoken more than a few words in the years since Jake had come back. Whenever Manuel walked up Water Street on his rounds of the village he would manage to be on the other side of the street as he passed Jake's yard.

With no boats up on the ways for weeks, and the workboat missing from the dock, Manuel knew Jake was away, so he had no compunctions about wandering through the yard.

"He still in Newport?" Manuel said when Bernardinho stepped out from the woodshed with a heavy mahogany plank.

Bernardinho nodded.

"They don't know him there," said Manuel. "What's he doing, trying to scrape up enough to save this yard? Maybe I can help him."

"You got a problem with your boat?" Bernardinho asked.

"If I did I wouldn't be here. I got yards up in Rhode Island where I can take a boat. I don't need Werth messing with my boat. I don't want him messing with anything of mine. Not the boat, and not Sera. He better know that."

Bernardinho didn't answer. He was trying to move planks from a high rack. He could have used two extra hands as he struggled to slide the heavy mahogany without dropping a plank. Manuel, in his clean pale green trousers, watched.

When Bernardinho finally got the plank down, flipped over, and in place on a lower rack, he said, "You got no cause to go on about Jake. If he hadn't come back to Stonington, half the boats in this fleet wouldn't be goin' out. No one else fixes boats without asking when he's gonna get paid. And there's nobody else who can fix a boat like Jake. Course there's some men who'd rather sink a boat for insurance than fix it."

Manuel stared at Bernardinho, then looked down at his trousers and town shoes, as if to say *You aren't worth soiling them.*

"It ain't boats I'm talking about. Sera's been acting funny lately. Mopes around, don't see nobody. I heard she got phone calls at the mill from somebody in Newport. It's all been since Werth went up there. If I find out that he's been with her, he'll be sorry he ever came back to Stonington."

Bernardinho picked up another heavy plank off the top rack, muscling it down. "You got no cause to talk about Jake and Sera neither," he said. "Jake hasn't been with Sera. Her troubles are with the other one. The Navy officer with the big car."

"What troubles?" said Manuel. "Who said she's got troubles?"

Bernardinho struggled with the heavy plank, catching his breath.

Before he could answer, Manuel said, "I hear anyone talking about Sera having troubles and they'll be sorry."

Josephina, who had learned when to steer clear, retreated to the kitchen when she heard Manuel's heavy steps on the wooden treads.

He stormed into the house, up the stairs, and into Sera's small room. Josephina could hear him slamming drawers and the closet door. Manuel liked to make noise when he was angry, as if he thought no one would recognize his anger without a loud commotion. Josephina was terrified to talk to him when he was in a rage.

He came down the stairs with a cigar box, slammed it down on the dining table, and took out a packet of letters tied with a ribbon. He had never been much of a reader, but he opened a few of the envelopes and held up the letters.

"You shouldn't read Sera's letters," Josephina said.

Manual waved her away, as if he were swatting a no-see-um. "You know what she done? With a Navy boy?"

"What did she do?"

"I heard she's in trouble."

"What kind of trouble?"

"You know what kind of trouble."

Josephina put her hands over her face. "Sera?"

Manuel folded the letters and put them next to the box. He moved the chairs around the table, so he had one side to himself, as if he were setting up an inquisition. He sat there, waiting for closing time at the mill.

When Sera came in the door, Manuel pushed the box across the table toward her before anyone even said hello.

Sera, recognizing the box, reached for it. Manuel quickly pulled it back.

"You had no right to look at my letters."

In a mocking voice, Manuel said, "You had no right to get in trouble with a fancy sailor."

Sera looked over at her mother, then reached for the box. "Give them to me."

"You won't need his fancy letters. You're going to marry him."

"What are you talking about?"

"You get in trouble, you marry him."

"What trouble? There's nothing in those letters."

"I know what's going on, you little whore."

Sera looked at her mother. Josephina stood to the side, looking back and forth from Sera to Manuel.

"No," said Sera.

"No? What, you're afraid of him? Well, I'm not afraid of a sailor. His big fancy car don't mean nothing to me. If he's in Newport, he should know not to mess with a Portuguese. I got friends there. I'll find him. He'll do what he should do."

"I don't want to marry him."

"You should have thought about that before you pulled down your panties."

"You're disgusting."

Josephina edged toward Sera, wrapping her arms around her. "Maybe she shouldn't marry the boy," Josephina said. "Maybe it was a mistake. Why should she give up everything for a mistake?" It was the first time since Manuel had moved in that Josephina had openly sided with Sera.

"So, what is she going to do?" Manuel shouted. "Live like that other whore, the one with the farm? You know what they say about her. And it isn't just Sera they'll be laughing at. I got a name to protect. She marries him."

Sera's eyes darted toward the door. Manuel saw her and blocked the doorway. When he came close to her, she pulled back, then twisted out of her mother's arms, grabbed the box of envelopes, and ran up the narrow stairs to her room.

Sera slammed the door and sat on the bed. She ran her fingertips over the perfect blue monogram on the flaps of the blue envelopes. The letters of the monogram were raised. She could read them with her eyes closed. She had never seen paper like that before, the surface as rich as fine fabric, with a watermark that showed through if you held the paper up to the light. She had wondered if she would ever write a letter on paper like that. The stationery was like the flowers at the ball, or the big car, or the perfect jacket that Russell wore to go shooting. They weren't part of her world.

When he had called at the mill, the secretary in the office thought it was an emergency at Sera's home—an accident on a boat, a brother or father who had gone overboard, or maybe a boat that was lost. She remembered thinking that if it was Manuel she was glad, and biting her lip at the thought. What else could a phone call be?

When she came back from the office, she told the girls who worked looms around her that it wasn't an accident. The girls giggled. They kept asking about him with winks and wry smiles even after she told them not to ask any more. They couldn't forget, and neither could she. In the privacy of her room she held the envelopes and felt the raised monograms with her fingers and wondered why she didn't cry.

From downstairs she heard an argument start up. Manuel was shouting in that manic voice he used when he felt threatened. Josephina's answers were meek, her voice apologetic. Sera tried to remember Josephina before Manuel had come, when her face was proud and beautiful, her long hair shiny black, her smile warm and easy.

She heard her name. Manuel's shout was so loud the name was indistinct. Then she heard Josephina outside the door, saying her name softly. Josephina's voice seemed more afraid than gentle.

"Sera, please come downstairs," Josephina said.

Sera stood by the door. She wondered how she could run from the house. Where was there to run?

"Manuel wants to talk," Josephina said. She stood on the landing with Sera. "He has an idea. He won't shout."

When Sera came down the stairs, staying a step behind her mother, Manuel's eyes were lit up, like when he told them he was going to buy a second boat, or had a new scheme for shares that would save more of the day's haul for himself.

"Maybe that sailor is no good for Sera," he said. "I got a better idea. She has to get married, but maybe it's better if she marries where she belongs."

"Where I belong?" said Sera.

"What does it mean?" said Josephina.

"Carlos," Manuel said. "My cousin from Newport. He'll come to Stonington to live. On Manuel Gomes's boat he'll make a good living. He's no fool like that brother of yours." Manuel looked proud of himself, impressed by his idea.

"She doesn't even know Carlos," said Josephina. "Today is not like the old days. A girl and a boy, they need to know each other today. She has seen him once, maybe twice in her life. They never even talked."

"She doesn't have much choice, does she? She's lucky he's there. And lucky I had such a good idea. Sera's better than he could expect, and he's smart enough to know that if he treats her right he'll drive Manuel Gomes's boat."

As much as she hated anything, even his horrible hands touching her, Sera hated when Manuel talked about himself that way, saying "Manuel Gomes's boat" as if he were talking about the bishop's cathedral or a king's castle. She couldn't even register the idea of marriage to his distant cousin in Newport. She hardly remembered Carlos, except that he had oily black hair and leered at her.

Sera looked up at her mother. "Mama?"

Josephina's arms wrapped around Sera, but her eyes were on Manuel. She lifted Sera's chin. "You know, Sera. Maybe it's not such a bad idea. Carlos isn't a terrible boy. He works hard. He'll be a good husband."

"Mama!"

"Sera, listen to me. There are different kinds of love. They say the best love is the one that grows. A slow love will last."

Sera glanced toward the door. It was a reflex. There was no place to run.

She looked over at the dining table, with its lace doilies and brass candlesticks. The scraps of one blue letter, torn into bits by Manuel, were lying on the polished wood. It didn't matter what it said, she thought.

24

Russell knew he was doing badly. He could tell as soon as they opened the game packets. All around him, men reached for maneuvering boards, steaming charts, and tables of fuel consumption curves. He went through the mechanical steps, as he had gone through the mechanical step of dressing for the game in the rubber-soled shoes that were required on the gaming floor. But his mind drifted. There was a procedure for assessing an initial fleet situation, checklists for evaluating fleet resources, even a protocol for breaking down the complex tasks. There was a four-part drill to assess strategic positions. The procedures took concentration, and Russell had already started thinking about Sera.

Men around him focused on the authorized scouting procedures, each laid out in prescribed detail: the *In-and-Out Method*, *Relative Movement Method "A,"* the *Sector Method*, the *Radial Double-Bank Method*, the *Limited Eclipse*. Those who had read up on scouting argued the merits of one method or the other, backing up their cases with calculations. The more he saw other men reaching for tables and charts and doing calculations with slide rules and maneuvering boards, the more Russell's mind drifted. He imagined walking with Sera along the bluffs of Adams Point, the breeze blowing her hair. He thought of Raymond's threats, and the hasty bet he had almost made with Robert Butler. He couldn't see Butler across the room—during the strategic phase of the game, before the two fleets had sighted one another, the screens were still up on the gameroom floor, blocking each side's view of the opposing fleet—but he knew the game situation was perfect for a bookworm like Butler. The luck of the draw had put Russell where he didn't want to be, on the defender's side.

Every war game was created with what the drafters intended as a predictable outcome. One side was either so much stronger than the other, or given a situation so much more favorable, that the outcome was effectively decided in advance. The play of strategy and tactics, the step-by-step moves of fleet and ship commanders under the pressure of the game clock, the outcome in ships lost and positions changed as the situation played out, was the real objective of the game—or so they said.

The situation for the fleet game was a classic tactical exercise, one more variation of the war strategies the Naval War College had been plotting for decades, ever since Theodore Roosevelt gave the Navy the order to prepare for war with Japan. Blue (the U.S. Pacific Fleet) was to launch a preemptive attack on the Marshall Islands to prevent Orange (the Imperial Japanese Fleet) from overrunning the Philippines and securing the oil supplies of the Dutch East Indies. In other fleet games the initial conditions might be defensive for Blue, and the venue might be somewhere else in the Pacific, but the basic assumptions of the exercise were always the same. Orange needed matériel to pursue the war, and Blue had to stop them from achieving that crucial, early objective.

The game on the floor unfolded in phases. During the strategic game, played behind screens, only the judges and spectators in the gallery knew the positions of the two fleets. With no enemy in sight, fleets steamed across hundreds or thousands of miles of open ocean to position themselves. Russell had always found the strategic game tedious, too cerebral, like the early moves of a chess game, when a player was supposed to think dozens of moves ahead. He was uncomfortable until the win-or-lose competition of the tactical game, when fleet confronted fleet, ship maneuvered against ship, salvos either scored or missed, ships survived or sunk, one side won the battle and the other lost all. In the early fleet game you couldn't see the impact of a move; in the tactical endgame, a single brilliant move could turn the table, defying the intended outcome of the game planners.

A full day into the game, Russell could see how badly he was doing from the expressions of the observers in the gallery. From their unobstructed viewpoint in the mezzanine above the tiled floor, the staff from the Naval War College and fleet officers who came to Newport for the game watched the men on the game floor below under the stress of battle. The observers were not discouraged from kibitzing; part of the challenge of the game was to distinguish useful information from the incessant and random noise of the kibitzers. Even when the observers said nothing at all, participants in the game put considerable energy into parsing the expressions on the watching faces in the gallery.

The game was its own world. Every three minutes, the game clock ticked off an hour of game time. It didn't take long before the clicks of the game clock were the only time that mattered. Men didn't eat or sleep when they were hungry or tired, but when the pace of the game allowed. Men napped, ate, and thought in game clock intervals. The only talk was of day three of the engagement, or eleven hours steaming time by the game clock. Day and night in the world outside, the rhythms and problems of the real world, no longer mattered.

Russell was assigned to the Orange side, with the task of defending the Marshall Islands from the Blue attack force. He was fire control officer on a heavy cruiser, not in the advance naval group that was supposed to defend the Marshalls, but in the main Orange fleet in the Java Sea, where they were supposed to be in a position to theaten Singapore, the rubber of Malaya, and the Dutch East Indies oil—the traditional targets for Japan in opening phases of the Pacific war. Around him, strategists were talking about the importance of seizing the Dutch oil reserves and neutralizing the British fleet and position at Singapore.

Russell heard the talk in a haze. All he saw was the main Orange force trapped, unable to engage the Blue fleet that was expected to attack. To join the smaller Japanese battle group

that was in a position to defend the Marshall Islands, the main
fleet would have had to sortie through the Makassar Strait between Borneo and Celebes. The game instructions were clear
on the hazards of the strait. It was one hundred miles wide, but
the channels were only twenty and forty-five miles wide. It was
assumed that Blue would send down a force from the Philippines to close off the straits. A few cruisers would do the trick:
fast, maneuverable ships with the firepower and the agility to
escape detection while blocking any chance of exit through the
dangerous strait.

The only other exit from the Java Sea was the Torres Strait,
between Australia and New Guinea, a passage so narrow that a
fleet would have to pass in single file. Russell saw the two straits
as the arms of a straitjacket. Without the backup of the main
fleet, the Orange forces outside the Java Sea were limited to
fighting a defensive action. A few observers in the galleries
might delight in the tactical fine points of a well-executed retreating maneuver, but everyone knew there were no prizes in
a defensive action. To make his future, Russell needed a victory.

What would Raymond demand next? Russell wondered. The
ball invitation that had seemed so innocent had blown up in a
disaster. After that debacle, it was almost predictable that Raymond would start on the money and threaten to report Russell
for conduct unbecoming. It might have been an idle threat, and
Breedlove might have defended Russell against charges. But he
could only count on that if he remained Breedlove's golden boy.

Russell knew his only chance was the tactical game. Once the
fleets sighted one another and the screens on the game floor
came down, it would be a battle of fleet against fleet, salvo by
salvo. In a tactical battle, even if he hadn't memorized the fire
control tables and the damage charts, he could play all out, like
a game of tennis or a race around the buoys. That was a game
he could win. If only he could get into the action.

He stared at the plotting chart. Around him men were working out solutions on maneuvering boards, and reading a steady
stream of dispatches.

"They have us outgunned," said a captain in the senior class.
"Sixteen-inch guns are what count, and Blue has enough big

guns to cut us down ship by ship. Our only option is a paced
retreat behind a smokescreen. We can hope to take some of their
ships out in the commotion. Then our cruiser force cuts their
supply lines. If they can't resupply, they can't protect the Philippines, and we're in position to threaten Dutch oil, English
rubber, and Singapore."

Around him, voices agreed. Russell said under his breath,
"We're wasting the main fleet."

No one responded.

He stared at the area chart. The powerful main Orange fleet,
bottled behind the Makassar Strait, easily outnumbered and
overpowered the smaller American fleet guarding the strait. But
at the opening of a strait, superior force didn't necessarily have
the advantage. A small group of cruisers could blast away any
ship that ventured out, or bottle the strait with mines.

He thought about an air strike, somehow getting Orange carriers up into the strait and using the mobility of planes to take
out the Blue fleet. An air strike would be Breedlove's dream.
But Blue would be on the lookout for planes. Russell had used
offensive aircraft to good effect in a tactical game early in the
summer. Then, there had been gasps from the gallery and loud
whispers that the tactic was ridiculous, but his attack had been
overwhelmingly successful, and the lavish praise from Breedlove
afterward had made air strikes a much-discussed topic. An air
strike would be no surprise this time. Even if Blue wasn't waiting with antiaircraft batteries at the ready, the length of the strait
took away any chance for surprise.

The other option was small craft, fast motorized torpedo
boats that with any luck at all he'd soon be running at the school
in Melville, close enough to see Sera every week. But the Makassar Strait was too long and too open. Even if Orange could
sneak torpedo boats up through the strait, there was too much
maneuvering room for the Blue fleet. Torpedo boats worked
when the opposing fleet was cramped. In the open water outside
the strait, the small boats would need reconnaissance to find the
waiting Blue cruisers, and while they searched, the small boats
would be like fish in a barrel—easy pickings for the long-range
guns on the Blue cruisers. It looked like Blue had them bottled.

"Forget the main fleet," he heard from all sides. "It's only there for the strategic game, to put pressure on the the oil and rubber, the Indies and Malaya. As long as the main fleet stays in the Java Sea, we keep our strategic options open. Think long: it's the future that counts."

"Future" was the only word Russell heard. *Yes*, he thought. The future was all that mattered.

He leaned over the chart table, taking in the entire strategic situation the way he would take in a fleet of Monohulls on a starting line. He stepped back until the details of the chart faded, so whole fleets were tiny specks amidst the blobs of land masses and seaways. The blobs of land became boats on a crowded starting line, when traffic would build up at the committee boat end of the line and sometimes there was no opening for another boat. There's always a smart move, he thought. You just have to look beyond the expected. In races, even when the line was slanted to favor the other end, everyone tried to start on starboard tack. It was the safe move. A port tacker could sneak in at the far end of the line and stomp the whole fleet. An unpredictable move like that would take the race at the start.

What about the other way around? he thought. Across the Banda Sea and out through the Torres Strait.

He traced it with his fingertip, then read the chart notation out loud. "The Torres Strait."

"Forget it. Read the first instruction packets."

"I read the packets. It's deep enough."

"It can only be transited by merchant ships. In places the channel is only two to three miles wide. The crosscurrent is three knots. That cuts maneuvering room to zero. The Torres Strait is impossible for a main fleet transit."

"Blue got the same game instructions," said Russell. "They don't expect anything. They'll have nothing there to stop us."

The senior captain, who had been aloof, turned to Russell. "You can't risk capital ships in a two-mile-wide channel."

"Why not? You ever sail through a gap in a sandbar at high tide, or port tack a hole in a starting line?"

"This isn't a yacht race, Westcott. Read the instructions. 'No fleet could possibly pass through this strait excepting in a long column. Merchant vessels can and do use it.' A battle fleet in column is sitting ducks."

"Only if there's a force waiting for them."

"It would be suicide."

Russell grinned. "Un-uh. It's my, *our* future."

The fleet maneuvering went on for three days on the game clock. With the ships hidden behind the screens on the tiled gameroom floor, each side could only guess at the position of the other fleet.

Then a Blue PBY Catalina, on a routine reconnaissance flight out of Port Moresby, spotted units of a main Orange battle fleet steaming at flank speed in the Coral Sea. The unexpected force was so large that the Blue officers receiving the report ordered a second PBY flight to confirm the sighting. Even the second confirmation sightings were greeted with skepticism on the Blue side of the game room.

Every eye in the gallery was on the tile floor when the contact officers certified that contact had been made between the fleets, and the screens that shielded the fleets from one another were pulled away, revealing the main Orange fleet (the metal ships on the gameroom floor were actually red, the traditional color of the "enemy" fleet) in the Coral Sea. The only possible explanation was that the main Orange battle fleet had transited the Torres Strait at night, battleships, carriers, and heavy cruisers defying a treacherous ship channel two to three miles wide, with a three-knot cross current. It was a move so audacious that gasps went up in the gallery. A few observers, including Horatio Breedlove, turned to find Russell on the floor below.

On the Orange side of the room, the initial silence of apprehension gave way to loud whispers, broad smiles, and rounds of handshakes. Across the room, expressions were suddenly gloomy. The confirmation of the situation in the expressions and animated chatter of the gallery was even more emphatic. The fleet game, planned to showcase a preemptive attack on the Marshalls by the Blue fleet, had turned instead into a potentially disastrous rout of the attackers by the main Orange battle fleet.

The beginning of the tactical engagement signaled a change

in the rules and style of the war game. Fire and damage tables came out, and the ticks of the game clock, which had seemed so painfully slow during the operational maneuvering, suddenly seemed to race as the long anticipation of the strategic game yielded to the adrenaline rush of battle. A salvo of fire from battleship guns required forty-five distinct calculations, derived from fifteen penalty tables and two hundred pages of fire effect tables. The probability of a hit from a torpedo firing was determined with the roll of big twenty-sided dice. Each tick of the relentless game clock was barely time to launch a torpedo or bomb. On each side of the floor, men were engaged in a life-and-death struggle, frantically identifying ships in the opposing fleets from profiles, looking up the opposing armor and armament, and planning their tactics. On the better-equipped Blue fleet, radar officers tried to correlate the readouts from the new-fangled devices with the visual sighting information, feeding combined information to the fire control officers who were planning their salvos. In the fury of battle, fleet commanders were expected to think like chess masters, planning enough moves ahead to predict the outcome of the game.

But even the sheer complexity of the tactical battle was not enough to distract attention from the dramatically altered situation. The Orange fleet that had so unexpectedly steamed through the narrow strait was overpowering. A single decisive move had determined the match. In truth, all that was left was the endgame. If it were a chess match, Blue would have been wise to withdraw. There is no gentlemanly withdrawal in war, and the rules of engagement for the fleet game demanded that the painful, one-sided battle be fought. As Breedlove had said ad nauseam, only in the full denouement of a battle could the observers and instructors in the galleries refine the strategies and tactics for the war they had been planning for so many decades.

Men would study this game for years. Fleet officers would use the game narratives to assess who had the intelligence, initiative, tenacity, and leadership to lead the fleets of tomorrow. Although instructors and visiting officers were quick to say that it was *how* the game was played out, not victory or defeat in the tactical battles that determined their evaluations, everyone knew the opposite was true. The glory of war was in victory, and heads in the gallery had already turned toward the Orange side of the floor. When it succeeded, brilliant initiative was the quality that stood out above all others. For a man like Horatio Breedlove, Russell's unorthodox, unexpected, and strikingly unanswerable tactic confirmed the theories of race, class, and breeding that were even more fundamental than the 160 pages of maneuver rules or the age-old, unwritten rules of conduct of the Navy.

With the screens down, everyone could see Russell, intense in his concentration on the brutal tactical game, his eyes flaming with competitive spirit as if he were slamming a ball across a net. For Russell, the war game truly was a game, which made his triumph even harder to witness.

Across the room, on the losing Blue side, the game clock seemed to slow down. Men like Robert Butler, who had studied hard, memorized tables, and prepared for what they thought was every eventuality, watched in dismay as the guns of the Orange fleet took their toll. Officers who had anticipated the sea battle now couldn't wait until the merciful end, when the referees would announce that the retreating Blue force was no longer within range of the guns of the Orange fleet. Then the exhausted officers would pack up their books, maneuvering boards, and instruments, and pad out on their rubber-soled shoes, eager for long-denied sleep. The infirmary that evening would greet a queue of officers with textbook symptoms of exhaustion.

Long before the room emptied, a smiling Horatio Breedlove caught up with Russell at the edge of the gameroom floor. From the corner of his eye, Russell could see Robert Butler watching them.

25

Breedlove would have gladly spent the afternoon and evening with Russell, regaling him with stories.

"Von Clausewitz got it right, Russell. Everyone knows his distinction between industrious and lazy officers."

"I've been called lazy before, sir."

"Jealousy can throw deadly arrows. They forget Von Clausewitz's more telling distinction between truly bright and mediocre minds. For the truly brilliant, those who bring an irreplaceable élan to the challenge, the feeble distinction of industrious and lazy no longer matters. When an officer has the gift of genius for fleet command, we must be wise enough to overlook all else."

Russell had too much on his mind to enjoy the praise. As much as he loved the tight action of the end of the war game, with the game over he thought only of Sera and Raymond.

"Could you excuse me, sir? I'm beat."

"Indeed, Russell. The surcease is well earned. When you're rested up, come around to the office and we'll talk about your next billet."

Russell went straight to the White Horse.

It never surprised him to find Raymond there. It did surprise him that Raymond was friendly, as if their previous meeting had never happened.

"How pleasant to see you," Raymond said. "I trust your game is over."

"You'll get your money, Raymond."

"Russell, please. We're friends, remember."

"Right. It will take me a little while to scare it up."

"Don't worry about it. You did well in the war game, I trust?"

"It's not a fucking tennis match, Raymond."

"Well, it's a game, isn't it? Games have winners and losers. May I assume you were a winner?"

"I told you before, Raymond, it's all bullshit. Breedlove and the others like offensive victories. They want Ts crossed and enemy fleets sunk. I got lucky, pulled a sweet move, and now Breedlove acts like I'm the greatest naval genius since Lord Nelson. Truth is, all I really knew was that we needed to burst out and engage. When the situation is desperate enough, you go for broke. This time it worked."

"What was the situation?"

"The situation? I needed a good rating in the game to get a decent billet. Once I'm at Melville, you'll get your money."

"In the war game, Russell?"

"What do you care about a stupid war game."

"I'm curious. I've always been curious about these games of yours. Your victory has piqued my curiosity."

"Well, you're going to have to stay curious."

Manuel had spoken to Carlos and arranged a dinner with Carlos's mother. It was done the way everything was done in the village, all back doors and buzzing whispers, so busybodies like Mrs. DaCunha wouldn't even guess at what really happened.

Sera tried to pretend it wasn't happening. She went to work each morning, took walks to the point, wandered past the shops and boatyard on Water Street, and fought memories. She tried to tell herself that it was all a mistake, a bad dream, that she would wake up and everything would be all right.

As she walked to the mill on Thursday morning, the day before Carlos and his mother were supposed to come to dinner, Sera saw Bernardinho loading Jake's truck with planks, boxes of fasteners, and tins of varnish. She detoured across Water Street and asked him, "Going to Newport?"

"Jake's starting another job. I never understand why he

doesn't bring the boats back to the yard. You'd think he likes it up there with those swells."

Sera glanced back across the street watching to see who walked by.

"Can I ride with you?"

"You got the day off?"

Sera shrugged, then winked.

"Sure. Always like company, especially a pretty girl."

Sera ran across the street and whispered something to Rosalie Esposito, who giggled; then she ran back and slipped into the passenger seat of the old Model A truck, slumping low in the seat until they were out of the village. Bernardinho drove recklessly—not fast, but with so little concentration as he alternately turned from the road to talk to Sera that she found herself cringing. She didn't sit up until they were on the Post Road, near the old road that ran down to where the Wequetequock Casino had burned down.

"Who are you afraid of seeing?" Bernardino asked.

"Manuel would kill me if he knew I was going with you. You won't tell him?"

"Course I won't."

"Promise?"

"I promise. I don't see much of Manuel anyway. He's sure 'round the village a lot instead of running his own boat, but I guess that's none of my business. They say a boat's unlucky when the cap'n ain't fishing her. He sure had some bad luck with that last boat of his."

Sera watched Bernardinho, looking for the wry grin that everyone else in the village flashed when they mentioned the sinking of Manuel's insured boat.

Bernardinho smiled. "Jake will be glad to see you."

"I'm not seeing Jake."

"No?"

Sera could see Bernardinho thinking and rethinking what he would say, turning toward her, starting to speak, then changing his mind. Each time he would lose his concentration on the road and swerve, so the truck wobbled down the road like a drunk staggering home. When he drove up onto the shoulder, pebbles

from the oiled road surface would bounce against the floorpan.
A few came through the holes in the floor. The load of mahogany planks made the truck so top-heavy that the truck would
dip and wobble as he fought the wheel.

Finally, he said, "If you aren't seeing Jake . . . ?"

"I have some business to take care of, Bernardinho."

"How come everybody's got business in Newport? Jake says
he's got business—a bunch o' fat-cat boats with little repairs
that don't even need to get done. What kind of business does a
pretty girl like you have in Newport?"

Sera didn't answer. A moment later, she felt tears coming.

"Doesn't look like good business," he said.

"It isn't good or bad," she said. "It doesn't matter anymore.
I'm going to marry Carlos."

"Carlos who?"

"Manuel's cousin, from Newport."

"You like that boy? I never seen him around except on Manuel's boat a few times."

"I don't even know him. I met him once, maybe."

"That don't seem right."

"Stories don't always come out right."

She watched out the open window, thinking of the night she
had come home from Newport on the bus and train. She remembered green fields and charming little farmhouses. The
open countryside had seemed romantic in the long shadows of
moonlight, the farmhouses alluring in the pale yellow-gray light,
the open fields vast and inviting. Now, in the harsh morning
sunlight, the farms seemed shabby. The fields were brown and
spiky with stubble. She saw a horse pulling an enormous load
of hay. She thought of Rosa's lonely farm, infested with weeds,
the fences patched with old boards and broken beds.

Was that what happened to every fantasy? she wondered.

When they reached the Jamestown bridge, she said, "Did you
ever build a sandcastle, Bernardinho? You start pilling up a little
sand and dripping some water and then before you know it
you're adding more sand and getting buckets of water and buckets of sand and the sandcastle is all you care about. You add
rooms and towers and you forget lunch, forget swimming. It

becomes a real castle and a whole world, everything you care about. Then a big wave that you don't expect comes and it's all gone and you know that what you dreamed can never be."

"I don't know about sandcastles. Just seems to me that you and Jake . . . I mean, I don't want to be a busybody and poke where I don't belong, but when you been around the village long enough you see things and know people and sometimes you can tell what's right and what isn't. Carlos, I don't know, maybe he's a nice boy and maybe not, but a boy you don't hardly know just don't seem right to me."

"If it were just me, maybe it would all be different. I could be like Rosa. I could open a shop. I'd like that. But Rosa had no family. I can say to hell with Manuel. But I can't do that to Mama. She's already afraid Paul will never come home. Even if he comes back to Stonington, he'll never really be at home again. What would happen if I ran away? Imagine what Mrs. DaCunha would say."

"Say about what? You lost me, Sera."

"I'm just tired, Bernardinho."

She found herself feeling strangely passive, as if her life were decided. She could imagine Carlos's mother. She would be a nice woman, shy, glancing over her shoulder to see what her sons or brothers thought before she said anything. Her house would have doilies on the table and dressers. She would be soaking *bacalao*, and there would be sweet bread in a box on the counter of the kitchen. She would wear a black dress, and have her hair covered, mourning forever the husband she had lost.

"I'll be done in an hour, maybe two," Bernardinho said when they drove off the ferry. "Soon as we get this stuff off and load up tools to go back. He won't care if I wait around. There's people I could see."

"Don't wait for me. I don't know how long I'll be."

"How will you get back?"

"I can take the bus and train. I've done it before."

"A young girl like you alone on the train?"

"I'll be fine," she said. She leaned across the seat and kissed Bernardinho on the cheek.

Guards with short-cropped hair and white leggings and belts, carrying rifles with white webbed slings, stood at attention at the gate of the Naval War College. Sera had walked there mechanically, as if she were walking to the mill in the morning.

One of the guards saluted her. Short blond hair peeked from under his white cap. It surprised her how much she liked the salute and the sparkling leggings and belt of the sailor's uniform. Like the rest of Russell's world, it seemed unreal, as if the sailors had dressed up for a ball. When she smiled, the sailor smiled back.

"Could I see an officer at the college?" Sera asked. "He's in the junior class."

"You're lucky you didn't come yesterday," the sailor said. "They were in the fleet exercise. I don't think the President of the United States could have gotten in here then. They're still on the review now. Junior class?—half of them are sleeping and the other half are in the infirmary."

"It's important. Can you get a message to him?"

"Who's the lucky guy?"

"Russell Westcott."

The guard's smile widened. "Lieutenant Westcott. I should have guessed. You're the one, eh? They weren't exaggerating."

Sera blushed. "Please," she said. "It's important."

"I'm not supposed to. Fact is, most of the junior class officers are so scared after that fleet game they'd probably die if they got a message from outside. Lieutenant Westcott might be different." He spoke to the other guard, then said to Sera, "Could you wait over there, miss? If anyone asks, you're just looking around." He walked briskly toward Luce Hall.

Sera liked the way the guard said "*Lieutenant* Westcott." She loved the neatly mowed lawns and perfect white paint on the buildings. Everything was so clean and orderly and neat.

Russell ran from the building. His hair blew in the breeze.

"They said you couldn't come," Sera said.

"For you, the rules are off." He reached out, taking her shoulders in his hands. "I've missed you so much." He tried to kiss her. She turned her head away.

"Sera! I was afraid I'd never see you again."

She pulled back. "You won't. I only came to say goodbye."

"Goodbye?"

"I don't want anything to do with you or that horrible world."

"You're angry because of that pervert? He's a hanger-on. He lives life by watching. I didn't know he would . . ." Russell led her away from the gate, down a path toward the causeway built over riprap stonework. Harbor wavelets lapped on the stones below them.

"It isn't just that," she said. "It was wrong."

"It wasn't wrong, Sera. Nothing could be more right. That's why I wanted us to wait."

"Not that. We're from different worlds. We don't belong together."

"Who told you that, your stepfather? What does he want for you? Are you supposed to wait every night for the fishing boats to come back? Wear a black dress, cook codfish, take care of crying babies?" Her silence made him turn her face toward him. Tears covered her cheeks. "Sera, you weren't meant for that."

She found herself curiously immune to the words that had once seemed so prescient. "Why not? I thought you and your world were so wonderful. I thought everything would be so beautiful. What did I get for it? I'm probably one of a hundred girls, right? What do you do, chalk us up on a list? Print a menu so your perverted friends can pick who they want to watch? Maybe that's your idea of fun. Not me."

"Sera, what happened was a mistake." He took her hands in his. She stopped trying to pull them away. "I didn't know there was anyone on the docks. I love you. I want you to be Mrs. Russell Westcott the Third."

"Why? Something else to throw in your mother's face?"

"She doesn't matter. I don't care about her. I just know it's the right thing. I've had time to think. God, for weeks all I've done is think. It's right for me and for you."

Sera pulled her hands away and held them up, palms out toward him. She shook her head. "Now you want to do the *right thing*. Do you think I'd walk up to Father Loftus with a belly out? For what? For a man who thinks love is a game for friends to watch?"

"Belly out?" He looked away, over the harbor to the south, then back at Luce Hall, and finally at her. "Did you say—? Sera, you aren't?"

"What difference does it make? I don't even want you to care."

"My God! Why didn't you tell me?" He turned in every direction, as if he were searching for answers. "It isn't a problem. There are people who take care of things like this. I'll find someone. I can get the money."

"I don't want your money. Where would you get it anyway, from your mother? You're like a little boy."

Suddenly she felt strong. She was as much angry at herself for falling for this man as angry with him.

"I'll get it."

"Where? From Raymond? Does he pay to watch you make love to women?"

"Sera, forget Raymond. The man is a fool. He collects gossip. All he cares about is which admiral is in and who is out. He asks stupid questions about the fleet exercises, likes to hear about families on Bellevue Avenue. If he's that much of a sucker—"

"Is he the sucker? I don't want his money. I don't want you to take care of anything. I don't want to see you again."

"Sera, trust me. I'll take care of everything."

Russell suddenly smiled. The sun was behind him, backlighting his hair into a halo. His pale blue eyes were as beautiful as ever. His half-smile was lovely. But his face was drained, as if he could not express emotion. He had once seemed so invincible, as if he owned the world. Now, he was a frightened boy.

Sera found it surprisingly easy to say, "Goodbye, Russell."

"Sera, we need to talk. I know where to find the right people. Just trust me. I'll take care of everything."

"Goodbye, Russell."

"Sera, I love you. Everything will be fine."

She had already turned away.

"Where are you going? I can get a leave. Give me an hour. I'll have everything worked out. Where can I find you? Where will you be?"

She walked back across the causeway without looking back. Memories of his smile and laughter and kisses, the easy joy of driving in the fast car, riding, swimming, dancing, watching him eat—tumbled through her mind. He seemed helpless standing at the gate of the War College. It was the first time she had ever seen him frightened, his self-confidence faltering. She tried to hold that image, but the other images flickered back. She saw his body naked, the smooth skin glistening in the moonlight, and then the hideous eyes watching them through the skylight of the docked boat.

She walked quickly back to Long Wharf, through narrow streets where multistory houses were stacked close to one another, each with a few clumps of flowers along the short front walk and clotheslines behind hung with men's work pants and undershirts and cotton slips. She could smell sweet Portuguese bread. She remembered that her uncle Georgio lived in one of these houses. Carlos would live in another, with his mother. Sera could picture the sort of room they would set aside for her and Carlos, with a pine chest and a mirror painted with scenes from the Azores, and a crocheted bedcover.

From the wharf she could see down the harbor edge, toward Brenton Cove. Yachts floated lazily at their moorings. The day suddenly seemed stifling, the air heavy and still, so little breeze that the boats drifted at random, pointing helter-skelter. At one of the commercial docks she thought she could make out Jake's workboat, tied up next to a sleek varnished yawl. It seemed strange to have the two men of her life so close to one another.

She sat for a long time on a bench on the wharf, looking toward the mouth of the harbor in the distance. Beyond was the open sea. When she couldn't stand the memories, she walked back to the docks where fishing boats were tied up, hoping Uncle Georgio's boat would be in port. She had first seen Russell from the deck of that boat. It seemed the right place to forget him.

26

"A Dr. Alden to see you, Mrs. Westcott."

Caroline Fiske, who prided herself in knowing every interesting man who appeared in Newport, had persuaded Sybil Westcott to see Alden.

"I don't want to buy any japanware," Sybil had told her.

"You don't have to buy anything," Caroline had said. "You'll like him. He's charming, has a wonderful English accent, dresses in divine tweeds, and can talk about anything. Zero sex appeal, but he'd make a perfect escort. Totally presentable, flawless manners, and he knows an arm is all he'll ever get."

"I don't need an escort."

"He's also helpful."

"You mean he discreetly sells off the treasures your husband spent a lifetime accumulating?"

"You always said you wanted a salon, with intelligent people making clever conversation. Just see Alden. What harm is there?"

Sybil met Alden in the entry hall. She took the calling card from his hand before he had a chance to drop it in the salver on the demi-lune table.

"Alden?" She said. He didn't expect a handshake, and she found his grip fey. "Surprised I wasn't waiting like the queen in a parlor?" she said. "I'm not like the rest of them."

"I can see that."

"Well, come in." She led him into the library. "Oh, and I'm not buying anything, if that's why you're here."

"Actually, Mrs. Westcott, I didn't come to sell you anything. I came because I've heard wonderful things about you and your son."

"Flattery will get you everywhere. What's Russell done now?"

"I hear he's done all sorts of splendid things. Although I suspect you already know that. I came here because I think I may have an opportunity for him."

"What sort of opportunity?"

"Mrs. Westcott—"

"Call me Sybil." She glanced down at the calling card. "Tell me everyone doesn't call you Professor. Even if they do, I refuse. And I'm not going to call you Brad either. You're simply not a Brad. If you don't mind—actually, even if you do—I'll call you Alden."

"Alden is fine."

"Good. Now go ahead with your flattery."

"Sybil, I'm sure you realize that there are remarkable opportunities today for intelligent, well-bred young men. When I say 'intelligent,' I don't mean a common sort of cleverness; that schoolbook quickness is a cheap commodity. I mean the judgment that comes with breeding, and if I can use a word that unfortunately is all too often disparaged today, *class*. I hope my visit is timely. I'm given to understand that Russell—and I suspect you, as well—would welcome a little *independence* on his part."

"Independence?" She pronounced the word one syllable at a time. "Nice euphemism, Alden. Actually, independence isn't what Russell needs; he's got too much already."

"I'll be frank. A Navy commission and trafficking with the sort of people he should avoid is far more *independence* than I want to see. What Russell needs is money. He unfortunately inherited his father's ability to spend money. It's a remarkable ability, mind you, but one I can't afford."

She smiled. "Spending money the way Russell and his father do is an art. Forget the flashy cars and vulgar furs and who knows what else that the parvenus splash around. Wes can walk into Purdeys in London and order a matched pair of skeet guns with hand-chased receivers as if they were shoelaces at the local

Woolworth's. Russell is no different. Their nonchalance is utterly enchanting to watch. Unfortunately, it isn't an indulgence I can support forever. It's been my fate to be the keeper of the purse, the ogre who doles it out and makes sure the source doesn't run dry. I suppose I can claim some success: we aren't in the streets yet. But if the purpose of my hanging onto those purse strings was to convey a notion of fiscal responsibility to Russell, I've failed miserably.

"Which is all by way of saying that whatever you're offering, it's got to be better than the Navy. Russell took that commission for spite: it was the one career that his father and I were agreed against. And he no doubt assumed those dress whites would turn every lovely young woman round-heeled. *Quel dommage.* He doesn't need a uniform for that—his way with women is another skill he inherited from his father. The Navy is just not the place for someone of Russell's talents. It's not the dreariness I mind, but the people he hangs around with."

"Indeed, which is why I'm here, Sybil. I must say, though, that Russell seems to have made at least one rather striking acquaintance despite the Navy."

Sybil raised her eyebrows. With a stranger, unlike with the Westcott men, she could hold her tongue.

Alden said, "That ball you gave last month is quite the talk these days. Newport clearly had been waiting for someone to save the Season, and word has it that you did a splendid job. I've heard nothing but lushly extravagant compliments for every detail. And not one person has failed to mention the extraordinary woman Russell brought. . . ."

Sybil pursed her lips. The skin on her temples tightened and pulsed with each controlled breath. "Why exactly did you want to see Russell, Mr. Alden?"

"Nothing more, or less, than what I said before: I'd like to help him. And I believe that he can help me."

"What makes you so sure he needs your help?"

"I've been told, on what I believe to be very good information, that Russell has fallen in with the wrong sort, and has incurred some obligations that could be a damper for a young gentleman. Oh, I'm sure this is nothing more than a youthful indiscretion, but the wrong problem at the wrong time can be a devilish burden for a free spirit like Russell.

"Of course you and Russell's father could handle the matter, but I share what I suspect is your view: a young man should take care of matters himself. Given Russell's social polish and intelligence, I think I have a way out of the situation for him. I'm quite certain this could prove to be one of those times when a little discreet help from a friendly quarter can work wonders."

Sybil offered a slow, viperous smile. "Really?" she said. "And what, exactly, do you want from me?"

"Actually, I'd love to be considered a friend. I hope that some-day I can interest you in some fine Japanese landscapes, which would complement your decor here splendidly. But for now, I'm seeking only an introduction to Russell, as a step toward a mu-tually beneficial relationship. No young gentleman needs un-welcome entanglements with the wrong sort of people."

Sybil looked Alden up and down, making no effort to shield her interrogating gaze. Was he a homosexual, she wondered, looking for a handsome young man? If anything, he seemed asexual, sterile, a hybrid that couldn't breed. Caroline Fiske was right: he would have made some woman a tame husband. Or a perfect eunuch escort, bright enough to converse, presentable enough to appear anywhere, and humble enough to know that the right to offer his arm was all he was going to get. It was exactly what some women wanted. Sybil had seen it a dozen times, could understand, and still wouldn't have touched a man like Alden with a ten-foot pole. For all the pain he had caused her, she wouldn't for a minute trade Wes for a man so con-trolled.

"You realize, Sybil, that I'm not the sort of person who is comfortable doing business in a tavern. I'm told meetings like that have gotten Russell into his current situation."

"Actually," Sybil paced her words, "Russell's problem started at a sailboat race. But never mind the fine points."

"Well, I have heard he's talented with boats, which is one reason I know he's the man I want. You understand that I'm not being charitable. I'm looking for information. Discreet, private information for a—shall we say *quirky?*—client. I need someone

who is well-connected here in Newport. The focus of my query
is ships and the sea. In return, my client would be quite generous. Certainly generous enough to make this current problem
of Russell's a thing of the past."

Sybil's lips pursed again. "What makes you so sure Russell has
a *problem*, as you put it?"

"Young men have their passions. As you said, Russell has a
gentleman's taste. That can be expensive."

Sybil felt her lips pursing. Her pulse throbbed. She couldn't
control her reaction. She had feared exactly this. How many
times had she tried to warn Russell that there were alluring girls
out there with entrapment schemes in their pretty young heads?
He had laughed her off. Now what would happen? Blackmail?
Scandal? A forced marriage? Russell ending up in those
wretched little married officer houses with a yard full of dirty,
screaming children?

Sybil looked away. She suddenly hated Alden, hated his
neatly creased trousers and his flawlessly straight bow tie and
his sweatless face as he sat there in the heavy tweed jacket. Why
am I finding out important information about my family from
a stranger? She knew the ball had been a failure—not one man
had looked at Lisa; they had instead talked about Russell and
the girl in the black dress. Now, it seemed, the world still had
reason to talk about them. And she was the last one to know.

She forced herself to lift her eyes. She stared through Alden,
less from embarrassment than as a retreat to privacy, a chance
to think. When she finally spoke, her thoughts were as far away
as her gaze. Words came out mechanically while her mind raced.
"You want to know about the sea?" she said. "It means so many
things in Newport: it's not just the yachts in Brenton Cove. It's
the Navy too, and the unfortunates who dangle lines off the
rocks on the shorelines for something to toss into the dinner
pot. And don't forget the Portuguese fishermen, those horrible
rotting boats over by the Oldtown docks. Newport is more than
you think, Alden."

"Indeed. Fortunately, my client is quite focused. We're looking for some very specific information. I'm sure Russell, with
his connections, is the ideal person for what we need."

Sybil pressed her lips together tightly, willing an end to the pulse she felt surging through her skin. Embarrassments had happened before. She knew how not to give in. "What exactly do you need?"

"I won't bore you with details. It's surely of no interest to anyone except my client. You know how it can be in the world of art: curiosity so easily turns to obsession. This client has developed an obsession about Newport. With the market for japanware in shambles, I have little choice but to indulge him."

"Russell is hardly an expert on Newport. I dare say that if it weren't for those games they play at the War College—Russell has a knack at anything called a game—he wouldn't have a whit of interest in the Navy and Newport."

"I've heard about these games. I suspect his experience there could be very useful to my client."

Sybil was conversing mechanically. Desperation made her mind race, grasping at a thousand frail ideas, until a a thought came to her like a ballooned IDEA! in a cartoon strip. Her pursed lips broke into an open smile. "Actually," she said, "Russell's not the one you want."

"Maybe I haven't been clear, Sybil. This could be a marvelous opportunity for him."

"I know, Alden."

"And I know this opportunity is timely. Mind, I'm not passing judgment. Youth will be youth. With a young man as winsome as Russell, it is certainly understandable that he has slipped in with the wrong people and has ended up saddled with the wrong sort of obligations. And, of course, for people of your standing, it's easy enough have these matters disappear. But are we really helping when we do? How much better to find a situation that can turn the experience into a profitable lesson."

Sybil's beaming smile had already contracted into a contented grin. "Look, Alden, I'm no fool. Actually I am, but that's a subject for another time, when we're better friends. You really don't have to say more. I know exactly what you're talking about." She placed a hand on Alden's arm. "Our views on Newport and the Navy are the same. And I appreciate your discretion. I've had to untangle my foot from my teeth enough times that this time, for a change, I'm going to pretend I'm a proper Newport lady. I hope you'll think of me as a gentlewoman. That term that doesn't get applied to Sybil Westcott very often."

Sybil winked, as if to to signal a shared intimacy. "I have no doubt yours is a generous and timely proposal. But Russell isn't the one you want. It so happens that I know who you should be talking to. Do you know Newport?"

Alden shook his head. He looked genuinely puzzled. He said, "I've had the privilege of calling on people in quite a few of the cottages."

"Nice Newport word. But it isn't a cottage you want; once they're dottering enough for a cottage, they're mostly watchers. You want Oldport, along the waterfront in the harbor. Do you know it? If not, look for the drunken sailors and the whore-houses on Thames Street. What you want is the commercial dock, which is only a long spit away. There are all sorts of pipes and tanks and timbers and engines piled up at the head of the dock. About halfway down, on the side facing Brenton Cove, you'll see a workboat tied up. Calling it a workboat really isn't fair. It's nicely finished, trim, a proper boat. You'll find a young man named Jake Werth there. He's the one you want. He knows everything you need to know." She winked. "And he's the one who can use some help getting out of an untimely entangle-ment."

"Are you quite sure?"

"Jake is the man you want, Alden."

"I take it he's also affiliated with the Naval War College?"

"Of course he isn't. The War College is a smug little nest of play-actors. Jake isn't playacting. He's been around and he's, well, let's just say that if I hadn't chosen to get myself tangled in this absurd Newport life, he's the sort of man I'd have killed for. Oh, those white dress uniforms dazzle, and there are plenty of empty-headed girls who will fall for them. But if you want real intelligence, you don't want the War College. A girl with a head on her shoulders, who isn't foolish enough to be taken in by Navy whites, would find her way to a man like Jake. Russell may have tried—he can never resist temptation—but Jake is the one who has what you want."

"Mrs. Westcott—Sybil—are you sure you understand what I'm talking about?"

"I haven't lived among these vipers for thirty years without learning a little about Newport and its secrets. I know exactly what you're talking about. Trust me, Alden, Jake is the man you want."

D iscretion above all, Russell," Raymond said. He and Russell were driving through Middletown in the Packard. Russell remembered the streets from the night they had gone to Raymond's club in Portsmouth. Do I have to put up with an afternoon of that? he wondered.

"The car is no problem," Raymond said. With an exaggerated wink, he added, "And I can busy myself for a while if you want the apartment. But a thousand dollars is a lot of money, especially on short notice." Without the slightest shift in his unctuous, all-too-civil tone, he continued, "Friendship is a two-way street, you know. Sometimes I need a favor too."

"What sort of favor?"

"It's nothing really. But ever since you told me about those old naval games, I've been curious to see them."

"What games?"

"At the college, the games you play."

"What are you talking about?"

"The war games, like the one you just finished. Or the fleet exercises you once told me about, with American airplanes attacking other American ships. I still don't understand what they're about, any more than I can understand the idea of a war college, but I suppose that's just me. I've said it before, Russell: I'm curious. Call it a perverse pleasure. I'd like to see them."

"I told you, Raymond. They're stupid, ridiculous. War games aren't like Parcheesi."

"I'm sure that's true. And it only makes me all the more eager. I'm talking about *old* exercises, Russell. You said some of them were quite fanciful. Impossible situations like Germany attacking the Panama Canal or Japanese ships attacking Pearl Harbor. Well, I'd like to have a look."

"Don't be ridiculous, Raymond."

"What is ridiculous about a favor for a friend? I've never called your requests ridiculous, including a request for a thousand dollars on short notice."

"The games are restricted material."

"Restricted? By whom? A bureaucrat at a desk somewhere? For what silly reason? Because the bureaucrat has nothing else to do?

"Have I ever asked you for anything else? Have I asked you to repay the money I advanced toward the pursuit of your lady friend? Oh, I mentioned it when you were being unfriendly, but you knew I would never really ask for the money. We're friends, remember. Even when we had a misunderstanding, you knew I'd still be there for you. After weeks of rather despicable behavior, you have no qualms asking me for a considerable sum of money. Now, just once I ask you for a trifling favor. And you balk because what I'd like to see is *restricted* material?"

"Why do you want them?"

"I'm planning on building a private navy and attacking Newport. Why do you think? Curiosity, Russell. Nothing more and nothing less. You know me well enough to realize that I have strange tastes and a passion for forbidden pleasures. I've never denied a fascination with the exotic. The more dangerous, the better. I've drunk absinthe. More than once, actually. I've tried hashish. I've done things with women that are, shall we say, out of the ordinary. I own books that cannot be sold in this country. When I went through customs with those books hidden in my bag, my heart thumped from fear. I'm not ashamed to admit that I enjoyed the danger of smuggling as much as I treasure the books themselves. It was exciting. The little people with their obsessions for *normalcy* call interests like mine perverse or abnormal. Why? Because they've never known the incomparable delights of forbidden pleasures, of doing or owning things that are truly unique."

"Raymond, it isn't that easy. This isn't like going to some private club. There are secrecy regulations."

"Which makes them even more deliciously wicked. A secret document, even if it's ridiculous and fanciful and impossible, would be utterly wonderful."

"Sera is right," Russell said. "You are a pervert. Ask me for tickets to a match at the Casino or Bailey's Beach. How about introductions at the Yacht Club, a woman, another ball, this time by the front door? Anything else and it's yours."

"No, Russell, I prefer the unique. Many go to the Casino and the Yacht Club. The beach is ugly and filthy. I've been to a ball now. The women of Newport are hardly a special prize. Even you went elsewhere to find your beauty. You know me well enough to realize that my vices are private pleasures: a rare wine, a hard-to-get woman, an irreplaceable artifact. Those games are what I want."

"How soon can you get the thousand dollars?"

"Drop me off at the White Horse and the car and apartment are yours."

"What about the money?"

"How soon can you get what I need, Russell?"

"What you *need*?"

"Want, need—is there a difference?"

27

J ake cleaned up the papers on the workboat with a vengeance. Every document he stuffed into a manila envelope was another loose end tied up, another thread of his temporary life in Newport that he would never see again.

Loose stacks of drawings and graphs were spread out on the engine box, sketches of release mechanisms, details of torpedo fins, trajectories of dropped torpedoes, sheets of graph paper with the results of tests and equations. Langer had never said anything about destroying the material, but after too many months in Newport, Jake couldn't wait to get rid of it.

Across the dock, a dragger was getting an engine transplant. There was enough noise from the groaning lift that Jake didn't realize he wasn't alone until a voice and face appeared outside the open companionway of the workboat.

The man was dressed in a tweed suit, white shirt, a hand-tied bow tie, and polished oxblood bluchers. "Jake?" he said. "Jake Werth?" The British accent was too affected, and the pitch of the voice too high not to sound out of place. "I'm Alden, Professor J. Bradford Alden. Sybil Westcott suggested that you and I talk. May I step aboard?"

Alden didn't wait for an answer. He climbed awkwardly onto the toerail of the workboat, then over the low lifeline to the deck, holding on to the metal guard strip on the edge of the workboat cabin and planting his leather-soled shoes hard, as if the force of his steps and the tenseness of his grip would keep

. him from slipping. When he had both feet on the deck, he said, "Bit tricky when it rocks on the waves."

The biggest wavelet in the harbor was about six inches.

Jake didn't hide his reaction. It wasn't the clothes. Langer wore the same tweed suits. But Langer wouldn't climb onto the deck of a workboat like a ballet dancer trying to avoid barnyard manure on her toe-slippers.

Alden flashed a polite half-smile, but looked unhappy with the utilitarian interior of the workboat, as if he expected varnished mahogany. "You are Jake Werth?" he said. "I'm told that you and I might do some business."

"Got a boat that needs fixing?"

Alden brushed his trouser legs with his palms, resetting the crease. His eyes searched the cabin of the workboat. Over the years Jake had rebuilt much of the boat. It was solid but simple, what his father, and he in turn, would call an "honest" boat.

When Alden's gaze caught the drawings and charts on the engine cover, he smiled. Jake had saved every graph, chart, plot, and sketch, holding on to even crude early sketches because he knew from long experience that sometimes the earliest idea ended up the best answer to a problem. Alden tried not to seem obvious as he stared. Jake could see him reading the upside-down papers.

Alden looked up, grinning. "Well, well. Our mutual friend is more clever than I imagined."

"Who's our friend?"

"Sybil Westcott."

Jake remembered a moment at almost the same place on the dock. He was working on James Putnam's motorsailer. Sybil had seemed to delight, even gloat, when she told him about Sera and her son, the lieutenant.

Alden picked up a sheet of graph paper with glide paths of torpedoes, and another with sketches of detachable torpedo fins. "Remarkable," he said. "Torpedoes configured for shallow water. Ship nets. Do you get a lot of queries to repair boats that have been torpedoed?"

"I like to be prepared when work comes along."

"Indeed. It seems very complicated, this new technology. Airplanes flying off of ships seems challenging enough. I'm told naval aviation requires entirely new strategies. These new weapons probably inspire quite a bit of gaming at the War College, wouldn't you think?"

When Jake didn't react, Alden filled the silence. "I appreciate your discretion. But let's not be too discreet. You appear to be a man of science. I admire that. I've been fascinated by Dr. Einstein's equations, the way he intertwines time and space. I like to think the same concept could be applied to time and money. All too often people with something valuable forget that what is priceless today can be worthless tomorrow."

"What makes you think I'm the man you want?"

"Our friend Sybil Westcott was not only perceptive about our mutual interests, but noted that you are eager to disentangle yourself from a situation. She was quite discreet. Reading between the lines I had the strong feeling it was a woman. In any case, the details are of no interest to me, but in years of dealing with unique artifacts, I have learned one thing: a sale requires only a buyer with sufficient funds and a seller in need of funds. The rest is technicalities."

Jake remembered when Langer first mentioned the possibility of spies in Newport. It seemed a joke then. Possible, but implausible. "Are you sure you have sufficient funds?" Jake said.

Alden smiled again, a quick flash of his teeth. "I find objets d'art for people, unique objets. Some are almost priceless. I assure you that my client has a very generous budget, even if his interests are unusual."

"How generous?"

Alden looked around at the workmanlike, battleship-gray interior of the workboat, with its exposed ribs and ceiling stringers, and frowned as if he had just smelled a rotten egg. "More generous than you can imagine."

"What exactly does your client want?"

"Has someone named Raymond approached you?"

"Raymond?"

"You would know if you met him. Foppish clothes, cannot discuss anything for five minutes without vulgar patter about his

so-called clubs and what he calls 'the beauty of human experience'—his shorthand for pornographic displays. The man has
the aesthetics of a scorpion and the ethics of a vampire."

"And you?"

Alden bristled. "Don't compare me with Raymond. He buys
drinks and pays for brothels for sailors. My client has arranged
a negotiable letter of credit. You know what that is? Effectively
a bank check, payable to the bearer. It cannot be traced. We
occasionally use the same instrument for purchases of artworks,
especially when there are overly curious authorities, or when
the provenance of a work must remain ambiguous."

Jake found himself snuffing his rising anger. He had a flash of
memory to when he was twelve and he watched his father let
three thugs with automatic pistols steal a rumrunner from the
yard.

"They didn't pay," Jake had said to his father. "You let them
take it without paying for the repairs."

"Should I argue and get us shot?" Sam had said. "Why? For
money?"

It had taken Jake years of wrestling with tangled feelings to
realize that his father had been right. But this wasn't just about
money. It also wasn't about Alden's smarmy affectations or the
tenuous but unavoidable connection that led back to Sybil Westcott and Sera.

Jake began gathering the papers on the engine cover into a
large manila envelope. "What are you looking for?" he asked.
"And how much are you willing to pay?'

Alden reached for a drawing, one of Jake's sketches of a torpedo. "My client's needs are very specific. He is particularly interested in fleet exercises in the Pacific. I believe there was a
game in 1938 in which an American carrier attempted an attack
on the naval base at Pearl Harbor. This would be of great interest. I have been authorized to be quite generous if you can meet
these needs."

Jake took the drawing from Alden's hand, tugging when he
felt resistance in Alden's fingertip grasp. Jake stuffed it and the
remaining drawings and charts into the manila envelope.

"And if the material is not for sale?"

"Mr. Werth, let us not be dissembling. Everything is for sale. The only question is. . . ."

The sound of rapid gunfire from somewhere outside, two quick shots followed by a third, cut him off. Alden ducked under the companionway, covering his head with his arms.

Jake laughed. "It isn't gunshots. I tell Bernardinho to let the truck cool down slowly, but he either doesn't hear or enjoys popping off a few backfires."

"Are you sure?" Alden composed himself, straightening the crease of his trousers after he stood up. "I've heard gunshots often enough that I. . . ."

Jake could hear Bernardinho's shuffling walk on the dock between Alden's words. An accident with a dragline years before had almost amputated Bernardinho's left foot at the ankle. It had healed but he still dragged the foot in a sliding shuffle when he walked.

Alden turned toward the companionway in time to see Bernardinho's face, with a three-day growth of beard, appear through the open hatch.

"Hey?" Bernardinho said. He saw Alden and froze up. He had always been wary of strangers, especially if they didn't look like boat people. "Didn't know you had company."

"It's all right," Jake said. "This is Mr. Alden. Bernardinho works with me in the yard."

"I better be going," said Bernardinho. "Just came by because I thought she might be here."

"She?" Jake said.

Bernardinho climbed down the companionway, leaned close to Jake and whispered, "Sera. I don't see her marryin' that Carlos. She don't hardly know him."

"Carlos?"

"Manuel's cousin. He's from 'round here. He takes Manuel's boat out sometimes. Manuel will do just about anything to keep from gettin' his hands greasy."

"Why is Sera . . . ?"

Bernardinho shrugged. "She said something about building sandcastles and a wave comes. Don't make sense to me. She never mentioned that other one, the lieutenant, but I think he's the problem. Manuel was sure fired up about him."

"When did . . . ?"

Jake hadn't finished the question when Alden grabbed the manila envelope off the engine box cover and bolted through the companionway, pushing his way past Bernardinho.

"Watch it—" said Bernardinho as he was jostled aside.

Jake climbed past Bernardinho into the open companionway. He watched Alden run up the dock, surprisingly fast for a man wearing street shoes.

"What's the matter with him?" Bernardinho asked.

Jake's gaze traced up the dock and along the seawall toward Long Wharf. A dragger was coming in, probably to take out a catch. Otherwise, the docks were sleepy. Out in the harbor boats drifted aimlessly on their moorings. The air was heavy and frighteningly still; it felt like the lull before a late-afternoon storm. At the head of the work dock he saw Alden slow down to navigate around the piles of machinery.

As Jake stepped onto the deck, he felt Bernardinho's strong grip on his arm.

"You going to look for Sera?" Bernardinho asked.

"This is more important," Jake said.

"More important?" said Bernardinho. "What's wrong with you? He don't even look like he's ever been on a boat. Even if he has, don't tell me that fixing boats in Newport is more important. Makes you sound more hardheaded than your father. That's crazy talk. A woman like Sera's more important than any of this. . . ."

He was talking to the wind. In two steps Jake was over the lifelines. He ran up the dock, skirting the pipes and coils of wire. Ahead of him, Alden was running along the seawall toward Thames Street with its warren of bars, tattoo parlors, and whorehouses.

Sera had no idea how long she had been daydreaming. She was on the afterdeck of Uncle Georgio's boat, looking out at the harbor. She had been lost in memories of the sailboat race months before. Everything had seemed so innocent then. A beautiful man sailing under the stern of the boat and smiling at her, showing up on the beach with that same glorious smile before she drove away with Jake. How easily it could have ended there. She had seen other glimpses of that world—the yachts and houses and fancy cars—envied them, and quickly forgotten them. From a distance, it was no different from the movies. Fun to watch, nice to fantasize, easy to forget when she went back to the mill.

The sun was low. A steady westerly breeze had started to fill in, driving away the still air and raising whitecaps in the harbor. The yachts that had swung aimlessly a few hours before were all pointing due west now. A few were starting to hobbyhorse at their moorings. *Hobbyhorse.* It was another word she had learned from Jake. She looked back at the commercial dock, squinting against the low sun. His workboat was still there.

She wasn't surprised to hear footsteps behind her. One boat had finished taking out a catch. Along the wharf, she saw fishermen securing doubled lines to some of the boats and putting extra tires over the sides as fenders.

She turned around, expecting her uncle.

"Sera! I was afraid I wouldn't find you."

"No, Russell. Go away. Leave me alone."

"I can't. I couldn't forget you if I tried."

"Please, Russell. Leave me alone."

"Just come talk, Sera."

She looked back at the harbor. For an instant the breeze felt fresh.

He put his hand over hers. "We have to talk."

"What is there to say?"

"Not here."

"Why not here?"

"Because I have to be alone with you."

"So someone can watch?"

"Sera, please."

She cringed when she saw the Packard parked on the wharf. The soft plush and leather seat was so familiar and comfortable. She couldn't help thinking of the worn seat in Jake's truck and the holes in the floor that let her see the road underneath.

He opened the door. In the middle of the seat was a blue duffel bag, the fabric worn and scuffed.

"I'm not going with you," she said.

"We don't have to drive. We can walk." He took the duffel and shut the door of the Packard.

"What is that?" she said, pointing at the blue duffel.

"This? Our future. Trust me, Sera. Everything is going to be all right." He tried to embrace her, still holding the bag.

"We don't have a future, Russell."

"Sera, you have to believe me. There are people who can fix things. I aced the fleet game. Breedlove was fawning all over me. That means my pick of billets. I've already told him I want Melville, right up the bay. It means plenty of time for us. I love you. What else matters?"

He kissed her, and she remembered the sweet taste of his lips, the gentle tiny kisses he would plant on the edges of her lips. She tried not to react.

"You know I love you," he said again.

She pulled away. "You don't know what the words mean. You don't love anything. Not me, not the Navy, not even your own family. Other men would be proud to wear that uniform, to be at the War College. Even the sailors at the gate were proud. It doesn't matter to you. Nothing matters to you."

"The hell with the Navy. You're what matters to me. But you're right: it's the first time I've ever cared about anyone or anything." He took her hand and started up a narrow street.

"Where are we going?" she asked.

"To a place where we can talk."

"I don't want to talk. I've said all I have to say." Yet she didn't walk away, didn't pull her hand from his. He smiled, and everything else seemed far away.

They walked past a tavern. The houses were wooden, built close to the street, without room for even a strip of grass or flowers. The maples in the crumbled sidewalk had already turned. The still air of the early afternoon was gone, gusts of breeze fluttered the leaves. The time, like the season, seemed suspended.

They stopped at a two-story house. Russell put the duffel under his arm so he had his hands free to unlock the door.

"Whose house?" she asked.

"A friend."

"Raymond?"

It was an old house, probably lovely once, now divided awkwardly into apartments. The staircase was narrow, and the second-floor apartment seemed stark, as if whoever lived there had never really bothered to move in. From the window in the living room, there was a view out over Goat Island. When Russell closed the door, he put down the duffel bag.

She remembered the fitted case he had for his tennis racket, and the fine leather case that held the shotguns they had used for skeet. When they had gone on a picnic, the food and plates and glasses were in a fitted basket. He never cared about the fancy fitted cases. Why was he so careful with this old duffel bag?

"What's in the bag?" she asked.

He smiled, taking both of her hands in his and trying again to embrace her. "I told you. It's our future."

"In a duffel bag?"

He laughed. "It's games. Stupid games."

"The ones you play at the War College?"

He mumbled as he nuzzled her neck. His sweet smell came back to her.

She pulled back. "You said those games were secret. Why are they here?"

"Because some people are fools."

Russell's forehead was covered with tiny beads of sweat. She had seen him like that after a tennis match. She remembered the salty taste of his sweat when she had kissed him. Why was he sweating now? "What does that mean?" she said.

"You've seen what a pervert Raymond is."

"What does Raymond have to do with war games?"

"I haven't told you a fraction of his weirdness. He collects pornographic books, goes to bizarre clubs, drinks things like absinthe. What an ass he is! I swear, after this I'll never see him again."

"After what?"

The phone rang in another room. "Give me a minute," Russell said.

She could hear Russell arguing from the other room.

"Why can't it wait?" he said. Then after a pause, "I don't count favors for friends, either. I'm just asking why it can't wait."

She stared at the duffel bag and pictured the shiny-faced sailor at the gate to the War College, remembered how protective he had been. He had said that during the war game they wouldn't have allowed the President of the United States through the gate.

She unzipped the duffel. Inside were papers in reddish-brown folders, held together with bent-metal clasps on the side. She slipped out the first one and opened the cover.

"SECRET. Strategic Exercise, 1938. Property of United States Navy. USE RESTRICTED."

The next page said, "Summary: A task force, comprising major naval aviation units, approaches the Hawaiian Islands from the northwest under heavy cloud cover. The force is not detected by. . . ."

Task force. Naval aviation units. It was like the games Paul and Jake had played with toy boats at the edge of the harbor. Something told her it was all wrong. These were more than games. Jake would know what they were, but there was no way to ask Jake. She missed him, realized she had missed him for a long time.

"Why can't it wait?" she heard from the other room. Then, "All right. We'll do it. Let's make it quick."

She replaced the folder before Russell came back into the room. She didn't have time to zip the bag.

"Sera, I have to do a quick errand. You can stay. We can telephone anyone if you need to. Tell them a story, anything. I'll get tomorrow off. We can walk on the beach and talk. Or go riding. Just us. We can plan a whole life together. We'll get this taken care of and have our whole lives ahead of us."

Sera glanced at the duffel bag, wondering if Russell would notice the open zipper.

"Stay right here. I have to change, then a quick errand and

the future is ours." He kissed her playfully, flashing the wonderful smile.

He slipped back into the other room. "I'll be back in no time."

She saw him grab a pair of dungarees and a thin sweater. She
had stopped thinking when she grabbed the duffel bag and ran
out the door of the apartment.

28

Whitecaps flecked the harbor. The sleepy haze of an hour earlier was gone. Dark puffy clouds scudded in front of the setting sun. Along the docks, men were doubling lines on the commercial boats.

She looked down at the duffel bag, not sure what was in it, not sure what to do with it, but knowing it mattered. She thought of the bus terminal, remembering the trip that night. The slow trip hadn't mattered when she only wanted to be away. If only she could get a ride with Bernardinho. The rattling truck with holes in the floorboards was somehow secure and friendly. She allowed herself a quick smile as she imagined Bernardinho driving, glancing over so often with talk and questions that he could barely hold the road.

She ran along the edge of the harbor from Long Wharf to the dock at the shipyard. What if Bernardinho had already left? He said all he was doing was dropping off some lumber and picking up some tools. At least Jake would be there, somehow making a home out of the crowded workboat. She remembered laughing at the workboat the first time she had ever seen it, thinking it reminded her of a rubber duck in a bathtub. It had started as an old dragger, before Jake rebuilt it and put a rack for the Monohull forward where the draggers usually carried a dory. He had replaced and reinforced planking, built up the samson post for towing, and replaced the old Lathrop engine with the diesel. Jake would know what the papers were.

It was a long run along the seawall. The walkway was rough, and the duffel, light when she first picked it up, felt heavy and awkward in her hand, banging against her leg as she ran. What would she say to Jake, after so many months? Then she had a different worry. What if he wasn't there?

She knew as soon as she reached the head of the dock that he wasn't on the boat. The sky was gloomy dark. It wasn't dusk yet, but thick clouds made the light luminescent close to the water and ominous above. There were no lights on the work-boat. If he had just gone out for supper, Jake would have left a cabin light on. With the wind whipping up in the harbor, he would probably have left marker lights too.

She found herself more relieved than surprised. There was too much to tell Jake.

What would Russell do when he found her gone? she wondered. She knew he would follow her, probably to the fishing boats. Would he look down here too? Did he even know Jake was in Newport?

She looked behind her, up along the seawall. She couldn't see anyone, but the sky was dark enough that she couldn't be sure.

The workboat was locked. She knew where Jake kept a key hidden on a hook under the deck vent. As she stepped into the dark cabin, she banged her shin on the foghorn. Instinctively, she reached for the master light switch, then caught herself. *Night vision*, she told herself. *Don't look at bright lights.* After a few seconds in the cabin, she could see well enough to find her way around.

Without thinking, she did what she had seen Jake do so many times—taking the blunt key for the tank filler cap and the mea-suring stick from behind the cabin door, stepping back up onto the deck, undoing the tank cap, and plumbing the tank. The oily glint of diesel fuel sparkled halfway up the stick. There were two spare fuel cans lashed behind the cabin. She tapped both with her knuckles. One was full, the other maybe half-full. She remembered Jake saying that half a tank was enough to get to Block Island. She tried to remember the charts. How much far-ther was Newport?

From the cabin, she looked back up toward the end of the

dock and then along the seawall that ran back toward Oldport, not sure who she expected to see. She saw a car pull up. In the dim light, the color of the car was impossible to make out. The outline, especially the long hood, was unmistakable.

She had never done it herself, but she knew how to start the diesel. She checked the oil, something she had seen Jake do dozens of times, then tried the starter. Nothing happened. She had forgotten the switch. She flicked it, and the ammeter and oil pressure gauge both jumped up. She tried the starter again. The engine groaned twice and died.

She knew what to do. It had happened before and she had watched Jake fix it. Under the floor hatch there were two huge batteries. The primary battery must be dead. She reached into the tool drawer and got a wrench for the battery cable clamp, trying three until she found one that fit snugly. She pulled hard with the wrench, but the bolt turned with the nut. She poked again in the drawer and found a second wrench to hold the bolt, and got one then the other cable off the terminals. When she moved the first cable to the new battery, matching the + on the terminal to the marking on the battery case, the terminal slid on easily. She tightened it with the two wrenches, then discovered that the second cable wouldn't reach.

She leaned down and tried to lift the battery. She could hardly move it. She got one leg down inside the hatch, then the other, so she could lift with her legs, heaved the heavy old battery onto the floorboards, then jiggle-walked the new battery across the compartment, moving one corner then the opposite corner, until the second cable would reach. A loud spark crackled when she touched the cable to the battery post. She used the wrenches to tighten the connector.

When she stood up again, her legs and back ached and her hands and arms were covered with grease from the terminals. Through the windscreen she could see two figures walking fast down the dock toward her. Maybe it was just imagination, but Russell's hair seemed to glow in the dim light.

She tried the starter again. The engine turned over but didn't catch.

Fuel, she thought. She pushed the throttle forward. On the next try the diesel caught. She ticked the throttle forward to a fast idle and listened as the rough sound of the engine smoothed out to a steady *puckety-puckety*. She looked up and saw the two figures running toward her. She remembered Russell running toward her at the gate of the War College, the broad smile on his face, his arms out toward her. And then later, when she was on Uncle Georgio's boat and it didn't seem a surprise that he found her. On the cabin sole next to her was the duffel bag that he had held so tightly, even when he put his arms around her.

As she stepped out onto the deck to get the lines, the work-boat was rocking uncomfortably in the choppy harbor swells. She had to hold on to the rail as she slipped the stern line off the piling and tossed it onto the deck. She had dropped mooring lines dozens of times, in winds worse than this, but usually someone like Jake was at the wheel, holding the boat steady with the engine so she could easily step from the dock back to the boat. When the wind caught the stern, the boat started to squirrel, the bow swinging in toward the dock.

She jumped into the cabin and eased the boat into gear, using the idling engine to hold the workboat against the spring line. When she climbed back onto the dock, Russell was close enough that she could see his long blond hair blown back over his fore-head. Another man—Raymond?—was running down the dock behind him, slower and ungainly.

She slipped the bowline off the piling. She had to think for an instant before she remembered the trick for the spring line, how she could hold one end around the piling and carry it back to the boat to cast herself off. She had the tail end of the line in her hand when she saw how close Russell was.

"Sera!" he shouted. "Wait."

There was no time for fancy tricks. She jumped onto the deck and pulled the boat out of gear, letting the wind blow it back enough to slacken the line so she could unwrap it from the deck cleat. Russell was almost close enough to leap onto the deck. It seemed incredibly strange to her that he was smiling. How fa-miliar his smile was, the wonderful million-dollar smile that she had never been able to resist.

She clicked the transmission into gear and pushed the fuel

lever forward. The diesel hesitated, picking up rpms slowly. She remembered Jake explaining that if you pushed the throttle forward too fast the prop would lose its grip on the water and spin like the milkshake machine at the pharmacy, kicking up a froth instead of pushing the boat.

As the boat moved away from the dock, the harbor swells caught her, quartering against the bow. Spray flew up against the windshield.

She glanced back over her shoulder at the dock. Russell was waving and shouting. With the wind ahead of her, she couldn't hear a word. The other man had already started back toward the Packard.

She tried taking the swells at different angles until she found a rhythm, turning into the swells to blunt the effect, then back to her course toward the mouth of the harbor. The fourth wave was bigger than the first three, and when it hit, she heard the heavy battery she had pulled out of the hatch slide across the cabin sole toward her. She jumped out of the way in time, but the battery slammed hard against the opposite side of the cabin. She knew how heavy the battery was, and remembered the warnings of what a spilled battery would do to the wiring of the boat. She looked around for a line to lash it and a fitting strong enough to hold the battery, wondering if she should slide it back into the bilge compartment.

The bow of the boat hit a heavy swell, and the loose battery careened back across the cabin sole, scraping the backs of her calves and smashing hard against the cabin door, splintering a panel. She tightened the wheel lock. She knew the boat wouldn't steer itself in the quartering sea, and might even turn broadside to the swells, but she needed both hands.

She tried to slide the battery back across the cabin sole, toward the bilge compartment. When the boat heeled toward the battery, it was too heavy to move; when the boat heeled back the other way, it took all of her strength to keep the battery from careening across the sole.

She held it in place by bracing her back against the steering pedestal and her feet against the battery, gradually easing the battery toward the hatch, reaching out with both hands to arrest it when the boat pitched back and the battery threatened to tip into the bilge. She saw moisture on top of the battery, and wondered if it was acid. Battery acid, she remembered Jake explaining, would destroy the wiring and maybe even the plumbing in the bilge. She grabbed at the hatch cover before it slid across the cabin sole and turned it sideways to make a ramp into the bilge compartment.

With the wheel locked, the boat had turned sideways to the swells, which was actually easier: the hull rocked in a regular motion, and she could time when to push the battery and when to hold it. The slick cabin sole, wet from water splashing in through the broken panel in the cabin door, made it easier to push the battery, but harder to hold or stop it.

Her first try missed. One end of the battery slid down her makeshift ramp, but a corner caught on the hatch and wedged. The boat pitched, and the hatch cover slid off the edge of the hatch into the bilge. *Damn!* she thought. The boat was broadside to the waves long enough that she wondered where she was heading. Wouldn't do much good to get the battery secure and run aground or smash into a dock.

"*I can do this!*" she shouted. With both legs braced against the hatch opening, she pulled the battery onto the bilge hatch and nestled it where it belonged. The hatch cover was caught between the two batteries, but another tug got it free. She jumped up, feeling the soreness in her legs from holding the heavy battery, and took the wheel.

The workboat was running straight across the harbor toward Brenton Cove. She missed the end of the long dock of the Yacht Club, but was aimed at a collection of moored yachts. Someone was shouting from the end of the Yacht Club dock. She couldn't make out what they were saying.

She loosened the wheel lock, brought the bow back into the waves and toward the open harbor mouth, and pushed the throttle foward. The boat pounded on the swells. The steering was rough, whipping her arms. Once or twice the wheel got away from her, and the spokes slammed into her forearms. But she was going home. At least they couldn't follow her. Even the Packard couldn't drive on water.

They had been running through the narrow streets for almost an hour.

Jake caught up with Alden as he was ducking into a sailors' bar off Thames Street. Jake had chased him up and down the narrow side streets of Newport, spotting then losing him, then spotting him again trying to hail a taxi. When he saw Jake, Alden ran from the taxi through a group of sailors lined up in front of a brothel, before he ducked into the bar. When Jake came in, Alden had his back turned toward the door. His tweed jacket and awkward hunched stance stood out like a bluefish in a barrel of bunker.

Alden was surprisingly docile. "This is outrageous," he said. "What do you think you're doing? Do you imagine for an instant that anyone would believe that I wasn't accosted by you? My God, with what's in that envelope, I should turn you in to the FBI. You realize who I am, I trust? And how ridiculous this will all sound?"

Jake dragged him to a phone booth, and dialed Langer's number with one hand while he held Alden's arm in a hammerlock behind his back with the other. No one on Thames Street was surprised to see one man dragging another man out of a bar.

While the phone rang, Jake lifted a wallet from the inside pocket of Alden's jacket, fine ostrich skin, silvery gray. Inside was a short stack of crisp new hundred-dollar bills and engraved business cards: "J. Bradford Alden, Ph.D. Department of Fine Art. Yale University."

"I thought better of Yale," Jake said.

"Look, I can explain," Alden said. "You didn't believe that bit of playacting, did you? I'm a tenured professor. What do I need with these silly games? It was a lark, part of a wager with a colleague. We do these high jinks all the time. I don't know who you are, have no idea what you're about. Let's call it quits and end this charade."

"Did you win the wager?"

"Really, that's all it was. I know nothing about this sort of nonsense."

There was no answer at Langer's numbers in Cambridge or

Annisquam. Jake knew there was no one he could hand Alden
to. The police would laugh, or lock Jake up instead. The Shore
Patrol on Thames Street, with their bright leggings and swinging
white sticks, were only interested in brawls and drunks. There
were Navy security police in Newport, and probably an FBI
office in Providence, or even Newport, but no one would know
what he was talking about. The more he tried to explain the
more he would sound like a lunatic. Even Langer hadn't believed enough to have a plan beyond "Call me."

He finally got an answer on the third call to Langer's Annisquam number. Langer was groggy. He had been napping. Jake
told him about Alden twice before he reacted.

"Yale?" said Langer. "I wouldn't have predicted a bad apple
in that barrel. They've got more people in this than we do."

The gray suits showed up in less than half an hour. Alden said
he was glad to see them, claiming that he had caught Jake with
purloined war games.

"What war games?" Jake said.

After the gray suits drove away with Alden in the backseat,
Jake called Langer again. This time Langer was wide awake and
excited.

"Your timing was quite fortuitous," he said. "I've just learned
that Washington and Tokyo are in a bit of an endgame. Their
side has presented demands that are virtually an ultimatum.
Both sides are doing the diplomatic dance for now, but war
seems inevitable, and sooner rather than later. It's not surprising
that their agent was desperate enough to mistake your sketches
for what they really need. I can't tell you how relieved we are
that their search got no further."

From the phone booth, Jake could see boats tugging at their
moorings. The sky was almost black, and a nasty chop roiled
the usually calm harbor. Jake pictured Sera on the deck of one
of the big yachts, eating canapés from a tray held by white-
gloved hands.

He walked slowly along the seawall. He wasn't even at the
head of the dock when he saw that the workboat was gone. One
dockline was still fastened to the dock.

Bernardinho? he wondered. No, the truck was gone. Bernardinho would never take the boat without talking to Jake. He had been at the yard longer than Jake, but he always thought of himself as an employee, always asked first. He would have closed the boat up and left it locked.

Only one other person knew where Jake kept the key. He told himself that Sera wouldn't have taken it unless she needed it. It was a comforting thought.

The breeze was piping up. Even in the harbor the chop was steep, with breaking whitecaps. Outside, with the clouds covering the moon, low visibility, crossing seas, and an onshore breeze, it would be rough conditions, especially for someone alone. *Sera can handle a boat*, he told himself.

Across the harbor, in Brenton Cove, a few boats that were normally tied at docks had been towed out to empty moorings. The spot where the big mahogany commuter usually rode was empty. Why would anyone take a boat like that out on a night like this?

He looked beyond the fleet, toward the mouth of the harbor, where rolling seas from outside were breaking into a confused chop. From the corner of his eye, at the edge of the fleet, he saw a heavy wake as a boat drove fast and hard through the confused chop. Under the darkening sky it was hard to make out the color or even the shape of the hull, until the boat made a fast turn into the channel, kicking up a rooster tail. Even at that distance, the symmetric rooster tail was unmistakable. Only one man built boats that would make a cut like that into rough seas.

He felt a flash of anger rising. He tried to remind himself that war was around the corner. The world was going to turn topsy-turvey. Against all odds, he had found the man looking for war games. How much did one broken heart matter anyway?

The Brenton Reef lightship stood out under an incredibly beautiful sky, deep gray, almost black above, luminescent below. Sera tried to remember what it meant. She knew some skies, like the greasy gray of a northeaster and the copper-colored sky that her father and other fishermen had seen before the big hurricane in '38. She knew the dark sky above on a fall evening meant a blow, but she wasn't sure which direction. She wished Jake was there. *No*, said the second thought. She was glad to be alone. And glad she was busy enough not to have to think.

Open seas hit her even before she rounded Point Judith. As the mouth of the harbor widened, she felt a cross chop bouncing the hull. "Old waves and new wind" was Jake's expression. Inside the harbor, the swells and wind had been westerly or slightly northwesterly. Outside, the wind was blowing hard from the southwest, knocking the tops off the swells that were still rolling from the west and northwest.

She tried to find a comfortable course, but the pitching motion of the workboat had become rough. The side door to the cabin blew open. She saw that the collision with the loose battery had broken the bottom hinge. She lashed it shut with one of the decklines, but enough water had come in to slosh on the cabin sole. When the boat settled down, she told herself, she would try the bilge pump.

She looked around the cabin sole and saw the duffel bag. One side was wet from the sloshing water.

She tightened the wheel brake and picked up the bag. The papers inside were still dry, but as a precaution, she wrapped the papers in wax paper from the galley drawer, and rolled the whole bundle up in an oilskin from the locker.

She put another oilskin on herself, and grabbed a sou'wester, tying the strap under her chin. She remembered when she was little and would put on her father's sou'wester and he would tell stories of the days on the banks. The sou'wester was black, and she remembered the superstitions that for her father had been stronger than law: never wear a black sou'wester, never take a dull knife on board, never whistle on a boat. She wondered if Jake had put a coin under the mast of the boat.

She loosened the wheel brake and tried to find a course through the seas. The motion as the boat climbed the waves was so violent she was afraid the prop would come out of the water. She remembered the routine Jake had once taught her: drop the revs down when the prop—what was the word?— *cavitates*. She put one hand on the wheel and one on the throttle and experimented. It took a few waves before she got the timing right. Once she did, she could thread her way through the waves. The routine was challenging enough to keep her mind off everything else. Salt spray covered the windshield. She waited for a lull to use her throttle hand to move the windshield wiper enough to clear a window so she could see the oncoming seas.

If it's like this here, behind the point, she wondered, what will it be like outside? She thought of turning in around Point Judith, through the Harbor of Refuge, maybe trying to wend up the channel to Galilee or Jerusalem. There would be fishermen there who would offer a line for a workboat, and she could find a telephone and call someone in the village. She even had cousins who fished out of Galilee. Then she looked at the bundle of papers, and remembered the warnings she had seen on the pages, Russell's grip on the bag when he took it from the car, and the look in his eyes as he watched her motor away from the dock.

She pictured his smile, the overconfident grin that he assumed would melt her and anyone he met. No, she told herself, she wouldn't go into a harbor. She needed to do this herself, to be alone on the open water. She needed the waves and wind to purge her of Russell and Raymond and that whole horrible world of Newport. It would be easy to throw the papers overboard. No one would ever see them again. But she wouldn't be free of Russell.

From watching the bearing to points on the shore, she knew she was making little headway. Am I steering that badly? she wondered. Or is this all the workboat can do? She concentrated and learned that she could thread her way through the seas by steering into the worst of them, easing back on the throttle when the bow dipped down at the crest and the prop would start to come out of the water. It was exhausting, but by concentrating she had the boat under control. She remembered Russell's amazement when she first drove his boat. What was so amazing? she thought. I'd like to see him handle these seas.

She knew the seas would be worse when she rounded Point Judith. They would have the open fetch of the sea to build up, and in the shallow water near the shore, the long swells would become ugly and steep. The quartering wind would blow the tops off the waves, making it harder to steer or hold a course. She glanced at the compass and then remembered a trick Jake had taught her on the sailboat: watching the spray off the top of the waves would tell her the true wind direction without having to estimate from the apparent wind and the speed and direction of the boat.

Once she rounded Point Judith the wind would be on the beam, blowing the boat toward the shore and rolling the boat with each wave. She watched the spray come through the broken cabin door as water from a breaking sea drained slowly through the deck scuppers.

She tried to imagine Russell out there, tried to picture him on a ship at sea. He was a Navy officer, yet she couldn't see him fighting seas and wind. She couldn't imagine him pumping the bilge or lashing the wheel to secure the loose battery.

The thought was cut short. She felt a sudden slam of wind. A breaking wave pitched the bow wildly off to the right. Before she could ask herself what had happened, she realized that she had cleared Point Judith. The motion of the boat was wilder than she had imagined. She had to steer her way up the face of each wave as if she were climbing up a child's slide at the park, jam the throttle back before she got to the top of the wave, and then push it foward again as the stern settled and the prop could finally bite solid water. After only a few waves her arms ached.

Her feet slipped on the soaked cabin sole, and she had to brace herself just to stand at the wheel. Through the broken doorway she saw the deck scupper. It was still clear, with water from the deck draining. Why was there so much water on the cabin sole? she wondered.

Holding the wheel with one hand, she lifted the bilge hatch. The water was halfway up the sides of the batteries. *A leak?* She remembered Johnny Cravinho's long gray face at the dance in the village, and the motion of his hand across his knees to show how deep the water was. She guessed the bilgewater would come to her ankles. She found the pump handle, fitted it to the pump, and pumped with her left hand while she steered with her right. The first strokes were easy, until the pump was fully primed. Then each stroke took strength. Her arm ached and she looked foward to what had been the exhausting battle of the wheel and throttle as a relief.

She had no idea how long it took to pump the bilge down. The pump got ahead of the water, and she decided it probably wasn't a leak, just water sloshing across the cabin sole through the broken door. When she put the handle back in the clip, she suddenly realized that she was sailing in the dark. No lights in the cabin and no running lights. She reached over to the panel and flicked the switches. Nothing happened. She tried the master switch, then the individual switches again. The wiring must have gotten wet or shorted, she thought.

It had started to rain, although with the spray flying and the rain blowing in horizontal sheets it was hard to distinguish rain from the froth off the tops of the waves. The visibility had dropped. She couldn't see the light at Point Judith anymore. To a coastal steamer or a dragger she would be invisible without running lights; they would run over her before they saw her. She knew there was a swinging kerosene lamp on the bulkhead, and emergency kerosene running lights and a tin of kerosene somewhere, but she wasn't sure she could keep a match burning long enough to get the lights working.

At least the engine was fine. She remembered Jake's explanation that once a diesel was started, it didn't need anything except fuel, clean air, and a clear exhaust. It would run underwater as long as there was fuel and clean air. As long as the engine didn't stop, she was fine.

She remembered that the main tank had only been half-full. The rest of the fuel was in two spare cans lashed behind the cabin. She would have to go out on the deck to fill the tank. The boat was handling the seas fine as long as she was on the wheel and throttle, but what would happen if she locked the wheel to go on deck? At least for now there was plenty of fuel. What about air?

She craned around, trying to get a look through the ports on the sides of the cabin. The air intake, on the cabin top, was as high as anything except the short mast and boom for the steadying sail.

Sail. Why didn't I think of that? In a beam sea, the sail would hold the boat at a steady angle of heel. Might even add a little speed. It would certainly make the steering easier. If she trimmed the sail right, she could probably get the boat to hold a course long enough to fill the fuel tank.

She locked the wheel and tied one end of a dockline around her waist in a bowline, lashing the other end to the narrow ladder on the side of the cabin. A few lights from the Rhode Island shore were visible off to the right, appearing and disappearing through the seas and spray. When she looked to the south, the sea was a maelstrom of churning froth, shorter waves breaking between the big swells, the tops of waves blowing off in stinging salt spray that mixed with the sheets of rain. The raw power of the storm was fascinating and beautiful enough that for a moment she held onto the ladder, staring into the wind, letting the soaking spray drench her as if it were a cleansing shower.

Hoisting the steadying sail was easier than she thought it would be. Jake had rigged the halyard so it could be hoisted and sheeted from the top of the ladder, without climbing up onto the cabin top. All she had to do was to remove the sail cover and toss it below, untie four sail ties, then hoist the halyard. The sail shook violently—she was afraid it would rip to pieces—until she trimmed in the sheet, pulling the boom down and in at the same time.

The motion of the boat immediately steadied. She eased the sheet just enough to lessen the angle of heel, then came down the ladder on the leeward side and for a moment enjoyed the steadiness of the deck under her feet, and the respite from the rain and wind. Still holding onto the ladder, she looked back toward Point Judith and Newport.

The sky was lighter behind her. The seas were confused, and the blowing rain and froth made it hard to see even the hint of a horizon. But with her night vision intact, she tried the trick Jake had taught her, using peripheral vision. She began to pick up what she thought were lights on shore. She concentrated and realized that it wasn't shore lights but running lights, one red and one green. They disappeared and reappeared with each set of seas. It was either a big ship, or close.

She thought again about putting out emergency lights on the workboat, to make sure they could see her. Then she wondered, what if it wasn't a ship? But if it wasn't, what other small boat would be out there?

29

S he couldn't stop thinking about the other boat.

Who would be out there at night? The draggers who were close enough had come in before the storm. She had seen them doubling lines at the wharf in Newport. The swordfishermen in Galilee and Jerusalem and Stonington would do the same, and the bigger trawlers would stay offshore until the weather blew through. No one was foolish enough to risk a boat along the shore in bad weather. The last thought made her smile.

With the steadying sail up, Jake's workboat was much easier to steer. She found herself handling the helm the way she would steer a sailboat upwind, using the wheel to keep the sail full and the angle of heel steady. It felt good to know that she had handled the situation. She remembered how Russell had congratulated her effusively when she did something well, like when she hit a clay pigeon or sailed a boat in a breeze.

The last two times she had looked for the running lights behind her she hadn't seen them. That didn't make sense. From the position of the lights, behind her and shoreward, she knew the boat was going the same direction she was, parallel to the Rhode Island coast. There was nowhere they could turn in after the Harbor of Refuge at Point Judith. The visibility was no worse than it had been before. The wind was still blowing spray off only the occasional tops of the waves, but the rain had mostly stopped. What could have happened to the other boat?

The windshield of the workboat was coated with salt spray; even the windshield wiper wouldn't clear it. She went on deck and with her back to the wind scanned from north to east, using her peripheral vision. She could only scan a short stretch of horizon before she felt the boat start to veer off course. When the sail started to luff, she would go inside to tweak the wheel back onto course. She was afraid to rip the sail in the heavy wind.

She didn't see any sign of the other boat. It had to be there, she told herself. She checked the compass to make sure of her own course. She had to look twice before she believed what she saw.

"That was stupid!" she said out loud.

She was making a heading of 190°, almost due south. The wind had swung to the south, and in trying to keep the steadying sail full, she had veered with the wind, taking herself offshore instead of along the coast. How long had she been going south? she wondered. She had no way of guessing how far offshore she was.

That explained what had happened to the lights. The other boat hadn't gone astray. She had.

She knew she should study a chart, but with no markers or ranges visible, what good would it do her? Her plan had been to skirt the Rhode Island shore, keeping far enough offshore to stay out of trouble. Now she had no choice but to turn north, to run in toward the shore, hoping she spotted a light or mark before she got too close.

When she brought the helm around, the boat heeled sharply. She turned back upwind, lashed the wheel, and climbed out through the broken doorway to ease the sheet on the steadying sail.

The motion of the boat was rough, and she had to duck her head when she eased the sheet and the boom ran out. She guessed how far to ease the sheet, cleated it, and ducked back into the cabin to take the helm.

As she bore off toward the shore a second time, the boat leveled off, no longer heeling from the wind on the sheeted-in sail. She thought her speed picked up too, as she ran with the wind on her quarter. But the steadying sail no longer damped the motion of the boat, and every third or fourth sea broke over the stern quarter, sloshing up the deck alongside the cabin and through the broken door onto the cabin sole.

She remembered to pump the bilge, and scanned the horizon, searching for the running light. She wasn't afraid of a collision. As long as she could see only one light the other boat would cross her course. If anything, the other boat was likely to be on course for Fishers Island Sound and the Watch Hill Passage. If she caught up with them, she could follow them home.

A few times she thought she saw a flash of red low on the water, but with the boat pitching and the spray on the window and water dripping from her hair into her eyes, she couldn't be sure.

Her arms ached from fighting the helm. At least the stern stayed in the water so she didn't have to work the throttle with each wave, but she could feel the exhaustion creeping up on her. Her legs were tired from bracing herself at the helm, and her arms were so heavy from fighting the wheel she could hardly lift them. She was tired enough to be mesmerized by the steady rolls of the seas. She told herself that looking for the other boat was a way to stay awake.

The wind was cleaner and steadier than an hour before, still what Jake would call a "double reef breeze." The howling fury and blowing spume of earlier had abated, but the seas were sloppy as the wind chopped across the direction of the waves. She ventured a look behind her, through the open cabin door on the portside. The sky was starting to clear, and she caught glimpses of an almost full moon. She stared at the streaks of moonlight on the wavetops until the boat pitched hard in a sea, and she had to fight the helm.

When she looked ahead again, there was a red running light in the clear off her starboard bow. The light dipped below the waves, disappearing and reappearing in the seas. A moment later she saw two lights, red on the right, green on the left. She glanced down at her hands, remembering the freckle on the back of her left hand, then craned to look at the lightboards mounted on either side of the cabin of the workboat for a check to make sure which color was on which side. Red was port, green starboard. It meant the other boat was coming straight at her.

She reached for the switch for the running lights, flipping it twice, but the power was still dead. She tried to remember where Jake kept the kerosene and matches. No matter, she thought. With the moon behind her, the other boat would see her without running lights. Especially with the steadying sail up, she would be silouetted against the moonlight. She looked over at the plunger of the foghorn, thinking that if they were too close she could pump the handle.

When she looked ahead, the running lights were brighter. They still appeared and disappeared behind the waves, but they were much closer. The other boat was pitching wildly in the seas, driving head-on into the wind, catching the swells just off the bow so it fought each wave. She tried to picture what kind of boat it could be. If the lights were low enough to drop behind the waves, it wasn't a steamer or ferry. Even the lights of a dragger wouldn't drop that much in the seas. What was a small boat doing out there? Anyone who took a small boat out in that weather was crazy. She laughed out loud. It felt good to be crazy, to be on her own.

When she looked again, she missed the running lights. Probably in the trough of a wave, she thought. As her eyes scanned the horizon, she glimpsed a bright flashing white light, almost dead ahead. She counted the flashes and knew it was Watch Hill. Almost home, she thought.

Then she saw the running lights again, dancing wildly now, darting from side to side, dipping and rising with each wave, as if the other boat were a bobbing cork, or maybe out of control. She glanced in the direction of Watch Hill, then back at the running lights. This time she could see a hull between the lights. Low, with no superstructure. The boat was pounding hard, leaping off the waves, crashing hard on the swells. She had never seen anything like it. She couldn't hear the boat—it was still downwind—but she could imagine the engines it would take to drive a boat like that.

It was only then that she realized it had to be Russell. There

was no other boat like that, and no one else who drove a boat
like that. She remembered the first night they had gone out into
Fishers Island Sound, when he gave her the wheel and the throttle, the sudden rush of escape and freedom that had so over-
whelmed her. Watching the boat touch the wavetops, she
thought of the times he had kissed her, the incredible sensation
of dancing with him, feeling their bodies touch and then slip
apart.

She glanced down at the duffel bag on the cabin sole,
wrapped in an oilskin slicker, and wondered: was he chasing her,
or the papers?

Sera turned toward Watch Hill and tapped the throttle forward. The steadying sail luffed as the wind came around to
slightly ahead of the beam. She lashed the wheel and went out
through the cabin door to tighten the sheet. From the deck, she
could see the low outline of the other boat as it skimmed over
waves. There was no mistaking it.

It surprised her to see how close she had come to Watch Hill
Passage. She tried to remember the ranges that her father had
once taught her. His favorite was Lantern Hill, where the face
of silica from the mining glistened in sunlight.

She remembered the hours she had spent watching boats go
in and out of the tricky passage. When she first went through
on a boat, it amazed her that day and night, fair weather and
foul, even through the pea soup fogs that seemed to gather there
like flies at a bait barrel, the boats uncannily picked their way
through the rocks. Jake explained that each fishermen had his
own trick, like holding the church steeple at a certain bearing.

When she looked back to starboard, the other boat wasn't
there.

Then she heard the engines coming up from behind. The
deep-throated roar was as familiar as the powerful lines and
peaked skylight ahead of the open cockpit. The boat came up
fast on her port quarter, slightly to windward, then slipped into
a trough, so she couldn't see the cockpit, only the peaked skylight, standing proud. The memory of the skylight hit hard.

A moment later the mahogany boat rose on the crest of a

following wave. Russell was at the wheel, bareheaded, wearing a wet oilskin slicker that glistened in the moonlight. She remembered how easily the big boat handled at speed; when she first tried the helm it had been almost too responsive.

On the starboard side of the cockpit, closer to her, another man was holding the frame of the windshield with one hand and a length of line in the other. He had a sou'wester tied under his chin, covering much of his face, but his fastidious manner, the way he held the line away from himself, told her it was Raymond. She felt a fluttering luff of the steadying sail, and realized that she had instinctively turned the wheel away. Why? she asked herself. Was she that afraid of what would happen if they touched?

Raymond looked like he was about to shout to her. Suddenly he lost his balance when Russell pulled back on the throttle. He grabbed for the windscreen and fell awkwardly back into the cockpit. With the roar of the engines, now to windward of her, she wouldn't have heard a word he said anyway. The boat sped up and turned to windward for another pass. She saw Russell handling the wheel easily, as if riding through the fifteen-foot seas were fun.

On the second pass, the boat came closer. This time Raymond held what looked like a pistol in his right hand as he stood on the passenger seat. He waved it in what was supposed to be a threatening gesture. His balance was unsure, and the pistol flailed in the air. When they were close alongside, Sera could make out that it was a flare pistol. She remembered when Paul used to get into trouble for stealing the flare pistol from their father's boat and shooting it off at the beach on the Fourth of July. For all Raymond's silliness as he stood at the rail and shouted words she couldn't hear over the roar of the engines, she admired how easily Russell steered the big mahogany boat, keeping exactly parallel to her and only a few feet away, even as the waves and wind hammered the two boats, driving them in opposite directions. She remembered how hard the workboat had been to handle before she got the steadying sail up, and knew the powerful mahogany boat would be even more squirrelly when it was throttled down. Jake had once explained that the rudders of fast boats were deliberately small, so they wouldn't oversteer at high speed; the small rudders made them uncontrollable at slow speeds. In that wind and with those seas, it would be impossible to bring any two boats alongside one another. The fishermen told stories about how impossible rescues were in a big seaway: trying to bring another boat alongside risked both boats.

Russell speeded up and went around in a third circle. Sera looked up again toward Watch Hill. She could see the Rhode Island shore clearly now. She strained to make out the low outline of Fishers Island through the salt-covered window. If she could see the shore, would a lookout at the Coast Guard station see her? she wondered. Why would they look for small boats on a night like that? It wasn't like watching for a load of Prohibition liquor sneaking inshore in bad weather.

The mahogany boat came around for a third pass. This time, it was steering erratically, riding up the back of a wave, then oversteering and turning abeam to the next wave. The engines shrieked as the boat pitched over the top of a wave and the props came out of the water. Russell was standing on the starboard seat, holding the windshield frame with one hand. Water streaked down his face. The wind blew his hair around his face.

The bow of the mahogany boat swerved hard toward the stern quarter of the workboat, lifting on a wave crest so that for a moment it looked as if it were hanging over the toerail of the workboat, ready to land on the deck.

Sera watched the sea drop down and back. She felt a tinge of pride that she understood that Raymond, at the helm, hadn't compensated for the wind. If he didn't know enough to do that, how was he ever going to steer that boat?

An instant later the boat was alongside her. Russell leaned toward the workboat, reaching out with his free hand. He was almost close enough to touch. She watched him brush the hair back from his face. His eyes caught hers, and held her in his gaze. With the moonlight glinting off his hair, he was the incredibly beautiful man she remembered from a hundred moments.

Russell waited calmly, judging the distance between the two

boats. He didn't shout, just held her in his gaze and smiled. She was amazed. The smile was exactly as she remembered, as if they were alone and carefree, the only people in the world. As the boats and seas and wind and the roar of the engines and the flutter of the luffing sail flooded back into her eyes and ears, Russell's smile suddenly seemed unreal, a gesture that refused to see the world, a flotsam of false emotion blithely ignorant of the maelstrom around them.

A wave came up under the workboat, and she watched Russell drop below the rail of the rising workboat. There was a soft crunch: she wasn't sure whether she heard it over the roar of the engines on the mahogany boat, or felt it through her legs from the cabin sole. A moment later she felt a second tap, further aft. She thought of turning the wheel, but knew the heavy workboat would respond too slowly to make a difference. Even with the deafening roar of the engines, she could feel the steadying sail luff. She instinctively backed the wheel to keep the sail full.

As the wave passed, the workboat dropped again. She watched the mahogany hull coming up alongside. It took her a moment to realize that Russell wasn't there. She looked aft, wondering if he had somehow leapt onto the workboat. He wasn't on the workboat, but when she looked back at the mahogany boat she saw that he had rolled over the edge, probably to avoid being crushed when the boats bumped. He was improbably holding on to a cleat on the rail and hugging the slick planking of the flared side.

She knew he couldn't hold on for long. She glanced at the life ring on the side of the wheelhouse and wondered, how would she turn back in those seas? She had heard stories of how impossible it was to fish a man from a rough sea before he was crushed or drowned. And that was without a madman who didn't know how to steer charging around in an overpowered speedboat.

The big mahogany boat turned wildly away from her, so she could no longer see Russell on the side. The turn threw up a rooster tail of spray as the stern pitched up on a sea until the props cavitated and the engines screamed in protest. She wasn't sure the boat would recover, but it turned back in an equally violent motion, throwing another rooster tail of spray until the stern was facing the wind. Miraculously, Russell was still holding on to the side, his arms and legs spread out as if he were trying to hug the planks. She waited for Raymond to find a course, to bring the helm back, but he seemed to panic. Then she realized that he was trying to cross in front of her.

She yanked back the throttle of the workboat and slammed the transmission into reverse, cringing as she heard the gears grate and then a loud clunk as the shifter found its detent.

In front of her, the mahogany boat loomed, rising above the bow of the workboat. She tried to decide whether it was better to put her helm hard to starboard or port, and knew it would make no difference. A wave rose under the bow of the workboat and she could no longer see the mahogany boat. *Maybe they will cross safely in front*, she thought.

For a long moment the workboat hung in the air, as if she had caught a strange syncopated wave that broke the usual rhythm of three small waves, then a big one. The sound of the engines on the other boat dropped in pitch and seemed to fade, as if the boat were far away. She felt the bow of the workboat start to drop, and looked at the horizon to confirm the sensation.

The first sound was like a giant foot coming down on the treads of a staircase. The bow of the workboat hesitated in its fall before she heard a louder crunch, a scream of heavy wood beams against splintering planking. The protests of the wood pierced even the roar of the engines and the wind.

The workboat bounced like Jake's truck on a bumpy road, pitching forward in jerks. She felt the motion in her legs, weird, staccato jolts that didn't belong on a boat. Holding onto the wheel for balance, she leaned out one side of the wheelhouse, then the other, looking ahead and to starboard, expecting to see the other boat emerge. It was only after the bumping stopped, and she left the wheel and looked aft past the wheelhouse that she finally saw what was left of the mahogany boat.

One, maybe both engines of the other boat were still racing, the ungoverned whine rising in pitch until it became the shriek of metal grating against metal. Then the shriek stopped. The mahogany boat was broken; the crushing destruction of the heavy wooden keel of the workboat was already hidden underwater as the two ends of the mahogany boat pitched up at impossible angles. For a moment Sera thought it was two boats, one sinking by the stern, the other sinking by the bow. The varnished planking glistened in the moonlight, and a slick of oil and fuel spread on the water. She remembered an expression about throwing oil on roiled seas, and in fact the waves seemed suddenly damped.

She felt a swell come up under the workboat, and heard the steadying sail flap. She tried to turn the helm, but the boat wouldn't answer. She looked down and realized that she was still in reverse, with the engine barely idling. She shifted the lever forward, waited for the transmission to click, and brought the throttle up. She felt the prop turning, and the boat start to move away. When she tried the wheel again, it spun too easily. She turned it all the way to the stops, from one side to the other. There was no response.

She didn't know whether it was the rudder or the steering gear, but she remembered Jake once explaining the emergency helm. She went out on deck and found the tiller secure in the clips along the rail aft. It was heavy, but fit easily into the slot at the head of the rudder. She pushed it in, dropped the pin into place to hold it, and steered the boat as if it were a sailboat. The sail was luffing, the sound suddenly loud with the noise of the big engines gone.

She thought she heard a voice, but when she scanned over the wreckage of the mahogany boat, all she could see was the stern section going under, forming a whirl like the drain of a bathtub. Beyond the whirl, the iridescent slick of oil and gas spread over the surface. The bow section still pointed up at a crazy angle, the skylights popped open as if someone were letting in air and light. She tried to guess where Russell would be, and cringed when she realized that his handhold had been in the section of hull that the workboat had crushed.

The luffing of the sail seemed like it would tear the workboat apart. She lashed the tiller to a padeye on the deck and went forward to the ladder for the sheet. She was deciding whether to sheet it tight or maybe try to lower the halyard when from the corner of her eye she caught a glimpse of what looked like an arm reaching up from the cockpit of the mahogany boat. She let go of the sheet, and climbed around the wheelhouse. She saw an orange oilskin before the horizon was filled with a flash. She instinctively closed her eyes, but even through her eyelids, the flash was as bright as the sun. An instant later she found herself lying on the deck, looking straight up. She couldn't tell whether the crash she had heard was her hitting the wheel-house, or an explosion. She squeezed her hands into fists, and reached for one leg then the other to make sure she was all right.

A moment later the workboat righted itself. A wave of searing heat, dry and acrid, hit her. She recoiled, instinctively covering her face. When she forced her eyes open again, the fireball was gone. She smelled burning fuel. Swirls of black smoke rose from the water.

She got to her feet and took heavy steps, misestimating the distance and direction like a drunk man until she found her footing. The motion of the boat, so familiar for so long, suddenly seemed unpredictable. Her head ached. She tore off the sou'wester and found a stickiness at the back of her head. Oil? she wondered. Fuel? She held on to the side of the cabin, trying to focus on the chaos of the charts, books, and tools that had come loose when the boat went over on her beam end. Shapes were moving too fast. She couldn't tell whether she was dizzy or the boat was whirling. She closed her eyes and tasted her fingertips. It wasn't oil. She blinked hard, and held her fingers up. Even in the dim light, they were the bright red of blood.

30

Dense gray smoke rose from the water. Sera remembered when Paul played war games with his toy boats, putting matchstick men into the boats and bombing them with firecrackers. After the firecrackers went off, they found no trace of the matchstick men. It was a superstition in the village never to talk about gasoline explosions on boats. An explosion was worse than a drowning or an accident with equipment. When the vapors from a ruptured fuel tank exploded, all that would be left was bits of wood and paper and rubber, scraps of what had once been a boat. There would be no bodies, at least nothing they could ever show in a coffin.

She felt her head again. It was still sticky, but the bleeding had stopped. Ahead of her she could see lights from the towns on the shore. She felt bruises on her legs and shoulders, but everything moved, enough to secure the tiller, climb the ladder to the cabin top, and finish lowering the steadying sail. It amazed her that the sail wasn't torn, and that the sail ties were right where she had put them, on a hook above the cabin door. She remembered that she had seen Jake secure the ties, making sure he would find them when he needed them. He was like that.

From the cabin top she had a good view of the wreckage. The water seemed strangely calm, cluttered with the flotsam of bits of mahogany and oak. It was worse than the stories her father had told her, worse even than Paul's toy boats after the firecrackers. Nothing looked like a boat. Only scraps of charred wood, an occasional glint of varnish from a scrap of planking, and the swirl of the oil slick. Patches of water were on fire. She motored around the wreckage in a slow circle, close enough to have to dodge flotsam.

In the smoke and roiled water, it was hard to make sense of what she saw. Twice she thought she saw something move, but a moment later she decided the swirls of oil and drifting smoke had been playing tricks with her eyes.

The second time around she thought she saw part of a slicker floating to the surface. She kept the helm over and circled a third time. People don't just disappear, she told herself. The oil slick had already started to break up, and the flickers of flame on the water had burned out. She started to go around a fourth time, and realized that she wasn't thinking, that she was steering the boat mechanically. *They're gone*, she told herself. *Gone*.

It was after she sat down on the rail, pushing the tiller away with her leg and reaching back to feel her head, that she saw something moving in the water. She stared at the spot, trying to make sure whether it was real or her eyes tricking her. She blinked, and when she opened her eyes Russell was floating alongside the workboat, his face barely above the water. Dull brown-gray oil streaked his face, but his hair glistened in the early light. She couldn't tell whether he was alive.

She reached out toward him, leaning over the rail. Her fingers almost touched his sleeve, but the workboat was moving fast and the freeboard was high. She made a stabbing reach, just touching his sleeve. She had to catch her balance before she slipped overboard.

With one hand on the tiller, she brought the boat around in a tight circle, shifting to neutral, hoping she could drift close. She remembered Jake explaining how hard it was to recover a person who fell overboard, how even two or three strong men couldn't pull a man in wet clothes over a rail unless they used a tackle from a boom swung out.

The workboat bore down on the floating slicker. She slammed the tiller over hard. Even with the scant headway she was making, the boat overcorrected. She pulled the tiller back, but by then the boat had lost momentum from the hard turns. She tried sculling the tiller to force the workboat the last few feet until she could reach out and touch the slicker.

"Russell! Can you hear me?" The boat started to drift away again. She leaned so far that she was tottering on the lifelines. The slicker in the water was covered with oil and hard to grasp.

"Russell?"

She finally got the oilskin in her fingertips and pulled toward the boat. A moment later she had his wrist in her fingers.

He looked up at her. His eyebrows were singed, and his face was smeared with oil. She couldn't believe that he looked like he was smiling.

She tugged on the wrist, but she could hardly lift his arm from the water. The boat heeled when she pulled. She held on with one hand, and with her other hand reached a length of dockline. *Bowline*, she thought. She remembered the time Jake had taught her to tie a bowline with one hand. "Why would I ever need to do it with one hand?" she had asked him. The ditty came back to her. *The rabbit comes up the hole, runs around the tree, then back down the hole.* She slipped the bowline off her waist and lowered it over Russell, threading his arm through, leaning precariously to work the loop down under his arms. She silently prayed for him to stay in the loop.

She loosened the sheet for the steadying sail, swung the short boom out over the rail, unreeved the sheet, and ran the dockline through the block at the end of the boom. Then she started to haul on the free end of the line.

The first few lengths weren't too hard, but once the slack was gone and Russell's shoulders were clear of the water, it was dead weight.

"*Come on!*" she shouted. "*Damn it, come on!*" She leaned her back into the line and began to gain lengths as the boat rolled toward Russell. *I can get one man aboard*, she told herself. She remembered her father's stories of men singing special songs while they hauled in miles of drop lines. *I can do this!*

She leaned back, putting all of her weight on the line again. It still wouldn't budge. "*Come on!*" she shouted again. "*Damn it, come on!*"

She looked up, exhausted, and realized that she had pulled

the bowline all the way up to the block in the boom. Russell's legs were still in the water, but his body was clear. She tied the free end of the dockline off and reached out to swing the boom inboard. It came easily, and with both hands around Russell's waist she swung him aboard. When she uncleated the line, he fell hard to the deck.

"Russell!" She cradled his head in her arms, peeled away the oilskin that had bunched up around his head, and brushed the hair away from his face. His eyes were open and looking at her. She said his name again and felt his cheeks and put her cheek close to his lips, hoping to feel his breath. It was impossible to tell whether he was responding at all.

"Russell!" She shook him, gently at first, then harder. She felt him move, not strong, but a twitch. She cradled his head and brushed the hair away from his face again. "Can you hear me?" she said.

Suddenly, he smiled, the lips parting until she could see a row of teeth. For an instant his eyes were glued on her, as if she were the only person in the world.

"Why, Russell? Why?"

She held his head gently, never taking her eyes off his. His eyes stayed open, the smile serene, as he went limp, and she knew he was dead.

The workboat wallowed in the leftover swells.

She didn't know how long it had been when she forced herself back to the helm, flicked the transmission into forward, and turned toward Watch Hill Passage. Even in a calm sea, she knew, Watch Hill Passage was tricky. She remembered what the fishermen said: *While the Good Lord was cutting that channel through Watch Hill Reef, the devil was busy behind his back, piling up rocks and trouble on all sides.* And she was planning to go through in the leftover slop from a storm, with only an emergency helm to steer the workboat.

She picked up a few markers, but the flood current was strong and she raced past the markers before she could identify them. She saw swirls in the water to her left, and instinctively pulled the helm over. When the boat didn't respond, she ran up to the wheelhouse and tapped the throttle forward. The engine picked up rpms, and the workboat surged through the passage, water swirling around the submerged rocks on either side. She tried to remember the tricks of lining up the marker lights, but found herself steering by instinct, as if from some atavistic memory. Off the starboard side of the workboat, waves broke over the underwater reef.

She had no idea how long it was before the surface was suddenly calm. She had thought about nothing but steering the boat, and now suddenly everything came flooding back. She remembered how her father used to say that he came home from every fishing trip in steps: The first was the moment when they decided they had a "trip" and hauled in the net for the last time. The second was when they came through the passage and were no longer at sea. Then there was the moment when they tied up at the wharf and shut down the engine. And finally came the only moment she remembered, when her father's footfalls on the front steps told her he was home.

As she motored past the commercial dock, she saw sleepy men loading ice and fuel in the dim early morning light. No one paid attention to the workboat. She wondered if anyone had heard the explosion or seen the flash. On the water it had been deafening and blinding. But the fishermen lived away from the dock, back in the crowded streets of the village. They came home bone tired. At sea they might turn in for watch sleep, with one ear tuned to the slightest change in the rumble of the engine or sounds of the boat moving through seas. Ashore, with no sea sounds to monitor, they fell into a dead sleep until it was time for another day of fishing. That's why they hadn't heard.

As she turned around the backside of the dock at the boatyard, she looked around the workboat. The deck was was filthy, the cabin a mess, the door smashed, the steering broken, the bottom scraped at least, the topsides smeared with oil slicks. And she had a body aboard.

She tried to remember everything: current, wind, which way the prop would twist the the stern of the boat. Her head hurt, her arms and legs ached, and she was so tired she had to tell her arms what to do: *Helm right! More! Straighten out!* She ran forward and eased the transmission into neutral, then realized she wasn't close enough and flicked the boat into gear to steer around in a loop for another approach. The second time she was too close. She pushed the helm over, but the rail of the workboat hit a piling, hard enough for her to lose her footing. That was all she remembered.

Sera woke up groggy. When she opened her eyes she recognized the inside of Jake's cabin. She was on the cot. Jake was sitting next to her on a straightbacked chair.

"Jake? Oooh." Her head ached. She tried to sit up, but was too dizzy. She felt his hands catching her. "I—"

She drifted off again. When she opened her eyes a second time, Jake was holding a mug of hot tea. He helped her sit up.

"Sip it slowly," he said. "You took a good knock."

"Did you find . . . ?"

"Yes. I'm sorry."

"Sorry? It's not the right word. Not for you. Maybe for me." She closed her eyes hard for a moment, turning her head away. "He . . . I don't know how to explain it. He was like a child: smart, and handsome and rich and good at anything he tried, but he didn't know right from wrong. I guess I didn't either. Is your boat okay?"

"The workboat is fine. What happened to the other boat?"

Sera sipped the tea. She closed her eyes for a moment and remembered. "It was horrible. That man was steering—Raymond. He cut across in front of the workboat. There was nothing I could do."

"Willy Estes went out in a lobster boat and brought in a few pieces. The Coast Guard is out there now. Some of the fishermen agreed to drag for bodies, but the way the tide runs in the passage, it could be weeks before they find anything. Was anyone else on the boat?"

"Just Russell and Raymond. Did you find a package of papers? I wrapped it up in oilskins."

Jake pointed to the other room.

"Do you know what they are?"

Jake nodded. "I think so."

"They're important, aren't they?"

"How did you get them?"

She sat up, adjusting a pillow behind her, and took another sip of tea. "That's a long story."

She reached back behind her head and found that there was no stickiness. Her neck felt clean. She looked down at her arms and legs. They had been washed clean. She was wearing one of Jake's blue workshirts.

She looked at Jake's hands. She had almost forgotten his hands. There were scratches on the knuckles. She reached out, and he took her hand in his. His touch was amazingly gentle. She pulled his fingers toward her, holding them up to her face.

"You smell like linseed oil," she said.

"I didn't have time to change."

"I like the smell."

"My mother and Manuel think I'm going to marry Carlos."

"I know."

"How do you know that?"

He hesitated.

"Never mind. It doesn't matter. I have something else to tell you, Jake. A lot of things."

Part Four

31

The pilots took off early on the morning of December 7, 1941, from a position two hundred miles northwest of Oahu. The torpedo and bomb attack achieved complete surprise. Before the morning was over, eight battleships of the U.S. Pacific Fleet had been sunk or put out of commission, scores of other ships had been damaged or sunk. Almost every Army Air Corps plane on Oahu was destroyed on the ground. In a few hours, over 2,000 sailors were killed, more casualties than the Navy had suffered in all previous actions in the twentieth century. The nation and the world were shocked.

Horatio Breedlove was one of the few American naval officers who was not surprised by the news of the Japanese air attack on Pearl Harbor. His first reaction was to ask about the American carriers. The early reports were confused, and it took a few days before he confirmed that none of the three American carriers had been in Pearl Harbor at the time of the attack. All three, he was delighted to read, were under the command of men who had studied with him.

It took Breedlove weeks to assemble enough information for an analysis of the Japanese attack. From the sparse details in the official U.S. Army and Navy sources from Hawaii and Washington, and the preliminary report that was prepared for the investigation into the conduct of the commanders in Hawaii, Breedlove's first thought was that the Japanese attack was modeled after Fleet Problem XIX in 1938, when the *Saratoga*, under the command of

Ernest King, had approached Pearl Harbor from the northwest undetected, and managed to launch a successful strike on the U.S. naval base without losing a single plane. Parts of the attack plan even resembled Fleet Problem VII, with the old *Langley* attacking Pearl Harbor with flour bombs in 1928, and Problem XIV in 1932, when the *Saratoga* and *Lexington* had simulated an attack on the fleet at dawn on a Sunday. The similarities didn't surprise him; if anything, they were a compliment to his authorship of the exercises.

He remembered that he had loaned his copies of the fleet problems to poor Russell Westcott, shortly before he was killed in a boating accident near Fishers Island. After the incredibly sad funeral—the Episcopal priest had poignantly eulogized Russell as a young man of enormous unrealized talent—Breedlove had gone to Russell's house. Russell's mother, almost inconsolable in her grief, pulled herself together to talk to him.

"I searched for those papers after your phone call," she said. "I found nothing. I'm sorry, but it was Russell's way. He wasn't careful with sails or papers or people. Or his own life."

The newspapers and radio commentators were quick with their analyses of the Japanese attack. Everyone, from the newspaper wags to the top brass in the Navy, cried over the lost battleships and called the Japanese attack a telling blow. Breedlove took two months to complete his own analysis. Although his report wasn't published, he would tell anyone who would listen that the commentators and battleship admirals were all wrong. Despite the ships sunk, the aircraft destroyed on the ground, and the shock to American complacency, by any real measure of naval strategy, the Japanese attack had failed miserably. The battleships they had sunk or crippled would hardly matter. What mattered was the American carriers, and the Japanese attack had missed all three.

Why? Breedlove kept asking himself. How could the Japanese have planned an attack so carefully, risked all on such a desperate move, and not made sure the most important target of all, the American carriers, were in port when they attacked. Didn't the Japanese pay attention to American war games and exercises? What were their spies doing? He smiled at the thought that if the Japanese had only studied the fleet problems he had prepared for the War College games, they would have realized that an attack that did not get the American carriers was a suicide mission.

Breedlove leaned back in his chair, smiling. He had studied and planned the war for so long that the reality was almost anticlimactic. He thought about his students: Ernest King, Halsey, Fletcher, Spruance. King, who had commanded the *Saratoga* in the fleet exercise, had already been appointed to a new post as independent head of the Navy in the Pacific. Spruance had been in command of a division of five cruisers, absent from Pearl at the time of the attack. At least *his* students had learned the lessons of naval aviation. It was only a matter of time before they would use the carriers that had been spared at Pearl to destroy the Japanese Navy.

He thought of Russell Westcott. Such promise, cut down too early. Russell should have been part of the ultimate, inevitable victory.

Sera was round and plump when she got out of the car at the office of Admiral Kalbfus, who had been promoted to Commandant of the Atlantic Fleet. The admiral's office was still inside the gates of the Naval War College, and Sera recognized the shining white buildings. There were more guards at the gate now, and a pivoted gateway had to be raised for each vehicle.

When she was ushered into the office, the commandant seemed surprised and embarrassed as he shook her hand. He asked her to take a seat across from the desk while he read from a paper on his desk.

"This is not a public ceremony, and nothing that happens here will ever be announced. But by order of the Secretary of the Navy, on behalf of the American people, I have the pleasure of thanking you for your act of extraordinary courage. I cannot explain the details of what was in those papers, but suffice it to say that some day, when the true story of Pearl Harbor can be told, you will be recognized as a heroine."

He looked up from the paper and said, "I have only one question to ask: Where did you learn to handle a boat like that?"

Sera nodded toward Jake, then reached out and held Jake's hand.

The admiral looked at Jake. "I've seen you here in Newport, haven't I? At the regattas? Or around the docks maybe?"

"I worked on some boats here."

"What kind of boats?"

"Yachts, mostly."

"What are you doing now?"

"I've been working on a design for fast attack boats."

"What kind of design?"

Jake nodded toward a pad on the admiral's desk. He pulled the stub of a pencil from his pocket, sharpened it with a knife, and began to sketch.